Martin Chimes is a veteran Australian businessman responsible for numerous business start-ups over the course of thirty years. Among his many achievements are building the largest stationery supply chain in the southern hemisphere and being recognised with the 2006 Ernst and Young Entrepreneur of the Year Award. He is also a popular speaker.

Martin's current passions are writing and fitness training and he is an accomplished triathlete. He approaches his writing with the same seriousness and dedication that he does everything else.

Martin lives in Sydney, Australia, with his best friend and wife Sara and a cast of children, dogs and relatives.

INTO THE LION'S DEN

MARTIN CHIMES

First Published by Harlequin Mira 2015
First Australian Paperback Edition 2015
ISBN 978 174369305 6

Published by
Harlequin Mira
An imprint of Harlequin Enterprises (Australia) Pty Ltd.
Level 4, 132 Arthur Street
NORTH SYDNEY NSW 2060
AUSTRALIA

Printed and bound in Australia by Griffin Press

MIX
Paper from
responsible sources
FSC® C009448
www.fsc.org

This book is dedicated to my wife and
best friend, Sara, without whose love, support
and help it would never have happened. And
also to our five wonderful children, Adam, Jake,
Natalia, Jason and Daniel, our daughter-in-law, Talya,
granddaughter, Stella and future daughter-in-law, Jenna.
I love you all with all my heart.

1946, Johannesburg

They had struck him like a pack of wolves, tearing him to pieces in seconds. Even mustering all his considerable strength, he was unable to stop them. Yet at least one of the cowards would always remember him.

It would not have happened if he stayed out of that alley beside the synagogue, or if once he'd entered it and seen the Brownshirts lounging about there, he'd turned around, but Abe Novak never walked away from a fight. Sometimes he wondered if that made him brave or stupid. Whatever the case, without people like him, Hitler would not have been thwarted, and he was glad to have thrown his fighting spirit behind the effort to stop the slaughter and rapine that dominated the world for the long years since the madman's rise to power. Back home in South Africa he wore his uniform with pride as he sauntered about Johannesburg.

Not everyone, however, was happy with the Allies' victory. The Brownshirts were among those who had sided with the Nazis. But Abe hadn't risked his life in Europe to live in fear at home, so he lengthened his stride and walked on, moving into the street to manoeuvre his way around the tangle of brooding hoodlums lounging against the wall.

'*Waar gaan jy, fokken Jood soldaat?*' One of them blocked his way, demanding to know where he was going, calling him a fucking Jew soldier. He was a tall, well-built brute and would have been good-looking if not for the sneer on his face.

'Get out of my way,' Abe ordered. He looked the blond giant in the eye.

'Suppose you make me?'

Whatever further repartee the thug might have had in mind was cut short as Abe's fist connected squarely with his nose. The stunned giant stumbled back and Abe took off like a hare. The gang were too amazed to react at once and he had a good head start. He was strong, fit and disciplined from his military training, unlike this rabble, and there was little doubt he could have outrun them … if only that cat hadn't darted under his feet, tripping him. The stray was black. It was said they were unlucky. Abe had never believed it until then. The alleyway was old and cobblestoned and he went down hard.

As he struggled to rise they surrounded him and blocked off any chance of escape, their eyes full of vengeance. Abe was already reeling under their assault when their bloody-nosed leader gripped his shirt and struck him with a mallet-like fist. Something broke in his cheek and he threw himself back desperately, trying to wrench free. His shirt tore and his assailant saw the Star of David on his chest.

'A fucking Jew, just as I thought.'

A crushing right hook sent Abe flying into a pile of rubbish heaped up against a wall.

'Leave him be,' the giant growled as his comrades surged forward, raining blows upon the fallen man. 'I want this bastard for myself.'

Abe tried to crawl away as a boot smashed into him, shattering ribs. They were going to kill him. He gasped with shock and fear, but in that moment he spied something amidst the litter that he hoped might help him even the score. He grabbed the jagged shard of glass from the trash as a pair of massive hands reached down and rolled him over.

Abe thrust his makeshift weapon into the elbow of his foe. The giant screamed as Abe wrenched his dagger back and forth, twisting it savagely, unconcerned about the lacerations to his own fingers. His final feeling was one of grim satisfaction as he sank into oblivion, vaguely aware of the police whistle echoing in the alley.

* * *

Although it seemed his appointment with Death would be postponed this day, in his world of pain Abe felt the blackness hovering nearby as the doctors and nurses worked on him. He wondered whether they could reconstruct his body. With every merciless blow he had heard his bones crack, felt them break. He could only imagine what his face looked like. Teeth had been smashed out and his crushed cheeks throbbed agonisingly.

After having lived through four years of desert warfare up north and in El Alamein and surviving numerous battles and injuries, how ironic that now, here at home, he should lie so close to death. Would he ever feel safe walking the streets of South Africa again?

Had it been worth it? Could he have avoided the fight? Only by staying out of the alley. His only option had been to strike first and hope to prevail. He had known that the moment he looked into the eyes of the giant. There was nothing to regret.

At least I didn't go down without a fight, he thought, as the anaesthetic flooded his veins. The white light and white coats blurred into one and darkness engulfed him.

CHAPTER

1

And So It Ends

2009, Sydney,
Tuesday 29 September, around 5:45 a.m.

That feeling of foreboding happens to everybody – a deadly sense of déjà vu, as if they've been there before in that moment where some unknown peril threatens. That's what Ben Novak felt.

The familiar switching sound came through his Blackberry, a pause as the overseas connection to Josh's phone was made. He could just about hear his son answering the phone with his trademark, 'Hey, daddy boy.' But his boy didn't respond – someone else did. Well, someone pressed the answer button, but silence followed.

'Hi, boykie?' Ben said. 'What's up?'

Still nothing but silence, and then that voice with its thick Afrikaans accent, vaguely familiar.

'And so it ends.'

Followed by more silence.

'Josh? Josh!' Ben urged again, but the only response was the sound of the phone disconnecting.

'That's strange,' he thought aloud, taking a moment to think. 'It must have been a wrong number.'

He checked the Blackberry. No, it was the right one. Perhaps all that switching on the overseas connection patched him through to someone else by mistake. Yet the Afrikaner accent with its vague tone of threat provoked a queasy feeling within him.

His mind began to race. *Why didn't he talk to me properly? What the hell does 'and so it ends' mean? Where do I know that voice from?*

Ben redialled. There were more sounds of switching … a pause … and finally Josh's voicemail: 'Hi, this is Josh. Leave a message.'

'Hi, boy,' he said. 'Call your dad.'

They often spoke to each other that way, he and his sons: 'Hi, boy' or 'boykie', Ben would say, while they called him 'daddy boy' in return. Saul, his elder, twenty-six, and Josh, twenty-four; his world revolved around them, even more so since Dahlia had died.

When they were younger they hated it if he kissed or hugged them, especially when their friends were around, particularly the girlfriends.

'Get used to it,' he frequently told them. 'I'll kiss and hug you all your lives and you'll get to love it and do the same with your own children and they'll love it too.'

Something about this is not right, Ben thought. *When he's away, Josh never switches off his phone. He knows I'm a bit crazy like that and I need to be able to contact him at all times.*

He phoned Saul. It was early, not yet six o'clock. He would just be getting up.

'Hi, boy,' Ben said. 'Sorry it's so early, but when did you last talk to your brother?'

'Not sure,' Saul mumbled sleepily. 'Maybe yesterday … why?'

'I don't know,' Ben said. 'Something strange happened. I called his phone and someone else answered and when I called back I got his message bank.'

'Stop worrying, Dad, it's probably a bad connection. Did you leave a message?'

'Yeah.'

'He'll call you back,' Saul reassured him. 'Sorry, Dad, you're worrying for nothing and I've got to get going to work.'

'Okay,' Ben agreed reluctantly, and hung up.

It was obvious that Saul was a bit irritated. Ben didn't really blame him. His firstborn was always so calm, so in control. A glow spread through him whenever he thought of his boys, each so different in their own way and yet so much the same. The emotions that had overcome him when they were born had never faded, the memories of the moment still burnt bright in his mind and in his heart.

'It's a boy,' the nurse had said, handing him the little bundle wrapped in a blue baby blanket.

Awestruck, he thought, *This is my son ... my baby.* He gazed at Saul's beautiful round pink face, his glorious long black hair. *Babies don't have hair! Babies are not beautiful!* And yet his was. Saul was exquisite – and he was *his* son. The infant was big and strong and he was his son. All that emotion, all that *love*, the unexpectedness of these feelings welled up in him and spilt from his eyes, the tears splashing onto his little boy's face.

In that moment, Ben had become someone else: father to a son, a daddy. An infinite capacity for love and care bloomed within him. Saul's pain would make Ben cry, his happiness would give him untold joy and his future mattered so much more than Ben's own. He laid his cheek against his infant's face. This boy conceived in Africa, born in Australia.

Ben came back to the present, sitting in his office at home in Sydney. He never liked it much when the boys went away. But when the destination was South Africa it really churned him up.

His beloved South Africa, the land of his birth; the root of so much love and so much pain. However deep his love for his homeland might be, it was a perilous place. At least if he were with them, he could mitigate the danger. He knew the country, the people, the way they thought there. He could see trouble coming, sense it before it happened.

South Africa is dangerous and Josh is there and his phone is not being answered. I have reason to worry.

The country wasn't always that way. There was a time when beautiful mysterious South Africa, with the rich culture and history of its peoples, with its extraordinary wildlife, was considered 'God's Country'. The suburbs were safe and houses had no dividing fences, let alone brick walls. Now all that was gone and homes sat locked up in gated communities, barricaded behind eight-foot-high walls and electrified fences.

I shouldn't have let him go alone, Ben thought. *I probably shouldn't have let him go at all.* But he had felt that Josh would be safe staying at Rick's, especially with all the security, the armoured car and his friend to keep an eye on him.

Rick. He picked up the phone and dialled, calculating the time there – 9 p.m. His friend would be up.

'Ben,' Rick said as he answered. 'He hasn't come home yet. It's a bit odd because Josh said he'd be early, but I thought maybe he met someone.'

There it was again, that sense of foreboding. *You're overreacting,* Ben told himself, as nausea gripped him. *Josh is twenty-four years old, he's probably having a night out on the town, it's not even that late and here I am, half a world away, panicking because I can't get my boy on the phone.*

But there was that ugly Afrikaans voice with its cryptic message.

'Rick, I don't know what's happening, I've got this feeling that something's not right. Some stranger answered Josh's phone. They said "and so it ends" and then hung up. I know it's not enough to justify this feeling of dread … but I'm afraid he's hurt or … I don't know what.'

'Hmm, that's strange. I'll try and get hold of him, Ben, and I'll phone you back. I don't think you have to worry too much.'

Rick was obviously trying to calm him, but his tone was not as casual as he tried to make it. Rick, too, was alarmed. Ben heard the worry in his voice. *This is South Africa. When people don't arrive when they're supposed to and don't phone to let you know, especially people like Josh, something is wrong.*

Suddenly Ben was sure; Josh would never stay out without letting Rick know. Josh of all people; he was thoughtful and considerate. To cause anyone unnecessary worry was contrary to his nature.

'I'm coming over,' he said to Rick. 'I'm coming to get my boy.'

CHAPTER

2

Edge of Terror

Johannesburg,
Monday 28 September, around 7 p.m.

Josh had never experienced fear like this. It overwhelmed him. He shivered uncontrollably. His heart raced, beating hard inside his chest. His pants were wet.

I've peed myself, he thought in shame. The gag in his mouth made it impossible for him to move his tongue and choked him. Getting air into his lungs was a struggle and the more he panicked, the harder breathing became.

Have to try and calm down.

Josh willed himself to take a long slow breath and attempted to orient himself anew.

Darkness ruled almost unchallenged in the car trunk but every now and then a brief red glow from the brake lights alleviated the abysmal blackness. He was lying on his side. His hands were tied behind him, elbows pulled tight together. A rope stretched between his wrists and his ankles, bending his legs back until his feet almost touched his hands. His arms felt as if they were being pulled out of his shoulders.

He sought desperately for a reason for his abduction, even as he struggled for calm. The taste of blood was bitter in his mouth, and with his bottom lip he felt the jagged edge of a broken tooth. A sticky trail slicked the back of his head, wet and warm.

The assault had been so sudden. He had been in the parking garage at Melrose Arch, heading back to his car after a night out. Without warning, there was a movement, a figure glimpsed from the corner of his eye, just before the blow struck. And then there was nothing.

Panic hit Josh as his awful predicament became clear: he was bound in the boot of a car and could die there – just like that. An overpowering desire to scream out for help assailed him, but his throat constricted.

Get a grip, he told himself and fought to slow his heart, control his breath.

Think! It was time to get his wits working. *If they've tied me up and put me in a trunk, they want me alive. But why would anyone do this to me? Why? Why? Why?*

The car hit a bump and his body slammed into the metal rim of the boot.

CHAPTER

3

Guide

Sydney, around 6:15 a.m.

Ben phoned Qantas. There was seating available so he bought the ticket for QF63 departing at 10:35 a.m. and then he went to wake Dahlia.

He paused. It had eluded him again, as it often did when he was distracted, that there would be no waking her. His beloved girl was gone. Yet sometimes, in the early morning, he forgot she was no longer there. He missed her terribly, needed her near, to share his troubles. Almost two years had dragged by since they had lost her. He was still dumbfounded by how quickly the cancer had stolen her away. The loss was incomprehensible and he eased the ache by imagining her still present, aglow and full of life.

What would she have said when he told her about this bizarre business? Would she have felt the same foreboding? Would she have supported his decision to go immediately to South Africa, or would she think it was an overreaction?

Dahlia always considered everything so carefully, but when it came to her children, she would do whatever was needed to ensure they were safe. The irony was that right now she was spared the pain of worrying about their son and it rested solely on him.

Yet he did not feel alone. She was his constant guide, a wise presence he invoked in imaginary counsel.

'Hi, hon, is it time to go already?' Her smile beams.

He is so used to waking her early with a cup of black coffee. She cannot function until the first sip. He chooses his next words carefully.

'Hi, honey, change of plan, we aren't going to the gym today.'

Surprise registers on her sleepy face, disturbed by this change to their ritual of waking early and walking the dogs before going to the Stadium Gym.

'How come?'

'I'm going to South Africa.'

She's on her second sip and still slow to react, but it's obvious she's processing this news, looking at him through the messy blonde curls falling over her face.

'What are you talking about?'

'I'm worried about Josh. He's not answering his phone. It's probably an overreaction, but I decided to go to South Africa. Just to see that he's okay, and then I'll have a few days break with Rick.'

Concerned now, she's sitting up. Dahlia knows Ben. It's not like him to simply up and go unless there is a real need.

'Tell me what's going on. You don't just suddenly say you're going to South Africa and that you're overreacting. What the hell are you talking about?' That was her, no bullshit.

'I called him, and someone else answered his phone, and I got a bad feeling about it, so I thought I would act on the safe side. I'm sure it's nothing, I'm–'

'Who answered his phone? Have you tried again?'

'I don't know who, that's why I'm worried, and of course I tried again. Also, Josh didn't get back to Rick's place after saying he'd be home early.'

Frowning with worry now, eyes piercing him, she says, 'That's not like Josh. What time is it there?'

'About nine-thirty in the evening.'

'Couldn't he just be out and have switched his phone off or run out of battery?'

'It's possible, but it's not like him. It's more the fact that someone else answered that makes me worried. That's why I need to go.'

'What did they say?'

'It was strange, ominous … something like, "and so it ends". And the worst thing is that I have a feeling I know that voice. But I can't recall whose it is.'

'What about me?' she says. 'Why am I not going with you? I want to be there, too.'

Oh! How he wished she could be there, too. To really talk to. To advise and support him. He needed her now.

'Honey, I don't know what this is all about. It may be nothing, I'm hoping it's nothing, but if someone has got Josh, I'm going to find him and I don't want to be worried about you.'

Still, all he wished for was that she could be there for him to worry about.

She does not mince her words. 'Ben, don't be mad. You can't go after him alone. You don't know who you're dealing with. If someone has him, you get the police, you pay professionals.'

After more than thirty years together she knew what he was thinking, sensed his every mood. However far apart they were, he could feel her as though she was there.

'You need to be careful, Ben. You know how dangerous South Africa is. You have to curb your impulsiveness, plan everything carefully, before you go acting too hastily.

'Bring our boy home safely,' she says.

CHAPTER
4

Au Revoir

Ben arrived at the airport earlier than needed. Impatient to get going, he could not sit around at home. Previously, Dahlia had always dropped him off whenever he went away.

She would have kissed and hugged him, held him tighter than usual, and he would have felt all her love and concern.

'Please be careful. I love you. I can't live without you. You are the best thing that has happened in my life and I need you until I'm at least ninety.'

She always spoke as though they would be together forever.

'Don't worry, my girl,' he whispered, 'nothing will happen to me. You know that I've got angels that watch over me. They've been doing it forever.'

A passerby, dragging a case behind him, gave Ben an odd look, which he ignored.

Dahlia was his angel now. She watched over him and waved at him; a little wave, a concerned wave like she knew something, as if she hoped it was only *au revoir* while praying it was not goodbye.

Ben tried not to think about South Africa, about all the reasons why Josh might not be answering his phone. Could he have been attacked by a *tsotsi*, hurt in a car crash? Was that thinking paranoid? An overreaction? Was it reasonable to suddenly drop everything and rush to South Africa, merely because of a strange message and an unanswered call?

But he couldn't ignore that feeling. That ominous sense of foreboding.

Is it possible that bastard is back in my life? he wondered, finally acknowledging the fear his conscious mind had refused to contemplate from the first moment that ugly voice had come over the phone. Could it be the phantom that haunted so many half-buried memories in the distant past?

*   *   *

The Afrikaner looms over him in a nightmarish reverie. His screamed words poison the air: '*Sleep dit, jy fokken jood!*' ('Haul it, you fucking Jew.') That's all he is to the platoon sergeant who haunts this hellish reverie; less than an animal and fit for no more than to be a beast of burden. In that bad dream the windblown sands of the Namib Desert choke him as he kneels bound to his tether in the sand. Grit sticks to his lips and in his nose, choking him with every breath. Caked on his skin with sweat and piss, inside his overalls the sand flays him, peeling his hide as he crawls on his belly. Invective streams from his tormentor's lips like a conduit from a bottomless pit of hate. Spittle spatters Ben's face.

Existence is fear that morphs into loathing.

A coarse rope coiled around his neck and shoulders bites into his flesh, burning as he drags on his cruel harness. Sprawled in the grit, he lifts himself and looks back under his armpit to see the burden at the other end of his tether: a tractor tyre filled with sand, half-buried and immovable.

Fuck him.

His torturer's boots are almost close enough for Ben to grab. In the reverie he sees them over and over again, tempting as El Dorado, unholy as hell.

But the master of this inferno knows precisely how much distance to keep and the point where his eighteen-year-old victim has passed caring and would gladly strangle him – if he could just get his oppressor in his hands.

'Come on, Jew boy, give me a reason,' he sneers in his guttural Afrikaans, his hand on the holstered gun.

Loathing evolves into vengefulness but the invitation is ignored.

I'm not that stupid, Ben thinks, in this dream. *I'm not going to die out here in the desert, in army detention barracks, when all my life is still in front of me and he can walk free detesting the Kaffirs and Jews.* Ben stays down in the dirt. *I can wait. I'll be patient, and I'll get out of here. And one day that devil will know what it's like to grovel helplessly in the dirt, while someone else has power over your life.*

* * *

Unencumbered by check-in bags, it took Ben only a few minutes to collect a boarding pass and get through customs and to the gate. He found a seat in the corner, away from the crowd of passengers, to wait quietly until the flight boarded.

He phoned Saul, knowing that his son, as always, would chastise him for being overzealous about their safety. Ben was grateful for his elder boy's attitude, though. For if Saul had shared his father's ill-omened sense, he would insist on going with him and Ben would be forced to argue him out of entering into danger.

'Saul, I'm at the airport on my way to South Africa,' he said casually.

'You're mad, Dad,' Saul answered, 'but that's no surprise. I'm sure Josh is all right.'

'I hope so, my boy, but I can't understand why he hasn't called Rick.'

The words slipped out despite Ben's resolve to downplay his misgivings.

'Saul, will you please do me a favour?'

'Sure, Dad, what do you want?'

'It's late in Joburg now, so you won't be able to do it right away, but please make a few calls to Josh's work colleagues and see if anyone knows anything about his movements after work. Maybe he went out with one of them. If you discover anything, send me a message by email or text. I'll pick it up when I land.'

'Will do, Dad. Be careful. I'm sure I'm right about Josh and this is just you being overcautious.'

'I hope so too, my boy. I would love to be wrong.'

Dahlia was so proud of her level-headed and caring son. At times she had complained about the special bond the three of them shared. It was not that they wanted to exclude her, but it was a man thing, and they found time to be together, just the three of them.

'What about me?' she used to wail. But despite the occasional little barb of jealousy that plagued her, she would never stand in the way.

Ben settled into his seat. He always chose an aisle seat near the front so he could be the first out, first through customs and through the terminal, never waiting for bags.

Normally he would relax and use the long flight to switch off from the world, read a book or watch the movies, pass the hours in a pleasantly mindless state – but not this time. He wondered how to get through the flight, how much time was being lost, what could or should be done. Fearful imaginings of Josh in peril or distress intruded upon his mind but he could not afford to let them set up residence there.

The thought of anything happening to his children had always been too terrible to contemplate. With Dahlia gone it had become worse, if that were possible. Still, he tried not to suffocate them.

Dahlia. He could never say she was dead. That dreaded word evoked the image of a corpse. That was not his Dahlia. Not even in death could he think of her that way. Always, he saw her as a bright spirit, smiling, hovering nearby. He courted that vision now, hoping to find refuge in the comfort of it, but other, darker thoughts intruded, forcing his angel out.

What if someone hurt my son?

Even as he struggled desperately for peace, a demonic rage simmered inside, crying out for retribution. Jaws locked, he gritted his teeth, fists clenched, veins popping in his neck.

It was still in him; the capacity for violence. He had hoped that part of him had been left behind in South Africa, almost thirty years ago when they emigrated, but he knew deep down it remained, a sleeping dragon.

Though there was no doubt that his warrior spirit remained intact, Ben wondered if he still had the ability to use it. What if he was no longer equal to the task?

He had kept to his daily fitness regime, even without Dahlia. He still bench-pressed 110 kilos, did thirty consecutive pull-ups on the chinning bar and hundreds of abdominals. He was strong and fit, especially for his age. Yet now a debilitating doubt haunted him: would it be enough?

Once he had been so sure of his strength, the power of his own will to overcome all obstacles, such doubts would never have occurred to him. Middle age changed things; he was no longer in his prime, his aggression was tempered. The years weathered everyone, mellowed them, too, if they were lucky.

Ben closed his eyes and concentrated on breathing and relaxing. With a fourteen-hour flight ahead, all he could do was try to shift his mind into a peaceful meditative place and say a silent prayer that everything was going to turn out okay.

He had trained himself well in this exercise. So many years in business, all the start-ups, had burdened him with constant anxiety and forced him to find the tools to cope with it. That stress had been the price he had paid for his success.

Now Ben sought after other things. He wanted peace and tranquillity, to get away from it all and find respite from the frenetic world around him. At this stage in his life he could afford that. For years he had been disentangling himself from his business activities and had been able to spend more time with his family and with Dahlia at their beautiful remote cottage on the water. The serenity invited him to reflect on his reason for being; on a higher force, God perhaps, and what really mattered to him: his family, his children.

Please, God, don't let anything happen to Josh, he prayed. *If you really are there, please don't let anything else happen to my family;*

don't spoil what I have left, my only joy, everything I have strived for my whole life.

Stilling his mind, he blocked the anxiety from infiltrating his being and focused on his breath – in and out – thinking about air as life force, a beneficent energy infusing his body. Breathing out, he exhaled the worry and the troubles. Slowly he let all thought cease, anxiety dissipate. Gradually peace and stillness regenerated him, refuelled him, energised his mind.

He felt the thrust of the aircraft and the backward tilt as the nose came up and it lifted into the air and turned its way towards South Africa; land of his origin, his heritage. *I am a white child of the Dark Continent*, he thought as a flood of images flashed through his mind: his beloved father and family, the brutality of his youth, the beauty and the cruelty that was, so often, just Africa.

CHAPTER
5

Red Earth

1960s Johannesburg

Ben was always the special one, the only son; the boy his father, Abe, had dreamed of. His mother finally delivered him: the heir who would ensure the perpetuation of the Novak family name. Abe was forty-four and the child was his pride and joy. At five years old, he was routinely accompanying Abe and his buddies around the golf course.

Their summer outings to Kyalami Country Club were unforgettable. They drove beneath the purple canopy of the jacaranda-lined avenues, amid the beautiful homes set in the lush gardens of the affluent northern suburbs of Johannesburg, beyond which lay the blacks' shanty town.

Alexandra Township lay huddled under the pall of grey smoke rising from the wood fires that fuelled the cooking pots of its denizens and provided their only source of warmth during the freezing months of winter. The settlement was a shadow city, not well known like Soweto, but just the same.

The hamlet of hovels fascinated Ben. The lives of its people contrasted so harshly with his own idyllic white-child's life. As they drove past he was able to look down the sandy pot-holed roads of the township and witness little black kids, half naked, playing in the streets, kicking their soccer balls, miniature billows of dust at their ankles as they ran.

'Piccaninnies,' his dad called them. 'See, my son, how different it is for black people in our country. Their houses are cobbled together from what we whites discard: old timbers and rusted corrugated iron. There's no electricity, so to cook and keep warm they have to use a simple wood fire, and that's why there's always smoke when we drive past. The little piccaninnies only have the street to play in. No parks and gardens, no football grounds and golf courses. Not like you. It's very sad.'

This little portrait fell far short of adequately describing the dark cesspit black Africans inhabited so near the prosperous haven of their white neighbours. Overcrowded one-room shacks accommodating families of four to eight people, children included, with no privacy for a man and his woman, no running water, no separate cooking area. No bathroom, just a large pail of cold water for bathing; no toilet but a secluded hole in the ground outside in a wooden shed. No sanitation, no electricity. The only illumination came from a paraffin lamp which, if spilled, as on occasion they were, could raze to the ground the shack they must call home.

Abe's son was not at the age where he needed to know that the trials of these people did not end with what they lacked. There were also the *tsotsis* to contend with: criminal thugs who wandered lawlessly through the township, pillaging; robbing the workers on payday so that the meagre reward for their work, won with blood and the sweat from their brows, was squandered in drunkenness in the cluster of *shebeens,* the illicit degenerate bars that peppered the streets.

This quagmire of deprivation that was the 'Kaffirs'' designated domain remained separated by a single street from a region that may as well have been Camelot, so immense was the contrast. The perimeters between these two zones were guarded by an implacable white police force determined to keep the impoverished and the privileged eternally apart.

The cruelty of apartheid did more than just separate the whites from the blacks; it divided the black mothers and fathers from their children. As if impoverishment were not enough, family life was destroyed with it. Although Abe did not wish to burden his son with such dark visions, sometimes he could not keep himself from expressing his fears of how all this would end.

'As you sow, so shall you reap. With their policies of exploitation, the whites have sowed seeds of hatred amongst the black people. It will not be pretty when the time of the harvest arrives.'

'What does that mean?' Ben wondered aloud, upon hearing this cryptic prophecy. 'What's *exploitation*?'

'It means that the black people have to do all of the jobs we don't want to do and for very little pay.'

'Like Elizabeth and Joshua,' Ben said, with a worried look on his face. 'Don't they like looking after me? Doesn't Joshua like to do the gardening?'

Elizabeth Tsitsi and Joshua Mokwana resided in the domestic servants' quarters at the rear of the Novaks' home. Compared to the citizens of Alexandra, they were handsomely rewarded for their duties.

Abe laughed and ruffled his son's hair. 'No, they love looking after you and Joshua likes to garden. We treat them well and pay them better than most. But not everyone is as lucky as them.'

'But still, they don't get to be with their children like you and Mom do with me. That's terrible.'

'It isn't good,' Abe conceded, 'but although our servants must work cheap, without these jobs they would have nothing: no money, no food or clothes to send home to their children.'

Abe felt some consolation in that, even if there was no justifying the magnitude of this exploitation of one race by another.

Past Alexandra the road turned toward Kyalami, leaving behind the shadow city for tranquil rolling hills. Motoring alongside the bubbling Juksei River, they meandered through gullies that lay bare the rich African earth. The ground was a vibrant red, as though stained from all the blood that had been spilt there. That crimson soil, seared in his soul, remained etched in Ben's memory forever.

Driving the Vauxhall, sitting on his dad's lap, the steering wheel gripped between his hands, stirred him; the feeling of control, of being able to guide and turn the whole vehicle. The sense of power. Later, when he learnt the complex coordination of clutch, gears, brakes and accelerator, Abe would let him drive alone, sitting on a cushion so that he could see over the top of the dashboard.

Fourteen years old, Ben took the keys from his dad's locker and went joyriding. He taught himself to broadside by accelerating around the corners on the gravel roads. But on a single-lane cattle-grid crossing, joy went out of the ride and turned to panic when he slid head-on into a Mercedes. Sitting in the car following the impact, Ben stared in dismay at the concertinaed front end of the Vauxhall, thinking, *Jesus I hope my dad's not going to notice*. And then, seeing his father running towards the wreck, remorse overcame him. Abe's face was wracked with worry, yet his only words were, 'Are you okay, my boy?'

Abe's love rained upon his son in forgiveness. Even Ben breaching their bonds of faith and trust did not diminish the depth of his father's affection. All he cared about was his wellbeing.

When Ben wasn't destroying the car, he was on the practice tee with a bag of balls, while Abe went to join his friends in a game of poker a few hours before tee-off.

All manual work was done by blacks, some as young as ten and others grey-haired and sun-wrinkled from their lifetime of labour. So the caddies, too, were black. On the practice tee, the golfers hit their balls while the caddies ran to retrieve them with no protective clothing or headwear. White golfers cared little for their plight and had no regrets when, on occasion, one was downed by a rogue golf ball to the head. Later, a more mature Ben was shamed and ached for the callous disregard of the whites for people of colour.

Notwithstanding, Ben's youth was a treasured time of warm sunny days, heady with the smell of the grass. Silence reigned but for the hum of the bees, the chirping of birds and the thwack of the clubs. Barely a thought was spared for the nation's brewing discontent. There was nothing but a sense of warmth and protection, his dad's mates throwing their old golf balls at 'Abe's kid' so he could become a golfing ace.

For Abe and his crew, the sport itself was secondary to the betting. They gambled on everything and with everyone, making team bets and side bets with other groups.

By anyone's standards, Abe was a man's man: handsome, big-boned and heavily muscled. He loved his kids, his mates, his gambling, his business and his women, not necessarily in that order. A genial fellow, he was always ready with a smile, a story or a jest. No one could resist his infectious mirth, and no one appreciated his jokes more than himself, his eyes lighting up as he bellowed with laughter at his own stories.

The Novaks lived in the comfortable suburb of Glenhazel, their house identified by an ornately decorated black nameplate, which proclaimed the residence's name, *Fromde Bois,* in an impressive silver script. Abe chuckled when people asked him about the mysterious, presumably French, origins of the moniker.

'I won the deposit in a card game,' Abe would explain with a big grin, 'so I named it *From the Boys.*'

Despite his geniality, Abe was renowned as someone who never went down without a fight, even when faced with overwhelming odds, like on the day he had fallen afoul of the Brownshirts. He had recovered from his horrendous beating and the ringleader would not forget him ever, of that much he was sure.

'You will never truly know yourself, or your strength,' he told Ben, 'until you have been tested by adversity. It's then that you find out if you are a real man or a man of straw.' Those words would resonate through most of Ben's life. That's what Abe was – a real man – and Ben aspired to nothing more than to be like him.

Yet despite his warrior spirit, his dad was a gentle man, well satisfied with his station in life, kindly to his family, his friends and employees, and unlikely to deny his children anything they would ever ask.

From his father Ben learned to love family above all else.

'Take care of your sister,' Abe told him. 'Brenda will always need you – you are the man of the family.'

Brenda, his older sister by fifteen months, had a slight intellectual disability that left her disenfranchised from regular society and desperately lonely. Ben's dad had worried over what would become of her. Ben's duty had been impressed upon him first when he was just five years old and a thousand times after that, until an enduring sense of responsibility was instilled in him. It was up to him to protect everybody.

* * *

Safe! Someone touched him, the veil of memory lifted and Ben jolted upright in his seat. He searched the faces around him, looking for Josh, hoping that he would suddenly see his son's face beside him, a gentle taunt on his smiling lips: 'Dreaming, old man?'

'I'm sorry I disturbed your sleep, sir,' the flight attendant said. 'Can I offer you something to drink? We'll be serving dinner shortly.'

She was young. *In her thirties*, Ben thought, *and pretty*. The name tag said 'Sandy'. She smiled at him, waiting for his reply.

'Please,' he said. 'Orange juice mixed with water.'

She turned to her trolley to reach for the juice carton.

'You got a fright when I woke you,' she said. 'I'm sorry.' He recognised her accent as South African. *On a Qantas flight?*

'I was dreaming and woke at a critical point,' Ben replied.

'Not a good dream?' she said, pouring his juice.

'Some good, some bad.'

'Ice?'

'Yes, please.'

So much of his past had flashed through his mind as he slept.

'Are you going home?'

'Yes,' he said instinctively. 'Sorry, I mean *no*. I've been living in Sydney a long time.' He was surprised that, even after all this time, he still thought of South Africa as home, however fleetingly.

'You can never get Africa out of your blood,' he said, thinking about its red earth and praying that his family's blood wouldn't be added to the stained soil; hoping that he would be able to bring Josh home alive, safe back to Australia. *Am I still up to the task if it comes to a fight?*

'Well, you certainly haven't lost your accent, Mr Novak,' said Sandy, handing him his drink and a small packet of pretzels.

'It's doubtful I ever will after this amount of time.' Ben grinned. 'Thanks for the drink.'

The smile dimmed briefly as he wondered how Sandy knew his name.

CHAPTER

6

Captive

2009, Johannesburg, around 7:30 p.m.

'South Africa is dangerous!'

God, how many times have I heard that? Josh thought. He had heard enough horror stories of people who had been attacked or lost a loved one. So often, such an incident was the final trigger for their emigration to safer lands. But those were things that happened to other people, not to him. His parents had the foresight to leave twenty-seven years earlier, when his mom was pregnant, to ensure the safety of the family they had planned. Both he and Saul had been born in Australia.

This was the first time Josh had come to South Africa alone, and Ben had irritated him with his ceaseless warnings: 'Don't drive unless you're in Rick's car'. *The armoured Land Rover hadn't done much good,* he wanted to tell his dad. 'Watch out when you're getting in and out of the vehicle. Look about and if you see anyone suspicious hanging around, don't go near.' *I should have listened to him more carefully.*

Another wave of gut-wrenching dread washed over him. *What if I'm wrong and they don't want me alive? What if they're just going to torture me and then …* The word 'kill' was too frightening to contemplate.

Oh, God! My poor dad. Poor Saul.

He was thankful that his mom would be spared the agony of knowing his fate. Teary eyes closed, he pictured her and was soothed by the image. The only thing powerful enough to drown his terror was the thought of his family.

What will they do? This is going to destroy them.

Besides being his brother, Saul was also his closest friend. So often they talked about the depth of feelings they shared. How privileged they were to have such a bonded family where they had both only understood love and support.

He will feel so responsible for having sent me here, Josh thought.

Saul was the operations manager at BRT Limited, a bio-tech company. They had a new clinic to set up in Johannesburg and Josh was sent to do the job. Staying at Rick's place, he had considered he would be safe enough. The house was secured behind five-metre-high walls and electrified fences with armed security patrols around the clock.

Rick will know something's wrong when I don't arrive home … For a moment, he relaxed. Even in his fear and pain, locked in the trunk, he found solace in the idea that someone would start to look for him. The respite from despair and terror was all too brief. A paralysing fear overwhelmed him once more. The sense of powerlessness returned and he felt bile rise in his throat, tasted it in his mouth.

The car had slowed almost to a standstill. He heard the sound of a gate opening and a voice with an African accent say, 'Good evening, baas.' They were passing through a security point. If only he could scream out to let the guard know he was trapped in the boot! But the best he could manage through the gag was a feeble grunt.

A minute later they stopped again – at another gate – and then there was the crunch of tyres over the gravel of a driveway and the car came to rest. A voice, thick, coarse and chillingly cold, grumbled an order: 'Johan, put him in the cellar.'

The boot opened. Strong hands gripped him under his trussed arms and hauled him out. Josh was a strapping young man but his 80-kilo frame was hoisted like a shopping bag. The hulk holding him spoke to a black man standing beside the vehicle.

'Don't park it, Benjamin,' he ordered, 'we'll need it to go out later.'

Josh tried to appeal to them, desperate for the gag to be removed from his mouth. But all that came out was a gravelly meaningless mumble. The men ignored him.

Slung over the shoulder of his herculean captor and carried effortlessly into a substantial house, Josh registered the solid bulk of a heavy front door. There would be no way of escaping through that.

Below him were highly polished wooden floors. Before they descended a flight of stairs to the cellar, he saw a table in the entrance hall with heavy wrought-iron legs and a half-circle marble top. Upon it sat a larger-than-life-sized copper bust of a man's head. The face was brutal and ugly, almost to the point of deformity.

A faint sound came from across the hallway. He twisted his head and briefly glimpsed an old woman emerging from a doorway. All he could do was appeal to her with his eyes. She simply stood watching silently, shaking her head, but whether the gesture was in response to him or merely a habitual sign of bewilderment was impossible to say.

They passed through another door and down the wooden steps of the cellar, where the big man tossed Josh onto the hard concrete floor. His head thudded against the wall, and the air was driven from his lungs. Panic threatened once more as he battled the terrifying thought that they would torture him before performing the unthinkable ...

Beneath the gag, he cried out in pain and gasped. *My dad will find me*, he thought in desperation, although he realised the notion was foolish. How would Ben know where he was? How could he get him? But the thought comforted him; gave him hope. For a moment, a lightness descended on him and he closed his eyes and let go, leaving his fear and pain behind.

CHAPTER
7
Under Siege

1963, Johannesburg

Ben had never been sure whether he was strong because he thought he was, or whether he believed in his strength because he was strong. Whatever the case, for as long as he could remember, he had always been the strongest. Whether play-wrestling with a friend or in a serious schoolyard dust-up, he won without fail.

He was intrinsically strong, that was all he knew. Wherever he went he carried the knowledge with him and it gave him a sense of being unconquerable. It lent him a certain presence and he always felt protected. For some reason, he was convinced that no matter what befell him, he would be okay.

Strong men recognise each other, like members of the same exclusive club, and they make comparisons. If you know this, you can see them thinking, *He looks strong – but I'm stronger.*

When one has strength one's aura radiates that; the expression, the carriage and walk, all telegraph this fact, as surely as a dog with its tail between its legs advertises its meekness to the world. When challenged, such people react in a predictable manner; their faith in their ability to win makes them dangerous because they will not be cowed.

Yet there are those who may have an imposing build and be physically strong but they don't believe in themselves. These characters often need to convince others of their toughness, and they become bullies. That is all they are, however, mere bullies, and it is in the nature of such beasts to back off when it comes to the crunch because their essence is weak and their toughness a mere facade. The art lies in identifying one from the other; the genuinely strong from the impostors.

Ben did not know all of this at age eleven when he was riding his bicycle through the alleyway between the Raedene shops and found Joey Elias and Patrick Mansur blocking the way. Joey was huge, with a terrible case of acne that made him look as if he were perpetually red with fury – an impression that was not entirely deceiving. And Patrick: if there were a human equivalent of a hyena, it was him.

'Hey, give us your bike,' Joey said.

Ben did not know that these two belonged to a Lebanese gang, and that 'the Lebs', as he came to know them, had a fearsome reputation for beating the shit out of little 'Okes' – as they referred to guys like him. Had he known this he may have reacted differently, but as it was he only said, 'Piss off.'

And just as it was Ben's instinct to say no, it was Joey Elias's to give him a *klap,* which was the smack in the head that swiftly followed that refusal. Knocked from his bike, Ben found himself sprawled upon the ground, skull ringing and eyes stinging. Then Patrick Mansur kicked him in the head.

After being 'hoofed', his cranium rang so loudly that Ben completely forgot how strong he was. Suddenly he went from being unconquerable to scared and in urgent need of escape. Springing up, he abandoned his beloved bike and sprinted perhaps a hundred metres, just far enough to get out of sight and then, to his chagrin, wept a few brief but bitter tears. Soon, however, he calmed himself and self-belief began to creep cautiously back. *Being strong does not mean being stupid*, Ben thought. After all, there were two of them against him and Joey Elias was a monster.

As Ben slowly made his way back, he decided there was a significant difference between cowardice and making a strategic retreat in the face of overwhelming odds. He was no chicken and would not give in so easily now that he had had a chance to regroup.

He was just in time to see them disappearing through the alleyway, so he followed behind at a safe distance, ready to duck for cover if they turned around. Finally Patrick went off in one direction and Joey went in another and, as he had the pilfered bike, Ben followed the thug. Now that Joey was on his own Ben felt confident enough to creep closer. Fear was replaced by anger and the determination to recover his property.

Ben had taken part in lots of wrestling bouts but had never had a klap before, nor had he ever klapped anyone. It was clear that state of affairs had to end and Ben was going to baptise Joey Elias just as Joey had baptised him.

'Hey, you!' he yelled as he closed in on his prey and Joey turned just in time to meet Ben's fist with his cheek.

It was a good punch, but not enough to take down a behemoth like Joey Elias who walloped him straight back. Ben wasn't exactly sure what happened after that because his head was ringing again and it continued to ring for some time afterwards. All he knew was that he and Joey had continued to trade blows, but at the end of it he must have given as good as he got, because his opponent backed off and Ben got his bike back. He felt exhilarated. He grew taller in the knowledge that his stubbornness and determination had scored him a 'win'. But his victory also produced a lifelong enemy, one that would torment him for years to come.

*   *   *

From that day, Ben's life changed. He was never able to go anywhere safely in his own neighbourhood. It wasn't a problem if he encountered one of the Lebs on their own; they would just avoid each other. The problem was when he met them en masse, which was usually the case. They hunted in packs and were always on the lookout for a solitary Oke. When they found one, he was forced to hand over his money or his portable radio or anything else they might want, and the Oke would be lucky if he got away with just the loss of his possessions. More often than not, a klap or a hoof was included in the deal.

Anxiety became Ben's bodyguard. He stayed well away from the area most frequented by Joey Elias and Patrick Mansur. They had become known for the terror they inspired, and he knew it was just a matter of time before they would get him again.

CHAPTER

8

Antjie

She felt strange, the old woman, Antjie, seeing that horrible Johan carrying the young man over his shoulder, yet another doomed soul. One more anonymous victim in a life filled with so many, herself included, until she saw his face. He looked straight into her eyes with an expression of mute appeal and for the first time a prisoner was no longer anonymous. He reminded her so of Joost. Joost, her firstborn, her baby, her son. Joost, brother to the fiend Petrus, who had ordered this boy captured. Petrus, whose scarred face mirrored the cruelty in his soul.

Yet he had not always been that way. Even now he was sixty years old, when Antjie looked at her son, she still wanted to see her little Petrie and tried to erase everything else that had happened to him since. She recalled the beautiful blond boy, clinging to her skirt, smiling; so happy and full of love, trusting her totally to protect him.

Now, beneath his disfigured features, the short-cropped grey beard and black eye patch, only a mother could imagine the habitation of anything good or pure behind such a hideous facade. Only a mother's love could account for her blindness to the lurking evil that so resembled the malice of his father, Gerrit. It was hard to remember that there had been a time when Petrus's father had seemed to hold that same potential for good that had once appeared so obvious in their sons.

She remembered seeing him at school, swaggering about, tall and muscular, as if Michelangelo's David had incarnated in this Boer's son. The other girls, grouped in their cliques, tittered when he strode by, barely acknowledging them, and they would gaze after him with longing. She wondered what it would be like to be with such a man – because even then, Gerrit had not seemed a boy like the others.

Yet why would he be interested in a quiet little thing like her? She had been named Antjie, which meant 'angelic', and that had been her demeanour ever since she was a baby. A quiet child with few friends, she loved to read. Sport held no interest for her and she shied away from the crowd.

Gerrit, on the other hand, always seemed to be at the centre of one. Sycophants and admirers revolved around him like planets in the grip of the sun. So her surprise was immense when one day he detached himself from his own universe and entered into her orbit. It would have been easy to imagine that she was merely some debris in the way of his journey, except that his eyes were locked on her as he approached. He did not pass her by on his way to some portentous business but stopped in front of her as she stood looking down at their feet.

'Hey,' he said. 'Up here. I know girls like shoes but mine aren't so interesting.'

She had always thought people laughed around him out of nerves but it seemed he had some wit. She glanced up shyly.

'You're pretty,' he said. 'I like you.'

He was so unlike those boys who seemed too awkward to string a sentence together around her. She'd never thought it might be because she was beautiful and smart.

'I'd like to take you out.'

'Out?' The concept was strange. Did he mean like walking a dog?

'Ja. Let's go see a movie? You like movies, don't you?'

'I suppose so.'

'Good, it's settled then.'

'My pa might not agree …'

'He'll agree. I'll talk to him.'

'Oh, okay.'

It seemed certain her father would agree. She was not the only timid one in her family, and it was hard to imagine that anyone would ever say no to Gerrit. He was someone who would get his way in life. She had thought that was a good thing at the time. He would get what he wanted for himself and for her.

And then he was gone, trailing his satellites in his wake, and she was left standing open-mouthed.

'What was that?'

She turned to find one of the other girls staring at her in fascination.

'He asked me out,' Antjie said.

'*Why?*'

'I don't know.' She was oblivious to the insult.

'Who are you, anyway?'

'I'm Antjie, we've been in the same class for three years.' It had always been that way, and years later when her ex-schoolmates looked at their old class photos, despite her beautiful face no one would have remembered her name, had it not been for Gerrit.

She could never understand what it was about her that had appealed to him. Maybe it had been her childlike manner, the thought of being with a woman who was not really a woman, more like a little girl. Had she been able to glimpse her future, it would have been even more unthinkable that she would have agreed. But that day in the school-yard her heart leapt and she wanted to scream with excitement, little realising that afterwards, all her screams would be of anguish and pain.

* * *

These days Antjie heard a lot more than she ever let on. Once she had been a nobody and was thrilled to suddenly be noticed as Gerrit's consort. But her sudden rise in status was the start of a nightmare. Now she had reclaimed her anonymity gladly; giving it up had been where she had first gone wrong. They chatted as though she was not there, speaking freely about weapon smuggling and the fortunes that were being made, and in a sense she wasn't there, for the strain of living with such a brute had resulted in a divorce from reality.

She could not remember a time when she had not feared him. He was so powerful he took what he wanted from everyone and no one dared challenge him, not even her father.

'I'm going to marry your daughter,' he said. And her dad, the man who was supposed to protect her, was too meek and mild to dare tell Gerrit to be kind to her, as most other fathers would have. Not that the brute paid any attention to anyone.

Even the government feared him. They'd had to intern him during the war because he was forming his own army to support the Nazis. It took ten men to detain him. Gerrit enjoyed the battle. The beast loved nothing more than to wade into a group of men and pound them into the ground, scatter them out of his path. The sound of snapping bones and cries of pain was a symphony to him.

Only once did anyone stop him. A hero decorated with medals, returning from the war, had defended himself and dealt the brute a terrible wound. Far from stopping his rampaging, it only made him worse. Raging against his affliction, Gerrit turned his wrath on his helpless wife and children.

How long could anyone endure that: living in fear and pain, eyes swollen, cheeks blackened and, worst of all, spirit broken? The beast took her, too, whenever he wanted. Took her from behind, turning her over and ramming himself into her like an animal, screaming, 'Take that you whore. You bitch!' until she felt she were nothing. Small wonder she went mad. All those years locked away in a padded room. They drugged her, and she sat rocking for weeks at a time in a dream state.

At some point they stopped the injections, but the madness would not let go, so they subjected her to an agonising regime of electric shock treatment. At times, her mind turned back to those vague phantoms of the past, her boys. What had become of them, with no one to protect them from that monster for all those years? On occasion, when they cleaned her, an old woman looked back at her from the mirror. Where had the young girl gone that she had come back an old woman? Antjie would wonder. And then she recalled, she had been to hell.

The old woman woke one day and the madness had gone, and she was just a shell, empty and lonely, and he was there, holding her hand. Gerrit!

'Ah, get away from me!' she screamed. 'Get away from me, you monster.'

'Ma!' the man who held her cried. 'It's me, Petrus, you don't have to be afraid.'

She looked at his face, so familiar and so strange. So like the man she had hated and the boy she loved.

'You're okay, I'm going to take you home. You'll be safe with me.'

'Where's your father?'

'Ma, it's okay,' he said, aghast at something. His eyes were moist with emotion. 'He's gone. He'll never hurt anyone again.' His arms went around her and she felt the terrible strength in them but also a gentleness that was hard to imagine, and she knew that with him she was safe.

Her madness was gone but reality was not sane for all that. For Gerrit was also gone and yet his spirit lingered on like an evil seed that bloomed in the breast of his son. Like some choking parasitic weed that she feared would one day overwhelm whatever goodness was within him, if it hadn't already.

*   *   *

Although she had returned from the asylum, Antjie thought that perhaps she had never quite fully returned to reality. How else could she have abided living in this house of torture and crime? In this surreal place the old woman had recognised well-known politicians among their visitors. She had witnessed bribes made to a man in almost the highest office in the land. The story was in all the newspapers: a case where the charges had been dismissed for lack of evidence.

Antjie had seen her son preside over a deal that involved selling electrical power to neighbouring countries for huge amounts of cash, paid to the chief minister. The arrangement led to power shortages and blackouts throughout the country. She overheard these potentates boast of the wealth they acquired by demanding part ownership of businesses and ensuring lucrative government contracts. They pocketed millions, selling power to other countries while there was not enough to keep their own people warm in winter. Her homeland was run by so few, who were supposed to serve so many but who served no one but themselves. And at the core of this evil was her own flesh and blood.

Anyone who challenged him disappeared into the cellar where they wore the terrible 'necklace', as Petrus called it. The smell of burning tyre rubber and flesh filled her nostrils as their screams echoed through the house. Her heart ached at their cries but what was she supposed to do? All her life she had been impotent against his father and now it was the same with him. Powerlessness had become a habit.

Inevitably, she blamed herself: Petrus was this way because of her. If she had not given way to madness and been removed from him in his infancy, he would not have turned out like this. He would not have been left with that devil whose heart overflowed with rage that he turned on her angels, trying to warp them into the mirror of his own twisted image. And now, it seemed, with Petrus he had succeeded.

Antjie heaved a heavy sigh, as she had each day for more than fifty years. *My poor Joost, my poor Petrus, what chance did they ever have with a father like Gerrit?*

She thought again of the prisoner slung over the shoulder of that oaf, Johan. The boy's head, blond like Joost's, hung down. He turned his sweet face towards her and for a moment she saw into his eyes. His expression reminded Antjie of the way her children had looked when Gerrit was gripped in a rage and she was powerless to succour them. That same look of appeal was in this dear boy's eyes and once again she was helpless.

CHAPTER
9

Fucking Jerry Lewis

1964

Ben and his friend, Rick, were going to the Saturday morning matinee at the Astra Cinema in Orange Grove. A week earlier, Ben had crashed his bike and broken his coccyx and the pain was excruciating.

'It will subside with time,' the kindly doctor had said, 'but you need to be careful to avoid bumping your bum in any way. So be sure to rest and take it easy.' So of course Ben decided to go see a movie.

The two boys got off the bus outside the Astra. Careful not to aggravate his injury, Ben alighted gingerly in his 'takkies', as the soft white tennis shoes were called. They made their way to the box-office queue to get their tickets.

'Look who's here, it's fucking Jerry Lewis in his takkies.'

The familiar voice terrified Ben. He looked up in horror to see Joey Elias and Patrick Mansur standing right there beside the box office.

His heart sank.

'I'm in deep shit,' he muttered to Rick.

'Who's Jerry Lewis?' Rick asked.

'He's a famous Jewish comedian who wears takkies,' Ben murmured to Rick. 'They're going to hit me – they hate me.'

A good friend, Rick was not about to stand by and watch these guys hit his mate.

'Leave him alone,' he said valiantly to Joey Elias. 'He's badly hurt.'

By now most of the Jewish kids knew enough about the Lebs to avoid them. Rick, however, was still a virgin in that regard. Otherwise he would probably have said nothing and kept himself out of the picture, good friend or not. But it was too late for that.

Joey Elias thumped him a horrible smack in his nose, at the same time Patrick Mansur kicked Ben, right in the coccyx. Ben saw Rick's nose implode and blood spray in an arc across his face about a millisecond before the pain from his posterior exploded in his brain like a great lightning flash, and he remembered nothing more until he heard the voice of an ambulance man asking, 'Are you awake?'

Rick's nose was smashed and needed to be surgically relocated to the middle of his face. Ben recovered slowly from his injury. The pain and difficulty lasted for months, fuelling his growing anger and frustration. He had not recovered from the humiliation. The fear of these assaults happening over and over plagued him, and he knew he would have to do something … but what? Jewish kids were not fighters. They didn't hang out in gangs looking for trouble, so there were no ready allies who he could take on the Lebs with and show any sort of power. The sense of helplessness frustrated him and he felt an overwhelming sense of indignation at the injustice of his situation. His dad had never shied away from fighting back and his legacy was one of courage to resist against intimidation. Had his dad been scared or felt pain at the time, or had he just reacted on the spur of the moment?

Ben was consumed with the need to find a rational solution to his dilemma. If he wasn't scared of getting hurt and could no longer tolerate being humiliated, then there was no reason for him not to fight back. If it was just one-on-one he could win, so what stopped him from becoming a hunter like them? What was there to prevent him from going out and awaiting the opportunity to corner them one at a time? Maybe, if they were beaten often enough, they would eventually leave him alone? At that early stage of his life, Ben decided that he was not going to allow his existence to be controlled by fear. Joey Elias would learn that every action had its consequences.

Joey had to be the target. Clearly, he was the instigator of the trouble and Patrick was merely the backup. Winning a fight happens in a second and the one to strike first is invariably the victor, especially if the blow is unexpected.

10

It'll Be Okay

2009, around 7:45 p.m.

Coming round, Josh swallowed repeatedly, trying to summon enough saliva to lubricate his parched throat. His head ached from a crusted lump behind his left ear where he was first struck. His right cheek had hit the concrete when he had been thrown to the floor and was now too tender to touch. Any sense of how long he had been there eluded him, but it dawned on him that his hands were no longer tied and he moved his feet to discover that they, too, were loose.

Finding himself unbound was a relief, even though his arms and legs were grazed and sore from the ropes. The jagged edge of a broken incisor had cut his lips and the taste of blood inside his dry mouth was sickening. Lying helpless on the low futon bed, he lacked the strength to lift himself up or move off its stinking rough coir mattress. He was utterly miserable.

Nothing in his sheltered existence had prepared him for the feelings coursing through him. In the hours since his capture, Josh had feared himself doomed to die, then allowed himself to hope for a reprieve. Terror and humiliation had immobilised him and the stench of his own urine shamed him.

Moving his head was so painful that even blinking hurt, so he lay motionless on his side, rolling his eyes to glance around the cellar. A single small window was set high in one of the sandstone walls. A meagre light filtered through garden leaves and a dirty pane to illuminate his subterranean prison. There was little else: a table and chairs and an open door to a small bathroom. No way out of this cold and gloomy place offered itself.

He closed his eyes, hoping his body might heal with rest. If his mind could just be stilled he might even sleep and hasten his recovery. It seemed his best chance of survival, if a thin one at that.

*   *   *

While Josh drifted in and out of consciousness, Ben was halfway around the world, on a plane bound for Johannesburg, his son foremost in his mind.

People often described Josh as 'gorgeous'. Not only because of his tall muscular body and angular good looks, but due to his gentle nature and vibrant personality. He stood a little over 180 centimetres, and with more recent training in the gym had built his weight to 80 kilos. His lithe, narrow-waisted physique had become powerful and well defined and bore the hallmark ruggedness of the Novaks.

Being the youngest member of the family, he was the most protected, and it was only when his mum, his ultimate carer, had died, that Josh began to grow up. Prior to that, Saul, two years older, had watched over him. At school, everyone knew he had a big brother who took no shit and this did much to clear his pathway of obstacles.

At twenty-four he was a psychology graduate and working for Saul, setting up laboratories that were testing brain function and analysing the results. He travelled rarely and had been looking forward to this trip.

For Ben, the love of his sons and the powerful connection he shared with them was the greatest of his riches, just as it had been with him and his dad. For his part, Abe had adored his grandsons.

'There is no way to adequately describe the love for a grandchild,' he had told Ben. 'It's different from what you feel for your own offspring, even more intense and yet without the same daily responsibilities. So it's even more pleasurable, if that's possible.'

Abe was unable to hold back the tears whenever he set his eyes upon his grandchildren. He mourned being separated from them. Ben and Dahlia's departure from their homeland had robbed him of his greatest joy. Nevertheless, he had agreed that it was the right thing for them to do. Australia was a land with a future, so he supported their decision to settle there even though it had stolen his time with them from him. Abe loathed having his son so far away and the fact that his two wonderful grandsons would never really know their grandpa.

Evie, Ben's mum, had told him that the last thing on his father's lips before he died had been his grandsons' names.

What would Abe have done? Ben thought. What would he be telling me right now?

The words came to him immediately, as if his father's shade spoke directly into his ear: *It will be okay.*

That's what he told me when I crashed his car when I was only fourteen.

He told me it would be okay before I had to go into the ring with Joey Elias.

'It'll be okay,' he said, when Saul was on the way. 'I'm sure you'll have all the joy from him that you gave us when you were born.'

Abe had been right; it had all been okay, at least until now.

Like any decent father, all Ben ever wanted for his boys was their happiness, their serenity, their comfortable acceptance of themselves, and their enduring peace of mind.

Throughout the years Josh remained a constant source of joy and love to those around him, a precious gift to the world. How could anyone possibly want to hurt him?

Ben's heart ached with fear for his son. The impotence of being strapped in by a seatbelt with so many flying hours ahead was akin to torture, an overwhelming pain and a sense of grief at the thought of Josh being hurt. His only remedy was to allow his fears to be supplanted by a primal urge to inflict pain on whoever might be responsible.

CHAPTER
11

Locked in Battle

1964

Ben was waiting on his bike for his nemesis when, haversack on his back, Joey came out of class surrounded by his friends. Ben kept his quarry in sight until he was walking alone, having turned down the street leading to his home. Oblivious to the sound of Ben pedalling at full speed, Joey sauntered nonchalantly along until Ben's bike ploughed into his back, sending him crashing face first into the ground.

Ben, exhilarated, saw the source of all his pain, anger and anxiety sprawled on the ground not knowing what had hit him. It was beautiful, Ben thought. He had his revenge and Joey wouldn't even know it was him. Maybe now the bully would think twice before he started smacking someone else.

The feeling of elation turned suddenly to horror as Joey roared, 'You are fucking dead!'

His face all bloody, the monster rolled over, bounded to his feet and dove straight at Ben. Both went down, fists flying.

Joey was intent on murder and all Ben's efforts were focused on self-preservation. But Ben's innate power began to work for him. On the ground at close quarters, he could feel he was actually more powerful than his bigger opponent. Keeping his quarry clutched close, he stopped him from swinging his arms and landing punches with those massive meaty fists and was able to scramble onto Joey's back. Then rolling onto his own back, with Joey clamped in front of him, he rendered the monster as helpless as an upturned tortoise. Ben kept his legs wrapped firmly around Joey's waist while his arms throttled him. Joey didn't stop cursing for a second.

'I'm gonna kill you,' he screamed. 'You're dead.'

All the while, Ben clung to him without any idea what would happen next.

This had not turned out as he had expected. The magnitude of Joey's rage was frightening. Ben could not let his enemy go for fear that he would make good his threat, but it was also impossible to continue lying there gripping onto him.

They had probably been trapped in that situation for only a few seconds while he tried to decide on a course of action, but it felt like an age. *I'm such a fool,* Ben thought, *I should have ridden straight off after knocking him down. That way he'd never have known it was me and he wouldn't have a quarry to go after.*

Ben decided there was no real need to fear his opponent over whom he now had the upper hand. Maybe if he let Joey get a few hits in it would be enough to mollify him, and the current impasse would be at an end. The idea was loathsome, but if Joey wasn't satisfied now, he would take his revenge somewhere else and it would probably be worse because his anger and hatred would have had time to build up.

Ben let go and Joey bounced up onto his feet. He turned, his face red with rage. 'You better run,' he snarled.

Joey was presenting him with an avenue of escape instead of immediately 'killing' him. The monster wasn't going to hit back after all. Ben's attack had obviously unsettled him. People didn't fight Joey. Usually they ran away or begged for mercy, but here he was on his own and there was nothing to be proved to anyone else. This match would just be between the two of them, and maybe the bully wasn't as sure of the outcome as he would be when his friends were around.

'Stay away from me, Joey, I don't want to fight with you anymore,' Ben said, as he turned and bent to pick up his bike.

Joey was a street fighter and had been gifted the opening he was waiting for. The moment Ben turned his back Joey pounced, throwing a vicious punch at the back of Ben's head before sprinting away. Once he was at a safe distance he turned to shout, 'You'll never be safe while I'm alive.'

Ben's head pounded. Joey hit hard, and the frustration he felt at creating this dilemma was almost as painful. In one way, little had been accomplished, because, despite his attempted payback, Joey seemed no less committed to perpetuating their vendetta. Yet in another way things were no longer the same. Ben had shown his enemy, and more importantly, himself, that he would not succumb to intimidation. He had drawn on the depths of his inner strength and proven his willingness to pay the inevitable price of holding his head high in defiance. Regardless of Joey's parting threat, Ben was determined to make his life safe from the likes of him and his gang.

CHAPTER
12
Critical Venture

2009

Despite the agony of waiting for the flight to end, in truth, it was a long time since Ben had felt as fragile or as vulnerable as he did right now. Events over the past few years had conspired to force him to re-evaluate his life. A succession of deeply personal setbacks seemed like a divine demand for soul-searching. That bereavement would exact its toll was only natural, but nothing could have prepared him for the unending sadness and loss that followed Dahlia's demise. A thousand images haunted him: her smile, her calm control throughout her illness, the memory of his powerlessness. She had accepted the inevitability of the cancer spreading through her with such grace and equanimity. But he denied it, railed against it, wanted to search the world for the elusive cure, and the rampant disease deprived him of the final peace she seemed to find with her capitulation.

He had loved her from that first moment when he saw her face in the university library. Strands of blonde hair had escaped from under the cap sitting on her high forehead to hang in front of her pretty face with its wide tapered eyebrows and blue-green eyes. Her cheekbones were high and perfectly proportioned. Her mouth and jawline were prominent, the teeth bright white, the bottom row slightly crooked. This last imperfection made her perfect, he thought.

The name 'Dahlia' was written on one of her books. He thought it was lovely and said it out loud.

'Yes,' she said, looking up at him. She studied him for a moment then asked, 'Do I know you?' She had an accent Ben recognised as Israeli. He found it irresistible.

'No, I just saw your name on this notebook. It's your name, isn't it? I like the name Dahlia.'

'Do you know any other Dahlias?' She seemed unaccountably amused.

'Actually, no, I just like the name,' he replied, and he felt a connection in the way she looked at him, a moment of enchantment.

'I like you, too,' he said, emboldened by that look.

She laughed. 'How do you know? You know nothing about me except my name.'

He liked the way she laughed, just a chuckle but it lit up her entire face and Ben could see she liked to laugh and was quick to do so when amused.

She wanted him. He knew it and he thought how marvellous it was the way nature had engineered everything to work. How the brain was tuned to analysing a wealth of minute signs detected by the senses. The manner in which she held her head, the tone of her voice, her aroma – a dozen little cues – allowed her to exude her availability to him, but in such a subtle fashion that their courting would not have been obvious to the uninitiated. Ben wondered if she was aware of it herself.

He put out his hand. 'I'm Ben.'

'Hi, Ben.' She took his hand and they both held on and, although he did not know for sure, he had a distinct feeling that this beautiful Dahlia was the flower he had been waiting for all his life.

'Sshhh,' the librarian hissed in their direction.

'Come for a walk with me,' he whispered.

'I haven't finished yet,' she said, and he started to feel a little crestfallen, but she smiled again and added, 'but it looks like I won't finish today. Where are we going?'

She told him about her family leaving Israel and coming to live in South Africa. In her opinion they had gone from the frying pan into the fire because, while living in Israel was tough, she saw no future in South Africa. The good life there was just a temporary seduction.

He felt an affinity with her on so many levels. He liked the fact that she seemed happy to be herself and live simply. This was not the norm amongst the affluent youth of Johannesburg, particularly the northern suburbs Jews. Theirs was a life of unbridled privilege. They saw little of what was happening in the world and less of what was happening in South Africa.

Ben shuddered, remembering one girl he knew complaining about her black servant failing to iron her jeans satisfactorily, a particularly thoughtless comment because she was going to a students' demonstration in support of Black Rights.

They had crossed over the main road from the university and wandered through a reserve that offered a little slice of nature in the suburbs. He watched her climbing over rocks and strolling gracefully along the sandy pathway. She was dressed simply in jeans and a singlet top with thin shoulder straps that barely hid the straps of her bra. Her breasts were small. Ben liked that, too.

They talked about relationships and she quickly made her requirements clear.

'Trust is everything,' she told him. 'If someone betrays my trust, I'm not the kind of person who can move on from that. I don't understand how people can. Even if I could forgive, I don't know that I could forget.'

Whilst he had never before contemplated being with only one girl and could not imagine himself being monogamous, with Dahlia that suddenly seemed possible. He could see an entire future with her. She had pulled ahead briefly while he daydreamed, and Ben quickened his pace to catch up with her and took her arm to slow her down. Her skin was so silky, so soft. He felt her breath catch as he placed his other hand on her shoulder and she pulled up.

Leaning forward, he rested his lips on her shoulder and brushed the bottom of her hair upwards with his hand so that he could kiss the back of her neck. She gasped and, tilting her head back, opened her mouth so that he could taste her sweetness. Her body pressed against his and she could feel his desire hard against her back. His hands brushed lightly over her petite breasts. She shared his hunger and neither of them wanted the moment to end.

'What's happening here?' he whispered while his lips brushed her ear.

'I don't know,' she breathed, 'but it doesn't feel like you're a stranger I just picked up in the library.' She turned, wrapping her arms around his neck, her lips against his and her heart beating wildly against his chest.

The chemistry was overwhelming, a breathtaking spell that did not lose its grip over time. Ben could never get enough of her. He would wait for the phone to ring when she was finished at the university and leave work to pick her up. She was completing her masters in psychology and he became her test case in therapy as well as her boyfriend.

She loved to talk about his family, its influence over his life and his resultant behaviour, which she thought needed a lot of working on. His history of aggression appalled her. She coaxed from him a gentleness he had all but forgotten yet still lay hidden within.

'The softest thing about Ben is his teeth,' Rick had once said.

Dahlia, though, soon perceived the other Ben, so different from the young man who had first charmed her in the library; the one who seemed to live as if primed for some kind of confrontation. Yet it was hardly surprising when she learned about his years of fighting guys in gangs and the outrages he had suffered in the army, to say nothing of the violence of daily life in a country that had ordinary people packing guns.

Dahlia was never in doubt as to whom the real Ben was, however, even when sometimes he expressed his own doubts about the finer side of his nature.

'Look how you care for Brenda,' she would say. 'You choose your friends according to how they respond to your sister.'

Ben's family adored Dahlia from the first moment they set eyes on her, and Brenda opened her heart and chatted with her like the friend she had longed for all her days.

Dahlia loved Ben's strength but it was his tenderness she treasured most.

'You are a *good* guy,' she always told him. 'You are so gentle,' she would whisper when they made love and she drew him to her, wrapped her arms and legs around him and pulled him in deep.

But if Ben thought he was tough, he found that he'd met his match when he inevitably had another random fight.

'You have this picture of masculinity that requires you protect everybody and defend your turf,' she chastised him. 'Your heroes have been warriors in battle and on the sports field, and you think they're fine role models, so you've become just like them. But they're not an admirable example and not the type I want for my kids. I want them to grow up being able to talk their way out of arguments. I also want them to learn karate so they can protect themselves if they need to, but it should be controlled. You just explode at any provocation and then you revel in it without thinking about the damage it does to the other person and the residue of anger it leaves behind.'

'That's not how you feel when you talk about Israel and the Arabs,' Ben argued. Sometimes it was impossible to resist poking the bear.

He could see the hair on her neck flare. For all her kindness and compassion she was still a feisty Israeli sabra, and he had to be careful when he got her worked up.

'That is in no way similar to what I've been saying,' she hissed. 'The Arabs want the Jews dead. They're taught in school that the only good Jew is a dead one and they have to drive them into the sea.

I've seen it firsthand; school buses full of Israeli children bombed and their little bodies strewn across the roads. They only respect power and cruelty, and regard any form of kindness as a weakness. There is no logic to this behaviour and it calls for an exceptional response.'

Dahlia saw the situation in the Middle East as a matter of the survival of her homeland and race, and could view it with a particular callousness that was not evident in respect to any other matter and quite contrary to her belief in God. And, then, if things weren't complicated enough, there were the angels.

She had been cautious in how she approached telling him about them and how they protected her and talked to her.

'My family think I'm certifiably crazy whenever I talk about it, but my angels have been with me for as long as I can remember. I can reach them whenever I'm sad or lonely, and they never fail to cheer me up or provide much-needed advice. These angels have lived lives before and are either waiting to return to the physical world or for some loved one to join them.'

Whilst Ben, too, had experienced feelings of being protected, which he thought must be like the feeling of angels that Dahlia described, he had never felt the actual presence of entities or conversed with them the way she had. So in the beginning he was sceptical, but she was able to tell him things about people he knew who had died that no one could possibly have known. Ben's mother, Evie, who was known for her own spirituality, told him that the young woman had a gift.

His life had become interwoven with Dahlia's. He was only content when he was with her. They shared the same thoughts and often, when he spoke, he noticed that she had just opened her mouth to say the same thing.

His friends complained that he had disappeared, but what could he do? Why wouldn't he prefer to be with Dahlia? She was beautiful and sexy, and he spent every moment he could in bed with her. She loved to love and was totally unabashed. They would play and experiment and laugh at all the positions they could get into. Her passion was as boundless as her heart. At other times, the tears ran down her cheeks and she would sob, 'I'm just so happy,' because she felt it unfair that she could have so much.

Since her passing he had been lost and it took all his strength to focus on the boys. Her words resounded in his ears: 'It's up to you now. You make sure that all's well with them. See that they find themselves good girls who will take care of them the same way I took care of you. And, Ben, you find yourself another woman.'

How could she do that? How could she say that to him? How could she believe that anyone could ever replace her in his life?

'Honey, you have to live your life,' she said. 'You have to resume it and run your business and find your joy and share it. And if I'm not there then you will have to share it with someone else. I love you and that means that I want you to be happy.'

Logically, he knew she was right, but a vast emptiness had come to dwell inside him. He had no desire for love and even less for being in business. Not at any level. Was it going to be this way forever or just a passing phase? Besides, he was tired of business. The cruel reality was that in that world you were only as good as your last deal and he wasn't doing that well anymore. No matter the lifetime of achievement behind him of developing ideas and putting in place the foundations for building successful enterprises. No matter that people followed him and successfully invested in his schemes time after time and had been well rewarded for doing so. Inevitably he would only be judged and remembered by the success or failure of his last venture.

There had been a myriad of calls from investors whose disappointment in him was difficult to conceal despite the fact that the Information Memorandum had repeatedly warned, 'This investment should be regarded as highly speculative,' and that, 'The forecast income is based purely on assumptions of how the consumer market will accept the new delivery technology'. In previous years he had been hailed 'a remarkable driving force' and 'a serial entrepreneur', and he had been lauded at gala dinners that acknowledged 'fertile minds' and their contribution to the Australian economy.

He had lost his Dahlia and now ProTech was struggling. Over and over in his mind, Ben had examined the business to see if he could uncover some obvious mistake that he had made running it.

'You don't need to be a genius to be a success in business,' he had always said. 'A thriving concern is built on good products or ideas that are "on trend" and distinct from their competitors.' But the most significant driver for success was a clear vision of what that business would look like in the years ahead. Only the venture's creator can have such a vision, can see it in their mind, can touch it in their dreams and articulate it in their plans.

Properly articulated, the vision becomes the driving force. From this the strategic plan is derived and how it should be resourced. Shared dreams would entice the team required for the execution of the strategic plan. Everyone wanted to be a part of the excitement of creation and the success that would follow. And with the vision, the strategy and the people, money was no object. The investors would come – provided that the man at the top had a track record. That is what you were judged on: the number of times you got scores on the board, the likelihood that it would be repeated. It was always at this point that you were only as good as your last deal. If the last one had been a success, the money would be there. If not, it wouldn't. Not from investors, the banks or financial institutions.

Now Ben had ProTech to contend with. The business needed his focus or it could fail and that would be his final legacy, invalidating thirty years of success. Still, he realised in a sudden epiphany that it no longer really mattered. There was no need for more money or challenges. He felt that the 'get up and go' that always made him a Trojan had 'got up and gone'. What he longed for now was Dahlia and peace of mind. He no longer had the appetite for waking up in the middle of the night with the next exciting idea or worrying about what had not been done according to the plan. The vigilance was gone. It was time for something new for him and for someone else to assume the mantle of all his past obligations. He wanted out.

The timing could not be worse. The subprime mortgage crisis had been the prelude to a collapse in value of the global stock markets.

Fears of recession and lower corporate earnings caused panic in investors and the bubble burst. Nothing new; history shows the cycle time and again, but timing makes the genius and Ben's timing was bad. He was reducing debt and selling assets in a market with falling values and seeing millions of dollars of hard-earned wealth disappear.

None of it mattered to him any longer. He had enough and he'd had enough. He was sick of a world dominated by greed and a one-dimensional economic perspective and increasingly bereft of concern for humanity.

Would he have been so contemplative had Dahlia been alive or ProTech had boomed? He liked to believe that, regardless of the circumstances, the time had come to reassess his deeper values, but he could not in all honesty find himself that worthy. Indeed, he too had placed an inordinate emphasis on economic prosperity as the ultimate yardstick of success. Maybe, Ben thought, despite all his rhetoric, he was just the same as those he deplored. The thought sickened him.

No amount of disillusionment, however, diminished the importance he placed on his children, his boys, his gift from Dahlia, his true joy. As long as they were okay he was okay. She would be watching him now. He knew that she would expect him to remain aware that, regardless of what else happened, there was only one thing that mattered, even if it was going to be his last big venture, and that was that he brought Josh home safely.

CHAPTER
13

Garden Boy Job

1968

As the police van appeared around the corner, Joshua Mokwana knew he was in trouble. His friends had more experience in these matters and they knew to scatter immediately, making it impossible for all of them to get caught. But he had been warned before that running had consequences, too. The white policemen would spill out of the paddy wagons and hurtle after the fleeing blacks, lashing out with truncheons and sjamboks. On occasion, depending on their mood, some might even pull out a gun to fire a warning shot.

This could have the effect of making the fugitives stop dead in their tracks with fear. Alternatively, it could give rise to panic and a desperate attempt to get away at any cost. This, in turn, could lead to the appearance of being guilty or of something more sinister than just being on the street without a pass. And that could provide the justification for a young Afrikaner policeman to shoot the 'Kaffir' rather than just firing the customary warning shot.

Dying for being in the wrong place was not uncommon in the streets of the white suburb of Lyndhurst that bordered the black township of Alexandra. Given these circumstances, it was not surprising that Joshua, who on this occasion was merely out walking with a few of his friends, should feel panic as the police van swung round the corner and switched on its headlights while its occupants bellowed orders in Afrikaans.

'Staan stil! *Geen niemand beweeg*!'

Being commanded to stand still and remain unmoving seemed to be an invitation for everyone to run. Yet while the others scattered before the charging police, Joshua stood frozen with fear in the middle of the road, stuck in the glare of the police van lights without his pass.

He remained petrified as the policemen careered around him in pursuit of his comrades, until the sjambok smashed into the side of his head, accompanied by a roared command: '*Le op die grond!*'

'Yes, baas! Sorry, baas!' Joshua cried, lying upon the ground as he was ordered.

How could he have been such a fool as to go out without a pass? Joshua wondered. Too many years of living in the relative safety and comfort of the Novaks' home had made him careless. He had forgotten that this was not the normal way of things with the Afrikaner.

How quickly the memories had faded of the harsh times he had endured after arriving from Islington, his black homeland, to live in Alexandra. Looking for a place to stay, he had been turned away by everyone because he was unknown to them, a stranger in a place where people were wary of strangers and weary from the toll of daily life. He had to 'borrow' a few planks from a building site at night, along with sheets of corrugated iron and used hessian bags, dusty with concrete powder, to make himself a shelter in the shantytown among the thousands who came to Johannesburg looking for work.

Joshua trudged for hours each day along Louis Botha Avenue. The busy artery that connected Joburg to Pretoria carried thousands of whites in cars and blacks on foot, or on bicycles or riding in Putco buses. In the white suburbs he searched for a job, any job, and a white person who would get him a pass and legitimise his presence in the busy metropolis. Joshua made friends with a fellow named Simon who worked for a family by the name of Katz and, one day, finally, Simon had good news for him.

'I have a job for you.'

'What kind of job is it?'

'A garden-boy job.'

'Is that a job for a man?'

'Ja, they just call it a garden-boy job, even though it's a man's job.'

'Is it the same as your job?'

'Oh no! Mine is a houseboy job, although sometimes I do garden work. But a houseboy job needs more experience and the money is better. I am sure they will train you to become a houseboy.'

It was a little too confusing for Joshua.

'And where is this job?'

'It is next door to my job. It was the neighbours who asked me if I can find them a garden boy.'

The interview was easy, and Joshua left his shanty for the luxury of the Novaks' servants' quarters in Glenhazel. In the eight years since he had been with them he had come to love little Ben as though he was his own son, and Ben's unabashed hugging allowed Joshua to believe that, as far as a white boy could love a black servant, Ben loved him too.

'Come, boykie,' he would say to the little boy, using the term his daddy used, and lifting him onto his shoulders to take him to the shops. Everyone called him boykie now.

'You have funny hair,' Ben giggled. Joshua felt the little boy's hands exploring the thick, coarse curls of his coir hair under the disdainful gaze of the passing white neighbours.

They rode together on Joshua's bike with the little boy sitting on the crossbar shouting, 'Go faster!'

'No, boykie. Too fast on a bike is dangerous and you can get hurt and then the baas will not be happy with me.'

'Please, show me how to ride by myself,' Ben pleaded. Joshua taught him, and the following week the boy persuaded his father to get him his own bike. Soon enough, fearless Ben mastered the art of riding around the neighbourhood at breakneck speed until no one could catch him.

When Joshua wasn't working in the house or the garden, they would go and dig in the mud together to find worms and Joshua showed Ben how to attach these to the sharp end of a bent pin.

'It must be hurting them to stick pins in them.'

'Ja, but the fish eat them, the same way that we eat the fish.'

With a nylon line attached, they fished in the dam at the bottom of the road, but they always let the fish go, for Ben could not bear to do them harm.

In the evenings, after the family had eaten their dinner, Ben would come out back to Joshua's humble room in the servants' quarters and share his pap of ground maize and gravy with him. The room was small and contained only the simplest of possessions. But it was cosy, especially when warmed by the paraffin heater in winter, and they treasured the hours they spent together.

Sometimes their conversation would be awkward. For even at an early age there was a distance in knowledge and education between the black man and white boy, which only grew greater as time passed. Nonetheless, they found plenty of information to swap and Joshua loved to listen to Ben tell of his days at school. He roared with laughter when Ben reported his pranks and scowled ferociously at the punishments of the headmaster.

Joshua told the wide-eyed child about life on the kraal and the *tokolosh,* a kind of gremlin. The black people stood the legs of their beds on bricks to prevent him from getting up on them.

Ben was worried. 'My bed isn't on bricks. They'll get me.'

'No, no, you don't have to worry.' Joshua hugged him. 'He won't get you because you're not black. I never heard of the *tokolosh* getting a white boy.'

'Joshua, will we always be together?' Ben asked him once.

Joshua frowned. How could he explain to young Ben that the servant of a white family was paid to relieve the parents of the grind of their daily chores but in no way intended to replace their parental love.

'Yes,' was his simple reply, because their relationship was both unquestionable and indefinable at the same time. It was so much more than master and servant, more than friends, and yet, so much less than father and son.

'What about your own family?' Ben asked. 'Why aren't you with them?'

Again Joshua struggled to describe the situation that required him to leave his loved ones in order to come to Johannesburg. The opportunities were few, and money was needed for their livelihood. But within himself he could not begin to explain his attachment to Ben and the love he had for him that filled a terrible void in his life and helped to stay the ache he felt for his wife and his little girl from overwhelming him. Nor could he tell Ben that he was now plagued by fear, that this new attachment doomed him to lose the love of either one or the other.

*   *   *

'I'm here for Joshua Mokwana,' Ben fumed indignantly. He had stormed down to Lyndhurst Police Station as soon as Simon had apprised him of the situation, cursing about apartheid all the way.

'His arrest is a mistake. I have his pass.'

Ben slammed it down on the desk in front of the sergeant.

'All you had to do was ask, and he would have explained that he had forgotten it at home.'

'Kaffirs must have their passes on them at all times,' the sergeant said, unimpressed. 'It's the *law*.'

'Well that's a stupid bloody law anyway,' Ben snapped.

'I don't make them, I just enforce them,' the sergeant said with a sarcastic smile. 'If you don't like it, get into politics, see how far you get.'

Joshua was brought up from the underground cells. At the sight of the livid weal along the side of his friend's face, Ben's subsiding rage returned, doubled.

'Who did this to you?' he demanded. Ben turned to the brawny sergeant when Joshua dropped his head, unwilling to answer. 'Who's the fucking bastard that hit him? I'd like to give him a klap myself,' he fumed, 'if he has the guts to meet me without his uniform on.'

'*Hoe jou bek, Kaffir boetie*,' yelled the officer, telling the 'Kaffir lover' to hold his mouth. 'You're not funny anymore. Or do you want to find yourself locked up in a fucking cell? Who the fuck do you think you are, loudmouth?'

Finally they released Joshua, eager to get him and his hot-headed defender out of their hair as soon as possible.

* * *

Years later Joshua explained to Sophie, his beautiful wife, that naming their new baby Benjamin would enable him to keep the white boy always in his heart, though it was inevitable that Ben and he would not 'always be together', regardless of his promise.

CHAPTER
14

Contact

2009, around 5 p.m.

Ben watched the familiar red earth flashing by on the final touch-down, and as they taxied towards the terminal, he dialled Josh's number. He sighed, disappointed when it went to message bank again. He wanted it to answer, one way or another.

He called Rick's phone.

'I watched you land,' his friend said. 'I'm waiting outside and will meet you in the front of arrivals in my car.'

'Thanks, Rick. Any word?' Ben asked, although he knew it was redundant.

Something had happened to his son. He accepted that now, it was the only rational conclusion, but what? He also knew that Josh was alive, but there was nothing rational about that knowledge. It was not clear to him how or why he knew this, he just knew it; in the same way that he felt a protective force, the one he had sensed all of his life and that Dahlia called their angels.

'People would think we are crazy,' she would say when they talked about it. Was it merely faith that made them both believe there was something beyond their earthly existence? Or was it just an unwillingness to believe that this life was all there was, with nothing to look forward to thereafter? Or could it have been that they were gifted with a perception that was denied to others?

'No word from Josh, I'm sorry, Ben,' Rick said. 'I've made an informal inquiry with the police. Generally they won't do anything before forty-eight hours is up and then they regard someone as potentially missing, although what they can do about it is anybody's guess. The crime rate here is out of control and there are no resources to deal with it.'

'How high up can we go with the police?' Ben asked.

'I'm sure I can go as high as we need, but I wanted to wait until you arrived and we discussed exactly what you want to do,' Rick replied.

'What I want is to find Josh, whatever it takes. That's all I've been thinking about, trying to work out a strategy the whole way over here. Wait there for me, I won't be long. I have no checked bags.'

'So what's new?' said Rick.

The conversation between them was easy as always. Friends since first grade, Rick held a rare position in Ben's heart. Rick had always seemed the yin complement to Ben's excessive yang. While Ben was playing rugby and competing in iron man events, Rick, the sophisticate, played tennis at the club. If Ben was racing his motorbike in the Trans Kalahari or canoeing the Olifants River, Rick would be skiing in Switzerland or Colorado. While Ben was butting heads with the Lebs, Rick was heading the debating team. Though they seemed at opposite ends of the personality spectrum, together they formed a strange symbiosis.

Ben found Rick waiting in his Mercedes Sports, directly outside the entrance, as he emerged from navigating through the dense, predominantly black crowd that awaited the arriving passengers.

'Still pretentious,' Ben said, eyeing the car, 'and a stupid prick. Why you would make yourself a hijack target is beyond me. And now you make me one.'

'Still the master of charm,' said Rick, rolling his eyes as Ben jumped in beside him. 'And, for your information, the Mercedes Sports is not a popular target. It's too noticeable and easy to trace.'

'Let's go,' said Ben, looking out at the clear late-afternoon sky and calculating. 'Josh's been gone for less than twenty-four hours. I want to talk through everything we know and don't know while we're driving.'

'Where are we en route to, the house or the police?'

'I don't know yet, just drive,' said Ben. 'Here's my thinking. Josh is alive – that much I know – and someone has used his phone to send me a somewhat disturbing message!'

'Okay,' said Rick, 'let's work on that assumption; there's no other ready explanation. We all know Josh. Who would want to kidnap him?'

'I don't know but I'm sure he wasn't grabbed at random,' said Ben. 'Whoever it was, they were specifically after my boy. If it were random they'd shoot him, right? If it was a carjack they would shoot him and take the car. No one randomly kidnaps someone.'

He felt sick saying so, but it was true. Just a few weeks earlier, the brother of one of his friends had been on the telephone with his son when the boy was shot in the head by a gang who had hijacked a vehicle. As they drove off, the gang saw him on the phone and thought he was calling the police, so they killed him.

'What a mad, fucking country! I can't believe I let him come here,' said Ben. 'This is not a hostage or ransom scenario, our family has no profile here and we're not wealthy enough to be a target, agreed?'

'Absolutely,' said Rick. 'This doesn't look like a random kidnapping, but anything can happen here. There was an article today in a UK paper about the state of the crime in South Africa. In the last twenty-four hours there have been 50 murders, 51 attempted murders, 99 rapes, 324 robberies, 575 assaults, 651 burglaries and 39 car-jackings. Those are representative figures, they repeat themselves every twenty-four hours. Most of it is random, so it's possible that what happened to Josh is too. But if it wasn't simply out of the blue, then it must be someone who knows him.'

Statistics like those were not really what Ben wanted to hear; sometimes he wished Rick didn't have such a good head for figures. They made it seem more likely that Josh's disappearance was mere happenstance rather than premeditated. He could not bear to subscribe to that right now. All his reasoning presupposed that Josh was part of some bigger plan, which guaranteed he would be kept alive. Ben had to believe that.

They were entering the freeway outside the airport and heading towards the city and the affluent northern suburbs. The swiftly moving traffic presented a daunting spectacle as drivers, horns blaring and lights flashing, changed lanes aggressively. Hurtling panel vans adapted as people movers, heavily overladen with black commuters, swerved through the tangle of cars, tempting oblivion.

'Will you look at these maniacs!' Ben shook his head.

'Ja.' Rick nodded. 'As if the crime statistics aren't crazy enough there's another thousand people who die on the road every week. The country is in chaos. Sometimes I think I must be fucking mad to live here.'

'Of course you're fucking mad.' Ben laughed grimly. 'Why else would you choose me as a best friend?'

'You're my best friend?' Rick joked. 'I guess you are. I never realised what a sorry sort of bastard I am.'

'Jeez, I could have told you that, if you were in any doubt,' Ben said, punching him in the shoulder.

Since childhood they had shared more than most men did – their innermost thoughts and feelings. Rick was the first person Ben had run to, to blurt out the tale of how he had lost his virginity. The news had been met with disapproval and thinly disguised fascination.

Nonetheless, it took forty years of friendship for Rick to spill the beans about being gay.

Ben's only response had been, 'So what else is new? I've known that almost as long as I've known you. I wondered when you'd get around to telling me.'

Rick had wept with relief and wondered himself why he had let his fear of rejection make him hide his true sense of Ben who had never been anything but accepting.

'Thanks for being here for me,' Ben said, squeezing his shoulder. 'It makes such a difference to have you here to greet me.'

'You've always been there for me,' Rick replied.

As they sat for a moment in silence, Ben's mind immediately returned to his son's disappearance.

'I just can't imagine anyone wanting to hurt Josh. He can't have any enemies. I have never heard of anyone who even dislikes him. You know how gentle and easygoing he is. I only ever hear praise of him.'

'Perhaps what's happened is work related?'

'It may be, but Josh is doing simple technical installation work for a medical technology company and working for Saul, there's nothing remotely sinister about the business or the work they're doing that could explain this. Nonetheless, I asked Saul to make some inquiries and let me know if he discovers anything.'

A disturbing feeling continued to nag at Ben, so painful he could hardly bear to give voice to it.

'If anyone wanted to hurt me, harming my family would be the best way to make me suffer. I think this is about me – about my past. I don't know why or what, but I think someone must be try-ing to get at me by taking my son.'

'If that's the case, why haven't they contacted you?' said Rick.

'We can only speculate,' Ben said with a shrug, 'but it's been less than twenty-four hours. If it is about me then, presumably, they would know that I'd have to come from Australia. There's no way I could have got here quicker than I did. At the very earliest I could only expect to hear from them about now.'

'Have you called Josh's phone?'

'Yes. That was my first call after landing. I just got voicemail. Rick, do you know where he went before he was due to come home last night? Did he say anything?'

'No, only that he'd be home early. I asked my housekeeper, Florence, if he'd said anything to her. She asked him if he was going to be at home for dinner and he said no, but didn't say where he was going or with whom.'

'It's imperative that we find out where he went and who he was with. That may give us some insight into what's happened. What do you think we should do about the police?'

'It's hard to say. There's so much crime and their resources are so stretched, I can't see them devoting any attention to a situation where someone has been missing for less than twenty-four hours. Still, we should report the matter anyway. I also know a private investigator we can talk to. He's well regarded and keeps up with all the latest technology like mobile phone tracking.'

'Great! That sounds really promising. Hopefully he's not too busy with other work. Let's get onto it right away. The clock is ticking.'

'Okay, I'll arrange for him to come to the house. What else?'

'I've got some messages on my phone that I haven't read yet because I was trying to get hold of Josh's phone and you. There's one here from Saul.'

Before Ben could open the message, the phone rang. He took a sharp breath when he saw Josh's number showed on the display and he answered quickly, 'Josh!'

'You will be responsible for your son's death if you do not do what I tell you. Do you understand me?'

It was the same deep-voiced Afrikaner with the heavy accent. He spoke slowly, his words filled with malice. Fear flooded into Ben's being at the idea of someone having his son in their power, caging him, hurting him. A terrible rage, beyond imagination, welled up in the wake of that cruel tide of emotion.

It took all of his resolve to bite off the venom that threatened to spew forth from his lips. 'Who are you?' he pleaded instead. 'What do you want from me? Is it money? I'll get you money, just don't hurt him!'

Rick pulled the car off to the side of the freeway and stopped under a large billboard.

'I'm not interested in your money,' said the voice. 'Go to your friend Rick's house and wait there for me to call you. Don't talk to the police. I'll know if you speak to anyone, the same way I know that you have arrived in South Africa, and who you are with … and which seat you sat in on the plane.' He disconnected before Ben could say another word.

With the discussion replaying in his head, Ben slumped back, staring blankly up at the billboard. A beautiful sexy black woman gazed back at him, a condom in her tapered fingers. The slogan proclaimed, 'If it's not on, it's not on.' If South Africans weren't being murdered or raped or killed in the carnage on the roads, there was a good chance they would die from the HIV/AIDS that infected thirty per cent of the population.

What has become of this godforsaken country? How could it have entangled me again? Ben thought.

Ben recounted the entire conversation to Rick, who looked appalled.

'I was right,' Ben said. 'This isn't random, but I would never have guessed that whatever is going on would be so organised.'

'Who the fuck are we dealing with here?' Rick swore. 'He knows who I am and who you sat next to on the plane. What kind of power gets someone that kind of information?'

Ben remembered the pretty South African flight attendant who had been so friendly. 'Sandy,' he mumbled, recalling her name tag.

'What?' Rick asked, nonplussed.

'Nothing,' Ben replied. 'But to answer your question, I have no idea who has the power to put a plan like this together.'

'Well, what have you been messing about with to attract this kind of attention? Here, in South Africa? It's not as though you spend much time here!'

'I haven't done anything,' said Ben. 'My life is quieter now than it's ever been. I'm retired and I don't know of anyone who'd want to harm me. Dahlia and I spent most of her last few years at our cottage in the middle of nowhere. This can't be about something I've done, certainly not recently.'

'Well, at least we know for sure that Josh is alive,' said Rick. 'Now we have to find out what they want in order to let him go.'

'The problem is,' said Ben, 'if they're not after money, then what else could it be? It has to be for some sort of leverage, to force me to do something that I wouldn't be prepared to do in other circumstances.'

'Let's go to the house,' said Rick, 'and get that investigator, fast.'

CHAPTER
15

The Big Fight

1969

It was the last days of high school, and Ben was destined to spend the following year in the army after he returned from a holiday in Cape Town.

'I can't imagine being in the army,' Rick said with a shudder, as they sat in Ben's room discussing the future.

'I think it'll be okay,' Ben said.

'I don't know.' Rick grinned. 'Maybe there won't be enough fighting for you, unless they send Joey and his mates along.'

'Yeah, I'll miss him okay,' Ben said. 'Thanks to Joey I feel I've already done basic training and more. If not for him I might never have been inspired to put all of those hours into the gym or taken up judo and karate. I mean, I'm inherently strong, but I'd never have become this unstoppable fighting machine without that bunch to motivate me.'

Ben stepped back, threw a couple of shadow punches and struck a body builder's pose for good measure. He wiggled his eyebrows.

'Yeah, the legendary Novak,' Rick snorted. 'And where do you get your modesty from?'

'Dunno, must just be inborn, too, like the killer fighting instinct.'

'I should have guessed. You know, Joey and his ilk also inspired me.'

'Really?'

'Yeah, they inspired me to keep out of trouble. You see, between these two ears, I have what's called a brain. It sends instructions to my mouth that help me actually get out of trouble, rather than into it.'

'Interesting,' Ben said. 'That sounds almost crazy enough to work.'

'You might try it sometime.'

'Hmm,' Ben mused. 'If I didn't know better, I'd think you were suggesting that, in some way, my dilemma is my own fault. I'm a legend. Can I help it that there's always some moron who wants to try to prove I'm not unbeatable?'

Rick sighed. 'I guess not.'

'Come on!' Ben protested. 'Have you ever known me to pick a fight?'

'No,' Rick conceded. 'I've also never known you to back away from one.'

'Well, I've got my reputation to think of.'

'Are you normal? What good is your reputation when all it does is get you into fights?'

'That's not all it gets me into.' Ben did the eyebrow thing again. 'It also gets me into a lot of girls' pants.'

'Yeah, they do love a tough guy, don't they.' Rick sighed as if he were jealous.

'They sure do,' Ben said, playing along. 'But it shouldn't bother you, right? You're still saving yourself for someone special?'

'Absolutely,' Rick said, folding his arms and looking out the window. Ben's bedroom was at the front of the house in what used to be the sunroom. His parents had let him move in there after his mum had walked in on him having sex with the girl from three doors up the street. The room had its own entrance and plenty of privacy and freedom to come and go without them knowing what he was up to. He had been pushing for the move for some time.

Ben had overheard them discussing it. His mother wasn't too pleased with his new hobby but Abe was more sanguine.

'Hon, he's horny,' he said. 'What do you expect at his age?' And there was no mistaking the sound of pride in his voice.

'You've had it pretty good here,' Rick said. 'Your parents let you do everything, and you've had me to help you through with your matric.'

'Yeah, you saved my derrière there.' Ben nodded.

His matriculation results had been a surprise to all, including Ben, who had spent seemingly countless hours of what should have been study time playing pinball at the Sydenham café. The little room at the rear of his favourite hangout was like a drug, and he couldn't get enough of the dimly lit smoky atmosphere, the dinging of the machines and cluck of the free games that were the reward of his conquests. Without Rick's help he would never have done as well.

'Still, my life's not entirely a bowl of cherries. Fucking Elias has been riding me worse than ever lately.'

Rick shrugged. 'School's nearly over and it's eating him up that he still hasn't been able to establish himself as top dog. Everyone else in the school is terrified of him. Time's running out for him to prove he's lord and supreme ruler of all he surveys. Just stay out of his way for the next couple of weeks and you're home clear. How hard can it be? Because if there's one guy you do not want to fight, it's Joey Elias.'

'No shit, Sherlock.' There were limits to even Ben's bravado. 'He's twice my fucking size and since he got serious about boxing he's become a good athlete, too.'

Over the years Joey had filled out even more and he now topped 190 centimetres, his bulky frame dwarfing Ben's. The acne was no longer red and raw, but it had left a field of craters spread across Joey's brutish face giving it the look of some angry planet. His aura signalled 'don't fuck with me' like a flashing neon sign the size of a building.

'Yeah, and he's a maniac as well. He could have killed that kid he bottled last week at Carl's party. I swear he's getting worse.

Whatever you do, do not get in a fight with that guy. Two weeks, remember, it's just two weeks.'

'Don't worry, I'm not crazy.'

* * *

Ben had never been more serious about anything than avoiding a fight with Joey Elias. Yet the tension was getting to him, and when two days after this conversation the mauler pushed in front of him at the canteen, instinct took over.

'Hey, get back in the line,' Ben growled, grabbing Joey by the bicep.

'Make me,' Joey snarled, pushing Ben in the chest.

Ben hesitated just a moment. A savage grin twisted the lips of the bigger youth. 'Well, Novak, are you gonna try and make me, or are you chicken?'

A crowd had grown around them and pressed forward with the usual mix of anxiousness and excitement that a looming fight stirred up.

'CHICKENNN!' shouted a voice from the throng.

Ben shoved Joey back. 'Fuck you! I'm not scared of you!'

Ben's heart pounded, and he could feel the adrenalin pumping. He was madly trying to concoct a way out of the fight altogether, without seeming to be a coward.

'In the gym, tomorrow. You and me, man to man,' Joey said.

A prearranged fight with Joey was a disaster in the making. *If it is going to happen, it should happen now,* his mind urged him. *Hit the bastard first. Get it over with.* Instead, he found himself saying, 'Fine, in the gym.'

'Great,' growled Joey. 'About time someone knocked your fucking block off.'

'Fight!' yelled a voice in the crowd. Some little turd who would shit himself in a brawl, but was keen to watch someone else get pounded. 'Big match in the gym tomorrow, Elias and Novak, great match!' he shouted, letting the whole school know. Ben wanted to hit him.

Suddenly it was locked in. Ben sighed at the idea of another battle.

'What is it with you?' said Rick. 'Did we not just talk about this! I'm sick of it.'

'What's it to you? You're not involved. It's not like you've ever swung a punch to help me in all these years.'

'Well, that's the point,' said Rick. 'I'm always feeling bad; like I should be doing something. But you get yourself involved in this stuff, and I'm left feeling guilty.'

'Rick, do me a favour and fuck off! I've known you since I was five years old. I've had a hundred fights. You've never had one. If you felt so guilty you would have stepped in and helped me at least once. One thing I've learnt is never to rely on you as a backup. I'm too busy thinking about Joey fucking Elias to worry about your fucking guilt complex,' Ben said, storming off.

He was furious. Not least of all because Rick was right about one thing: the battle could have been avoided. How was it that one guy went through his entire life never having a fight and another one never stopped fighting? He had deliberately cultivated his macho persona. Although there was more to him than just muscle and grit, he had buried the kindness and tenderness deep within himself so that only a rare few would ever recognise it. He had armoured himself in a macho shell, largely as a response to the long drawn-out vendetta. There was never a night out or a party when one of his foes didn't turn up. If they set eyes on him, a battle ensued. The struggle had profoundly changed him, forcing him to be wary and on guard all the time.

If there was one thing that growing up around the gangs had taught him, it was that there is no such thing as a fair fight. He was not proud of many of his actions, but he would use any means at his disposal to win. In the final analysis there was only a winner or a loser. Once, when he had been on the ground fighting Joey, one of Joey's gang had kicked him in the face and literally almost knocked his block off. Any lingering attachment to the concept of a fair fight was knocked out of him at the same time. A smashed nose and broken teeth were hardly badges of honour. He vowed that would never happen again. He decided the use of any handy weapon, be it a stick or a stone, or any tactic, was justified. Kicking and biting were particularly effective.

Knowing that made this fight with Joey Elias the biggest mistake he could make. He had got himself into a scheduled battle, losing the element of surprise and sacrificing his only advantage against that monstrous bully.

Joey Elias wanted a 'fair fight' in the gym with boxing gloves, in controlled conditions, no kicking, no biting, where he had the size and weight advantage and all his training as a boxer. What was fair about that? It didn't suit Ben; no one won a battle by letting his opponent choose the circumstances.

Fucking idiot, he said to himself, *agreeing to fight in a gym.*

*   *   *

Ben was lying on his bed cultivating a sense of lightness, of his body floating, letting it soothe his mind and ease the panic gnawing away in his stomach. There was a light tap on the bedroom door, and Abe entered.

'What's going on, my boy?'

His dad had this uncanny ability to read him. He always took his time and chose the right moment so that when they conversed, it never felt like an intrusion. That they were so close was a testament to their relationship, even though Abe was relatively old as a parent.

'I'm shitting myself,' said Ben. 'I got into an argument with Joey Elias again and it finished up that we're having it out in the gym tomorrow. He's going to kill me.'

'That's no good, boykie! Why don't you just refuse to fight?'

'I wish I could, Dad, but it's gone too far for that. In any event, I wouldn't be able to look at myself in the mirror if I took that way out. He called me chicken, and if I don't go through with it, that's all everyone will remember, that I was chicken.'

'Ben, the only person you need to worry about is yourself. It's irrelevant what other people think. You know that. You've always stood up for yourself. It depends on how important this is to you. Is it worth getting a hiding over?'

'Probably not, but I know that I'm not going to back out, so I also know that I'm going to get beaten up. I'm just trying to get myself prepared. Why did I do this? I'm such an idiot.'

'Yeah, probably.' Abe laughed. 'But it's not entirely your fault. Fighting is in your blood. I always told you how my brothers and me never backed off. Maybe I should have kept my stories to myself. But I'm proud of what we did. That Uncle Les of yours.' Abe chuckled. 'Joining the army to fight the Germans and then deciding he wanted to be in the air force and become a pilot. So he deserts from the army, changes his name and trains as a pilot, and all the while the military police are looking for him as a deserter. And then that's not enough for him. After the war ends, he has to be one of the first to go to Israel and become a pilot in the War of Liberation.

'All of that, Israel's entire struggle for survival following the Holocaust, the struggle of our whole race, is part of your identity. Look at these books you read.'

Abe tapped a finger against the spines lining the little bookcase set into the head of Ben's bed. *Exodus* and *Mila 18* by Leon Uris. Abe was right, those novels had left an indelible imprint of their people's suffering in his young mind. And one question burned in his brain above all others: why had so many of them gone so meekly to the gas chambers? Why didn't they rise against their oppressors when they knew they were going to die? What had happened to make them so apathetic about their own survival? Plagued by these thoughts, Ben had become determined that he, Ben Novak, like the others of his clan, was one Jew who would never go quietly.

'So long as you're not a bully,' Abe said, 'I think it's a good thing that you aren't afraid of fighting. Sometimes, it's the only noble thing to do.'

He ruffled Ben's hair. 'It'll be okay, my boy. You can't get too hurt with gloves on.' That was Abe; he always had an unshakeable belief that everything would be okay. Right now there was little else he could do other than reassure his son that the choices he made were his own and the consequences were ultimately his personal responsibility too. Yet Ben knew that behind the veneer of calm and comfort, Abe worried, too, and despite his faith that all would turn out well in the long run, he still wept in secret for every pain his son suffered in the meantime.

Abe patted his shoulder and left him to his thoughts. Ben felt comforted by his father's concern and the words of reassurance. Yet one thing bothered him still. His father was right: sometimes to fight was the only noble thing to do. But if he were honest, there was more to it than that. There was a part of him that revelled in the challenge, the primitivism of it. He didn't seek violence but he never avoided it either, and he wondered how much that, too, was part of the family heritage, or was he the only one with a mean streak?

This was no time to be pondering the possible flaws in his character, however. If he was ever going to improve himself, he would have to survive the coming battle with this goliath first. All he could do was visualise Joey Elias's horrid face; meditate on it as a target for his wrath to be delivered at the hard end of his fists. *I'll retaliate first*, he thought. *And hit hard.* Ben insulated himself from the idea of losing with the understanding that the pain of defeat would be temporary but the memory of winning would last forever.

*   *   *

At 11 a.m., the start of the morning tea break, Ben arrived at the gym building to find it jam-packed with students, all shoving to get a view of the boxing ring. The entire student population, it seemed, had managed to escape class to be there. All those unable to squeeze inside the doors strained at the windows to see the outcome of this highly anticipated event.

Ben had spent the morning feeling sick in his stomach and weak at the knees. This experience was not new to him, but previously the nausea had lasted only for a few seconds prior to the adrenalin rush at the beginning of a fight. This time it had dragged on through the night and the morning as the dreaded moment drew inevitably

closer. Still, pushing his way through the crowd, Ben was comforted by the chorus of cheering. Students jostled one another to
slap him on the back, and the familiar faces of his friends beamed
at him with encouragement and support. To discover just how
many people wanted to see him put an end to Joey's reign of terror
was somewhat overwhelming.

'C'mon, Ben, finish him off quickly!' someone yelled.

Joey was already in the ring with his gloves on and did not seem
to be suffering any of Ben's anxieties. As he danced around, shadow
boxing, his gloves sliced through the air with lightning-fast jabs
left, right and centre.

By the time Ben had stripped off his shirt, he was actually glad
that within the next few minutes it would all be over, one way or
another.

Mr Van, the gym master, called them to the centre of the ring.
Joey was studying his opponent's wiry muscular physique and Ben
was pleased to note a flicker of concern flash across his pockmarked
face.

'Where are your gloves, Ben?' asked Mr Van.

'I'm not fighting with gloves,' said Ben. 'I'm not a boxer.'

'What do you mean you're not wearing gloves?' said Joey, his
look of concern deepening. 'You have to. I am.'

'You wanted the fight,' said Ben. 'You chose the time and the
location, but don't tell me what to wear. If you want to fight with
gloves that's fine by me, but I'm not.'

'That's not fair,' Joey wailed against the background ruckus of
the crowd.

'Well, take your gloves off and we can both fight with bare fists,'
said Ben. 'That's fair, and I won't kick you either,' he added, to the
concern of both Joey and Mr Van, neither of whom had considered
that as a possibility.

'Take them off. Take them off,' the crowd began to chant, impatient for the action to begin.

Ben stood steely still, his body tensed and his muscles flexed,
while Joey took off the gloves, his entire demeanour different, his

arrogant confidence undermined by the changed rules of engagement. By all accounts the odds should still have favoured Joey with his longer reach, larger size and weight, but Ben had settled and was focusing his mind and his gaze on the acne-scarred face. The crowd, too, had sensed the shifting dynamics and had quietened in expectation of the start of the bout.

Reciting his customary routine, Mr Van told them to return to their corners and come out fighting. Ben had no intention of returning to his corner or sizing up his opponent and circling him to see how the battle was going to play out. He exploded, seeing only Joey's face and counting the number of times he could slam his fists into it. In a blur of speed, he launched his vicious attack and had Joey back-peddling. With Joey's greater height and longer reach Ben struggled to get at his head, where he could do the most damage.

Knowing that the longer the fight continued, the more it would favour his opponent, Ben's instincts took over and, forgetting his promise, he kicked Joey, twice. The first was a roundhouse that caught Joey in the side, bruising his ribs. Ben danced back and came in again, throwing the kick higher and landing it with precision on the side of his enemy's head. Joey's ear was bleeding, and Ben could almost see the wicked impression on his temple. Joey dropped any pretence of being a boxer as he covered his face and head from the multitude of blows that rained on him from all sides as Ben buzzed around him. It took just seconds to obliterate the titan.

Some of the crowd, probably Joey's mates, were booing, but they could hardly be heard above the roar of cheering.

'No kicking!' Ben heard Patrick Mansur yell. 'You're a dirty fighter, Novak!'

'Fuck you!' Ben screamed back. 'There's no points for losing.' He had put up with too many years of Joey's bullying to feel any remorse at finally giving him some just compensation.

The match was over and the crowd was gone, and all that was left was Joey with his injured head and his injured pride. Although in some ways his victory seemed pointless, Ben was glad he had won, and he knew that his swift and ruthless conquest would become fabled at the school.

Nonetheless, as Ben grew older, he grew doubtful about the value of a victory attained through violence. He had come to think that this urge in him, which persisted regardless of his intellect, his understanding of human nature or his compassion, diminished him in his own eyes, even while it glorified him in the eyes of so many others. He had begun to consider that there might be other ways to resolve his conflicts that did not necessarily involve brutality, but this approach would still need a bit of working on.

At the same time, however, Ben pondered how he might not have fully appreciated the residue of anger left in Joey and the malicious desire for revenge that could fester for years to come.

CHAPTER
16

Rocco

2009

Rocco Petersen's résumé included stints as a mercenary, bodyguard, policeman and lawyer. Currently, he wore the hats of a private investigator and specialist in electronic surveillance, and they were an excellent fit. For everything Rocco revealed there were just as many closely guarded secrets. He looked like a body builder, almost as wide as he was tall. His short-cropped salt-and-pepper hair and authoritative manner lent him the air of the military man.

Ben's confidence in Rocco grew as he found himself thoroughly interrogated by a man possessed of an impressive degree of ingenuity and assertiveness. He liked his swift penetrating analysis of their situation and his determination to gather all the facts before considering any plans for action. Even Rocco's straightforward and matter-of-fact manner regarding his fee pleased Ben, for although it was exorbitant, it came with a commitment to do 'whatever it takes to get the result we want'. In the end, that was all that mattered to Ben.

'They want something from you,' Rocco said, looking intently at his client. 'We know they are South African, and we'll gain a lot from ascertaining how it became known that Josh was your son and visiting here. Could it be through someone at his work or from his immediate associates?'

Ben shook his head, bewildered.

'Other than work, where has he been in the last week?' Rocco asked.

Rick answered, 'Josh arrived last Friday and we went straight to our game lodge for the weekend. Then he went to work on Monday.'

'Tell me more about the lodge.'

'We named it Makanyi,' said Ben. 'It's part of the Timbavati Game Reserve in the Lowveld. We bought it about eight or nine years ago with the profits from a technology company that our army buddy, Harry, had floated. Acquiring the lodge provided a wonderful opportunity to share an enduring part of the African bush and leave a legacy for our children.' Ben's voice filled with fervour as he recalled the reunion with his motherland.

More than twenty years had passed since he and Dahlia had left South Africa and, as much as he had tried to leave Africa behind, a deep yearning remained stubbornly lodged in his heart. The times spent with his friends at university in the early seventies were impossible to forget. At every chance, they went travelling throughout the southern part of Africa. They had lived so many unforgettable experiences on these expeditions, their canoe trip down the Olifants River being among the most momentous.

In 1978, inspired by the riveting movie *Deliverance*, Harry and Ben procured a sponsorship from *Scope Magazine* and tackled the mighty river in custom-made canoes similar to those in the film. Accompanying them on their six-day adventure was Robert, a friend they had met on their travels and who had grown up in the Timbavati. No one knew the bush like him and only his knowledge of the habitat enabled them to safely negotiate the fast-flowing, rocky river that bristled with crocodiles and hippos. Their adventure had not been without incident, for the Olifants fought them like a thing alive, challenging them at every turn, and on a particularly treacherous stretch it bucked them so fiercely that Harry was catapulted from his canoe and swept away with no hope of rescue from those following behind.

Meanwhile, Robert had already safely negotiated the white water to their destination only to find himself alone in a pool filled with young hippos and their mother. Hippos are responsible for more human fatalities than any other animal, and protective females with calves are the most lethal. Heart in his mouth, Robert made straight for shore and hauled his canoe to safety. Desperate to warn the others, he sprinted back through the bush to discover Harry floundering in the raging waters that were no less vicious than the hippo mother awaiting their arrival. On an impulse that later seemed inexplicable, he had brought a rope with him from his canoe. Not stopping to ponder this serendipitous fortuity, he plunged into the river and fixed the rope around Harry, saving him from a sure death. For, had he not drowned before reaching the hippos, he would have lacked the strength to elude them.

As the others joined Robert to help Harry safely ashore, he told them of the danger lying ahead and they left the water well before it arrived at the pool. Approaching cautiously along the bank to see if they could recover Harry's canoe, they found that it had managed to reach the hippos unmanned, where it had been chomped in half by the warlike mother. They cautiously salvaged what they could from the broken vessel, and retired to a safe spot to build a fire. Late into the night, in the rarefied beauty of their remote haven, they sat drinking Black Label scotch straight from the bottle and gloating at their triumph over nature. It was then that Ben and Harry made a promise to each other that remained forever etched in their minds.

One day we will own a precious piece of this sanctified soil.

'We celebrated our good fortune by consummating a pact we made together many years ago. We bought three thousand hectares of the Timbavati Reserve. As you no doubt know, it's wonderfully rich in wildlife, and we gave our friend, Robert, and his wife, Margaret, lifelong jobs as wardens and caretakers of this dream of ours.'

'Hmm,' Rocco mused. 'Is it possible that Josh might have met anyone there who could somehow be connected to his disappearance?'

'On Sunday evening,' Rick replied, 'Robert and I had a meeting with our neighbour, De Jager, who owns the tract of land southwest of Makanyi. He'd seen Josh in a Land Rover near his border and asked about him. I don't think he's a nice guy. He can put on the charm when it suits him, but it always seems a facade to me. Thinking back on it, when we explained who Josh was, he repeated the name "Novak", almost as though it was familiar to him. I didn't think it meant anything at the time but …'

'Tell me more,' Rocco urged instantly, suddenly alert as a hound that scents a hare. 'Who is this De Jager? What was your meeting about?'

'We've been a thorn in his side for years,' said Rick. 'We're strenuously opposed to any form of hunting in the region. De Jager has been there for about six or seven years and has, to the contrary, always allowed hunting on his property. In more recent times, our lobbying with the National Parks Board and other owners in the region has gained momentum. This has infuriated our pugnacious neighbour. Essentially, he's been telling us that no matter what we do, he'll continue to hunt, but we would be better off if we kept our opinions to ourselves rather than rallying against him.'

'That could be significant,' said Rocco. 'This dispute may have motivated him to seek some form of leverage. As lacking in finesse as it may seem, it is a possibility. What else do you know about De Jager?'

'Not a lot,' said Rick. 'He keeps a low profile but he's rumoured to be well connected. I have no direct knowledge but the word in the local area is that a lot of senior government people go hunting on his farm. We're pretty sure that's why our initiatives are regularly blocked.'

'Hold on,' said Ben. 'If he wanted leverage, why would he have an interest in Josh? How could he know that we have any ownership in Makanyi? Our financial involvement is through an offshore company, and none of us has ever met him. How would he even suspect we are related?'

'Ben,' said Rick, 'I think Robert may have mentioned that Josh was the son of one of the lodge's proprietors.'

'It's him!' said Ben. His every instinct cried out that this was the case. 'He must be the one. He's got Josh.'

'Whoa, hold on!' said Rocco. 'Don't go jumping to conclusions. Just because there's been some trouble with De Jager, it's still highly unlikely that he or anyone else would abduct Josh on the strength of an altercation over land that hasn't gone particularly far. Still, it's a lead worth following up.'

'It's the closest thing I can see to a reason for what's happened,' said Ben. 'I have been racking my brain as to why anything should happen to my boy, and this is the only sniff of a motive that comes to mind. I want to go and see this guy.'

'Relax, Ben!' Rocco interjected. 'Abduction is a very serious offence and the consequences are dire. When someone embarks on this course they know the risks they're taking, and they're likely to be extremely dangerous. You can't go waltzing up to a suspect without being adequately prepared. If they're not involved you may unwittingly telegraph our intentions to the real perpetrators, and if they are connected you expose yourself and your son to a danger that can well be avoided. So, please, let's stay calm and think things through logically and with a minimum of emotional distraction. I understand that this isn't easy for you, but we have to do it my way. Let's face it, time is of the essence and if De Jager is a red herring it will be a setback if we go chasing it.'

Ben paced the room, his brow furrowed with worry. He unclenched his hands and rubbed his head in frustration.

'Ben,' Rocco said. 'This is one of those times when you have to think like a man of action but, more importantly, act like a man of thought.'

Ben halted. 'You're right,' he said. 'But it's my *boy*. This is fucking hard for me!' Nevertheless, despite his anguish, Rocco's firm sense of purpose was reassuring and Ben surrendered to his good sense.

'Rick,' said Rocco. 'Let's go back to De Jager's interest in the name Novak. You said he repeated it as if it were familiar?'

'Ja, that's right.' Rick nodded.

'Well, if De Jager knows you, Ben, chances are you know him. Does his name mean anything to you?'

Ben shook his head. 'Not at all. But that's not something I have a good memory for. What does he look like?'

'Not pretty.' Rick grimaced. 'He's an older guy in his sixties and very tough. He wears an eye patch; must be missing an eye.'

'Not the sort of face you forget,' Ben mused. 'I can't say I recall anyone who fits that description.' Yet there it was again, that ominous feeling. 'I wonder why he would seem to recognise my name.'

'Well, you're not the only Novak,' said Rocco. 'Maybe he knows someone else by that name. Gentlemen, our enemy said he would call you back. We have to wait for that call. In the meantime, I'm going to leave you here while I organise a triangulation on the phone and see if I can get some more information about De Jager. His name is very common, however, and I would need to have some more specifics on whom to look for. Also, I must caution you not to expect too much from the triangulation. If these people really are as smart and organised as they appear, they'll know that the location of the mobile phone can be detected, so it's unlikely they'll continue to use it. But call me as soon as he phones and make a careful note of everything he says. In these cases, and I know it sounds clichéd, but the devil is in the detail.'

'You are right about the devil,' said Ben grimly. 'Anyone who would abduct another man's child is a devil. I just want to see him in hell, where he belongs.'

He accompanied Rocco along the forty-metre long passageway that led from the office to the cavernous entrance of Rick's house. Once there, Rocco would have to drive to the private guardhouse to be ushered out of the grounds. After that, a guarded barricade that sealed off the homes of the elite Pioneer Avenue Estate from the grand suburb of Sandhurst remained to be negotiated. To top it off, the entire gated community was sealed off from the city of Sandton. Sometimes it seemed there was no end to the barriers in South Africa.

As they walked, Ben gazed around at the opulent monument Rick had built to himself. Spanning sixty metres, the magnificent edifice of modern architecture appeared to float on a series of pools and fountains that cascaded towards the north. Facing the sun, it overlooked an emerald expanse of manicured lawns bordered by gardens.

Rocco also had noticed. 'Ja, all this for one man alone, in a land where so many have so little and so few have so much,' he said, shaking his head. 'In my professional life, I've seen it all. I've had so many opportunities to acquire wealth over the years, if I had just been willing to make a few compromises. I always prided myself on the fact that I have never been tempted.'

'So being the ultimate professional has always been enough reward?' Ben quizzed.

'The excesses that I have seen within my clients' realm have seldom brought them happiness or contentment and I have never coveted any of it. My satisfaction is in working every job through to its conclusion, no matter what the odds, and in succeeding where many others would have tried and failed.'

Ben liked everything that he had seen about Rocco. He did not need much convincing. His intuition also told him that while he may have thought of himself as a smart tough guy, he was in well over his head and his need for a professional's help was far greater than he had realised initially. In this regard, Ben felt quietly content that Rocco was the best he could get.

CHAPTER
17

You're in the Fucking Army

1970

The recruits received their draft papers during their matriculation year, a few sheets outlining their army number and the name of their regiment. Ben was joining the Transvaal Scottish, which had been founded in 1902 following the conclusion of the Boer War. He was told his army number was the only information he could ever disclose about his training.

No details were provided about their future activities, just a short list of items to bring along with them, like underwear and socks, sports shoes and an iron. Everything else would be supplied when they arrived at their destination: Walvis Bay in South West Africa, the one place you didn't want to get drafted to.

It was rumoured that a year in the army would be a good time to catch up on reading and rest following the stress of studying for matriculation. Ben, therefore, had pictured himself relaxing on a bunk, reading books and smoking cigarettes pretty much at his leisure. The five-day train ride to Walvis would merely be a brief interlude of discomfort until they reached their vacation camp. Such laughable naivety.

Amongst the South African Jews there was a network of successful upper-middle-class business people. In Johannesburg many lived in comfortable houses in the avenues of the northern suburbs. Other Jews were well integrated in smaller country towns and villages, and many owned concession stores that operated in the vast mining communities, where much of the early wealth of South Africa originated. But wherever the Jews were, they retained a distinct communal identity, their lives centred around their synagogue and their kin.

The acquisition of a good education and success in business were the ambitions most Jewish parents had for their children. These were the pathways to freedom and insurance against the event of another forced migration. They were never sure how long the good life in South Africa would continue. The influx of Holocaust survivors impacted the consciousness of many South African Jews. After Hitler had 'cleansed' Europe, they no longer believed that anywhere was quite safe.

The massacre of blacks by police in Sharpeville in 1960 was a stark and bloody reminder of another rising well of anger and dissatisfaction; this time the black people against the whites, the have-nots against the haves. The Jewish youth growing up in their segregated and insular communities were far removed from the poverty and brutality of the real life of the country. This separation did not adequately prepare the boys for the army, where they would be exposed to the harsh and brutal world of the Afrikaner whose heritage was a myriad of savage wars. Initially with the indigenous people during the first century following white settlement, and then in battle with the cruel British forces during the Boer War.

Of the seven hundred recruits boarding the train that day in January 1970, a handful were Jewish boys from around Johannesburg. Many had been at King David, a Jewish-only private school. They represented the few whose parents had not exerted sufficient influence over the drafting authority to keep them away from South

West Africa and closer to home. Whatever the reason for their presence, they searched for each other, finding comfort in their sense of
shared identity.

Gossip and stories had circulated of Ben's battles with his Lebanese nemeses and, therefore, he was generally regarded as a pariah
by most parents and a character their child would do best to avoid.
But on the eve of leaving for SWA, word was out that Ben was on
the train. For a rare moment in his life, there was a jockeying for a
position to share his company amongst that handful of Jews who
were comforted by the idea that there was at least one kid among
them who could take care of himself and maybe them too.

Five of them had settled into a compartment together, briefly
encountering the guys in the compartment next door: all Afrikaners, loud and belligerent, none more so than a giant named Attie
Fourie. At nineteen years, Attie was a bull of a man. He had spent
his entire life on a farm where he worked from sunrise to sunset,
except for the few hours a day that his 'Pa' allowed him to go to
school. Even that was considered a waste of time because, according
to his father, 'all the Fouries work the land and there's no need for
this school crap'.

Attie was at least 200 centimetres tall and, if that wasn't intimi-
dating enough, Ben estimated his weight at 105 kilos. With the size
of his thick neck, he was Springbok front-row rugby material all the
way. Attie was also mean and hated the Kaffirs.

Ben, on the other hand, had grown to love black people. His
direct experiences with Elizabeth Tsitsi and Joshua Mokwana had
given Ben an affectionate view of the original inhabitants of his
land. To Ben, they were gentle loving carers who had looked after
him from his infancy, alternating between the roles of minder, play-
mate and surrogate parent.

Yet in the apartheid era racism was rife, and Ben was only ten
minutes on the tracks when he experienced his first real taste of
right-wing Afrikanerdom.

All the recruits' heads were craning out the windows, watching
the sleepers flash by, the steel wheels going clickety-clack as they

crossed the railway joints. Crowds of piccaninnies stood beside the train lines begging for morsels of food from the rich whites. Attie thought it was a great joke to pelt the little ones with plastic bags filled with water. At high speed, they struck like missiles.

Witnessing this wanton cruelty, Ben was consumed with fury.

'Hey! Stop that,' he bellowed.

Attie barely looked up.

'*Fokof,*' he said, and threw another plastic bag.

When a brute the size of Attie Fourie tells you to *fuck off,* it would only be stupidity to do anything else, but rage can make smart people do stupid things. In this case Ben made his own water bomb. Attie's compartment was downwind from his. When the giant next stuck his head out to let fly again, Ben released his own missile, which exploded wetly in the middle of his back.

Attie didn't say anything. There was no swearing, no shouting. He just bolted away from the window. Ben was in no doubt that, in a moment, Attie's rage would bring him to the door to their compartment and he would descend upon them like the spirit of vengeance itself.

In a moment of desperation, Ben remembered that on the short list of items he had brought with him was an iron for pressing his uniform. It sat just a metre away on the top bunk. Snatching up the implement, he held it at head height in the doorway just seconds before Attie exploded into the compartment. He collided face first with the iron, bounced off it and crashed headlong to the floor.

Ben was sitting on the top bunk, Attie was lying face down on the floor, not moving, and Steve was saying, 'Ben, what the fuck have you done? We are going to be dead long before we even get trained how to fight.'

All the jockeying for position to share a compartment with Ben seemed to have had the exact opposite effect to what was intended. Instead of feeling a little safer, Ben could see from the looks on their faces that everyone was horrified. They expected Attie to rise at any moment, and then it would be them flying out of the window rather than water bombs.

'Jesus, what are you going to do?' Bernard said to Ben.

'What do you mean what am *I* going to do?' he replied. 'I'm going to tell him that *you* hit him with an iron.'

'Are you fucking insane? He'll kill me!' Bernard cried.

Attie's companions crowded the doorway, gazing in stunned wonder at the hulk lying on the floor, perplexed as to what had happened to him.

Then it occurred to Ben that Attie hadn't seen the iron. He had burst in so fast he had virtually knocked himself out without any help. The other guys from Attie's compartment could not have seen anything either, so they would be thinking that someone in Ben's compartment had flattened the gorilla.

Ben's heart was racing but his head was working. 'Keep cool, you guys,' he told his buddies and climbed down from the bunk. He picked up a bag of water and rolled Attie over. He was starting to stir, so Ben poured the water over his face. Whilst his foe lay there, still groggy, Ben put his knee against Attie's neck, got close to him and said, '*Attie, kan jy Engels praat?*'

The Boer could, indeed, speak English. He blinked and gave a little nod.

'Listen carefully,' Ben said to him. 'I am not looking for a fight with you, but when we get to Walvis Bay, all they are going to do is teach us how precious water is to a desert platoon.'

He shook him. 'You hear me?' he said. 'You're lucky! You're getting off lightly this time. When you're in the desert, nobody throws fucking water about!'

Still confused, Attie nodded, and Ben could breathe again.

'*Kom, maat,*' Ben said to him, as if they really were mates, and helped the confused goliath to his feet and out the door back to his compartment.

When Attie was gone the boys burst out in a fit of nervous laughter.

'Shhhh!' Ben did not want Attie and his friends to feel humiliated. This was not a guy he wanted as an enemy.

'I can't believe what just happened,' Bernard whispered.

'Hey,' said Jack, 'he was just stunned. In a few minutes he's going to be back. You better hide or find another compartment.'

They were enjoying the moment. So was Ben. He felt a buzzing in his head. He had put down Attie Fourie. That was going to make him a legend. He was smiling to himself, until he saw Gary.

Gary was lying on the middle bunk and had turned his face towards the wall, but as Ben climbed up to his bunk, he glimpsed the look of pure dread on his face.

'Hey, Gary, what's wrong?'

Gary didn't answer and curled his legs up. It was weird – him lying there like a foetus.

Ben signalled the others. 'Something's wrong,' he mouthed silently and Steve stood up and reached over to touch Gary's shoulder.

Gary shrank away from him.

'I can't stand this,' he blurted in anguish. 'You're reckless.' Gary pierced Ben with a look. 'That guy is not going to let this go. He's going to come back for you – for all of us. I'm not cut out for this,' he moaned. 'I'll never make it through the army.'

The boys exchanged uneasy looks. They had all shared the same privileged sheltered life as Gary. He seemed the living emblem of their new sense of vulnerability.

'C'mon, Gary,' Steve said. 'He won't come back – you'll see. He'll never figure out what happened.'

'Take it easy,' Ben said. 'You'll be much more settled once we get to the camp. You'll get used to it in no time.'

'Yeah … maybe you're right,' Gary breathed. His body relaxed and unfurled. He looked at his friends with gratitude. They could easily have ridiculed him for his frailty, but the small group, united by empathy and a shared sense of identity, had transformed the moment into one of camaraderie. In such a short time they had become a unit with a ready acceptance of each other.

No one was fooled, though. Gary was right. Attie was going to be back for Ben. It was just a question of time. In the ensuing days they stayed mainly in their compartment. Their safety lay in numbers, and they made furtive trips to the bathroom at odd hours to avoid encountering the disgruntled giant. He had a wicked bluish-purple bruise on his forehead and puffy eyes and remained mystified as to what had befallen him, but it was apparent that he was seething and waiting for the time and the opportunity to '*maak goed*' with his enemy. And that making good was not going to be good for Ben.

* * *

The distant sound of whistles blowing became a mad cacophony. The 'roofs', as the new recruits were known, were shocked awake. The half-light reflecting from the clock on the station platform showed 4:30 a.m. Non-commissioned officers – corporals and sergeants – strutted the platform yelling, '*Klim uit, tree aan!*'

'You're in the fucking army!' the NCOs screamed, with no suggestion this was any reason for joy. The prospect of a holiday camp was dimming by the second.

Dazed and half asleep, the roofs stumbled out of the train, dragging their gear and forming up on the platform to be loaded into Bedford army trucks and transported out of town to the South African military base. They had arrived.

South West Africa is home to the Namib Desert. One of the oldest deserts in the world, and situated off a barren and inhospitable stretch of Atlantic coastline, it has endured arid conditions for fifty-five million years. The Namib was home to the Second South African Infantry – 2SAI – at Walvis Bay, a solitary place, huddled amidst a sea of sand dunes. The dunes, some rising over 300 metres, trapped the freezing morning fog that shrouded the camp until the sun burnt it off later in the morning, but neither the mist nor the sun did anything to rid the area of the unending stench of dead fish from the nearby fisheries. It hung in the air, permeating their clothes and their lives.

NCOs bellow, they roar, they rant and scream. They do not speak, not to roofs at any rate. Awash in the atmosphere of yelled orders and directions, the recruits assembled in straight lines along the parade ground. Standing on the hard flat salty crust of desert in the early morning gloom, Ben could see the lights in the distance, coming on in row upon row of prefabricated bungalows where they would live for a year.

They huddled together in the cold pre-dawn darkness, under-dressed and unprepared for day one in the military. Gary stuck close to Ben. He was obviously in awe of the way Attie had been handled and the fact that Ben had the audacity to make a stand against a monster like that at all.

Ben liked Gary. He wasn't a guy who stood out in a crowd. On the contrary, with his skinny gangly frame, it seemed his mission was to remain nondescript, apart from the black rings around his dark eyes. He was quiet and measured every situation carefully. Although never quick with an answer, when he did speak his words were well weighed and the intensity of his gaze underlined their substance.

Being adopted as his protector, Ben had the mantle of the wor-rier draped around his warrior's shoulders. It was not the most com-fortable fit.

'How long will they leave us standing here doing nothing and freezing?' Gary muttered contemptuously to Ben. 'All they do is make you hurry up and then wait.'

'Well, I guess we have a year to get used to it.'

Gary shrank visibly. 'Great! Thanks for that. Let me know next time you have another deep insight!'

'It's not that bad, you know,' Ben insisted. 'A year out of our lives. It'll give us time to get to know ourselves and make some good friends.'

'It may not be that bad for you. You aren't the type who gets picked on. You can stand up for yourself. You're not consumed with fear.'

'I've been shit scared plenty of times, but maybe you can try to see this as an opportunity to learn to confront fear. Fear is just about always worse than the reality anyway.'

'You mean this is an opportunity different to any other in my life? Like I've never had to confront fear before? Look at me, for Christ's sake, that's all I've ever fucking done.'

'I don't think it's going to be easy, Gary, but getting through this time will make you stronger.'

'That's if I get through it,' Gary replied hopelessly.

'Of course you will,' Ben said in an attempt to be reassuring, though he realised he was hardly qualified to tell Gary how to deal with his anxiety.

The sun rose and the process of dividing them into groups began. Gary stayed close to Ben. Every command or question was in Afrikaans and they struggled to understand what they were expected to do, which meant they were screamed at even more vigorously.

'I think everyone goes through the same initiation,' Ben said to Gary.

'Never volunteer for anything in the army,' warned Gary.

And volunteer they did not.

As the sun rose higher the mist disappeared and they began to fry in the early heat of the desert, looking for hats or caps in their kits to protect their heads from the cruel blaze. The chefs, drivers, medics and clerks had been whittled out of the morass of manpower melting on the parade ground, until only the dregs were left. They would form the various infantry companies and special platoons to handle mortars and anti-tank operations.

'I have a feeling we might have been better off volunteering,' said Gary, pale at the idea that he may have been wrong. 'It looks like the cushy jobs have all gone.'

They were in smaller groups, each under the control of a corporal who was instructed to 'sort the men from the boys'.

'What am I going to do now?' Gary said, stricken. 'Do you think we can organise for me to get into the same area as you?'

'I'm not sure,' Ben said, not wanting to be laden with the responsibility of eternally watching out for Gary. He was adjusting to the fact that the year was not going to be the picnic he had originally thought, and his hands would be full merely looking after himself.

CHAPTER
18

Namesake

Northern Transvaal, Lowveld

They lived at the bottom of the great escarpment, where the land poked through the clouds and the rivers dropped their water in a thunderous roar amidst rainbow-filled mist. Their homes were on the plains amongst the thornbushes that were rich and green and thick with edible fruit. They cultivated the red soil from which the vegetables sprang. There were small animals in great abundance that were easy to snare and ensured that no one would go hungry.

The walls of their houses were made from mud, dried and baked and painted in bright colours, with a roof of thatch and a hard floor made from dung that was polished until it shone. The house was lovely, shielded from the heat by the dung floor and thatched roof in the height of summer and warmed in winter by the fire that burned in the hearth.

This was the home where little Benjamin lived with his mother and his two sisters, and he was the luckiest of them all, for he was the son. Every father must have a son, and when his father came, two times each year, from the city of Johannesburg, he brought gifts for his children: sweets and toys, and once a mattress to replace their sleeping mats. But always Joshua came with something special for his son. The boy's sisters were never angry or jealous, for they too knew that, for a man, his son carried his name, and it was the boy's birthright to be preferred above his sisters.

When his father came it was a memorable time for him, for it was then that he taught Benjamin the things that a man ought to know. How to make a catapult from the rubber of the tube out of a car wheel and a V-shaped branch from a tree, and how to aim and shoot the rounded pebbles straight enough to bring down doves and even small buck and rabbits to fill their roasting pots at night. Benjamin had become a very good shot. He sat with his father at night by the fire when they cooked with their three-legged pots, and Joshua told him of life in the city and about the need for his son to obtain an education, which would provide this thing called opportunity.

Opportunity was the reason why Edwin Meies was the only child from their village to ever go to university and come back as a doctor. Now he was able to help all the sick people of their small tribe. But education was very hard to come by, for it cost a lot of money, and so, without the money there could be no opportunity.

Little Benjamin always missed his father when he went away and worried about him, because he had heard that where he worked the white men were very cruel, and it was a dangerous place for a black man to live. But although he had learnt early in life to distrust the white men and their 'apartheid', he came to realise there were good whites too. There was one in particular who had a unique position in his father's heart and also in his own.

As long as he could remember, Joshua had extolled to him the virtues of the Novak family for whom he worked as servant and garden boy. When he was younger, Benjamin had been entranced by the stories of the young Ben Novak and was proud to be the bearer of his name. His father had told him about his love for this young white boy who had captured his heart. A fearless young warrior who dismissed the colour bar of race in the height of the apartheid era, and who had loved his black servant and carer like he did his own father. The Ben Novak he knew about was wild and exuberant, a magnet to the kids in the neighbourhood who congregated to witness his daring exploits.

He charged them a shilling to watch him climb to the top of the majestic pine trees that graced the borders of their white home. Opening his arms wide, the young daredevil plummeted from his dizzying perch, rolling down the outstretched branches to retard the speed of his descent until he dropped to the ground unharmed amidst the noise of the neighbours' applause.

He was a boy who was never cowed by bullies. Once he had waded into a motorcycle gang that had congregated threateningly outside his front gate. He grabbed their leader and dragged him from his motorbike, breaking his arm and knocking him senseless before turning on the others, who decided on an inglorious retreat rather than facing his wrath.

And yet, in the absence of threat, Ben was a gentle boy who could not kill the fish he caught at the end of his rod. A smart boy who went on to graduate from university and become a success in business but who, in all the years away, had never forgotten his old servant. Prior to immigrating to distant Australia, Ben had implored old Joshua to ensure that his young son, Ben's namesake, received a proper education, and he had provided the financial endowment necessary to facilitate this request.

Benjamin vividly recalled the times he saw Ben, when his father took him to the home where he worked. The boss had swept him into his arms and hugged him tight, kissing his face, before lifting him onto his shoulders saying, 'Just like this, Benjamin. This is how your daddy carried me when I was a boy like you. Just like this!'

Benjamin chuckled uproariously while Ben carried him inside. Here he received a hoard of presents and mementos that he took home and kept for years. In those innocent days of early youth, he felt that being named Benjamin was a unique honour. It empowered him to believe in his own great future and the possibility that he would do noble deeds of his own.

But this happy state of innocence was not to last. Benjamin's education opened up a window to knowledge and opportunity denied to so many of his kind, and it deepened his awareness of the injustice that had ruled his land for so long. And with that understanding his contempt for his father and the Novak family who had bought his allegiance, and a clean conscience for themselves, also grew more profound. Benjamin knew that, like so many others, his father was a pragmatist, who did not bother himself with what should be, but only with what was and felt grateful that his place in the scheme of things was relatively good. But Benjamin was an idealist. The extent of the injustice his people had to suffer tortured him. He bled for each and every one of his black brothers, and could not be satisfied until all of them were free to enjoy the same privileges as the whites. So his great compassion for his countrymen – his true countrymen – turned into an all-consuming hatred for the white exploiter.

Benjamin remembered his history and political science, and thrust the Novaks from his mind. His studies would pave the way for him to power within the African National Congress. His education would equip him to deal with people of influence and gain their attention, their respect. Eventually he would reach a plateau that would enable him to play a part in righting the wrongs of the past and building the South Africa of his dreams.

How had it all gone so wrong?

He had been such a fool. As a rising aspirant within the party, he had sought the most desirable political bedfellows and had been introduced to De Jager with no regard as to how this might have been contrived. Benjamin thought himself a Machiavelli in the making. Of course he didn't like De Jager. He saw through the man's veneer of charm to the cruelty beneath, and through his culture to the crudity. But Benjamin did not like any white men, so that was not a problem. De Jager's unpleasantness only made it easier to exploit him. So he would pretend to be fooled by his overtures of friendship.

De Jager had money and money was power, and the Afrikaner always dangled that carrot so persuasively. Not to mention the promises of information and introductions to powerbrokers. In the meantime there were the parties, the women, the drugs and the booze. The excursions into satisfying his little cravings meant Benjamin became increasingly dependent. De Jager kept him so befuddled it became easy for him to think that he was really there biding his time, not simply addicted to the power and the powder. After spending nights being screwed by high-class whores and high on coke, it was easy to imagine that De Jager, who had supplied all this, wasn't such a bad guy after all; that the job offered him was really based on the savvy De Jager claimed to see in him.

Maybe De Jager really did prize their association. To have the attention of such a mover and shaker flattered Benjamin's ego. If the drugs and the women had been the first things De Jager intoxicated him with, in the end it was his ego that manacled him. And that was the most hazardous drug of all.

Underneath all the charm there were still those lingering hints of contempt. Upon first noticing it, Benjamin didn't take it personally. De Jager, he realised, actually hated everybody. Benjamin had been a misanthrope himself for so long that he felt a certain kinship with the Afrikaner in that respect. Initially, he had just hated the whites, and the blacks who colluded with them, like his father. But as he sank deeper into the quagmire of politics he discovered the dark side of ambition within his own race. For everyone who strove to liberate the people just because it was right, there were a dozen who merely saw a change of power in the wind and were determined to be at the front of it. So many of them wanted a new order, but only if they, personally, were at the top of it.

His cynicism flourished, while his idealism wilted and went into hibernation. Power, it seemed, was the ultimate seducer that no one could resist. De Jager had an abundance of that, and so, for the time being, Benjamin would throw in his lot with the Afrikaner, for as long as it suited him.

Yet, by imperceptible degrees, De Jager's mask had slipped more and more. It was becoming harder for him to hide his contempt for the 'Kaffirs' and the fact that, to him, Benjamin was just another Kaffir, though, perhaps, his pet one.

Contemplating the capture of young Novak, Benjamin understood something. He had always known that De Jager was using him, even while he was attempting to position himself to use the Afrikaner. But now he knew why. It was not that he was a young black man of promise who could help De Jager negotiate with the new black power in South Africa, it was for this petty act of revenge. The whole thing had been about getting back at the Novak clan. Somehow, De Jager had known of their connection. Maybe he had thought the relationship in itself would provide the opportunity for his revenge. But with Josh's arrival in South Africa for totally unrelated issues, he had decided it would be sweeter still to involve those allied to the Novaks by time, circumstance and familial love. Yes, that would appeal to his twisted mind.

Benjamin felt besieged by a wave of nausea as the realisation dawned of how fully, right from the start, he had been no more than a puppet in a sinister plot in which De Jager pulled all the strings. He cast his mind back and remembered how they had become acquainted. Now it was clear how the Afrikaner had engineered their introduction. That pretty girl, Denise, whom he had only just met, had gone to a lot of trouble to get him to the party where the man with the patch had been. She had not let on that she knew De Jager, but the look that passed between them had puzzled him. It had also seemed strange how she had gone from being besotted with him to completely losing interest shortly after the party.

Why had he never connected the two events? But putting that aside, at the party he had found himself talking to the big white guy with the deformity that drew his curiosity.

'So,' De Jager had said casually, after the introductions were made. 'Do they call you Benjamin or Ben?'

'A bit of both,' he replied. 'But I prefer to be called by my full name.'

'I agree with you. Benjamin, that's the name for a man – it's more sophisticated – and I know you're an educated person. I've heard about the excellent work you did at the Congress of Trade Unions, pushing for antiretroviral drugs and the treatment of AIDS.'

He had caught me so easily with a little flattery, Benjamin realised, and he used me for so long. That bastard knew how to push all the right buttons. De Jager had organised for his father to work on his estate.

'Benjamin,' De Jager had said, his twisted face filled with a false smile, 'I think it's time for your father to retire. They are killing him with work at the university gardens. I have just bought into a lovely game reserve in the Timbavati, and he can live very comfortably there and tend the grounds. His duties will be light, and he'll have lots of support. You owe it to him to use your connections to give him a peaceful time in his remaining years.'

God! I was so naive. *Connections!* Yes, let's pretend I'm a big shot now. Could I actually have believed that the wellbeing of an old Kaffir could be of any consequence to De Jager? Was I that strung out on coke and my own ego? I was being manipulated, like everyone else. Once he had my father, he knew he had completed his hold on me.

There was no mistaking that he was well and truly in the centre of the spider's web. How he wished he could clean himself up and extricate himself and his father from it. But De Jager was powerful. And after all, he thought, what did it really matter? So, De Jager had outplayed him. He had long since stopped believing in justice. Perhaps it was too late now to think of changing sides.

19

Blood Steyn

1970, Walvis Bay

'Blood Steyn' was his nickname and he loved it. The solidly built sergeant with his cold blue eyes and aquiline nose had the sort of good looks that easily distracted the gullible from his serpent nature, when it suited him to hide it. He was mean and dangerous enough to warrant his foul reputation, which included a rumour that he had cut his own father's throat. Close on his ankles was a creature even more menacing than its master, if that was possible: Hitler, his black German shepherd. Steyn reached down and patted him affectionately.

'Look at them, boy,' he said. 'Another fucking bunch of roofs. God, I love this job!'

Steyn did. He loved the power, the way they regarded him with fear and trembled when he came near, and he revelled in his reputation for being totally without qualms. He'd heard himself described as a 'ruthless cunt' more than a few times. Far from being insulted, he found it intoxicating.

He loved the sense of power and the fear he inspired because it kept anyone from questioning his activities. He trafficked in armaments captured in the Caprivi Strip from the forces of SWAPO: the South West African Peoples Organisation. The weapons were transferred to Walvis and then, supplied with falsified documents, the disguised goods were shipped to Mozambique, where funds were paid into his clandestine bank account. Mostly he loved the money and he was making plenty of that, every day.

The arrangement was perfect, playing the tyrannical platoon sergeant and unarmed combat instructor by day and armaments dealer and trader by night. Not having the time to spend the loot didn't matter to him, it was all accumulating and an abundance of time lay ahead. This arrangement was too lucrative to sacrifice for partying and pleasure.

With his hands resting on his hips and his feet planted, Steyn barked at them, 'Fall in!' Hitler echoed the command with a snarl, as if they were joined in some savage duet.

'God, I love this dog!' the sergeant gloated, rubbing his mane. 'You are beautiful, boy, and so fucking mean.'

'Oh, shit,' Gary mumbled as the Land Rover pulled up next to Steyn. It was loaded with a pile of harnesses and un-primed mortar bombs.

In Afrikaans, the NCO barked at them to put on a harness, fill it front and back with six bombs and start running around the parade ground. The fully laden harnesses weighed about 30 kilos in total. 'Last one sleeps in the desert!' he roared.

The process of sorting the men from the boys had begun.

'C'mon, Gary,' Ben encouraged him, seeing the panic in his eyes. 'Let's just do it and see how we go.'

They helped each other put on the harnesses, but when it came to filling them, Gary's legs began to crumple.

'Just put two missiles in the front and move,' Ben said. 'I'll run close behind you so they can't see your back. Go quickly.'

They ran in their shorts, T-shirts and takkies, the harness straps biting into their shoulders and the weight of the bombs banging against them. The circular route around the ground's perimeter was about two kilometres and Ben could see that Gary was not going to make it, despite the lightness of his load. They had lagged behind as most of the others passed them.

'Ben, just go,' Gary said with little conviction. 'I'll never get around here. I won't be able to keep up with you.'

Ben was tempted. If Gary could not make it they would realise he was unable to manage physically and they would move him into another unit more suited to him. It would be a relief to escape the responsibility.

But he could hear his father's voice, 'Ben, it's up to you to take care of Brenda,' and strangely, though he was a world away from home, he felt that abandoning Gary would, in some way, be like abandoning his helpless sister. So he hung in with him until they heard the sound of the approaching Land Rover, Hitler snarling and Steyn screaming.

'What the fuck's going on with you two pansies?'

Gary stopped to explain.

'Keep running, you fuck!' Steyn screamed. 'You move and talk.'

Hitler growled in agreement.

Gary started running slowly, seeming to shrink as he went. 'Sergeant,' he groaned, 'I just can't do it.'

'He's not strong enough for this, sergeant,' Ben said.

'Who the fuck are you!'

'His friend, sergeant.'

'If you were his friend,' he said, 'you would shoot the fucker now and put him out of his misery, like a dog. Hey, boy?' Steyn added, turning to Hitler to seek the canine's agreement.

Gary stopped and simply stood there in the sun, wilting. Ben halted beside him and Steyn screamed, 'What's your fucking name, you piece of shit?'

'Private Novak, sir,' Ben said, using his official designation for the first time.

Steyn's head jerked towards Ben, his eyes narrowed, piercing him with his gaze. 'Say that again. What's your name?'

'Private Novak, sir,' Ben replied, uncertain now as to whether his use of 'private' was correct.

Steyn's face darkened and Ben had a fleeting sensation of something untoward. The NCO sneered at him. 'I am not *sir*.' His tone was all the more chilling for being so quiet. 'I am *Sergeant Steyn* and you better start *fucking* running or I will tie you and your *fucking* little friend to the back of this vehicle and drag you over the fucking sand dunes before I feed you to my dog.' He pointed towards the imposing bulk of the shifting sand dunes of the Namib and ruffled Hitler's neck.

Gary looked at Ben, his face ashen, his hands gesturing outwards, helplessly. 'There's nothing more you can do.' Silently he mouthed one more word, 'Go.' In its own small way, the gesture seemed heroic.

Ben had to concede that he was, indeed, powerless. They had been warned that disobeying a command from a higher rank would have dire consequences. Impotently, he started running again. The memory of Gary's haunted face filled him with guilt and he feared that the sense of culpability he felt over abandoning him would never leave. Seconds later, he glanced back to see the pathetic figure stripping off the bomb harness, standing meekly before the towering frame of Steyn who sneered, 'Hey, Hitler, what's the use of a Jew like this?'

Ben kept running, despairing in his powerlessness.

For the recruits, 'sorting the men from the boys' meant an endless grind of running around the barren fields, climbing rope netting and crawling on their bellies through obstacle courses built from old truck tyres, all the time weighed down by the mortar bombs strapped to their backs. They were exhausted, abraded, bleeding and blistered, but they had been classified and the strong sorted from their weaker counterparts for whom there was little sympathy and to whom the greatest punishment was meted out.

The smart guys stayed beneath the radar and did as they were told, unquestioningly, the general idea being to remain unremarkable and average to avoid drawing any kind of attention. Ben had blown all that. Steyn knew his name and had taken an instant dislike to him. His aggression towards him was inexplicable and Ben grew to detest the NCO as much as he did being ordered about, yelled at continuously and snarled at by his equally psychotic dog. Under their relentless assault, feelings of inferiority and worthlessness began to well up in him, but his integral sense of self-belief rose to meet these unfamiliar emotions, forcing them back down and into their place.

The military is the ultimate system of giving and taking orders. Unquestioning obedience to every command was obligatory. Ben was destined for trouble, regardless of his actions, his fate sealed by getting on the wrong side of Steyn. Anti Tank was a crack squad requiring specialised training and the highest level of physical ability. Unwillingly, Ben found himself assigned to its ranks. The objective, once they were trained, was the annihilation of enemy tanks, and the intense preparation they undertook was designed to produce a nimble roving platoon equipped with a customised Land Rover, six-pounder cannon and RPG rockets. The elite of their group would receive further specialised training on the French ENTAC guided missile system.

Steyn, the reputed patricidal throat-cutter, was their platoon sergeant. 'You are lower than shark shit,' began his opening address to the newly formed unit, 'and it is my unfortunate job to turn you into something less than the dregs of humanity that you now are.'

There were sixteen 'dregs' in the platoon, all of them Afrikaners except for Ben and one other 'Englishman'. Ben was the only Jew. It wasn't only the language that represented a barrier to the integration between English-speaking South Africans and Afrikaners. They were divided by culture. The Afrikaners referred to the others as *soutpiele*, which meant 'salt cocks', a term derived from the Boers, who hated the British South Africans who they regarded as having one foot in England, one foot in South Africa and their members hanging in the briny sea.

Few of the Afrikaners willingly spoke any English and it was up to the English speakers to become proficient in Afrikaans in order to communicate. There was little friendship or understanding among these factions. The Boer War and the cruelty of the British concentration camps had formed an impenetrable divide, and the Afrikaners still carried vestiges of hatred and resentment from their defeat.

Racial discrimination was endemic in the Afrikaner mentality. From those in the platoon who had never met one, Jews drew a measure of curiosity that was frequently combined with a great deal of hostility, for many subscribed to typical anti-Semitic attitudes, including the belief that the Jews were guilty of the death of Christ their saviour. Against blacks, the discrimination was enshrined in the policy of apartheid, which segregated every aspect of life from the workplace to the bedroom, even though the whites were dependent on the blacks as a workforce and as servants.

With the Jews it was hardly more subtle. The Nationalist Party came to power in 1948 under the leadership of DF Malan, and the Jews had reason to be wary. He had been a leading figure in the opposition to Jewish refugees and Holocaust survivors from Germany entering South Africa. In promoting legislation to prevent immigration, Malan told parliament in 1937: 'I have been reproached that I am now discriminating against the Jews as Jews. Now let me say frankly that I admit that it is so.' This statement legitimised a growing anti-Semitism that only grew stronger with the Jews' rise to prominence and prosperity.

Afrikaners saw the Nationalist Party's election victory as liberation from the bitterly hated British rule. The concentration camps of the Boer War may not have matched the genocidal horror of Hitler's death camps, but the memory of the demise of 25,000 women and children from disease and starvation was as deeply rooted in Afrikaner nationalism as the recollection of the Holocaust was central to the Jewish sense of identity. The lesson for the Afrikaner was to protect their interests or face destruction. The Afrikaners of apartheid South Africa had the biblical notion that the land was granted to them by God, and their pioneer forbears had established the myth that there were no black people in South Africa when they first settled in the seventeenth century. In truth they had colonised by force of arms and terror in a series of bloody wars of conquest.

All of this notwithstanding, Sergeant Steyn regarded Ben with a particularly virulent malice. Whether it was because of his personality, his name or just the fact that he was a Jew, the recruit could only imagine. The sergeant's evil temper seemed focused on him at all times. As if Ben's distress at this plight was not high enough, he soon discovered that the person he most wanted to avoid was also in Anti Tank: Attie Fourie, all 200 centimetres of him, still crimson-faced. The giant smirked hugely when he saw Ben and mumbled in Afrikaans, 'You fuck, I'm going to drown you in the fucking desert water.'

Ben had not seen Gary or any of his friends. He felt lonely and isolated and, once again, he would have to be eternally on his guard. Steyn referred to him pointedly as 'Jew – Novak', thereby presenting to the Afrikaners yet one more reason to hate him.

CHAPTER
20

Know Too Much, You're Dead

2009

A voice whispered in Josh's head, like the echo of a distant phantom. 'Wake up,' it said, over and over, getting louder as he came back to the present, though his head still ached and urged him to sleep on.

But the voice was persistent. 'Come on, you need to get up.' He felt himself being lifted into a half-sitting position. 'You smell like shit. Come on, get cleaned up.'

It was the black man, Benjamin, standing above him and pointing to the bathroom, handing him some garments. 'Have a shower and change your clothes. You'll be seeing the boss,' he said. 'It's too bad you got hurt.' The sentiment seemed grudging but Josh felt comforted nevertheless.

He struggled to his feet and made his way shakily to the bathroom, where he guzzled water from the basin tap. The light from the window was beginning to fade and he wondered anxiously how long it had been since the attack in the car park. It felt like days, but he doubted it was more than one.

Making an effort to shake off his funk, Josh shuffled over to
the shower. Soon the water was steaming off the cold tiles and it
seemed one prayer at least had been answered. Standing under the
hot soothing stream helped ease the shivering that had taken control of his body following the combined assault of shock and cold.
A modicum of vitality coursed back into his veins.

An overwhelming feeling of trepidation threatened to engulf
him. The last time he had allowed himself to believe he was going
to be all right, he had been hurled onto the floor. Now he feared
that the next encounter could have similar consequences.

He scrubbed his whole body and took stock of his injuries. His
head was bruised and sore, and the large bump at the base of his
skull and his cheeks were tender and swollen. He turned his face
into the spray and winced as it washed the blood from his mouth.
With his tongue he probed around his broken tooth. His right hip
hurt and his ribs were also sore, but already he felt better, encouraged by the realisation that his body was quite resilient.

It was his attitude that he had to be wary of.

'I will not allow any negative thoughts,' he said quietly to himself. 'I am going to get out of here.' Looking around though, he was
not sure how this would be possible.

Josh dried himself and put on the clean clothing: underwear,
socks and a fleece-lined grey tracksuit with a hood. They were all
new, from Woolworths, he saw from the labels. Hunger made his
guts growl. He walked around the cellar inspecting it for any way
out but soon gave up in frustration and sat down to wait at the table.

The wait was short, for after a few minutes he heard a key in the
lock and three men came down the stairs. None of them sat down
so he stood up. The man in front was older, in his sixties. His face
was twisted with hatred and an eye patch added to the general aura
of deformity that hung around him. Josh immediately recognised
him from the statue he had seen when he was first carted into the
house.

Jesus, what had happened to his face, and why would he have it
immortalised in a bust?

Thick neck, Johan, and the black man, Benjamin, were in tow. Benjamin stood back from the others, his eyes darting furtively around the cellar. Was it his imagination, Josh wondered, or was he somewhat ill at ease, perhaps even afraid?

'Why are you doing this to me?' Josh demanded.

The man with the patch seemed hard and cruel and capable of unspeakable acts. Fear overtook Josh again. There was no need to wait for an answer to know that no compassion would be forthcoming.

Thick-neck's demeanour didn't exactly exude compassion either. He looked like the type to carry out any order, the more ruthless ones being most to his taste. Only in the black man did Josh think that he could detect a hint of hesitation. Or was it just wishful thinking to hope that he only feigned being comfortable with his white cohorts' actions so as not to come under their baleful gaze?

The ugly man spoke English with a strong Afrikaans accent. 'So you are Joshua Novak, correct?'

'Yes, sir, but everyone calls me Josh.' He added a smile to the ingratiating tone but if anything, the glint in his captor's eye only hardened more.

'I'm not interested in what you're called!' he spat. 'You're the son of Ben Novak?'

'Yes, sir.'

'I see.' The maimed man paused for a moment. 'Do you want to live or die?'

'To live!' Josh whispered, horrified.

'Well …' A grim smile made the twisted face more twisted. 'That will depend on how you conduct yourself whilst you are here. Everything has a purpose, none of which is necessary for you to know. If you do what I tell you, there is a good chance you will leave here alive within a few days. If you don't, you will die. Do you understand me?'

'Yes … yes, sir,' Josh stammered. 'I understand. But what could I possibly have that you want?'

'What I want is for your father to come and get you. It's him that I'm after. You'll stay here until he arrives. If he doesn't come, I will kill you. If he does, you may live.'

The way his captor mentioned murder so matter-of-factly was terrifying to Josh, as if his life had no significance. What could connect his dad to this monster who wanted to kill him?

'Who are you?' he felt compelled to ask but was unable to keep his voice from trembling. 'Why do you want my dad?'

'It's not necessary for you to know that. All you will do is wait here until he comes. Anyway, if you know too much, you're dead. *Kom, jongens*,' he said, turning to leave.

The black man was the last to obey and locked the door behind him as he exited, but not before glancing at the prisoner. Josh's eyes met his with mute appeal, but Benjamin turned away, leaving the captive to ponder whether it might be with sorrow or indifference. To even contemplate the slim hope of the black man's favour was probably foolish. His boss was clearly the type who made his way through life with corruption and brutality. It seemed impossible to Josh that Benjamin could work for him and still be squeamish. He would find no friends here, only greater or lesser degrees of evil.

CHAPTER
21

Piss Parade

1970

'Hi, I'm Harry,' the stoutly built soldier said, his hand stuck out in greeting. His skin was olive and a smile never seemed far from his handsome face. Being among the very few other English-speakers in the platoon, it was natural they would befriend each other.

Ben grabbed his hand, delighted with the warm open greeting.

'Hi, Harry. Thank God there's another English speaker here. I'm Ben and I really could use a friend!'

'Well, it looks like you just got one. We seem to be a small minority of "*Engelsmanne*" here, so we'll probably wind up needing each other a lot over the next year.' Harry had no illusions that 'Englishmen' were any more popular than Jews. Unfortunately for Ben, he was considered both and therefore doubly hated.

Harry's surname was Pappas, and his family came from a small town called Bethal. He was easygoing and good-humoured with a big-hearted laugh that made people smile, even if they didn't know what he was laughing at.

'My family are Greek immigrants,' he said. 'We're a lot like the Jews. The Greeks place a huge emphasis on family and education.'

Ben found it easy to connect with Harry and told him about the experience on the train.

'You're the guy who floored Attie Fourie!' Harry whistled in awe. His face filled with concern. 'You better watch it. That guy is a mean son of a bitch and I can see he's gunning for you already.'

Ben also told him about Gary. He hadn't seen him since the parade ground.

'I'm worried about how he'll cope on his own. I feel I abandoned him by leaving him with bloody Blood Steyn.'

'Ben, there's nothing more that you could possibly have done. In the army it's every man for himself and he's going to have to learn to cope. As soon as we get a break, we can go and find out where he is.'

Together they went to the quartermaster's stores, where they collected their gear and piled it into a metal trunk or trommel. They had to carry these to their assigned bungalows a long way across the parade ground, all the while enduring Steyn screaming, 'Get your shit over there and wait for me.'

Struggling along with the rest of the platoon, Ben and Harry were carting and dragging their trommels across the salt-caked grounds when they heard, '*Hey, kom hierso!*'

Wondering who commanded their presence, they turned to see a fat sweaty corporal, beer belly drooping over the top of his belted overalls, standing at the entrance to a large marquee tent, beckoning them.

Leaving their gear, they approached the Afrikaner who, from his shape, was no platoon sergeant but more likely from the Support Services Group.

'*Ja, meneer,*' said Harry, speaking for both of them and addressing the officer as 'sir'.

'There is no "sir" in the army!' he bellowed at them in Afrikaans. 'I am a corporal!'

'*Ja, korporaal,*' they both replied.

The corporal continued to snarl in Afrikaans, 'Do you see that marquee over there?' They nodded. 'You see all those tables and chairs stacked in the corner?' They nodded again. 'Well unpack the fucking things and lay them out in a straight line!'

He waddled off, leaving the two of them standing there, laden and weary, their gear lying in the fading heat of the afternoon sun. The prospect of the bungalows had became a lot more inviting than spending the next few hours unpacking a tent full of tables and chairs.

'Hang tight,' said Harry, a twinkle in his eye, as he walked towards another two recruits staggering across the sands.

'Hey, you lot!' he called out commandingly in Afrikaans. 'Come here!'

Exactly as Ben and he had done, the newcomers dropped their gear and came running over.

'Yes, sir?' said one of them.

'There is no "sir" in the army!' Harry snapped. 'I am a corporal!'

'Yes, corporal!' they answered, and he took them through the same routine they had been through a few minutes earlier.

Leaving them bemused at their new task, he turned to Ben with a new command. 'You! Come with me and bring that trommel!' He pointed. 'You can come back for the other one!'

The door to their bungalow opened a few hours later, and the two weary roofs who had just spent the last few hours unpacking a tent full of tables stepped inside.

'Fuck it,' said Harry. 'Look who's just turned up. You've got to be kidding. Those guys are in our platoon.'

'They're going to be pissed off,' said Ben, as the newcomers started into the room towards them and the two empty beds.

When the new arrivals realised how Harry had tricked them, the mood turned hostile. The taller of the two strode over to confront the bogus corporal.

'Do you think you're fucking funny?' he snarled at Harry.

'Actually, more bright than funny,' said Harry, hoping to deflect his anger. 'We never expected you to be in our platoon. You have to see the humour in all this.'

Billy Critchley sized Harry up, deciding what to do next. The deed was done and all that remained was the choice of seeing the joke and making a friend, or resenting the prank and making an enemy.

'Billy,' he said, putting out his hand to shake. 'You owe me one.' He turned to introduce his friend. 'And this is Brent MATTARD!'

He always called Brent 'MATTARD!', pronouncing his surname emphatically. Because of Billy, no one ever called him Brent. He became known as 'MATTARD!', and vehemently so.

The English-speaking contingent had grown to four. They occupied the last five beds of the nine on the left-hand side of the bungalow. Swanepoel, a short fat blond Afrikaner, had taken the middle bunk between them and had no interest in moving despite being surrounded by Engelsmanne.

'Call me Swanny,' he said in passable English. He lay on his bed on his back and lifted his legs, rolling them back towards his head so that his anus became the apogee of his body and farted, a long controlled expulsion of methane gas to which he applied the flame from his lighter, creating a flaming *whooooosh*.

They needed the laugh and Swanny had timed it seconds before Steyn and Hitler came through the door.

The recruits had been issued their R1 assault rifles, a South African-manufactured version of the Belgian FN 7.62mm semi-automatic, and Steyn gave them a sermon on its significance. 'This weapon is closer to you than your family. It goes wherever you go, whether you are eating, sleeping or shitting. You don't let it out of your sight and you make sure it's always as clean as a whistle. When you need it, it will be to save your life, as little as that's worth.'

He went on to demonstrate how to strip down the rifle to its individual components, how to clean and oil it and then reassemble, impressing upon them the importance of ensuring that their lifeline would not malfunction or misfire. He handled the weapon with more tenderness than they would ever see him handle anything else besides his dog. This was their first lesson and arguably an infantryman's most important one. Ben soaked it in, feeling the beginnings of his own sense of attachment to the lethal implement of cold steel.

Before he left, Steyn made a special point of going over to Ben's bed. He walked around, lifted the blanket, opened his cupboard, poked through his possessions and had Hitler thoroughly sniff and check him over. It was obvious that Ben had been specifically singled out. When he had finished his inspection, he spun on his heels and strode out of the room, Hitler on his heels.

'What's going on with you?' Harry demanded. 'How come this guy is so fascinated with you?'

'I don't know,' Ben said. 'He's had it in for me since he saw me helping Gary. It's as though I've done something to him and he's looking to get back at me. He's an arsehole and I hate it that he's fixated on me.'

'All these Permanent Force are pricks,' said Billy, 'but fucking Blood Steyn is the prize. And how's that fucking mongrel of his? What kind of prick calls his dog that?'

'Obviously he loves the fucking Germans,' said Brent. 'Anyway the whole of South West Africa is fucking German, or fucking the fucking Germans, from what I hear.'

It was a well-known fact that there were a lot of blonde German women in the region, particularly the whores who serviced the armed forces.

'In fact,' said Harry, 'South West Africa was a German colony since 1884 until it was confiscated during the First World War by the League of Nations and put under South African control.'

'Jesus!' Billy exclaimed. 'We've got a fucking historian here. Where did you get all that shit? Anyway who cares? I just want to fucking eat.' They had heard the bugle announcing dinner and went off to find the mess. Ben searched for Gary, unable to shake the guilt of leaving him with Steyn. There was no sign of him.

The mess was a huge hall with row upon row of tables and benches. The din created by hundreds of soldiers talking, shouting and clanging their utensils on steel platters was unbearable. He was amazed at the number of Afrikaners. Although he had expected that Afrikaans would be the more dominant language, he had not anticipated the relative proportion to be so overwhelming. It was as though he had moved to some foreign land, it was so different from the predominantly English-speaking world he had always known. At least he had found Harry and the others in his platoon.

It had been a long wearying day and they longed to eat and get back to the bungalow to get some sleep in anxious anticipation of the 4:30 a.m. rollcall that would herald the start of their second day in Walvis.

*   *   *

The blaring of the megaphone was like an electric jolt to their worn-out bodies. From dreamy sleep they were instantly awakened in the glaring light as a group of rowdy '*ou manne*' stormed through the bungalow tipping them from their beds and yelling, 'Piss Parade! Piss Parade!'

The ritual of 'old men' waking the roofs on their first night was meant to disorientate and humiliate the new arrivals and was regarded as a great joke. These troops had been newcomers on the receiving end the year before and this was their chance to dish it out. They moved systematically through the bungalow, forcing the new recruits to leap out of bed, do push-ups and then run off to the toilet block to take a piss, come back and do more push-ups.

They were halfway down the row towards Ben's bed and he was seething.

On later reflection he considered that he must have a significant character flaw or simply be bloody stupid, because anyone with half a brain would know that in a situation like this you just go along with what's happening. It's only a bit of fun. But there was something deep down inside him that loathed it and as they approached his bed, he felt a familiar feeling of nervous tension, an adrenalin rush that came from knowing that he was one dog that wouldn't jump through hoops on command. Harry, who was last in line, had seen the look on his face and said, 'Don't even think about it.'

'There's no way I'm getting out of bed,' Ben said to him.

'You fucking get out or get thrown out,' the reply came from the closest *ou man*. He reached over to get a grip on the side of the bed and Ben swung his arm and brushed the *ou man*'s hands away. The men were determined. They had served their year and would be leaving the next day, and there was not going to be any consequences for their actions that were part of the tradition of clearing out – *klaar uit*, as they called it. Resisting was not an option and within seconds a group of them had surrounded him. Ben still had time to get up and avoid the confrontation.

He looked around and saw the reaction of the guys in his bungalow.

'Ben, it's only a few press-ups,' said Harry.

Ben saw Attie grinning, waiting. He had come around from the other side of the cupboards to see his enemy 'get it'. None of them was telling the behemoth to go and take a piss. *If I capitulate now, Attie will see that I'm intimidated*, he thought, and clung onto his bed.

A bunch of them upended him, bed and all, together with his absurd principles, and held him down. One *ou man* hauled out his member and pissed on him to the sound of laughter, not only from the *ou manne*, but also from the guys in his platoon, Attie most loudly.

'Thanks for fucking helping,' Ben said to Harry and Billy who were standing nearby. He was infuriated that none of his 'buddies' had made any move to intervene.

'If you're going to be an idiot, don't expect me to get into a fight for you,' Billy retorted. 'I'm glad to get involved for something worthwhile, but it's just fucking stupid to do anything other than go along. What are you trying to prove?'

Ben did not answer but it was a poignant question. He had just met them and it was probably unreasonable for him to expect that one of them would jump to his aid. But, in his mind, they were thrown together for the next year and would be the only Engelsmanne amongst a whole group of Afrikaners. His expectation was that they would stick together. He was convinced that, had one of them been held down and pissed on, he would have done something to help.

On the other hand, he was not blind to the fact that his resistance had been futile and unnecessary and fated for a predictable outcome. Grudgingly he began to admit to himself that they were right and that any escalation of the situation would have been pointless. Maybe it was wiser to weigh his pride and the desire to stand up for his views against the difficulty it invariably caused him. Did his stubbornness relate back to his sensitivity about the Jews going knowingly and quietly to their deaths without a fight? Or was it just plain ordinary stupid pride? In all the ruminating, he remembered Edmund Burke's words, 'All that is necessary for the triumph of evil is for good men to do nothing.'

Although, obviously, this was not about evil, it was a bizarre ritual that forced everyone into a mindless conformity. That was what he resented. In some ways he felt that his resistance was motivated by a desire to avoid being guilty of 'doing nothing'. How often had people succumbed to intimidation, especially when a confrontation was expected to lead to violence? Granted, there are many people who are not physically equipped to make any significant stand against bullying or thuggery. Perhaps it was fortunate for him that he was strong and had the ability to stand up for his beliefs. His strength was a gift, but his determination to use it was a virtue. But so was the ability to know when action was needed and when acquiescence was the lesser of two evils. Maybe, this time, he'd got it wrong.

A sense of misery overcame him. It seemed he had needlessly alienated himself from his new friends. This cruel sergeant with his psychotic dog seemed determined to persecute him and the ogre Attie was bent on revenge. On top of all that, he felt revoltingly wet, reeked of piss and was in desperate need of a shower and some sleep.

CHAPTER
22

Atonement

2009

He had looked so youthful, hardly more than a boy, Antjie thought.
Just a young man, handsome, like Joost. This was not the first time
she had seen that brute, Johan, take someone down into the cellar.
They kept the door locked.

She knew where the key was kept, on a high shelf in the kitchen
pantry. There was something about this young man that reached
deep into her heart. It was time for her to do something. For too
long she had been a bystander, closed off from feeling anything.

Even in that brief moment when she glanced at his face, she
could tell that he did not understand why he was there. The confused look, the appeal on his face, made him appear so helpless.
She perceived his gentleness. It reminded her of her own lost son,
another innocent, fallen victim to unreasoning hatred. No matter
what this boy had done, he did not deserve this.

The way he looked at her, too, seemed like a real communication.
As if he perceived her own gentle essence, while everyone else saw

only a useless old woman who had mostly lost her mind. There was no censure in his eyes, only a glimmer of hope. She could not disappoint him; could not abandon him too. Not like her own boys.

It must be cold and dark down there, she thought, and an enormous sadness at the young man's plight ran through her. She had never been down there, although once she tried to look into the window from the garden bed outside, but it was dark in the room and nothing was visible except the bars on the windows. *It's a prison,* she realised. She shrank at the idea of what may have happened to the others that had been consigned to it. Somehow, at the time, she had been so numbed that her concern was muted. Everything had become unreal … her own pain and the pain of others. But the sight of the young boy had awoken something inside her. A profound sadness.

It was tempting to shut it down again, but she couldn't. Not this time. In reality, the ache in her heart was preferable to the zombie-like existence she had retreated into for so long.

I have to help him, she thought. *It will make up for what I did to my sons. This time I won't allow them to hurt him.*

Of course, Petrus was also her son, but sometimes she found it hard to remember that. It was as if the child she had loved had become possessed by the malevolent spirit of his father; that very same hatred. As though Gerrit had the boy in the cellar. If he died it would be that beast all over again. The same cruel story, just with different names.

She knew what it was like to be in prison. More than half her life she had been locked in a cell and, worse still, once those barred walls had been left behind, she remained a prisoner in her mind. She would wait until they were all out of the house and she could use a chair or the short ladder in the kitchen to reach the shelf and get the key.

Antjie had seen Johan collect the key and open the door so that the three of them could go into the cellar. They had left the door ajar and she moved closer to the entry so she could hear their voices. Standing quietly by the door she listened to the conversation. Now she understood why the young man was there. He was a lure to bring his father. There was little hope that he would leave this house alive if she did not help him. As soon as the sound of their footfall upon the steps reached her ears she shuffled away from the door and, as always, became invisible to their eyes.

She waited until they had their dinner. They all ate separately. There was no friendship in that house. Petrus had supped in the dining room, Johan in the kitchen, the black man in his own quarters. She herself had eaten in the kitchen earlier. She had heard Petrus tell Johan to have the car ready at eight and that they would go to Sandton.

That would be the time, she thought to herself. She would open the cellar door and let the boy out.

Antjie thought about Petrus's reaction. Would he be able to forgive her, or would he consider her actions such a betrayal that he would send her away? She did not really believe that her son could harm her. He was ruthless and many people had died because of him, but she did not believe him capable of hurting his own mother. Not that it mattered any longer; she had already made up her mind. She had been a silent observer for too long. Now she accepted that she, too, had blood on her hands. She had said nothing and done nothing and became, therefore, equally culpable.

Besides, she bore him. He had emerged from her loins and she was responsible for her issue. She still wanted to believe there was good in him. He was always decent to her, if not tender, but there was no mercy in him for anyone else. None that she had ever witnessed. Slowly she had come to acknowledge that the beautiful blond boy she had borne was no more. Now he was nothing more than the spawn of Gerrit.

She was tired. At times, Antjie felt that she had lived longer than she deserved. Despite all her hopes for her children, she had failed, and the bottle full of capsules in her room would allow her peace. *Peace,* like her name. She had just one final matter to attend to. Although she had not been able to save her own offspring, maybe she would still be able to save someone else's son.

CHAPTER
23

Emasculation

1970

The reveille bugle brought Ben back from his restless dreams. The nightmares so vivid when he first awoke were no more than a vague memory moments later, but they left him with a residual sense of unease. The details eluded him, but Gary and Attie and Steyn were mixed up in there and it wasn't surprising that a cocktail such as that should cause him stress.

'It still stinks of piss around here,' Harry grumbled as he stumbled out of his bed, weary from lack of sleep. He tiptoed around the floor where Ben had been humiliated. Harry was still annoyed about Ben making a bad situation worse.

'ATTENNNNTION!'

The first person to notice the arrival of Steyn shouted the command as the sergeant stalked through the door.

The troops lined up at the foot of their beds, bodies erect, arms smartly by their sides, eyes facing forward.

Steyn sauntered along the edge of beds, checking every crease on the squared blankets, the polish on every boot and the cleanliness of the barrels of their R1 rifles. The slightest flaw would be cause for *afkak* – 'shit off', or punishment. Boots not shining: fifty push-ups. A creased bed: run around the parade ground. Steyn barked out each command like a rabid dog.

Facing forward, from the corner of his eye Ben could see his nemesis approaching. The hair bristled on the back of his neck in anticipation. Little doubt Steyn would find a reason to berate him and there would be ample opportunity for him to do so, for he was with them virtually every waking moment. Their entire existence was centred on Steyn's actions and reactions, subject to his every whim.

To him we're like dogs who must jump at his command, Ben realised, glancing at Hitler, who sat attentively watching his master, waiting for his orders. *No, we are less than dogs, because at least that mutt gets treated decently.*

'Wet your bed did you, sonny?' the sergeant said, sniffing the air with its faint odour of urine. 'Or did you have some other kind of accident?'

Steyn knew about the 'piss parade' incident.

'It's all in order, sergeant,' Ben replied.

'Nothing is in order!' he snapped. 'Your bed's a disgrace!'

His bed had been painstakingly prepared, sharp-edged all around.

'I squared my bed, sergeant,' he said.

'You call this a squared bed?' Steyn ripped the blankets off.

'No, sergeant,' Ben replied.

'Get moving!' Steyn roared. 'Around the parade ground. And you can join him!' He pointed to Harry.

Harry shook his head and sighed.

Punishment being meted out to Harry just for being beside him really worried Ben. The last thing he needed was to have one of his few allies alienated. He relied upon their friendship and camaraderie to survive.

'What won't kill us will only make us stronger,' said Harry, grinning. 'We've got to find some means of staying out of his way.'

That one little word, 'we', made Ben's heart leap for joy. Harry was not going to let the sergeant divide or polarise them, as he so obviously desired. They were in it together. Ben could have hugged him.

'Anyway, we're not the only ones having to do this,' Harry said, nodding towards the other troops on the track, and even as they looked, still more roofs were spilling out of the other bungalows. 'Obviously the purpose is to give us as tough a time as possible in the beginning. It's the breaking-in period.'

Ahead of them, Ben saw Gary wearily shuffling along and he called out to him as they drew near. Gary looked back, his eyes blank, face haunted. Ben groaned inwardly.

'Hi, Ben. Hey, it's good to see you,' he said faintly.

His hopelessness was so apparent another wave of remorse swept over Ben.

They slowed their pace. 'This is Harry. We're in Anti Tank together.'

'Good to meet you, Harry.'

'You too.' Harry nodded.

'I'm sorry I didn't see you yesterday,' said Ben. 'There was no opportunity to speak to anyone. What happened with Steyn and you after I left?'

'He's a prick!' Gary moaned. 'I can't stand him. And that fucking dog of his is as vicious as he is. He hates *you*.'

'What do you mean, he hates me?' Ben was alarmed.

Gary hesitated, as if he had said too much. 'I dunno, he just asked a whole lot of questions about you.'

'What sort of questions? Why was he grilling you about me?'

'I don't fucking know,' Gary said, head lowered and eyes averted. 'He just asked general stuff like where you came from and how did I know you.'

'What did you tell him?'

'Nothing. What's to tell? I told him we came from Joburg and met on the train.'

There was more, Ben could feel it. Why else was Gary being so evasive?

'Did you tell him about Attie?' Ben asked.

'Are you kidding! Why would I tell him about that?'

Gary changed the subject. 'Anyway, I'm in C Company with Steve and Bernard now.' Something had happened the previous day that he wasn't prepared to talk about. 'And as you can see, I have my problems. Slogging around this track with you guys isn't exactly my idea of fun. I hate this entire place but at least I'm with people I know and I'll probably survive. And I see Attie hasn't killed you yet.'

'Not yet,' Ben said ruefully. 'But would you believe he's also in Anti Tank? And guess who happens to be our platoon sergeant?'

'Not Steyn!' Gary said. 'Please tell me it's not Blood Steyn.' It was almost a prayer.

'Yeah, ol' Blood Steyn. We've got him *and* Attie to contend with,' Ben said.

'And,' Harry added, 'our good friend, Ben, is not doing well on either count.'

'I can imagine,' said Gary. 'He's not much of a diplomat – way too much aggression. Anyway, maybe I'll see you guys later. You better move along, I'm slowing you down and that can only cause you grief.'

Gary tried to create the impression that he wanted to avoid bringing trouble down on others, but Ben was convinced he just wanted to avoid continuing the conversation about the previous day.

'We'll come find you during lunchtime and catch up properly,' Ben said, thinking that a positive person like Harry would be a good influence on Gary.

'Yeah, great,' said Gary without enthusiasm.

There was a definite rift. The friendship they had developed on the train was now strained. Maybe Gary did feel abandoned by Ben. Although there was nothing Ben could have done to help, maybe he blamed him regardless. The depth of Gary's trepidation at the whole situation was evident. Was he just being self-protective? It was all a worry.

* * *

Only a few days later, any lingering doubt about how much Steyn revelled in the abuse of his power was laid solidly to rest. Ben's platoon were lining up when an unfortunate Billy made the cardinal error of moving while standing at attention. Steyn was on him in a second.

'What the fuck are you doing, soldier!' he yelled, his face thrust so close that spit sprayed into Billy's face.

'Sorry, sergeant, my gun moved.'

Steyn erupted. 'HAVEN'T YOU LEARNT A FUCKING THING!' he screamed. For one of his first sermons had warned them emphatically that the R1 was a rifle and calling it a gun amounted to sacrilege.

'THIS IS YOUR RIFLE!' He jabbed a finger at the weapon.

Then Steyn stepped directly onto Billy's boots and headbutted him. Eyes blazing, he grabbed Billy's crotch. 'AND THIS IS YOUR GUN.

'THIS IS FOR SHOOTING!' He pointed viciously at the rifle. 'AND THIS IS FOR FUN!' He savagely squeezed Billy's genitals.

The recruit dropped his rifle and collapsed.

Steyn glared down on his victim, and then turning to face the platoon, he pierced the rest of them with a vicious stare. 'AND DON'T FUCKING FORGET IT!'

The surreal image became etched in Ben's mind. Steyn standing there, red-faced and wheezing, and Billy leaning back, helpless and in agony while the sergeant crushed his manhood. Nor would he ever forget Steyn's words.

'Fucking Blood Steyn!' Billy snarled later when the four of them were together. 'He's a brute and a bully. Someone has to teach that fucker a lesson.' He was sore and walked tentatively to avoid unnecessarily rubbing his testes. His pride was hurt too. There is something fundamentally humiliating about someone squeezing a man by the balls and Billy was bitterly angry.

'Steyn staged the whole thing,' Ben said. 'Other guys were moving around as well, but he was waiting to get one of us English-speaking guys.'

'There's no doubt that he hates us,' said Billy. 'But do you think it's just because we're Engelsmanne or is it also because we're Ben's friends?'

'C'mon guys! Don't hold me responsible for everything,' Ben protested, though the question was more curious than accusatory. 'That's exactly what he wants.'

'I don't know what he's got against me,' Ben said, 'but I can't stop breathing, and that seems to be the only way to get him off my back. If you think he's picking on you because of me, then maybe you should keep a distance.'

'Cool it,' said Harry. 'No one's accusing you of anything, and no one's going to avoid you. Steyn is our problem, not only yours, and we've got to come up with a solution together.' Harry was one in a million.

'What solution? There is no solution. You've seen the power this guy wields. The other NCOs are scared of him. He drives around in a Land Rover when the others walk. He's the only one on the base who has a dog. How come? It's like he owns the place.'

Ben was getting worked up but what he was saying was true, and the others had to acknowledge that Steyn was not like the other NCOs. They had definitely drawn a short straw having him as their platoon sergeant.

'We have to get some leverage against him,' said Harry. 'A guy like him must have some dirt. If we found it, it might force him to ease off on us.'

'Yes, and it could make him even more dangerous,' said Ben. 'If he's that bad, then nothing is beyond him and he won't be intimidated by us.'

'But it's worth a try,' Harry appealed.

'Oh well! Now we're a bunch of fucking detectives,' said Billy.

They laughed.

'It can't do any harm,' said Harry. 'Let's keep our eyes peeled and ears to the ground and, MATTARD, you better keep your fucking eyes wide open.'

Brent had been staring vaguely off into space. He jerked back to attention.

'What? Why me?'

'Because you'll look fucking stupid walking around with them closed, you dick,' said Harry, roaring with laughter at his own joke.

Harry's guffaw was so infectious it got the others going too. They were a good team, the four of them: Harry and Billy, friendly and sharp-witted, Brent a little more reserved, but they all got along well and their trust in each other was growing. They remained mostly ignored by the Afrikaners.

This would have to change when they went to the border. There, their reliance on one another could make the difference between life and death. As a platoon it was expected that they would act together in each other's interest and for the greater defence of their country. They should be sharing a common goal, galvanised by their leader, and yet all Ben could see was divisiveness and mistrust. Even worse, he feared for his safety amongst his own colleagues.

24

Contraband

1970

If going to the Caprivi was not an idea that Ben relished, his immediate problem was surviving Steyn. Luckily for him, his friends were
almost as keen to be free of the sergeant as he was. They had already
decided they required leverage over the tyrant, and the most fertile
line of inquiry seemed to be to track the persistent rumours of his
involvement in illicit arms trading. On Wednesdays the NCO left
the base dressed in his civilian clothes and a quiet observation vigil
was founded to stalk him.

The spying was a nerve-racking business that involved following
him out of camp to Walvis Bay. To achieve this Ben and Harry
were forced to risk obtaining a bogus pass from a clerical friend that
allowed them off the base for two hours under the guise of performing census work for the Bureau of Statistics.

When they caught up with Steyn, he was locking a roller door on
a garage adjacent to a furniture shop. From a safe distance, unnoticed, they witnessed a well-dressed civilian approach him. The pair

chatted amiably for a few minutes before the stranger handed Steyn an envelope that he pocketed before returning quickly to base.

'That has to be cash,' said Ben. 'Did you see how quickly he concealed it and the way he checked around to make sure no one was watching? We have to find out what's inside that garage.'

'Are you out of your mind!' said Harry. 'We can't go into that place. We've got to get back to the base. This guy is up to no good.'

The rumours about Steyn involved an investigation into the disappearance of weapons that had led nowhere.

'If this has anything to do with missing weapons,' said Harry, 'we're into dangerous material. Gun-runners don't mess around. We've got to be careful or we'll wind up dead.'

Ben, however, was already facing that possibility, and the chance of finding something incriminating to free himself from Steyn's harassment was too tempting. Although he had no clue as to what he would do with the information, having come so far he could not contemplate leaving without looking inside the garage.

'If we get sent to the border, it will be the end of any chance to pin something on him. And that would be a shame because I think we're on the verge of getting some real evidence. Our ticket out of this predicament may be in that garage, Harry. There won't be another opportunity. We have to find a way in.'

'You're mad, Ben. I'm not doing this. Please, leave it alone. Let's go back to the base.'

'You stay here. I'll go. I just want to see if there's any way in.'

Creeping through the shadows, Ben scaled a rear wall separating the building from the neighbouring property and climbed onto the corrugated-iron roof. He pried open a loose panel and slipped through onto the timber roofing trusses inside. He was in – easy – looking at dozens of timber crates that could only be loaded with military weapons. He closed the loose corrugated sheet over his head, dropped to the ground and checked to ensure he could get out through the side door. It was latched from the inside, so he wedged a piece of timber in the frame to keep it open before collecting Harry.

'It's exactly what we thought. Blood Steyn's a fucking gun-runner!' he whispered, as he crept up on his friend through the shadows.

'Jesus! Don't do that!' said Harry, jumping with fright.

'Sorry. There's a garage full of crates. I'll bet your balls they're full of weapons. I left the door open so we can get in. No one will know we've been there. Come on, let's just open one crate and see what's inside.'

'Bet your own fucking balls,' grumbled Harry. 'You've got more than is useful.' But he followed Ben back to the garage, nonetheless.

With a crowbar they pried the top off one of the smaller crates to find an RPG: an anti-armour man-portable rocket launcher that served as a primary anti-tank weapon. 'Bingo!' shouted Ben.

'Ssshhh!' Harry smiled. 'This explains why a lowly sergeant in Anti Tank is so powerful,' he said, marvelling at the gleaming weapon nestled in its bed of straw along with four lethal rockets, two on each side. He looked around at all the crates in the garage. 'This lot is worth a fucking fortune!'

'Harry, I know you are not going to like this, but we're taking this crate out of here and we're going to bury it somewhere nearby as proof. Unless whoever's involved have a very particular inventory they may not even miss it, because no one will ever know we've been here.'

'You're nuts … but I like it,' said Harry. He helped Ben close the lid and carry the crate out of the garage by its rope handles. After making sure that the garage door was secured behind them, and with no trace of their having been there but for the missing crate, they took off once again, hugging the shadows, and made their way quietly back towards the base with their prize. They found a deep furrow a short distance off the road, and they excavated a hole deep enough to properly hide the crate. They left it well covered and scuffed the dirt around it to ensure that, in the unlikely event that anyone would be walking in the area, there would be no evidence of their buried treasure. After carefully noting where they had left it, they headed back to the camp, dirty and sweaty.

'Don't say a word about this to anyone, Harry,' said Ben. 'If Steyn finds out, we're dead.'

'Do you think I'm out of my mind?' said Harry. 'I never want to see that fucking thing again in my life. And another thing, what do you think you'll do with the "evidence" now that you've got it?'

'No idea,' Ben acknowledged. 'Having evidence is one thing, but doing something about it is another. We're in way over our heads. This is a big-time racket and no one is going to let us fuck it up for them. So we just sit tight and see what happens.'

'You don't have to convince me. I hope nothing happens. Besides, we wouldn't know whom to trust in order to bring any charges. Just about any one of the senior officers could be in on it. How else would Steyn be able to get the goods off base without detection? He must be in cahoots with others who can cover his tracks.'

'Shit,' said Ben. 'Can you imagine that? We go to all this trouble and risk to get the goods on these guys and then we're too fucking scared to use it.'

'Or too smart,' replied Harry. 'I'd rather be alive with the secret than dead with the evidence.'

Ironically, they both felt that deploying to the border was going to be a relief and looked forward to the imminent change of environment. For Ben, the escape from Steyn was going to be a blessing. The sergeant would be staying in Walvis to initiate another bunch of recruits and keep himself out of the firing line, while most of the other NCOs were being sent to take part in the unpopular Border War.

Going into combat with an unknown enemy was a terrifying prospect. Still, Ben was already losing a battle to a known enemy who was supposed to be on the same side, and that seemed an even less desirable destiny. At least with Steyn remaining behind, he would only have Attie to contend with at the front. *The sooner the better,* he thought.

CHAPTER
25

Freedom

2009

The feeling of helplessness was awful, even worse than the fear.
Despite all his resolutions Josh felt his courage crumbling, the thin
thread of hope beginning to unravel. He was imprisoned with no
prospect of escape. Still, if he remained where he was, his father
would come for him. Undoubtedly his captor would have contacted
Ben by now, and Josh felt sure he would already be on his way. As
soon as he knew that his son was in trouble, he would do everything in his power to rescue him.

If Josh did nothing, his dad would die.

As long as he could remember, his parents and Saul had watched
over him. It wasn't something he was conscious of each day. In fact,
it was so ever-present that it was easy to take it for granted; the
unquestioning support, the care and love that kept him safe, always.

Now it was his turn. His need to preserve his dad's life was stronger than his terror. Letting his father die was not an option. He had
to warn him. He had to find a way out.

Josh checked the bars on the little window. They were solidly bolted into the concrete and didn't give at all when he wrenched at them with his full weight. Even if he could procure something hard enough to dig into the concrete he would be unlikely to shift them, and anyone who entered would quickly see what he was up to.

He inspected every section of wall and corner of the cellar, the surface of each sandstone block. He tapped the walls here and there, but the entire room seemed solid and impenetrable.

The only way out was through the door.

He felt its solid timber and shook the handle. Peering through the keyhole revealed nothing but another wall. But with his ear against it, he could hear the faint sound of voices, but nothing of what was said. The only sure way out was through the door when it was unlocked, and then he would have to get past the giant with the keys. Josh had no chance against a massive brute like him. Unless, perhaps, he had some weapon? A rock or a pipe. Something that would give him the advantage.

The thought sickened him. He had never before been confronted with the need to hurt anyone. But he had to do something.

Examining his surroundings and planning an escape gave him focus and a fresh sense of purpose he had not felt in the long hours of worry and terror. He felt curiously powerful. Again he scoured his prison, searching for some opportunity. In the bathroom, he thought about removing one of the water pipes below the basin. But they were fixed solid as rocks. Maybe he could work one of them loose over time? That might succeed.

He searched about for other options. In a moment of inspiration he turned over the bed and discovered pine slats nailed to supports. Maybe he could prise one of these free, and split it to fashion a stabbing weapon? He would do it right now!

Using the mattress to muffle the noise, it took only a few minutes to kick one of the slats loose. The typical crooked grain of the pine and its relative softness made it ideal for manufacturing a crude weapon. A single well-aimed stomp and the board split lengthways into two pieces. One part had followed the grain off the edge of the board and terminated in a point. He grimly considered his weapon. Its deadliness vastly exceeded his expectations and after grinding it vigorously on the concrete floor, the point looked wickedly sharp. But he could still improve its handiness.

From the underside of the mattress, he ripped some cloth and tore it into strips. These he bound round the thick end of his spear, creating a firm hand grip that would protect him from splinters. He stood in the centre of the room and practised a stabbing action. Though satisfied the weapon would serve its purpose, he remained sceptical about his ability to use it. He had hardly ever hit anyone and cringed at the idea of actually stabbing another human being. Yet he had to make himself able to. These men were going to kill him and his dad! He pictured himself attacking.

Even then, he could not visualise himself inflicting a wound severe enough to stop the giant in his tracks without actually killing him. A direct stab to the jugular would achieve that. Despite everything, he still preferred the idea of incapacitating his jailer. With a heavy object like a club, he could deliver a good blow to the head and knock him unconscious. That seemed far preferable. Perhaps he could make a bludgeon by binding slats from the bed together.

He kicked off two more slats and split them so that they were thicker at one end and tapered sufficiently at the other for him to get his hands around easily. The narrower end he bound tightly with more strips of cloth to make an excellent grip. Swinging his new weapon experimentally, Josh found that he had indeed made quite a heavy club and felt confident he could floor a man with it.

Pleased with his work, he righted the bed and replaced the mattress so that there was no evidence of his efforts. He hid both weapons under the futon and considered the best time to strike. As he imagined what he might do, his heart beat faster and his body tensed with an adrenalin rush. Then another feeling overcame him: a sharp pain in his stomach. Hunger. It had grown dark, and he guessed the time at well after 7 p.m. He had eaten nothing for more than a day. *Surely they'll bring me food soon*, he hoped.

That would be the time to make his move. Whoever brought his meal would turn around to go back up the stairs and he could use his club while they were unaware. But then what? The weakness of his plan was that the front door to the house would probably also be locked. What use was it escaping from the cellar only to remain imprisoned in the house? But there were no other options. He would have to deal with that bridge when the time came to cross it.

As he sat waiting, the silence of the room took over and a dreadful anxiety claimed his mind and soul. Being active had been so much better. His heart dipped further into despondency when he heard a motor start up and a car drive off. When would someone come back to the cellar? A few minutes later he was surprised to hear the key in the lock. His heart started racing. Silently, slowly, he reached under the futon. The idea that he could die flared in his mind. He extinguished it immediately.

Then he looked up in amazement as he heard a frail voice calling, 'Are you there?' The old woman was slowly making her way down the stairs. Any thought of attack disappeared. What was she doing here? Was this some sort of trap? Were they luring him into trying to escape?

She stood in front of him at last, gazing at him kindly, as if she knew him in some way. 'What is your name, young man?' she asked. Her voice was gentle.

'I'm Josh,' he said cautiously.

'Listen to me, Josh. We don't have a lot of time. I'm going to let you out of here.' She spoke softly as though it was difficult to deliver the words.

'You must be hungry.' She held out a packet of sandwiches. The boy was ashamed to find himself grabbing the provisions and wolfing them down. She gazed at him intently, meeting his eyes.

'The men who locked you up here are very dangerous,' she said. 'I will let you out of the house – but after that, you have to be careful not to be seen. We are surrounded by walls and fences, and you'll need to find a way to get over or through them. This property is so large that I've never seen it all, so I can't help you find the best way

out. In fact, I don't know much of it apart from this house. You
must hurry.'

'This is incredible, thank you so much!' he cried. 'But what will
they do to you when they find out I'm gone? Is there anyone else
who could have let me out? Will they know it was you?'

She chuckled. 'They'll know because I'll tell them I let you go –
as soon as they find out. I'll tell them that I hope you get away
safely.' She looked fierce. 'I won't be quiet any longer. I lost my life
to these people. Here, take this blanket with you. It will help you
get over the fence.'

Taking the blanket, Josh bent down and slid his hands underneath the futon, located his homemade assegai and bludgeon,
and rolled them into it. He did not want the old lady to see his
weapons. What would she think of him if she saw such wicked
instruments?

Quickly, she led him up the stairs and past the bust.

'That's my son,' she said sadly. 'He looks just like his father,
except for the eye patch. He keeps this statue to remind him to be
angry. His anger has made him dangerous and powerful, but also
very, very rich.'

At a side door, she turned off the lights so they would not be seen,
then opened it just enough for him to slip through. She pointed
to the guardhouse at the driveway exit. 'Don't try that way. The
guards have guns, and they'll shoot anyone who tries to enter or
leave without authority.'

Josh saw the long brightly lit driveway sloping down to the
guardhouse located beside an electronically operated sliding steel
gate at least four metres high. The gate stood between solid walls
topped with barbed wire that was probably electrified. Beyond, he
could see the lights of neighbouring estates. If he could somehow
climb the walls and get to the lights, he would be safe.

'Go now,' she said to him. 'Be careful of the wires on top of the
wall. Throw the blanket over them so that you don't have to touch
them when you go over. That way you'll avoid being shocked.' She
gently caressed Josh's cheek. 'I wish I could do more to help you.'

Then she disappeared behind the door, leaving the boy standing in the dark clutching his weapons, a blanket and a faint hope that this nightmare would soon end.

The darkness of the gardens and the sound of the night closed in on him as he headed downhill towards the wall and away from the guardhouse lights. A light drizzle was falling and the ground felt soft beneath his feet. Glancing up he spied a half moon, partially obscured by clouds, which threw its silver-grey light over the terrain. A breeze that brushed his skin seemed to chase the clouds across the surface of the glowing orb.

Josh was glad to have the hooded sweat top and pants. A slight shiver shook his body, more from the apprehension he felt deep in his stomach than the damp cool of the night. *At least I'm doing something rather than just sitting in the cellar and waiting to die ... or have my dad die ... or both of us.* He unrolled the blanket and gripped his weapons. Hanging the blanket around his neck he crept on, club in one hand, spear in the other.

Approaching the wall, he glanced back at the dark shadow of the house and estimated it to be at least 300 metres away. The grassy ground had given way to more bushy terrain, which grew denser as he neared the wall that loomed ahead, ominously high. He stumbled against a large reel with a thick garden hose attached to it on the fringe of the brush. The idea of having to go into the dense foliage filled him with loathing. Being a city kid, Josh had always feared spiders and snakes, and peering at the dense scrub it was easy to imagine himself crawling into a web or putting his hand on some deadly snake. Yet there was no way around the fact that getting close to the wall offered the best chance of finding some way to escape.

He pushed his way through the scrub, and crouched to get under the branches that caught at his clothes and forced him to put his hands into the soft undergrowth. Stopping to listen, he heard only the sound of nocturnal insects. In the silence of the night, the crickets seemed to be screaming. Maybe the cacophony was just in his head? He reached the wall and sighed in desperation. He could never spring high enough to get a hold on the ledge.

Josh peered up and down the length of the wall for something that would enable him to ascend. There was nothing. He trudged on along the wall, heading away from the gates, searching for a way out. The branches clutched at his clothes and held him back. He slashed at them awkwardly with his weapons, venting his frustration and fear on the obstructing foliage. 'This isn't fair,' he moaned to himself, hating the whining tone he detected in his own voice.

The ground dipped down a slope and in the silvery glow of the moon Josh saw the black shadow of a huge tree protruding from a small clearing close to the perimeter wall. *At last*, he thought, *I can get up the tree and climb out on a branch to reach the other side of the wall.* He started off down the slope, pushing his way through the bushes, heading towards the tree and freedom.

26

Slippery Character

1970

The months passed at an astonishing rate. With basic training complete, marching had become second nature and the recruits were more familiar with their rifles in the dark than they would be with their girlfriends. Even blindfolded, they were able to dismantle and reassemble their weapon in seconds. During the past six weeks their training had concentrated on the six-pounder cannon, RPGs and the French ENTAC guided-missile system in preparation for mobilisation to the Caprivi Strip.

Friendship and banter alleviated the grind of army life and, in Ben's case, helped him keep his morale high despite the constant battle against Steyn and Attie. He was grimly determined not to be lured into a confrontation with either and prayed that, in time, they would find other outlets for their malice and let him be. But as much as he took solace from his comrades, Ben was full of woe at the sudden disappearance of Gary, who had gone AWOL during his first weekend leave.

It was Steve who gave Ben the news.

'How could this happen?' Ben demanded, his own sense of guilt tinging his words with anger.

Steve shrugged uncomfortably. 'He'd been distancing himself from the guys in C Company and becoming increasingly solitary. He'd sit for hours on his bed, lost in thought, or go off wandering around alone in the sand dunes. We tried to befriend him but he kept everyone at an arm's length.'

'So it wasn't just me?' Ben said.

'No, it was everyone. In the end we had to leave him to fight his own demons. We said we were there if he needed us. So we were happily surprised when he asked Bernard and me if he could join us on our first weekend pass to Swakopmund. After an early beer on Friday night we went back to our hotel room to collect him for dinner, only to find he'd scarpered.'

'Did you try to find him?' Ben demanded.

'We didn't realise he was AWOL,' Steve said miserably. 'At first we just assumed that he was unhappy at the hotel. I mean, he was a moody bugger. But when we got back we realised what had happened. I came straight here to tell you.'

'How could you leave him alone?' Ben demanded. 'Fuck it, he's been tight as a wire for weeks. Surely you would know to keep a watch on him.'

'I swear, we never thought for one minute that he'd be crazy enough to go just like that ...' Steve fell silent as he saw the rage creep into Ben's eyes.

'I'm sorry, Steve,' Ben said, forcing himself to calm down. 'I shouldn't have said that. A fragile, gentle person like Gary isn't cut out for military life. I'm just pissed off because I felt some bizarre obligation to watch out for him. But once we were separated, I couldn't. It really wasn't anyone's fault. Gary isn't your responsibility.'

'He's not yours either.'

'No, he isn't.' Ben smiled sadly. 'But that doesn't stop me from feeling bad and worrying about what will happen to him when he's found.'

'Well, let's just hope he isn't,' said Steve. 'Anyway, besides the occasional game of cards, I barely saw him. But he did seem to be coping better. Walking in the dunes seemed to give him peace. Except for when he set eyes on your sergeant. He hates that bastard.'

'I know how he feels. He does that to me too, but could Blood Steyn have made him miserable enough to want to split like that?'

'I think it was the whole army thing,' said Steve. 'The guys in C Company treated him okay, but he stuck pretty much to himself. I don't think he ever wanted to burden anyone by being too friendly with him. But the more I think about it, it wasn't just hate he felt for Steyn, it was loathing and revulsion. He looked like he was going to vomit when he saw him.'

'That fucking arsehole picked him out on our first day here, you know,' Ben said. 'I was there and couldn't do a thing about it. I just remember running off leaving him with that prick. Whatever happened that day, Gary won't talk about. If I ever raised it or asked him anything, he brushed me off.'

'Well, he's in bigger trouble now. When they find out he's gone they'll go after him, and he'll go to Detention Barracks when they find him.'

'You mean *if* they find him! He's not that strong or brave, but Gary's smart and I don't think he'll make it easy for them to catch him. Once he's out of here and relying purely on his own wits, it's going to be a wholly different story. Fuck, I almost wish I was with him.'

'He's going to have to leave the country, though,' Steve said. 'Now he's AWOL, they'll never stop looking for him.'

'I don't think he was planning on living in South Africa anyway,' said Ben. 'I just don't understand why he didn't go before. It doesn't make any sense that he'd actually turn up, do months of training and then take off after Basics when the hardest part is over.'

'Probably because he needed the weekend pass to give himself enough time to get far enough away before they found out.'

'Yeah, maybe.'

* * *

The C Company guys closed ranks and the disappearance only became known at Monday morning rollcall. They paid a heavy price for covering for Gary; their platoon sergeant drilled them mercilessly for twelve hours straight.

Ben had so much to contend with in his own life that there was barely time to dwell on it, so he just parked all his feelings about Gary in anticipation that one day, somewhere, they would meet up again and have a good laugh about the whole experience. What else could be done? In the short period they had known each other, they had become friends and Ben really liked him. Maybe in different circumstances, if he had not felt so responsible for him and Gary had not been as needy, they might have grown much closer. Guiltily, Ben felt a sense of relief that Gary had made the decision to run and freed him of the burden of being his protector. Perhaps that was Gary's intention anyway, even though he had imperilled himself in the process.

* * *

There were mixed feelings in the platoon about the prospect of their deployment to the Border War. Most of them didn't understand the first thing about the conflict, but amongst the Afrikaners it did not matter. As long as they were in the army and had been trained, they were looking forward to the battle.

'Ach, man,' Attie Fourie had been telling his mates, 'up there, there's a communist behind every fucking bush and we should kill the whole fucking lot of them.'

'The guy is a natural-born killer,' Ben observed ruefully. 'He can't wait for the fighting to start.'

Having finally admitted to himself that Attie scared him, he had come to sorely regret challenging him on the train. Because of that one stupid impulse, Attie's considerable aggression was focused squarely on him. There was no way to stop him and Ben found himself having to endure a daily routine of jibes and threats from the giant, that was seemingly sponsored or endorsed by Steyn.

The constant menace of the duo and his inability to neutralise their venom had eroded Ben's confidence. Anxiety affected his sleep and he had taken to rising early and going to the shower block before the rest of the platoon awoke. He liked the solitude of that hour. It was calming, standing under the hot water before it ran out when the other guys arrived en masse.

He had just stepped under the water and was squirting shampoo into his hand when Attie arrived. No one else showered that early, so this was no coincidence. Attie was there for him and Ben's senses were on full alert. He attempted to look nonchalant whilst he fathomed a way to get past the titan and out of the block. Perhaps there might be some way to minimise the damage that was now patently unavoidable.

All at once, he was gifted with a glimmer of inspiration. Ben waited for Attie to draw his T-shirt over his head, and when the moment came, he squirted shampoo from the plastic bottle onto the tiled floor beneath the adjacent showerhead. Having finished undressing, except for his briefs, the giant turned towards him and sneered.

The time for the long-awaited reckoning had come.

'This is it, Jew boy,' Attie spat, his voice full of menace. 'Plenty of water here, hey? Enough for you to drown in.'

Ja, this is it, thought Ben. Was there any last chance of appeasing him or redirecting his anger?

'C'mon, Attie. I'm sorry about what happened on the way here. I never thought we'd be in the same platoon. We should be comrades. We're going to the border soon and there are real enemies up there. Can't you save your anger for them?'

'I have fuck-all interest in being your comrade,' Attie snarled. 'I want to know what the fuck you did to me on the train and then I'm going to break your fucking neck.'

Attie's massive member was outlined clearly in his briefs as he moved towards Ben, who stood naked and self-conscious, his own manhood steadily shrinking with fear. There was no merit in telling Attie he had hit him with the iron. The truth would incense him.

'Attie, it was an accident. Can't we just forget it?'

All the signs pointed to an impending fight and in normal circumstances Ben would have taken the initiative in order to get in the first blow. But he did not believe he could hit hard enough to stop this hulk, and his 'retaliate first' strategy would merely incense him further. Now his focus was purely on vacating the shower block with as little injury as possible.

'Ja, we'll put this all behind us,' said Attie, 'as soon as I get even with you.' And he swung a haymaker at Ben's head.

Although he anticipated the attack, Ben was not swift enough to fully deflect the blow. It struck him on his left shoulder, bounced into the side of his head and spun him around, smashing his face into the shower wall. Terrified, he realised the true magnitude of Attie's power and how much damage a single, well-placed blow would do. Stunned and scrabbling to find a foothold, Ben felt the blood streaming down his face; saw it wash down his body, mixing with the water running towards the drain. He pedalled out from under the shower and away as Attie stepped into the shampoo on the floor between them and lunged after his intended victim.

Attie's feet slid out from under him and he landed with a thud on the tiles. Ben seized the chance to escape, and using the wall for leverage, propelled himself away from his tormentor. But Attie, still on his back, got his feet against the wall and shoved himself off. Sliding through the shampoo he grabbed Ben's ankles. Ben crashed to the floor and Attie pounced, clasping his huge hands around his enemy's neck. Ben struggled desperately to wedge his fingers beneath his attacker's as his life was choked away. Blood covered Attie's massive straining arms; it seemed to be everywhere. Through his crimson-stained vision, Ben saw Attie bear down on him, his red face twisted with murderous determination. Ben turned his head to the side trying to get his teeth into Attie's flesh but to no avail, and he felt himself slipping towards oblivion.

'Enough! You've had your fun. Let him go.' Ben dimly heard the command and immediately he was sucking air back into his lungs.

Steyn was there, leaning against the wall as though this was just another day in the office, another ordinary event in the life of a soldier. Attie backed off and rose to his feet, covered in blood-bubbled pink shampoo. Ben lay on the ground, naked, battered and hopelessly defeated. The previously suspected connivance between his tormentors was now obviously fact. Ben placed his hand on his head to feel a gaping gash on his forehead.

'Is this it, Attie?' Ben growled. 'Are you satisfied now? Does this make you even?'

For reply, Attie stepped forward and kicked him viciously in his side. 'Fuck you, Jew! I haven't even started on you. I've got the rest of the year to complete the job.'

'Get out of here, Attie,' said Steyn.

'What's the matter, Sarge?' said Ben. 'Why don't you let him finish the job? You're both having too much fun, hey?'

'Finishing you off is not his job, Novak, it's mine. All in good time. You think about that. Every day, you just think about that. When I am ready, you will know all about it.'

Steyn left Ben lying on the wet floor. He rinsed the blood off and made a compress of his towel to arrest the bleeding, before heading for First Aid. Nothing he could do was going to stop them. Any complaint from him would be denied. There were no witnesses. No one would take notice of a few cuts and bruises arising from a disagreement, and who would believe he didn't just slip in the shower if that was what they claimed.

Terror engulfed Ben at the idea of what lay in store for him, but he also feared his growing sense of frustration: the rising anger at being cornered with nowhere to go and no alternative but to start fighting back. He would have to retaliate first, find the right time and use overwhelming force to put an end to their campaign against him. Yet where would he find the opportunity?

There had been an escalation in the number of skirmishes in the Caprivi Strip, and Ben's battalion was under pressure to add reinforcements to the troops already being sent up. They were next in line to join a war that most of them knew nothing about, other than they were headed for the hotspot of all the insurgent activity emanating from Zambia, where the military wing of South West African Peoples Organisation 'SWAPO' had established its base and which was also the launching pad for the South African operations into Angola. Who knew what might happen in a theatre of war, Ben mused. An accident might befall his enemy.

There was small comfort in the idea, and his spirits were not at all improved with the realisation that Attie was probably thinking the same thing about him.

CHAPTER
27

No Sacrificial Lamb

2009

At 8:15 p.m. Rick's home phone rang and Ben answered the expected call.

'This is Ben Novak.'

'Ahh, Novak, I see you've been waiting on me,' came the familiar voice with its guttural Afrikaner accent. 'You'll notice that I'm not calling you on your cell, nor am I using your son's phone. This call can't be traced or triangulated, so don't waste any effort in that respect. We'll meet tomorrow. You'll be waiting on the corner of Corlett Drive and Melrose Avenue at precisely twelve noon. I'll send a car to collect you. The driver will bring you to me. Do not speak to him. He'll tell you nothing. You will come alone. No one is to follow the car.'

'I hear you,' said Ben. 'Please, just tell me what this is about. How do I know that my son is okay? How do I know that I can trust you?'

The chuckle on the other end of the line was chillingly sinister. Ben could hear the relish in the other's voice, the pleasure he took from the agony he inflicted. 'You *don't* know,' he said. 'You can only hope. One thing you can be sure of is that the only chance of survival that your son has is for you to do exactly what I tell you.'

The whole situation was bizarre. Ben felt as though he were an actor playing a role in some pathetic Hollywood movie with a feeble abduction plot. Except that this was real, and his son's precious life was in jeopardy. The man was right: it made no difference whether he knew with certainty that Josh was alive, he would do as he was bidden.

Ben put down the phone. How could he wait until the next day? Endure another night of suffering and worry? He was exhausted, had hardly slept, and yet the concept of sleep was impossible.

Rick put a gentle arm around his friend and led him to his room. 'Rest,' he said, 'we'll need our strength tomorrow.'

Taking off his shoes, Ben placed them neatly in the cupboard and lay down on the king-size bed, luxuriating in the welcoming softness that beckoned him to sleep. He wanted to call Saul just to hear his voice, but it was still the early hours of the morning in Australia. And what could he say? He loathed the thought of telling him how futile his efforts seemed, how powerless he felt.

Instead, he called Rocco and recounted the conversation with the abductors. 'You were right about the triangulation,' he finished with a sigh.

'Wait up, Ben,' said Rocco. 'While I still believe we shouldn't pin our hopes on it, the technology is quite sophisticated and gets better all the time. I'll know more about that in the morning. Personally, I wouldn't write it off just yet.'

'Is there anything we can do between now and tomorrow?' Ben asked, hoping for some task to break the long night ahead.

'I don't think so,' said Rocco. 'At this stage we don't know who we're dealing with, so finding them is a problem. If I'm careless in my inquiries, it's likely it will get back to them and that could endanger Josh, if they're serious about their threats. In the meantime, they've already found us, so I think it's best to wait.'

Ben was not cut out to be a sacrificial lamb. Just passively surrendering himself to these people was anathema to him. He would gladly forfeit his life to ensure Josh's safety, but there was no certainty of that outcome and he desperately needed to figure out a way of changing the odds so that they were not stacked totally against him.

Eyes closed, he began to doze off and get a bit of the rest he so badly needed in order to prepare for the following day.

CHAPTER
28

Acharei

1970

Anger and resentment at Steyn's treatment gnawed at Ben. That the evidence to terminate the tyrant's criminal existence was in his hands frustrated him no end, but he was unable to use it for fear of his life. Meanwhile, if Steyn had been wicked before, he seemed now to be possessed. Bizarrely, he had begun to creep up on the troops during their time-out, listening to their conversations, perhaps seeking some insight into their minds. If the sergeant knew about the missing RPG, he never let on, but the relentless harassment reached new heights. By slow degrees, paranoia invaded the troops' minds.

'I can't do this anymore,' Ben said to Harry. 'There is no justification for the way he victimises me.'

'Yeah, but what can you do? You realise of course that it's taking its toll on me as well. I mean, he doesn't rest with just picking on you, he picks on me, Billy and Mattard as well.'

'Yes, I know, but please don't try to compare the abuse he dishes out to me with how he treats you guys. Besides, you know he only picks on you because you're friends with me.'

'Yep, there are lots of other English speakers around the camp; he doesn't like them but he leaves them alone. There's no question. It's because of you. You're a fucking liability.' Harry smiled.

'What bothers me is that his fucking stripes give him such immunity,' Ben grumbled. 'If he wasn't a sergeant he wouldn't be so tough.'

Ben was feeling sorry for himself and sick of Steyn berating and belittling him. He could not envisage any other situation where he would allow someone to demean him to the extent that Steyn had.

'I want to thump him so badly. Give him a taste of his own medicine for once.'

Harry shook his head. 'Ben, you have to stop thinking like that. If you touch him they'll lock you up and throw away the key.'

'Fuck, Harry, I almost think it would be worth it. Can you imagine the shock he would get?' Ben was visualising it. '*Bwah*! One hit! Right on the fucking nose. He wouldn't get up from it.' There was a certain vicarious pleasure in the image of striking Steyn that lodged itself stubbornly in Ben's mind. His tormenter was fixated on him and something had to be done to break that cycle.

'Do you think any of the other guys feel the same way? I mean, like wanting to wallop him?' Ben said.

'Nah, they don't like him,' Harry replied. 'He's not the sort of guy anyone can like, but no one would dare think about hitting him. In any event, he's a fucking tough guy, you know. He's a trained unarmed combat instructor. Remember all that stuff we did during basics, when he threw the guys around like they were little kids?'

'Yeah, I remember,' Ben answered. 'But there's a big difference between a street fight and when you're on a training field or in a boxing ring. In a real brawl anything goes. There are no rules, there's just a winner or a loser. I'll win. If I have to, I'll kick or bite, use anything as a weapon. Just knock the fucker down and win.'

'Well, you won't get a chance with Steyn,' Harry said. 'You may as well get used to the idea. He's going to push you around the entire time you're here. You're an English-speaking Jew, and he hates everything you stand for.'

'Yeah! It's a double whammy all right. But it's more than that, Harry, I swear. I can feel it, that guy hates me. He's fucking obsessed. You've seen it. Him and Hitler, wherever I go, they are sniffing me and snarling at me. I love dogs, I love all animals and can relate to them, but that dog is like fucking Steyn, he sees me and he bares his teeth. It's not normal. Steyn is goading me to do something.'

'Well, if you're right, it's because he wants to stick you in Detention Barracks. So for once in your life, just be smart and keep your cool. There is absolutely no good that can come from you doing anything ...'

Harry fell silent. Steyn was creeping around again.

'Sounds like you are snivelling, shithead.'

Steyn looked at Ben. He and Harry had been sitting against a wall drawing warmth from the early morning sun and he began to get back onto his feet muttering to himself, 'Not as much as you'd be,' thinking about how Steyn would come off if it came down to an actual fight.

'What!' said Steyn. 'What did you say, prick? Did I hear you say I'd be snivelling?'

Ben just glared at him. He was seething but he kept his mouth shut. Steyn wouldn't let it go, though. He put his hands against Ben's chest and pushed, while Hitler growled fit to freeze the blood. Ben could smell the sergeant's foul breath.

'Did you fucking-well say I would be snivelling like you, Jew?' It was the shove that infuriated Ben, even more than the distasteful way his tormenter sneered the word 'Jew'.

Ben knew he needed to stay quiet. He knew that everything Harry and he had agreed upon only moments before was true. Steyn wanted nothing more than for him to go over the edge. That would give the NCO the excuse he longed for to put Ben away. Yet, knowing all that, Ben said, 'I would never snivel like you, sergeant.'

Steyn went ballistic.

'Me snivel, you little cunt! You think you could make me snivel!'
He pushed Ben in the chest again, harder this time. 'You want to
try?' he said. 'You want to take me on?'

'Not with your stripes on, sergeant,' Ben said calmly.

Steyn laughed in his face. 'You think you can handle me? Come,
boy, let's go, into the dunes. I'll give you a shot. I'll fucking take
these off!' He pointed to his stripes. 'And you can take your shot.'

Ben was not sure what Steyn expected. Did the NCO believe
it would be completely one-sided, because Ben was only eighteen
and he was, perhaps, twenty-five or thirty? Did he believe that after
Ben had been pushed around for months without retaliating, he
never would? Or did Steyn think that, because he was an expert in
unarmed combat and Ben was just in his first year in the army, it
would be a walkover?

Whatever his reasons, Steyn ignored all the essential rules of a
street fight, because as they walked into the sand dunes he turned
his back on his opponent to remove his jacket with its sergeant
stripes, and Ben spun him around and struck. One blow, right on
the nose, just as he had pictured it. Steyn's head snapped back and
his arms were thrown apart, leaving him wide open for Ben to drive
his fist deep into the man's solar plexus. His breathing crippled,
Steyn was left gasping for air. Just like that, it was all over.

It's rare to win a fight after receiving a solid punch right on the
nose. Anyone who has been hit there knows that. The lights go off
in your head, your vision disappears and it hurts like hell. For at
least thirty seconds it's impossible to fight back, and when you can't
breathe at the same time, it's game over. Ben had been in many a
fracas and knew the importance of that first telling blow.

Ben felt a surge of elation at the ease of his victory. The thrill was
somewhat mitigated by the knowledge that the battle with his foe
would now escalate.

In that split second with Steyn staggering about, Ben thought
about his friend David in the Israeli army and the letters they
had exchanged. David told him about the word *Acharei*, which in
Hebrew means 'behind me'. But it implies so much more: that 'I go

before you', as your leader – I do as I expect you to do. It signifies the respect that the leader has for his follower. David also told him how, in Israel, the wellbeing of the soldier comes before everything else.

How different it was for Ben, in the South African army with Steyn. There was no leadership, no consideration for the wellbeing of the soldiers. There was no 'Do as I do', just 'Do as I say'. There was nothing about Steyn that Ben aspired to. He commanded no respect. He preyed on the weaknesses of others and inspired only fear and loathing. In that same split second, while the thought of Acharei and David in Israel was in his mind, Hitler attacked him.

Ben saw the black flash coming from the corner of his eye and by reflex, threw up his arms to cover his head, probably saving his life, because Hitler's teeth sank into his right arm instead of his throat. The entire weight of the snarling canine's huge lithe body hit Ben and bowled him over in the sand. The dog was all over him, wild and frenzied, savaging his arm.

'Get him off me!' Ben screamed.

Even while he stood there wheezing, his hands cupped over his face and the blood from his nose dripping through his fingers, Steyn gasped out a yell, 'Hitler, stay!'

This was a serious matter for the sergeant. It was against standard procedure for anyone to be allowed a dog in the army, and whatever concession had been made in his instance would never be known. For the dog to savage a recruit, regardless of the reason, was going to cause him immense trouble and with all his hatred Steyn loved his dog.

Hitler backed off in an instant, but stood at the ready, poised to strike, his lips curled back in a silent snarl, his mane spiked, watching Ben's every move. Ben stayed on the sand cradling his arm, which was already causing him agony, while Steyn held a handkerchief to his nose.

An odd lull hung over the scene, as though there had been an explosion that had taken them both by surprise and they were standing in the aftermath examining the damage. Ben had achieved his desire but knew that, in the long term, he would pay a heavy price for the satisfaction delivered by the two blows with which he had laid Steyn low. The sergeant understood that Ben wasn't going to say anything about Hitler biting him, and they both realised that the situation was, for the time being, a stalemate.

'Here, boy.' Steyn called Hitler over to his side. 'Get the fuck out of my sight,' he snarled at Ben. 'Don't think you'll get away with a fucking liberty punch.'

But they both knew that he had underestimated his opponent and had lost because of that. If Steyn had been in a combat situation and there was no Hitler around, he would have been helpless.

'Sergeant, there's no reason why you should persecute me,' Ben said. 'I try hard to be a good soldier but nothing I do satisfies you.'

'You're a piece of shit,' Steyn sneered. 'That's all you'll ever be.'

Ben realised then that he could never win with Steyn, no matter what he did.

The first person he saw was Harry, his face peering over the top of the neighbouring sand dune. He was there with a few of the other guys from their platoon. Harry must have signalled to them to come and watch. Among them was Attie Fourie. *Fuck it*, Ben thought, *he must have seen me liberty punch Steyn, and now he's probably thinking that's exactly what happened to him on the train. Oh God, this never ends. It's a constant nightmare. I go to sleep worrying about Attie and wake up worrying about Steyn.*

The pain in his arm was excruciating. 'How am I going to get this fixed up?' he said to Harry, who patted him gently on the back. 'If I go to the medics, they'll know it's a dog bite and will want to report Hitler, and then this whole debacle will come out.'

'No problem.' Harry flashed his boyish smile. 'What's his name – Goldstein? That Jewish guy in C Company, he's halfway through his degree in medicine and he's got a complete medical kit. I'll get him to fix you up.'

'Thanks, Harry,' Ben sighed gratefully, 'you're a real mate.'

Examining his arm, he noticed there were deep lacerations. 'It's going to need stitches and I'll need a tetanus shot.'

'He's organised. He knows all the medics and will get the material from the hospital. Don't worry about it. I'll take care of it. Go back to the bungalow. Steyn's not going to worry you today and I'll go get Goldstein.'

Harry had become an amazing friend. Outwardly, he coasted through life with a smile and a joke, but he also had great substance. Perceptive to the core, he had an uncanny ability to connect with all kinds of people on different levels. Ben felt lucky to have forged so strong a friendship with him and be in the same barracks. Harry's loyalty and sense of humour made the trials he was forced to endure bearable, and he would have been lost without his support.

CHAPTER
29

Hitler Number Five

2009

The dog had been bred from a long line of black German shepherds to be a defender. His name was Hitler, the same as all the others who had served his master. A working dog, large and intelligent, he was trained to obey without hesitation. When he was stationed each night at the clearing by the tree, he knew that anyone moving around out there, besides his master, posed a danger that it was his life's work to fend off.

He had been taught to wait silently until his quarry came within his zone, from which, given his speed and deadly power, there could be no escape. He had been watching, poised, trembling, his lips curled, his growl a silent rumble in his chest, the fur on his neck bristling, waiting until his prey broke through the bushes. His excitement got the better of him, and he let slip a short growl just as he launched.

Josh felt he had already been to hell and back that day and his senses were hyper alert. Everything slowed down like a replay on

The group of four terrorists ahead of them on this incursion had already taken three soldiers' lives in a savage ambush, and Ben's platoon had been on their trail for the past six hours. If the pursuers were detected, the terrorists would just melt into the bush, wait for them to pass and then come at them from the rear in yet another ambush.

Notwithstanding all their training, the South Africans were still rookies compared to these SWAPO insurgents who had spent a lifetime in the bush. They were born with guns in their hands and the South African troops were taking a beating. They were deficient in numbers and poorly trained to take on their veteran foes.

Sergeant Beets had immediately recognised Ben's aptitude and utilised him as a scout ahead of the platoon, to ensure they would not stumble into a trap. Beets was similarly aware that Attie's exuberance posed a danger to them all, but limited manpower prevented him from leaving the giant behind as a rearguard. They needed a full force to overcome their adversaries.

The plan was for Beets and Ben to advance on each flank ahead of the others and come in like a pincer, while the rest of the platoon closed in slowly from the rear. For the strategy to succeed it would need to be closely timed, and the two scouts would have to remain undetected until the moment of engagement.

'Think like them, act like them,' Ben whispered to himself. *They must know that we are in pursuit. Gary should have had the chance to learn about avoiding pursuit.* As it happened, it had not taken the military police too long to capture him. Rumours were that he had committed suicide the day of his capture and return to Walvis, just weeks after they arrived at the border. It was said that he had hanged himself with his bootlaces after spending just an hour with Steyn, but that was unconfirmed. The news was devastating. Everyone had truly believed that he would outsmart the military police and escape the country. The only certainty was that Gary died because of Steyn. Whether the brute killed him or tormented him to the point where he took his own life, the sergeant was responsible, and Ben swore that he would make him pay. Right now, though, he needed to stay focused on their prey, who were quite able to strike right back at them.

The SWAPO thugs had spread themselves wide, making detection of their position and number more difficult for their pursuers. Beets' advance group glided towards the crest of a hillock, crawling low through the underbrush, remaining unseen even though they had moved to higher ground. They scrutinised the terrain, searching for any movement of a branch or an anomalous shape in the bush.

An almost imperceptible movement revealed Ben's enemy's position. The ambusher, silhouetted in the foliage, faced the advancing platoon. He'd raised his arm to signal a comrade and Ben strained to see the other's response, hoping that he, too, would betray his position. The scout saw the answering wave. The insurgents had acknowledged each other. This was the lair from where they would make their savage assault – a thick clump of trees and bushes skirting an open plain. The place had been chosen well, it was a natural killing ground. The moment the South Africans were in the open, they would be fired upon. The SWAPO agents had positioned themselves so their crossfire would come from all directions. Hopefully, Harry would recognise the danger instantly and hold his group back.

The terrorists would not anticipate Ben and Beets attacking them from their flanks. Ben had spotted two of them, Beets at least one from his side. Because he was downwind, unless movement revealed his position, Ben would retain that essential element of surprise.

Sliding low, he raised the R1. The rifle was muddied so there would be no shine, no glint of metal to reveal him. He drew a careful bead on the still form, 180 metres away by his estimate. If they played it carefully, it could be a rout.

His breathing was slow and measured despite his elevated heartbeat. On the fringes of the clearing he saw a faint movement as Harry signalled his group to stop and dropped low out of sight.

'Thank God,' Ben sighed with relief.

He searched for Attie, aware he was in danger, wanting to shout a warning but not able to for fear of giving the entire game away.

Then the bull burst into the clearing, as Ben had feared. Instantly there was a puff of smoke as a third insurgent opened fire, revealing his position. Ben fired almost simultaneously and saw the first insurgent jerk and drop. He swung the R1 towards the other who had looked briefly sideways, surprised at his comrade's fate, a mere instant before Ben's second bullet ripped his throat apart.

Turning towards the clearing, he saw Attie on his knees, one hand on his chest and the other open in front of him, red with his blood; his face quizzical with disbelief. Ben started running towards Beets and where the other two insurgents had been. He saw a form detach itself from a tree and take two steps forward before falling. Beets materialised from the bush and crouched on one knee, his rifle against his cheek, firing successive rounds at the blurred movement of the last of their quarry weaving away in full flight. With Attie down and three of the insurgents dead, no one was going after the lone survivor.

Attie's eyes were barely open, and yet he remained unrepentant as his life drained away in dark red rivulets through his fingers. 'Where the fuck were you okes?' he said, as though Ben and Beets were responsible for his plight.

He looked directly at Ben. 'Were you waiting specially for them to get me?'

Ben knelt beside him. 'Sorry, Attie,' he said. 'We were almost in place but your charge made them show themselves, and we got the buggers. You're a hero.'

Attie smiled. 'See, I told you,' he said with his last breath.

* * *

'That was a decent thing you did,' Beets said to Ben later, clapping him on the shoulder. He had witnessed the final exchange between Ben and Attie.

'What do you mean?'

'I mean you didn't have to give him a hero's send-off. I know there was no love lost between the two of you. And knowing Attie, if the situation had been reversed, he would have spat on your wounds.'

'It was a small thing,' Ben said. 'If you can't offer a white lie as a peace offering to a dying man … well, you're a sorry excuse for a human being, aren't you?'

'Ach,' Beets said. 'The Boers are a tough breed. They've been fighting something ever since they arrived here. The blacks, the British, the beasts, even the bloody land. You can't expect us to be overflowing with compassion. Not that we don't have our own share of bleeding hearts.' He laughed.

Although Ben couldn't ignore his sense of relief to have the threat Attie posed removed from his life, he felt guilty about it and deeply saddened by the giant's loss.

'It's such a waste, all this bloody fighting and killing,' he said mournfully. 'It's true Attie and I had our differences, but I'd rather have had him alive as a comrade than dead as an enemy.'

'I don't know that you had that choice,' Beets observed. 'But you're right, it's a bloody waste. The soldier's fate is like a lottery in which life and death are the stakes. All we can do is try to improve our odds.'

'I'll remember that,' Ben said.

CHAPTER
31

Premonition

2009

De Jager could tell from the moment he walked through the front door of his home that things were not as they should be. His instincts had always given him that little edge: the nudge that forewarned him so he could emerge from a confrontation with the upper hand. Lately his mother had been listening more intently than ever, asking questions. The behaviour was unusual. Mostly she hovered quietly, listened, nodded and then moved on. There was something about young Novak that had piqued her interest. She was certainly more curious than he had seen her before. After leaving the house he had dismissed the idea. But now, suddenly, the strangeness of her behaviour came back.

Then he saw the cellar door brazenly open with no attempt to hide her act of treachery. Novak was gone.

'Ag, Ma!' the scarred man cried. '*Wat het jou gedoen!*' What had she done, indeed? In that moment, as his fury consumed him, he reached for the razor-sharp blade in the scabbard that never left his side.

This was his mother, the only human being who had ever meant anything to him, other than Joost. He wasn't sure whether what he felt for her might have been love. For him, love was a word, not an emotion to which he could relate. Not like hatred or anger. Those feelings stirred him. Those he knew and understood. Where was she? He could not let her get away with this with impunity.

'Johan!' he shouted 'Novak is out. Find him! He can't be far.'

He knew it was only a minor setback and that the boy must still be hiding somewhere nearby. There was no way out.

'In the meantime, I'll phone his father and arrange his pickup for tomorrow morning.'

'Sure,' said Johan, pleased at the idea of a hunt, especially with such easy prey. 'I'll bring him back.' Wheeling his enormous frame around with extraordinary lightness, he disappeared through the door. The speed at which the big man could move was surprising. Johan was swift and deadly as a serpent. De Jager calculated that his offsider must have also been over sixty by now, and he had known him for more than forty of those years. Johan had gone from being his subordinate in the army to becoming his most trusted employee.

Although not De Jager's smartest man, the giant had plenty of native cunning, an excess of power and seemed loyal without question. Back in '69, during an illicit diamond smuggling operation in the desert, De Jager had saved Johan's life and earned his eternal gratitude. The following four decades of service and dirty deeds had been rich with rewards and perks, enough to satisfy a king, let alone an uneducated soldier of fortune. Johan had grown into his constant companion, as close to him as a brother.

CHAPTER
32

Torment

1970

'Something special just for you,' Steyn gloated, as he pushed Ben through the gate and locked him in the cell. 'Your mate gave up on his useless life here. You may as well share your last days with his ghost.'

The sergeant couldn't have been happier. At last he had Ben precisely where he wanted him. There would be no consequences for whatever he did to him here; there was no accountability in this merciless system governed by soulless brutes.

'Make sure I can see my reflection on the fucking floor when I get back.' Steyn's parting words echoed amidst the fall of his boots reverberating on the polished concrete floor.

In the gloomy darkness of the cell, looking through the small barred window above his head, Ben could see the distant lights of the base. A place of comfort compared to this cell. A year ago it had appeared so arid and hostile. Now accustomed to it, it beckoned differently. He longed to be out there.

'It's just what you get used to,' he comforted himself.

Standing there, in Gary's cell, he closed his eyes and pictured the sense of futility and despair his buddy must have felt, to end it all, here in the desert, so far from his family, so removed from civilisation.

Ahh, Gary, my friend. In the silence of his mind he talked to him, felt the comfort of his lost soul that was surely with him right now.

What sort of person does this? Ben asked Gary's shade. *Who makes war on us when we are not even the enemy? That prick tortured you. I understand that, we all know that. I wish you hadn't died. I wish you could have prevailed a little longer.*

He could feel Gary there, the calmness of his presence, and knew that he was at peace. No one could hurt him any longer and there was nothing more for him to fear.

Whatever was in store for him in the weeks ahead, he knew that peaceful presence would be there, held in his heart, guiding him through the tough times.

Ben had tried everything to stay out of Detention Barracks. 'Plead guilty and you will get two weeks,' his military defence attorney told him, somewhat knowingly for a first-year legal student. 'If not, they will put you away for a month.'

A month didn't seem like such a long time, but in DB it was a lifetime, an interminable torture. The possibility of reducing the sentence was so tempting that virtually everyone pleaded guilty, just to be done with it. Ben pleaded guilty with extenuating circumstances in the hope that he might get some reduction – a week, a day, anything. But Steyn had it all under control, exactly as he had with Gary. In this area, he could act with impunity. No one questioned him, and there had been no inquiry into why Gary had died within hours of his return.

'A history of violence,' Steyn reiterated at the proceedings, 'along with a pattern of disobedience,' and the trial was over before it began.

Steyn's witnesses attested to the fact that Ben had sworn to punch '*Speknek*' if he ever touched him with his steel spoon. Speknek was

Steyn's buddy. His real name was Corporal Johan Greef, and Steyn had procured the corporal his job running the kitchen. He, too, was a giant of a man. *Where did they find these guys?* Ben wondered. His neck was so thick it seemed joined to his chest, giving him the appearance of a gigantic boar, hence his name '*Speknek*' or 'Bacon-neck'.

Anyone not standing properly while waiting in line for their food to be slapped on their plate was subject to a klap. This was Speknek's unique little ritual, delivering a whack on the hapless roof's *staaldak* – steel helmet – with his ladle to deliver an ear-ringing thud. Angered by this callous practice, Ben had once declared that he would 'smack him back' if he ever touched him, but that was months before 'the assault'.

They were not long returned from Caprivi and the horror of the Border War, when Speknek had singled Ben out for a surprise klap on the *staaldak*. Having just spent months perpetually on the alert for danger, it was not surprising that he was edgy. Caught unaware, he acted instinctively in defence. But the tribunal judged that the corporal's actions did not amount to assault and dismissed Ben's claim of self-defence as specious. The fight with Steyn was not listed in his history of violence but, no doubt, unofficially he was being punished for that as well. His reputation, it appeared, demonstrated that the assault on Speknek was consistent with his dubious character.

In fact, Ben was advised he should consider himself fortunate that other violent incidents were not taken into account that would extend his sentence even further. Twenty-eight days' incarceration was a modest punishment for a villain of his ilk.

As it was, Ben was mortified at the length of his sentence. This was much worse than he had anticipated, and there wasn't much to hope from an appeal either. The tribunal showed no sympathy when, during his defence, he raised the 'Jew baiting' he had been forced to endure. They greeted his indignation with indifference if not hostility. After all, if the majority of the Afrikaners had had their way, South Africa would have been with the Reich rather than the Allies. That situation was only narrowly averted by wartime

Prime Minister and Honorary Field Marshal Jan Smuts, who had swung the marginal votes towards joining the Allies in 1939. The former PM was regularly referred to as 'that fucker Smuts' by the many Afrikaners who were strongly anti-Semitic.

Full of misery, Ben found himself standing on the mirror-polished floor of his cell. Just a few metres square, it was completely bare but for a rolled sleeping mat and a grey army blanket. The reflection of the bars in the concrete magnified the signs of his incarceration wherever he looked. Desolately, he unrolled the mat and lay down, covering himself with the woollen blanket. Although cold, hungry and emotionally exhausted, he knew that being left alone in the cell was soon bound to become the happiest moment of each day.

Steyn had made sure his boots were out of reach, outside his cell, along with the belt from his dungarees. 'I don't want you to hang yourself,' he said. 'Not before I've had my fill of you.'

How could Gary have done it? Ben wondered morbidly, searching to see where he might have tied his laces to hang himself. The only possibility was the bars on the window. He would have tied himself to them and simply flopped down and died. *God, what am I thinking!*

This macabre spectacle within his mind made him conscious of how close death was here. It almost seemed like an option he might try; an easy escape from what lay ahead.

Lying forlornly on the floor in that miserable place, wrapped in the single blanket that barely shielded him from the bitter cold of the desert night, Ben drifted into a troubled sleep.

The next morning, he silently followed the other prisoners to the shower block. Communication between inmates was forbidden and Ben had been warned that a solitary word might mean the loss of the next meal. Food was scarce in DB, so the threat was ominous.

The other two inmates whispered introductions, their hushed voices shielded by the sound of the running water.

'I'm Schalk. You have to be careful in here, if you want to get out, man,' the taller one hissed furtively. He limped on his one good leg, gingerly dragging the other, with its swollen bruised ankle, along the ground. Haunted eyes stared from the dark-ringed sockets of his gaunt face, cheekbones protruded starkly. His demeanour reeked of defeat.

'Henrik,' said the other, patting Ben on the back. 'Anything goes here,' he whispered. Compared to Schalk, Henrik beamed reassurance. Perhaps it was his powerfully built frame that had helped him weather the tempest.

'We try and help each other a bit,' Schalk murmured, 'but we're not allowed to talk. No friendships. They break us down by keeping us isolated and in constant fear of what might happen next.'

'How long have you been in here?' Ben asked.

'Three weeks,' said Schalk. 'I get out tomorrow, if I make it.'

'Me too,' said Henrik. 'You better shower quickly. They'll be here in a few minutes.'

Ben splashed cold water on his face, shivering under the onslaught of the icy water. With no heating in the prison, the inmates warmed themselves by swinging their arms wildly and rubbing their bodies vigorously to keep their circulation going. After dressing in their overalls, they headed for the mess, where a breakfast bowl of cold lumpy porridge and an apple was served to fortify them. It was 4:30 a.m. The day was about to begin and time, as Ben knew it, was about to end.

*   *   *

One minute you are a person with an identity, and then suddenly you are nothing, a nobody.

'*Haal dit, jou jood fok!*' Steyn's words, 'Haul it, you Jew fuck,' were like poison in Ben's ear. He felt a profound change within himself, his heart hardening as he knelt, head bowed, mouth half buried in the windblown sands of the Namib Desert. Sand and grit stuck to his lips and in his nose, choking him on every breath. It flayed his skin, caked with sweat and piss, inside his overalls, peeling his hide as he crawled on his belly. Steyn poured his hatred out in a steady stream of abuse, his mouth deafeningly close to Ben's ears. His spittle spattered his victim's face.

Fear became loathing.

The dry rope coiled around Ben's neck and shoulders bit into his flesh with a burning pain as he dragged on his cruel harness.

'*Haal!*'

Sprawled in the dirt, Ben lifted himself and looked back under his armpit to see the burden at the other end of his tether: a tractor tyre filled with sand, half-buried and immovable.

'*Haal!*'

Fuck him.

Steyn's boots were almost close enough for Ben to grab.

But the master of torment knew precisely how much distance to keep, knowing he could push his victim to the point where it no longer mattered; where the eighteen-year-old would kill him – if he could just get his oppressor in his hands.

'Come on, Jew boy, give me a reason,' Steyn sneered in his guttural Afrikaans, his hand on the holstered gun.

Loathing became vengefulness.

I'm not that stupid, Ben thought. *I'm not going to die out here in the desert, in army detention barracks, when all my life is still in front of me and he can walk free detesting the Kaffirs and Jews.* He stayed down in the dirt. *I can wait. I'll be patient and get out of here, and one day Steyn will know what it's like to grovel helplessly in the dirt, while someone else has power over your life.*

*   *   *

There came a point where the pain was so intense that Ben was no longer able to partition his mind. His consciousness was consumed with the agony of his blistered hands and feet, the burning from the salt that covered his lacerated body. At times, he was able to elevate his awareness as though he had transcended his corporeal self and was in another dimension looking at himself from there.

At those times, although a part of him knew that his body endured pain, with his awareness removed to that other place, he did not actually feel it. There, he could understand how people were able to endure torture. But it was impossible to remain in

that sphere, and when he returned to reality, the suffering was
there to greet him, even more tortuous than before. It felt impossible for him to bear the agony for even a minute longer. His body
screamed at him to stop. All he needed was to close his eyes and
sleep. But that small mercy was withheld. Even at night. It seemed
that the moment he managed to fall asleep, despite the pain in his
body and the discomfort of his mat, Steyn would be there, abusing
him, assaulting him. He knew where to strike the body without
leaving visible evidence, and where the maximum pain could be
inflicted, leaving his victim to retch and throw up. In the end, only
bile remained to dribble from his lips for he had already disgorged
everything else.

Steyn arrived the day Schalk and Henrik had been discharged.
His appearance heralded the onset of a nightmare that Ben knew
full well he might not survive. It seemed that Steyn was able to set
aside all his other duties to focus on the pleasure of Ben's trans-
formation from man to wretch. Ben wondered how his tormentor
could have so much power that he was able to switch roles from
platoon sergeant to military policeman, seemingly on whim. All
Ben knew was that, despite how bad DB had been before then, it
became manifoldly worse.

Steyn's capacity for venting anger and hatred was inexhaustible.
He belittled Ben unrelentingly, making him strip and run naked
and barefoot, on the spot, in his bare cell. Steyn guffawed at the size
of his victim's shrivelled genitals.

'Your *pille* is too tiny to piss out of, let alone satisfy a woman. You
Jews, you cut the tip off before you know how short it's going to be.'

Unsatisfied with mere insult, Steyn whacked Ben's balls with
his sjambok, leaving him screaming and writhing in agony on the
floor.

Steyn forced his prisoner to run in the heat of the day up the
soft sand of a dune, carrying a timber beam, arms stretched above
his head until he could hold it no longer and his burden dropped
from his grip, striking his head and knocking him blissfully unconscious, until he was shocked awake by a bucket of icy water. His

body railed at him to capitulate and submit to Steyn, to beg him for mercy, but his spirit prevailed on him to resist and deny his tormentor the satisfaction of seeing him bow.

During his recuperation, he was made to dig a hole, two metres square and similarly deep, provided drinking water only when the hole was dug and again when it was refilled. On his hands, the unhealed blisters burst and bled, while even more erupted from beneath his damaged skin. The days blurred repetitively and agonisingly, and Ben no longer knew how long he had been there or whether he would ever leave. His body withered away under the constant toil, lack of sleep and the meagre nourishment.

Although it had only been a few weeks, he felt his life force dwindling, yet he refused to yield. The more he resisted, the more Steyn sought to make him capitulate. As a soldier, Steyn could have grudgingly acknowledged his prisoner's fortitude and demonstrated some compassion, but his heartlessness was unbounded. The actual military police, at least, became uncharacteristically mellow with the captive, unable to meet his gaze when he pleaded for an explanation for Steyn's appearance and his motives. Ben's look made them complicit in the demon's actions and, hardened as they were, they were no longer willing accomplices.

Steyn persisted in provoking Ben to retaliate in their presence so as to justify shooting him in the guise of self-defence. Ben feared he would torment him until he died, and he would never understand why. Nothing could remotely explain the sergeant's desire to torture him so relentlessly, and he wished Steyn dead. He found himself fantasising, imagining himself surprising the fiend when his back was turned and ensuring that, if he were destined to die there, his jailer would be dragged down with him. Longingly, he pictured his hands around the evil bastard's neck, laughing as the breath left his body; his tormentor begging for mercy until the moment he died right there on the floor in his cell.

But the onslaught on Ben's body had taken such a toll, he was not sure it retained enough power for him to succeed. In any case, it was just a dream. *How much longer do I have to stay here?* he would wonder. *Only a few more days to go. Not long now. Hang in there. I'm going to be out of here and out of the fucking army.*

*   *   *

As though Steyn had been eavesdropping on his thoughts, he arrived at Ben's cell door to taunt and gloat, his face suffused with hate, his foul breath laced with alcohol.

'Not so tough anymore are you, Jew boy?' he slurred through the bars.

Exhausted and weak from lack of sleep and food, Ben could not answer, nor did he want to.

'I told you you would pay for that liberty punch, you fucking coward. You fucking hit me when my back was turned.'

Ben kept his peace, yet his contempt was writ large across his face. He had endured so much from Steyn there was nothing more that he could do to him.

'What's the matter, hey?' Steyn goaded, determined to provoke a response. 'You want some revenge? Come, I'll give you another chance.' Fiddling with the key, he inserted it in the lock and the door swung open.

Ben stood up expectantly, excited. Maybe this was his opportunity. Even in his weakened state, he welcomed it, regardless of the consequences. All he wanted was payback.

Ben could see that this time, Steyn was not taking any chances. The readiness in his move would have told Steyn that he'd finally got the response he desired from his adversary. As the cell door opened and Ben attacked, Steyn swung the truncheon concealed behind his back. There was the sound of wood crunching on bone and Steyn watched with satisfaction as his foe collapsed, eyes bloodied from the vessels bursting in his head.

CHAPTER
33

Out on a Limb

2009

Scouring his surroundings, Josh noticed for the first time that the lower branches of the tree had been sawed short and did not extend sufficiently to enable him to reach the other side of the wall. The tree was huge and, above the lopped limbs, massive branches reached out well beyond the perimeter but they were too lofty to be of any use. Jumping from there would result in broken limbs at the least, if it did not prove fatal. Josh buried his head in his hands and wept. All his effort had been for nothing.

Kneeling on the moist earth, he considered all that had transpired; the seesawing of his emotions between despair and hope, fear and anger, torment and triumph. Yet he still could not succumb, dared not fail. The moon illuminated the tree and the impossibly high branches that stretched so tantalisingly over the wall to liberty. Then he remembered the garden hose and his heart leapt.

Full of hope once more, he ploughed through the bushes back up the hill to where he had stumbled against the hose reel. Concerned about how much time had elapsed since his release, he noticed the glare of the lights of the returning vehicle as it rolled along from the guardhouse towards the mansion. A wave of dread washed over Josh, and his mind raced. It would not be long before they came searching for him. Would they switch on the outdoor lights and expose him? Maybe they wouldn't check to see if he was in the cellar? There was no reason to suspect that he could escape, so perhaps there was still enough time. But the old woman had seemed eager to tell them she had defied them at last. Maybe she would spill the beans before he could get away?

Worming his way back quickly, he became aware of how easily the trail left by his passage through the bush could be traced. The hose reel was firmly clasped to a submerged tap and refused to come free until a furious kicking made it release its stubborn grip. Frustrated at the loss of time, Josh picked up his prize and ran back to the tree. In the clearing, he unrolled the hose. It was thick and strong and could easily take his weight. He studied the best route up the tree; where it would be easiest to climb. Carrying the hose to within reach of one of the higher limbs would enable him to reach the other side. Once he had crawled out there, he could secure his makeshift rope to a branch and descend to safety. He looped one end of the hose around his waist.

Heavy and inflexible, he realised the hose would make climbing dangerous. Plus it would be too difficult to take both weapons at the same time. Choosing between the spear and the club was not much of a contest. He tucked the club into the back of his pants, grabbed at the branches and pulled himself up into the tree. His injured arm was of little use, and soon his other limbs ached almost as much, as he strained to heave himself higher. The drag of the hose became greater as he climbed, so he had to stop and pull it up with him. Josh rested a few loops in the junction of two boughs, making sure that it would not snag. He heaved himself higher, eventually reaching one of the massive limbs that extended beyond the wall. He dared not look down: one slip from that yawning height was sure death. The branch of the magnificent tree was his sole lifeline.

Josh clung to the mighty bough, exhausted from the effort of hauling his own weight and the hose. Slowly he dragged himself along its perilous length, crawling forward inches at a time. All at once the expression 'out on a limb' had taken on a vivid reality it never had before.

Finally, he reached the spot where he could safely descend. Clinging precariously to the branch with his legs, he anchored the hose securely. The lights of the neighbouring property glowed brightly not too far away, signalling freedom, and as he descended the rubber cable his spirit soared. Success was his – against all odds he had found the strength and the courage to escape.

Josh hit the ground running and raced towards the lights of the house, towards liberty, closing the distance between him and the neighbours. Suddenly his world was flooded with a blinding light and the deafening wail of an alarm assaulted his ears. Shocked, he stumbled to a standstill. A four-wheel drive stood between him and the house, and he was fixed in the beam of its floodlights. In front of the open door stood the massive frame of Johan, the big man with the neck like a bull. A double-barrel shotgun rested in the crook of his arm, pointed at Josh's chest. Staring at the barrels of the gun, anticipating the blast that would rend his flesh, he felt almost calm, accepting of his fate. He had done all that was possible and there was nothing more for him to do.

CHAPTER
34

Gorilla

1980

Every year, at the German Keller, in the Johannesburg suburb of Hillbrow, Adolf Hitler's birthday was celebrated by elements of the Afrikaner Broederbond. This 'brotherhood' was despised by the South African Jews. Amongst the Wits University rugby fraternity, a small group of Jewish objectors had determined to put an end to the annual celebrations of these zealots. In the absence of any form of hindrance by the authorities, this sickening annual ritual gathered momentum, exacerbating a growing anti-Semitism.

Errol Cohen, affectionately known to his friends and not so affectionately to his opponents on the field as 'Gorilla', agitated to confront the threat. Aid was solicited from any able-bodied Jew unafraid of a fight and willing to put himself at risk for the cause. Ben received his call at around 6 p.m.

'Novak, it's on tonight,' Gorilla said. 'We need you with us. To the best of our knowledge there will be no cops, so we'll be there instead. About twenty of us. We have to make sure they don't get away with it again without any consequences.'

South Africa's love–hate relationship with its Jews was a recurring source of concern to the community. Notwithstanding the significant contributions made by the Jews in business, medicine, the cultural arts and philanthropy, there remained a constant undercurrent of resentment that frequently spilt over in anti-Semitic victimisation. Left unchecked and with the polarising influence of the Afrikaner ancestry, there was always the potential for an escalation of racial persecution. The Jewish Board of Deputies vigorously advocated Jewish rights and took substantive defensive measures in government and the press. But a violent confrontation had become inevitable, particularly because of the disdain shown by the police each year towards the complaints lodged by the Jewish people against the vulgarity of the Hitler's birthday celebrations. This year promised to be different, due in part to the Board of Deputies succeeding in having the potential skirmish highlighted in the *Sunday Times*. There was a heightening of both the awareness and the tension surrounding the event.

'Don't worry,' Ben said. 'I'll be there.'

Dahlia was not at all happy about the idea. She screamed at him to leave it alone, and when that didn't work she begged.

'Please, Ben. No good can come of you being there. You know what you're like. You need to keep away from the violence and retribution. We have a good life now. Please don't risk changing that.'

But he would not be dissuaded.

Gorilla's small group had already gathered outside the Keller when Ben arrived, but no one was game to try entering for fear of being isolated within the hostile crowd inside.

'I know it's risky,' said Ben, 'but if someone doesn't go inside and determine who the organisers are, then we may as well go home. We have to single out the ringleaders. They are our targets. We can't take on the entire pub, we'll get massacred.'

'If we can find out who they are,' said Gorilla, 'we could start a ruckus outside. We can wait out the front and pick off the cunts that started it. Enough of a public disturbance will cause the police to disband the whole thing.'

It seemed like a workable plan, all it needed was someone stupid or daring enough to enter alone, reconnoitre and identify the ringleaders.

'I'll do it,' said Ben. 'Once the crowd outside is sufficiently riled and the arrival of the cops is imminent, I'll go inside.'

The timing was perfect. As Ben descended the steps into the Keller, one of the 'Krauts' jumped onto the bar counter and unfurled his swastika to a roar of approval from the crowd. Completely distracted, the crowd gathered around the counter, leaving Ben's entry virtually unnoticed. Outside, the police had arrived and were in heated discussion with Gorilla about dispersing his group. He implored them to recognise that the real problem was the Nazi sympathisers on the inside, not the demonstrators on the outside.

Ben found a quiet corner, where he remained obscured behind a concrete pillar. He witnessed a number of men bearing Nazi banners and waving them about to the accompaniment of the chant, 'Heil Hitler'.

The man standing on the bar, shrouded in his vile flag, turned towards him, and Ben saw the evil visage of his tormentor, Steyn, the source of all his hatred. It had been nearly ten years since his crippling final days in DB, but his fury was unabated. He had managed to secrete it away so as to lead the semblance of a normal life. But the fact that it had remained could not be denied – an explosive force lying dormant, waiting until provoked; waiting for this moment. Ben looked around at the rising fervour, fuelled by Steyn, who swept along the bar counter. Only striking like lightning would provide him with the opportunity of getting to his enemy and escaping alive.

Sprinting the short distance to the bar, Ben whipped the concealed baton from his sleeve, sprang onto the counter and swung it with all his strength at the oblivious Steyn. For a second, shock registered in the Afrikaner's face before he spiralled off the counter, pole-axed by a bone-crunching blow to the side of the head. Ben ran along the bar, leapt to the floor and headed for the stairs and the relative safety of his gang of friends. Stunned by the swiftness of the vicious attack and the horror of seeing Steyn's face impaled on a beer tap, the crowd's retaliation was momentarily stalled. Then pandemonium broke loose as they bolted towards the stairs chasing Ben.

He was brought down just metres from freedom. Fists and boots rained on him as he crouched low, trying to cover his head and protect his vital organs from the onslaught. He glimpsed the flash of a steel blade. A desperately swung arm blocked it, and he felt the sting of it slicing his arm to the bone. Through the haze of pain, Ben distantly heard Dahlia's chilling warning against revenge. Suddenly he felt the strong arms of Gorilla grasp him, and he was lifted from the madding crowd and spirited up the stairs to safety.

The papers in the following days headlined a call for the police to do more to prevent the annual outbreaks of violence that led to so many people being injured and hospitalised. There were no specifics on the number or the nature of the casualties, but his friends had it go mostly their way.

For Ben, the night had opened many old wounds. Had Dahlia, indeed, been right? Had no good come of it for him? He had not been seriously injured, and although the brief encounter had released all his suppressed anger against Steyn, his satisfaction was muted as he reflected upon the damage done. His enemy had been dealt a devastating blow; in fact, Ben feared that he might have killed him. The result of that would be disastrous, and all he could do was hope that it would not find its way back to him.

At last he could no longer consider the brutality of his country and that within himself as part of the future he wanted for his family. He was sick of the undercurrent of violence that permeated every aspect of life in South Africa and the hopelessness he felt about its prospects. Sadly, he saw his land rent apart by its people, inculcated with prejudice, the roots of which were rarely understood, but that manifested itself as unremitting anger and hatred. Alan Paton's *Cry the Beloved Country* had compellingly revealed the complex social and racial alignments that wove the fabric of South

Africa's human experience. Paton's novel eloquently portrayed the story of a man who is murdered by those whom he had dedicated his life to helping and who unwittingly chose him as their victim. The story was an exposition of the fundamental ailments of the apartheid system. Paton described what was tolerable and what was not in a land built on exploitation.

After reading the novel, the full clarity of keeping men unskilled for the sake of unskilled work had finally dawned on Ben, along with the tragedy of the goldmining compounds that separated these men from their women and children, disintegrating the native family life in favour of poverty, slums and crime. In the novel, Paton had declared that such exploitation, whilst permissible in the early days, was no longer permissible when its true cost became known, and the tale of the beauty and terror of human life, published in 1948, saw Paton reviled by the apartheid regime that perpetuated these crimes. Thirty years later, still nothing had changed in his country. Ben saw no solutions and needed his conscience freed from its burden. If that meant not having to think about it and ultimately forgetting, then that was what he wanted to do. It was time to leave. Increasingly, over the years, he had come to recognise that the longer he stayed in South Africa, the harder it became to sever his ties to the good life enjoyed by his fellow white countrymen, from a financial perspective at least. The prestige and lucrative earnings Ben won in his ascent up the corporate ladder gave him all the trappings of success. Yet even while they brought much freedom with them, they chained him more tightly to the abhorrent system of discrimination that shackled the conscience of white South Africa.

For Ben, it was no longer a question of *if* but *when* he was going to leave the country of his birth, and he knew that Dahlia was ready too. She was ready to have their babies, and they were not going to be born there.

The cathartic sight of Steyn's body spiralling off the bar closed a terrible chapter, freeing him from the labyrinth of violence that characterised his past and allowing him to start afresh. Somewhere else, he could become someone else.

'I'm sorry,' he said to her, when he stepped through the door with his bandaged arm to see her eyes swollen and cheeks stained with tears. 'You were almost right about no good coming from my being there. But there was some good. We're leaving this place and going to live in Australia.'

He took her in his arms and brushed his lips over her face as she moved against him. He pulled her closer, holding her tight, feeling her warm tears on his cheek. 'I love you,' he whispered, 'let's make babies.'

35

Chained Again

2009

There was no explosion, no crash. Johan just stepped forward and swung the butt of the gun into Josh's ribs. As he buckled, Johan followed up with another short jab to the side of his head. *I must be getting used to this*, Josh thought, in the brief moment before unconsciousness claimed him, *it doesn't even hurt.*

His whole body hurt like hell when he woke up, though. The pounding in his head and aching in his ribs vied with the damage that Hitler had done to his forearm for the honour of being the most agonising injury. He groaned as he lay on the ground where he had fallen. It seemed that he had not been unconscious for too long. Without moving his head, he could see that brute, Johan, standing at the door of his car talking into his phone. Josh knew just enough Afrikaans to make out the gist of what he said.

'Ja, I got him. He's knocked out. Stupid little fuck didn't consider that we might own the surrounding properties. You should have seen the surprise on his face. I'll bring him back to the house … Sure, we'll move him to Green Thorn.'

Fuck you, thought Josh. *They haven't killed me yet, and what doesn't kill you only makes you stronger*. He figured that all the dangers he had faced recently *had* made him stronger, because in that moment he felt braver than he could have imagined he ever would in such a situation, and he felt unshaken in his decision that there would be no capitulation from him.

Some of Josh's best childhood memories were of Ben regaling him and Saul with tales of his life. The two of them would lie tucked in their beds every night, waiting for their dad to come home. Ben would lie down between them and pick up where they had left off the night before. They loved to hear about his battles and rejoiced in his victories. Through these stories, they learnt about the advantage of surprise and getting in that first telling blow, and the vulnerability of a man's nose.

Josh considered all of this and watched through slitted eyes as the big man finished his conversation. And while he thought and watched and listened, he surreptitiously removed the bludgeon from the back of his pants and hid it beneath his body. When Johan bent down low to lift him, Josh applied all that he remembered and threw his weight into the momentum, swinging the truncheon out of hiding into Johan's face, shattering his bulbous nose. Grunting in pain and disbelief, the giant dropped his phone and clutched his face. A torrent of blood squirted between his fingers.

Josh grabbed the phone. It was a mistake. He should have hit Johan again. He hadn't counted on the strength and determination of the giant, his lightning reflexes and killer instinct. Johan whirled and dived into the cab of the vehicle. There was no doubt he was going for the shotgun. Josh spun on his heels and bolted out of the arc of the lights. The darkness was his greatest ally.

Maybe he should have gone after Johan with his bludgeon, climbed onto his back and clubbed him senseless before he got his hands on the gun. But Josh had no confidence in his ability to bring down that bull of a man. He had already underestimated him once. Still, he was proud of himself. He must have done some damage for there was no shot following his retreat, no engine gunning to life, no footsteps on his heels.

When he reached the safety of the bushes he risked a glance around. Johan had the shotgun all right, but he did not look in a fit state to use it. He was leaning back in the open doorway of the cab, the barrels pointing outward, his head lolling and body swaying side to side. Disorientated, he was unable to aim at anything. If the flow of blood from his nose was not staunched soon, he might faint. Josh could only hope. But Johan was deadly as a cornered lion so long as he held the firearm.

The youth surveyed his new surrounds. In the distance, he could see more walls and barbed wire. No doubt there was another gatehouse there and more security personnel. Apart from the fact that it was brightly illuminated and he had to get past Johan to reach it, there was little chance he would find help there. Just more lackeys of the man with the patch who would gladly give him over. The situation seemed hopeless. But he did have Johan's phone in his hand …

Crouching in the darkness, Josh punched his father's number into the luminous keypad and said a prayer. The phone rang once.

'Dad,' Josh said urgently, as Ben's voice came over the line. He could hear the shock in his father's response.

'Josh! Where are you?'

'Dad! I got away, but they're going to get me again. I don't know who they are but don't come for me. They're going to kill you.'

In the distance, Josh could see the big man moving unsteadily away from the vehicle. With one hand he held a handkerchief to his nose, in the other he held the gun. He was peering around the compound.

'Josh,' Ben said urgently, 'describe where you are, quickly. Tell me everything you see. If you're recaptured, hide the phone and leave it on. Don't do anything to antagonise them.'

Johan began to move in Josh's direction.

'I've only got a few seconds,' Josh whispered. 'The houses around here are on big grounds, and they have lots of security. We're not far from the city, I think Sandton. I could see the lights. They're going to move me to a farm. They mentioned the name of it. Oh God, what was it? Green Thorn! They're taking me to Green Thorn. He's almost here. He's got a gun. I have to be quiet …'

Josh tucked the phone inside his pants. Johan's great shadow fell over the bush where he crouched.

'Come out of there, you stupid little fuck,' the big man growled. 'I could see the light of the phone. You might have thought of that. If you're not out here in two seconds, I'm going to shoot. The boss wants you alive but after you smashed my nose, I really don't care. I'll square it with him … tell him I had no choice. You're as much value to us dead as alive.'

Josh didn't doubt the deadly seriousness of the threat. He stood up bravely, facing Johan, with his smashed nose and blood-spattered clothes. The barrels of the shotgun were pointed at his heart.

'The phone,' Johan said, holding out his meaty hand. Josh didn't like to think what a blow from one of those would do to him. But his face only showed defiance as he handed over the device.

'Oh, so you're a tough little fucker,' Johan spat.

Josh was pleased his defiance was evident.

'We'll break you, though. We'll break you so you'll never be fixed and you won't be bringing any more little Novaks into this world.'

Suddenly being a tough guy didn't seem so great, or the best way to ensure one's survival.

Johan's anger had kept him too diverted to notice that the phone was still on. With a scowl of annoyance, he switched it off. Whoever was on the other end could have heard nothing of use. He jerked the gun towards the vehicle. 'Get going.'

As Josh walked warily past Johan he received the blow he'd feared. But it wasn't too bad. He'd thought Johan would hit harder. Either the Afrikaner was weakened from blood loss or he was holding back, but the boy collapsed to the ground anyway, letting Johan think he was knocked out.

*   *   *

Johan was not taking any more chances with his captive. Josh had been laid on the back seat of the big Land Cruiser and his hands manacled together above his head by a set of handcuffs that had been passed through the handgrip of the car door, rendering his arms immobile. His feet had been similarly restrained, and he found himself shackled between the vehicle's rear doors. Physically exhausted and emotionally drained from the failed escape attempt, he was content to feign unconsciousness for the moment. Perhaps he would hear something useful.

The tyres crunched to a standstill on a pebble driveway and then came the chilling voice he recognised as that of the man with the eye patch.

'What took you so long? And what happened to your face?'

'He broke my fucking nose,' said Johan.

'What are you talking about? Ach, look at you ... you idiot! How did you allow this to happen?'

'He caught me by surprise,' Johan said. 'You know how these Jews have a way of catching you when you're not looking.'

'Ja,' the ugly man said. 'That's certainly true.'

'He had a club hidden on him. He got away but couldn't escape the grounds, and I caught him in the bushes.'

Johan fell silent. He didn't mention anything about Josh getting his hands on his phone. Despite the familiar way he spoke to his boss, he clearly feared his anger. Evidently the temporary loss of the phone was of less consequence to him than the ugly man knowing the extent of his blunder. *Good*, Josh thought. Ben knew he was being taken to Green Thorn, but the mastermind of this scheme and his lackey didn't know that. His dad would take advantage of the fact.

The boss snapped an order. 'You're a mess! I can't send you to Green Thorn with him alone. You better take Benjamin with you.'

'I don't need him. I can manage on my own.'

'You're hurt and I don't want him to find a way to outsmart you again. Just do what I say, but don't leave the two of them alone.'

'Why? You think he might care about him, because his dad was a family servant?'

'I doubt it. Benjamin has little love for whites. It's the only reason I like him the little that I do. But I'm not going to take any chances.'

'Then why involve him at all?'

De Jager sighed. 'Well, that's the difference between you and me, Johan. You have no finesse, no culture, no sense of irony. If you don't understand the piquancy of using Benjamin against the man who paid for his education, then I can't explain it to you.'

'I might not understand what the fuck "piquancy" is,' Johan replied, 'but I understand revenge, and it should be quick. All this elaborate game playing is not necessary, but if you want to involve Benjamin, that's okay, it just means I have to keep a good eye on him too.'

CHAPTER
36

Covert and Immune

Knowing that Josh was recaptured caused Ben's heart to sink. Although the muffled conversation had filled him with dread, he felt slightly compensated by hearing his son called a tough little fucker. The boy's resistance pleased him, even while its consequences terrified him. The rest of the tirade, however, brought him to the point of despair. The ugliness, the merciless evil in the voice, made it hard to believe there was any hope of a good outcome for Josh ... his Josh, his son ... in the hands of such men.

Breathing hard to stifle the rage that burned inside him, Ben no longer doubted his ability to kill. He knew he could do it. Given the chance, he would execute his son's assailants on sight. Once the primal instinct to protect his offspring was fired within him, his inability to act upon it became torture. But mingled with all this anguish was that feeling of pride that Josh had fought back, that he wasn't allowing whatever this was about to transpire without taking any steps to save himself. Knowing Josh's gentleness, Ben could only speculate on what suffering he must have endured to compel him to risk all to deliver his warning, the desperation he must have felt.

The identity of their enemy could no longer be in doubt. They were going to Green Thorn.

Immediately Ben dialled Rocco.

'It's De Jager,' he said, and told him everything that had just occurred. 'Between now and our rendezvous tomorrow, we need to gather as much information as possible about that prick and be forewarned about who he is and what he wants with me.'

'Ben,' said Rocco, 'I've already found out a lot about the guy and he's bad news.'

'Tell me,' said Ben.

'A friend of mine in private security and investigative work used to be with the Security Police and knows of him. His full name is Petrus De Jager. Somewhat intriguingly, people know of him but no one really knows too much about him.

'Apparently he's been involved in weapons dealings for years. It's a clandestine world, so he operates under a number of aliases, which doesn't help when it comes to piecing the information together. De Jager has the logistical set-up to supply the contraband in many of the covert wars taking place all over Africa.

'He's been involved for decades, originally in Mozambique and Angola, but later the Congo, Rwanda, Uganda et cetera. He was also into apartheid sanction busting in the eighties. His other interests are smuggling diamonds and ivory. That's what a lot of the wars in Africa, covert and otherwise, are really about. The power elites are happy to sacrifice half the population to get their hands on diamonds and ivory. So he supplies the arms to do the killing and then sells the contraband. You name it, he's in it. In a nutshell, he's an evil bastard.

'Hey! Are you still there?' he asked.

'Ja, I am,' Ben replied, digesting everything he'd just heard. 'Is that it?'

'No, not quite. You know I've been doing this investigative work for a long time, and I'm surprised that, with all De Jager's underworld and criminal activities, I've never heard of him. It's an uncanny capacity, to remain so secretive. He's never been arrested or charged with anything, so I figure he must be really well connected. Now I hear that he goes directly to the top. I don't know any names but it appears he has some of the top boys in the ANC in his pocket. They go to his house and his game reserve and ensure that everyone keeps a wide berth from him. Covert and immune is how I would best describe him. A rare individual and, unfortunately, I wasn't able to find out where he lives. That's like a state secret. But, anyway, we know about his farm.'

'Jesus!' was all Ben could reply, stunned at the scope of power and influence possessed by Josh's captor.

The intuition that had previously seemed improbable, that all this was related to Steyn and his past, could no longer be dismissed as paranoia. What he had just learnt about Josh's kidnapper sounded too reminiscent of his old enemy and confirmed, for him, that Steyn and De Jager were one and the same.

Everything made sense now. Steyn's arms dealing back in the early seventies had paved the way for his criminal life.

'Ben?' said Rocco. 'Are you still with me?'

'Yes, but I need to know something. You mentioned De Jager used a lot of aliases. Would you know if Steyn was one of them?'

'Ja,' Rocco said. 'That name was mentioned. But that was a long time ago.'

'I know him,' Ben said. 'I had a vendetta with him. I thought it was all over when we left for Australia twenty-nine years ago. He was my platoon sergeant in the army. A bloody sadist. He made my life hell for no reason I could discover, other than that I'm a Jew. He came near to killing me, then ten years later I was involved in an altercation with neo-Nazis celebrating Hitler's birthday. Steyn was there, and I took the opportunity to thump him. It happened very fast, and I thought he never knew who or what had hit him.'

'Incredible,' said Rocco. 'So, if he found out it was you, then he must have held a grudge all this time.'

'It also means he's planned for this moment and positioned himself to know when I would be vulnerable so he could strike. Josh being here was the exact kind of thing he was waiting for.'

'Hmm, that's a long time to wait for revenge.'

'Yes, it is, but that's the nature of this beast. He gets pleasure from other people's pain. He named his dog Hitler. That tells you a lot about him. Kidnapping someone's child is about the cruellest thing you can do to a parent and is precisely the kind of action a person like Steyn would take to satisfy his revenge.'

'But if you look at what he's risking to do this, it must mean a lot to him,' said Rocco.

'I couldn't understand the depth of his malevolence then, so I can't begin to imagine what's driving him now. Whatever it is, though, we have to stop him once and for all.'

'I'm surprised you hadn't thought of him earlier, given the impact he had on your life,' said Rocco.

'Oh, I did think fleetingly of him,' Ben admitted. 'As soon as I heard the Afrikaner voice over the phone a sixth sense warned me that it could be him. But in my mind, bringing up things that happened thirty years ago seemed so unlikely that I dismissed it.

'I was never an angel, Rocco, but Steyn brought out the worst in me, and I was glad to leave it behind when we left South Africa. I tried to forget everything about him, especially knowing the kind of evil he is capable of. Besides, it was too confronting to connect him with what's happening now. De Jager's résumé sounds so unmistakably like Steyn, except that he didn't have any deformities and that, I think, permitted me to remain consciously unconscious of him. In hindsight, maybe he received those injuries at the Keller that night. I hit him in the head so hard that he went flying off the bar, and I never stopped to look at what happened. All I was concerned with was getting out of the place alive. There were reports in the newspapers of people being badly injured but no details or any names. It would certainly help explain why his hatred of me seems to have festered over the years.'

'Well,' said Rocco, 'it's as intriguing as any mystery, but knowing why he hates you won't help us. What we really have to figure out is our next move.'

'If we know who the man is, surely we can find out where he lives, get the police involved and have him arrested?'

'Involving the police would be the worst thing we could do, Ben. De Jager means to win this at any cost. If his only motivation is hate, which seems likely, his main goal is to destroy you. If he can't kill you, he'll kill Josh quickly and cover his tracks. We have no proof, and even if we did, De Jager is too well connected. He's operated on the wrong side of the law for decades without being touched. It's not possible to escape prosecution this long without having men on the inside of government. If we got lucky and managed to avoid anyone in his network, even a well-intentioned police effort might not achieve anything but getting your son killed. He wants you, and his belief that you're playing along is all that's keeping Josh alive.'

'So what am I supposed to do?' Ben snapped in frustration. 'Simply surrender so De Jager can kill me? Do you think he'll let Josh go after that? Not likely. He'll murder him too. He's not going to leave my son alive, to either accuse him of a crime or risk that, sometime in the future, Josh will find a way to go after him.'

'He's no fool, Ben. So there's just one thing we can do.'

'Yes? What?'

'We have to go after him,' said Rocco.

'Yes, of course, and I see why you're hesitant to involve the police, but with all your connections, can't you locate some reliable cops? The chance of success would be much greater if we worked with the authorities.'

'No, really, forget the police,' Rocco insisted. 'Sure, I know some honest people. But if there's any official involvement they'll want to do everything by the book and we'll be sidelined. They'll take control of the situation and we can't have that. Or do you want to risk handing this over to someone you don't know, who may be too reckless or too timid? Who may tie us up in red tape? Who's as worried about keeping his job as saving your son–'

'Enough!' Ben shouted. 'You're right. Where do we begin?'

'There aren't a lot of choices. From what you told me, they're probably already underway to Green Thorn with your boy, so that's where we should head.'

'Okay, but De Jager is expecting me to meet him tomorrow at noon. If I don't show up he may carry out his threat to kill Josh. Whatever we do, it has to be before the rendezvous time.'

'Oh, it will be,' said Rocco. 'That's going to be our advantage. He may be ready for us to try something when the two of you meet, but we'll surprise him with a pre-emptive strike well before that.'

'What if he figures out that the best way to hurt me is to kill my son and leave me with that on my conscience for the rest of my life?'

'He already knows that,' Rocco said. 'That's why I said he'd murder Josh if he can't get to you. He knows that's the easiest way to ruin your life, but he wants you in his hands. I just didn't want to underline that point. But you've mentioned it now. He hasn't killed Josh yet or even harmed him sufficiently to have knocked the fight out of him. He wants *you*. But we can't take any risks with this guy. As you said, he's a sadist.

'Let's put ourselves in his shoes. If he really wants to destroy you as cruelly as possible, he may plan to execute Josh in front of you. He may have already decided neither of you is going to live. If you haven't entirely ruled out the idea of an exchange in your mind, I would now. Our only option is to take the fight to him. He'll think he holds all the cards, keeping Josh at the game farm. It's out of town and isolated, and he'll believe he has all the time in the world to do what he wants.'

There was no arguing with Rocco's logic, but Ben felt tortured. Tackling De Jager head-on was dangerous, but what other option was there?

'Okay,' said Ben. 'Let's go to the farm. When should we leave?'

'Right now,' Rocco said. 'Whatever else the plan entails we should attack in the early hours of the morning when they least expect it and the guards will be tired.'

'All right!' Ben agreed. Amidst all the turmoil, Rocco's composure was a godsend. 'If you don't mind, I'd like to do the driving. It'll take my mind off everything and I'll feel that I'm doing something useful.'

'No problem, Ben, of course. I'll be back to pick you up at 10 p.m. We'll work out the finer details of our strategy in the car.'

Ben found Rick in the kitchen making sandwiches. His bemused maid, Florence, hovered over his shoulder like a dog watching her puppies, while an obviously anxious Rick made his contribution to the mission. Ben gratefully grabbed a tuna sandwich and, between bites, informed Rick of their plans, probing him for an alternate viewpoint on the sensibility of their proposed plan. His friend listened carefully and nodded in assent.

'I can't see any other options either. You go with Rocco to Makanyi. I'll let Harry know what's happening, and I'll fly there in the morning. With Harry and Robert on hand, at least we have some extra manpower.'

CHAPTER
37

Born Bad

1960

'Kick the ball, Petrie! Kick it straight into the goals,' Joost yelled, as his fourteen-year-old brother ripped down the centre of the soccer field. Petrie feinted to the left to avoid the last defender and, when he took the bait, went right. Rolling his left foot over the top of the ball, he lined it up for the shot. Shifting his weight and getting his body over the ball, he booted it just above its centre, exactly as Joost had taught him. It went like a bullet, curling to the left, brushing past the outstretched fingers of the diving goalkeeper and ricocheted off the back net before rolling to a standstill in the corner.

'Yeah, boetie!' Petrie could hear his brother screaming from the sideline above the noise of the crowd, all the cheering mothers and fathers. 'You've done it, bro. You are the champion!'

Joost ran forward, arms thrown wide to embrace him. His teammates and their parents mobbed him, hugging him and slapping his back. They had just won the final. The trophy was theirs again, and they had Petrie to thank for it. For the second year in succession, he had scored the winning goal. The entire town would celebrate his accomplishment and lavish friendship and love upon him. Everyone would acknowledge him except his mom, who couldn't, and his dad, who wouldn't, the prick. But at least he had Joost.

His brother was always there for him. He had taught him to play soccer, rugby and cricket; to ride his bicycle and jump it over the ant hills in the veldt next to their house. In fact, there wasn't much Petrie valued that hadn't been taught to him by Joost. He had even taught him how to cover his head and body and roll with the punches whenever their father went into one of his frequent rages.

The art of protecting himself from the hideous beatings had been hard-won by Joost. Petrus recalled the times his older brother had stood in front of him and his mom like a shield to keep Gerrit away, ducking and weaving as the drunkard staggered after him, unleashing his stinging blows.

As brutal as Gerrit was at the best of times, he was even worse in the summer when everyone else was having a ball, living their festive lives. The sun blazed hotly and the sweat dripped from the men's faces and spread in big wet patches across their shirts, saturating their armpits. The women in their light cotton skirts packed up their kids and headed for the municipal swimming pools. There they all gathered and some of the fathers, too, everyone under umbrellas, with ice bags full of sandwiches and cold drinks. They put down their towels, laying claim to a spot from where they could watch their kids running and jumping, splashing and screaming in the cool blue water. Frolicking in the pool with his brother gifted Petrus with some of the happiest moments of his life. He even dared to dream of how the other kids must feel when their dads threw them high into the air, screaming with laughter and diving back into the depths.

Yet their father was conspicuously absent. Gerrit would never go to the pool and strip off his clothes and play with his kids. Not since he had to take that claw with him.

No, he would rather go to the *drink winkel*. Once ensconced in the pub, he would sit there on his barstool with his one good arm on the counter and his claw waving at the barman, ordering him to 'load me up and keep them coming'. As the day passed into night, Gerrit clung to his perch and railed against the heat and the poor service of the Kaffirs. The more the beer flowed, the more he found to lament.

'What's the country coming to? Where is it all going to end? What a shame the fucking Brits won the war ...'

On and on he went, but no matter where his diatribe wandered it always ended at the same destination.

'This fucking *claw* ... will you *look* at this *fucking* thing I'm saddled with. *All because of that fucking Jew*. He's the cause of it. Why is he still fucking *alive*? Eh? You tell me that! And why is it that that *Jew's* family is alive, when me, Gerrit Burger, a real Afrikaner's life is such a waste of fucking time? I'm lumbered with that useless bitch wife and her two useless piss-weak kids. I see them looking at my fucking buggered arm, my *claw*, as if I'm some sort of disgusting monster. They should *all burn in hell*. In fact, I think I'll help them on their way there just as soon as I get home!' It was always Joost who stepped up to the plate then, steered him away, talked him down and coaxed him to silence, patted him on the back and told him that he was loved and that his family would do anything for him.

* * *

As the brothers headed home that day after Petrie's victory, Joost's arm went around his younger sibling's shoulder. The simple embrace was full of warmth and strength.

'That was a great shot, Petrie. You've really mastered the game now. If you keep this up you may make selection to the provincial team.'

'Ja, I know, but I'm still not sure whether I love soccer more or rugby,' Petrie replied. 'Soccer is more refined but the ruggedness of rugby is fantastic, the speed and power and the rumbles, you know. Soccer is not the same. I know I can play, but it doesn't excite me the way rugby does.'

Joost was troubled that Petrie's aggression inclined him towards rugby. What he referred to so lightly as 'a rumble' was really an opportunity to pummel his opponent. With Petrie, the game was not merely rugged; it was brutal. He was often sent off the field for offences, but his behaviour was tolerated by the coach because his fearsome reputation intimidated their opponents, and his team was often victorious as a result. The rugby field was the perfect arena for his brother to rid himself of his frustration at Gerrit, but it pained Joost that Petrie relished inflicting pain on his opponents because of what he was enduring in his home. Joost preferred to see his sibling play soccer, where he was forced to exercise greater control. Petrie needed to rein in his emotions.

'Ja, no, you better make up your mind though, because if you want to be at the top you have to focus on a single sport and, to me, you have the makings of a soccer star,' he said, trying not to push his own point of view too hard.

Petrie looked over at his sibling as they walked. Joost always made him think about the essential things. He had this way about him, never forcing anything, merely asking a question and then leaving his younger brother to make the decision, after his own careful consideration.

'Ja, you're right,' he replied at last. 'But right now we just won the league and I don't have to decide yet. I'll make the decision next year, before we start training.

'You know, boet,' Petrie said to his brother, 'I see all the other kids at the games with their parents, and I think of how I never had a mom or dad there, ever. It's always been you. You've been watching over me since we were babies, and sometimes I think, like, who's been watching over you?'

Joost smiled. 'Petrie, I can still remember the day you came back from the nursing home where you were born. I was only three and I had a baby brother! I was so excited, man.'

His mom had been telling him how good it was going to be for him to have someone else around when she went away. He did not really understand what his mother was talking about when she said she was going away, but she had made him acutely aware of the importance of his brother.

'I was so lucky,' he said. 'I also had time with Mommy that you never did. I had time to experience her kindness. She always tried to protect me from him.'

But that was not really correct. He never really felt fortunate. Quite the opposite, in fact. He felt unlucky, cursed to have been born. No matter what his mom had tried to do, no one could have protected him from his father, that evil brute who inflicted unspeakable things upon them. When he was paralytic drunk and wanted nothing more than to kill or abuse someone, there was no one else to stand in his way but Joost. It had to be him. He had to make sure that Gerrit never got close enough to his mother or his brother to do any real harm.

Burdened with the responsibility for his younger brother whom he loved with all his heart, he tried to shield Petrie from experiencing the same things his father had inflicted upon him. The secret and the shame of that, he would have to carry on his own.

'You are my brother, Petrie, and my best friend. I loved you from the day you were born, and I've felt your love for me. You are my 2IC – my second in command – my mate, and I would never let anyone hurt you. They would have to kill me first.'

Petrie cloaked himself in Joost's words as if they were a protective blanket. They engendered a profound sense of security within him, despite their father's depredations. Feeling valued and cherished, his life gained a meaning it would otherwise have lacked. Whatever confidence he had was owed to his brother. Looking at him with pride and wrapping his arms around him, he said, 'I love you too, boet, I'll always be your 2IC.'

All the while, Joost remained terrified that Gerrit would molest his brother too. The unending anxiety frequently grew close to intolerable. *What will become of Petrie?* he wondered. *Despite my promises, how much longer can I protect him?*

They never spoke of Gerrit as 'Dad'. How could they possibly refer to him that way when he had never shown them any love? All he ever did was abuse them, bully them and beat them at the slight-est provocation, and often for none at all.

'When you came along, I was never lonely again,' Joost said to his brother. 'It became my mission to take care of you and ensure that you would always be around.'

'Sometimes I think we would have been better off as orphans,' Petrie said. 'You know they could have put us in a home with other kids, and we wouldn't have had to be frightened of that prick. I hate him so much. I still can't understand why he had kids when he completely loathes them.'

'It was Mum who wanted kids,' said Joost. 'He just wanted her. I don't think he cared about us or anything else after the accident with his arm ... having to live with that claw.'

'Still, it's one thing to not want to have any ankle-biters, but it's another to be a shit to them all the time. I've never heard of any kid that gets as many beatings as we've had. When he points that hook at us, he looks like the devil. Do you think he's always been evil?'

Joost considered his brother's question. This was not the first time they had discussed evil. Did a person become bad, or were some people just born that way? The topic was of more than academic interest to Joost because he was concerned about Petrie's inability to control his anger.

Once they had had a budgie named Ruby. The cute little creature used to climb all over them, sit on their shoulders and walk on their hands. One day it had bitten Petrie's finger and drawn blood. Petrie grabbed their pet and tore its head right off.

Joost was frozen in horror and Petrie ran off. Joost found him a few minutes later, sitting on the veranda with his head between his hands, sobbing.

'I killed Ruby,' he sobbed. 'Do you think I'm like *him*? Some-one who hurts the ones he's supposed to love, just because he gets angry?'

Joost chose his words carefully. 'I don't think he was always so cruel. I think he's beside himself with anger because that Jew stabbed him and he lost his arm. Mom once told me the whole story. He was never the same after that. When he came out of hospital he started drinking a lot and feeling sorry for himself, and then he became angry with everyone. Prior to that he mainly hated the Jews, the Kaffirs and the British but he controlled it, except when he was with the Brownshirts. They used to beat up soldiers because they supported the British in the war.

'Petrie, you have to learn to control your urges. Even if people have bad thoughts, it's their actions that they're judged on. It would be better not to ever want to harm another, but if you do have such impulses, you should never act upon them.

'The problem with him is that he can't control himself. I think he grew up always getting his own way, and now he just does what he wants without thinking. When he's angry, he doesn't think about the consequences to those he hurts.'

'I don't know,' said Petrie. 'I think you're wrong. It's not that he doesn't think about the consequences, he just doesn't care. That bastard knows exactly what he's doing but he doesn't give a fuck. He made Ma go mad. The way he treated her. If the prick had cared for her even a little bit, she wouldn't have gone nuts. Ma's in that place because of him. She would never have left us. She was so scared and didn't know what to do and she went mad. She's so messed up, and it's because of him. I swear one day I'm going to kill that son of a whore.'

'Calm down,' Joost said. There it was again. That anger that simmered within Petrie. This was not the first time he had sworn to kill their father. Joost knew that the worst thing to do was to fight back against Gerrit, because doing that meant somebody would definitely get killed.

Joost was quite sure his father had killed before and doubted that Gerrit could control himself enough to not slay his little brother if it came to a fight.

'I think we've had enough talk about him for one day. Let's just have a good time, hey!' Joost said, punching his brother playfully in the arm. Petrie punched him back and they began to wrestle, laughing and hugging.

Petrie had become incredibly strong. At fourteen, handsome with chiselled features, he had filled out and was scarily muscular. He did countless press-ups daily and used the chestnut tree in their front garden to do pull-ups until the muscles in his arms and chest had become tremendously powerful and well defined. A chill ran through Joost's body as they grappled like two young bears. If his brother was not tamed, one day he would be as deadly a predator as their father.

CHAPTER
38

Named in Honour

2009

At first appearances, the black man, Benjamin, had seemed out of place amongst the likes of De Jager and Johan. Had it just been wishful thinking, Josh wondered, to believe that he had picked up a subtle tentativeness that was not apparent to the other two? Josh smiled inwardly; his mother would have said it was the black guy's aura. His father and brother liked to tease her for her 'spookiness', nonetheless she had always impressed them with her intuition and how she could read signs of character that no one else noticed but were later proved to be uncannily correct. Deep down, despite all the teasing, he knew his father had been changed by her, and a significant dent had been placed in his scepticism even if he didn't always let on about it.

Sometimes she had expressed the hope that at least one of them shared the gift. Now Josh prayed devoutly that it was him. Hearing that this Benjamin was the same one his father had spoken of was a shock. How could it be? This was the son of his dad's old servant, Joshua, whose education Ben had paid for. However improbable the news seemed, hearing it fuelled some hope in his heart. It might also explain the man's initial tentativeness about his capture. Perhaps De Jager had some sort of hold on him and had ensured that Johan was there to keep an eye on them. That Benjamin would be a willing participant in all of this was inconceivable to Josh. Perhaps he could appeal to him? He would have to be careful that this was not just another strand in the web intended to snare his dad. To think that hope was possibly within reach, as near as despair, maddened him.

He was thankful he had not been gagged again, nor was there a hood over his head. From where he lay Josh had a clear view of Benjamin's face, but he could only see Johan when the Afrikaner turned towards him. The sight of his battered face gave the young man a measure of satisfaction.

'He won't wake up too fast from the klap I gave him,' Johan spat.

'Yeah, you really showed him,' Benjamin said, with a hint of irony that Josh thought probably went right over Johan's head. Clearly there was no love lost between these two. Emboldened, Josh opened one eye a slit in time to see Johan pop some pills and raise a bottle of water to his lips.

'Jesus, he did some damage to me,' he snarled.

'Maybe you should go to the hospital,' Benjamin suggested. 'I can handle this little whitey by myself.'

'And you think I can't?' Johan growled.

'I didn't say that.' Benjamin shrugged, but his tone certainly had.

'I don't need a hospital,' Johan grunted. 'Not yet, at least. I've had worse than this.'

But despite his protests, the Afrikaner was clearly fatigued and not inclined towards conversation with his black companion. Johan settled back in his seat and said no more. Nor did Benjamin disturb the silence. Josh watched out the window as the dark sky, filled with the bright stars of the South African heavens, flashed by. He was mesmerised, and before too long, under the hypnotic power of its influence, he tumbled into slumber.

* * *

Josh jerked awake. How much time had passed? The scene remained exactly the same, with the stars flashing by in the sky outside his window. Benjamin and Johan sat as before, both silent, each isolated in their own thoughts. Or was Johan, maybe, slumped a little deeper in his seat? Josh strained his ears. Was there a faint snoring coming from the big man? Had he succumbed to his pain and blood loss and drifted off to sleep under the soothing power of the painkillers?

'Benjamin?' Josh hissed, on a sudden impulse.

'So, you're awake,' Benjamin replied, making no attempt to lower his voice. Josh winced as Johan grunted and snuffled and stirred before lapsing back into sleep. 'I wondered if you were faking.'

'For a bit, but then I fell asleep,' Josh admitted, hoping to create a sense of intimacy with this little confession.

'You were better off in your dreams,' Benjamin said. 'The waking world holds no joy for you, I'm afraid.'

The cold response dampened any hopes Josh had of receiving this man's aid. But still he had to try.

'You know who I am?' he said.

Benjamin grunted. 'Oh yes, the son of my benefactor, the great Ben Novak. My poor father decided to honour him by naming his son after him.'

'Why the sarcasm?' Josh replied. 'My father loved your father. He reciprocated by naming me after your dad, Joshua.'

'Huh!' Benjamin mumbled something incoherent and derisive in reply but Josh forged on.

'And he loved *you*. He told me vividly of how your father brought you to their home and how beautiful he thought you were. How he picked you up and carried you on his shoulders and you screamed with delight!'

'Well, I guess we should forget all about apartheid then!' Benjamin said bitterly. 'Your dad carried me upon his shoulders! My father carried him a thousand times. You probably think that evens the score because that's how you whites calculate everything, isn't it? You take our land, our resources, our culture, our soul. In return, you give us the crumbs of wealth from your table.'

'Of course it was wrong!' Josh said, understanding his hatred. 'But it was a different time in a different country to now. My father always hated apartheid, that's why he left.'

'Ah, so that's why it ended,' Benjamin sneered. 'I never realised that was the best way to finish it. How brave of him. You really think he was any better than the rest, in any way that actually mattered? Oh, I remember my dad's endless stories of the mighty Ben Novak, with all his bravery and smiles and fine words. When I was young, I was under the spell of that delusion, as well. But I'm not the simpleton my dad is. I've had an education. I understand how the world works. Your father exploited us like all of the whites.

'I suppose he left here empty-handed? No! He left here rich, didn't he? And where did his wealth come from, if not from exploitation? There is no wealth without exploitation. There are no haves without there being have-nots. That was the entire basis of apartheid and why the white South Africans would bust every black head in the land if it would prevent it from crumbling. So the Novaks run off with their wealth. They go somewhere where they don't have to be confronted with the source of their money under their eyes every day. Your father isn't good, he's just squeamish.'

'That's not true!' Josh asserted, wondering how he could possibly dam this flow of vitriol. 'I'm sorry you feel this way. Growing up as the son of a servant in a racist country must have been awful for you. I understand your anger towards white people, but that doesn't change who my father is and the fact that he can be white and a good man at the same time!'

'Well, that's touching,' Benjamin said. 'That's truly touching. But I'm afraid I don't share your belief in human goodness. Don't you know your Machiavelli, your Hobbes, your Marx and your Darwin? Life is the survival of the fittest. Spend a little time living here and you'll learn that.'

Josh could understand the depth of Benjamin's anger and contempt. He decided it would be better to try a different tack.

'What about your father?' he said. 'He can't approve of what you're doing? My father helped provide for him as well as for your education. Surely–'

'Don't you dare mention my father!' Benjamin roared. 'Do you really think I care what he thinks! Oh, I did once, like every boy. I thought he could do no wrong, but then my eyes were opened and I saw how despicable his doting love for his white baas was. My father's gratitude filled me with shame.

'He was no better than the whites who were satisfied for inequality to rule so long as it served them. *He* was okay and happy to play the black lap dog and abide by the rules of apartheid, content at being just a humble servant while his own people suffered under the hands of more ruthless exploiters than the saintly Master Abe and Master Ben. Yep, old Joshua huddled happily in the relative safety of the Novak home while his neighbours were beaten and starved and worked to death.

'Gratitude! Don't speak to me of gratitude. Your father left this country wealthy. So, he left behind a pittance to help an old Kaffir educate his son! I'm sure you had it tough. Was there enough left over for your private schools and the holidays in Europe?

'I spit on your blood money! Oh, I took it all right. On behalf of the disenfranchised, I took that pittance of a down payment of what was owed them, so I could get an education and work for their betterment—'

'For Christ's sake, will you keep it down!' Johan grunted, shocking both Benjamin and Josh. 'Get off your soapbox, Benjamin. No one bloody well cares. Fuck, I thought you were over all of that nonsense years ago.' He snorted. 'Been long enough since you actually did something practical for your lot. I guess you're still biding your time, eh?'

Johan wrapped his arms around his chest and settled himself deep into his seat, intent on getting some more sleep. 'And you, you little fuck, stop stirring up the natives. If I hear any more out of you, I'll gag you again. I'm just like you in one respect, you never know when I'm really asleep or just pretending.' Johan mimicked a snore, chuckled to himself and was still.

Josh swallowed hard, his tears smarting. Benjamin's face held nothing but resentment, which, he guessed, was not entirely undeserved. He had tried to sway him and failed. What hope was left to him now?

CHAPTER
39

The Art of War

The white Land Cruiser sped easily along the freeway at 130 kilometres per hour towards the Timbavati. Vaguely aware of the township lights and those of passing cars, the silence weighed heavily on Ben's troubled mind. Rocco, on the other hand, gazed nonchalantly out the car window, seemingly unperturbed by the imminent dangers that lay ahead.

'What are you thinking about, Rocco?' Ben asked, hoping some conversation would give a modicum of respite from his unease and the silence.

Rocco sat motionless for a few moments as though his client's question had gone unheard. At last he responded slowly, 'I'm actually trying not to over think. You know how it is. Sometimes straining and exertion becomes counterproductive. The conscious mind is a great tool but at times the best ideas come when you allow your thoughts to rest for a bit, then inspiration comes of its own accord.'

Ben nodded in agreement. 'I had some of my best ideas while running on the beach thinking of nothing more than the sand and the sea.'

'Once we hear from your mate, Robert, we can apply our minds more actively to a plan,' said Rocco. 'What kind of a guy is he? I mean, is he cut out for this sort of action, and to what extent can we rely on him?'

Ben took a moment to consider the question, and when he spoke there was fondness and admiration in his voice. 'In our early varsity days, we spent every spare hour we could in the bush with him. Harry and I did this same trip most weekends. Rob was always around with us and became our guide. He was brilliant and taught us everything we know about the bush.

'He grew up in the Timbavati. His father was a game ranger for twenty years or more. Rob was able to speak almost every black language before he spoke Afrikaans or even English. You should hear him mimic the sounds of the animals, and it's incredible to watch him tracking. He taught Harry and me to read the minute telltale details of one spoor crossing the path of another, whether the animal was being hunted or escaping, the change of their direction and where they scuffed the dirt in their anxiety. "See this bent grass," he'd say, "that's where they lay in wait."'

Ben's reminiscence was cut short by the blaring of his phone. He turned it on in speaker mode.

'Hello?' Ben said.

'It's me, Robert.'

'I thought it would be. Speak of the devil ...'

'Hmm. Well, that would be De Jager, then.' There was an odd tone in Robert's voice. 'Rick tells me it's him for sure. I'm really so sorry about what's happened to Josh.'

'Thanks, Rob, I appreciate that. Yes, it's De Jager who's behind it. So what more can you tell us about him? Rocco is also on the line.'

'Well, you would know him better than the rest of us, though I understand from Rick that he was named Steyn then. I remember you talking about him. From that point of view, De Jager has done a pretty good job in hiding quite how repulsive he is. I guess, as his ambitions grew, he couldn't be so openly warped.'

'Ja, maybe,' Ben said. 'But in the army he wasn't too careful about who he revealed his brutality to.'

'Yeah,' Robert continued. 'So I don't think I have anything to tell you that you don't already know about his character. But I can tell you all about his compound, his resources and his security. I've been there and seen his operation. We had to discuss our various policies and try to persuade him to at least refrain from breaking the law, especially on our land.

'That's when I experienced how he could really lay on the charm and that he'd stop at nothing to get his way. I could have got very rich off his offers.'

'You never mentioned that before,' Ben said.

'Hah,' Robert snorted. 'If I went to Harry or you every time someone like De Jager offered me an incentive, we'd never talk about anything else. And I'm not the kind to boast just because I *didn't* do the wrong thing. It's just expected we'll do right by one another, hey?'

'Of course,' Ben said. 'Who else would we trust with Makanyi?'

'Tell us about the compound,' Rocco interjected, keen to get back to business now they had Robert on the phone, 'and the men there, too.'

'I'm not exactly sure how big his crew is, maybe six or seven, and they're well armed. Maybe four game rangers and three ex-army. You can tell the army guys even without talking to them, they look the part.'

'Thanks, Rob, that helps,' Rocco said. 'Ben mentioned you speak a lot of the local lingo. I guess that encourages them to open up.'

'Not really, I hardly have any interaction with them. Occasionally we meet along the fence line but they're not very sociable. Anyway, he has more men than would usually be required for a property like his, and they operate all over the farm on shifts. There are usually at least two army types at the compound, sometimes more depending on who his guests are. He has three permanent rangers who also have guns. They're not as likely to get involved in anything violent but the possibility can't be excluded. De Jager pays them very well, according to rumour at least. The ex-soldiers always gave me the impression that they're dangerous. They look tough and mean and never go anywhere unarmed.'

'What about the perimeter of the compound? Many of the lodges only have hard wall structures near the front gate and guardhouse. The rest of the perimeter is often constructed with soft fencing made from bamboo or blue gum slats with electrified wires to deter the elephants and other large animals.'

'Ja, it's the same there. The fences offer privacy to the lodgers, and the animals stay well away from the electric wiring so there's no reason for brick walls.'

'So,' said Rocco, 'if we drive off one of the roads in a heavy vehicle it would be possible to bust straight through the fence into the compound, rather than through the guarded front gate?'

'Yes, quite possible,' said Robert.

'And we'll be able to breach the perimeter in more than one place simultaneously?'

'Yes again,' said Robert. 'And that also means, once we get Josh into a vehicle we can get back out, either through the same hole or a new one.'

'Do you think you could draw us a map of the buildings in the compound, the fences and the general terrain of the surrounding area, and have it ready for when we reach Makanyi?'

'Sure can. I'll start drawing while I talk to you guys. I've got some local maps that will help, too.'

'Great, thanks. Quite a coincidence,' Rocco observed to Ben, 'De Jager owning a farm next door to you.'

'I doubt it's chance,' said Robert. 'Of course luck and coincidence do exist, but it seems much more likely that De Jager bought the place because he knew Ben owned Makanyi and one day he'd come here. Then he'd have his chance.'

'Incredible, isn't it?' Ben said. 'That someone could be so obsessed with revenge that they would go to such lengths, and bide their time so long.'

'You know the Italians have a saying that revenge is a dish best served cold,' Rocco mused. 'Some people like it even more when they can cook it as long as possible before it even begins to cool. Anticipation is the most delicious part of a meal for many people.'

'Okay ...' Robert's voice came over the speaker again. They heard him arranging his paper, reference material and pens. 'I'm going to describe the place to you as I draw it. It will help me clarify it in my own mind and may help you understand the drawing better when you get it.'

As he drew, Robert gave a running commentary, providing Ben and Rocco with a precise mental picture of the entire property and the layout of the compound, detailing the approach roads, the size and shape of the walls and fences and the most likely points of penetration. He mapped all the buildings he could remember and the direction they faced.

'Rocco, when do you expect the rescue to take place?' Robert asked, when the map was completed.

'A pre-dawn strike will produce the greatest element of surprise,' Rocco said. 'People are most deeply asleep early in the morning and that's when the guards will be least vigilant.'

'It's also the quietest time of night before the animals begin to stir and the sound of vehicles is most audible,' Robert cautioned.

'Well, it's a start,' Ben said. 'Now we know who we're up against. We understand the where, and we've worked out the when. The only details we're shaky on are the how.'

'I have a few ideas,' Rocco said. 'But I think that's enough for now. We can plan the details of the attack when we get to Makanyi.'

'Okay,' Robert agreed. 'Harry will be here then and we can all work it out together.'

'Whatever plan of attack we come up with,' Rocco said, 'it will be fraught with danger. Our planning has to be as precise as any military operation.'

'I also have a few ideas of my own, so drive safely and I'll see you guys soon,' said Robert, and hung up.

Enlivened by the discussion, Ben felt a renewed sense of hope. Plans were in place, events were underway. Yet Rocco's warning hammered home the stark reality of the situation. It seemed unlikely they could pull this off without someone being maimed or killed. He thought of his 'angels', as Dahlia called them, and prayed fervently. *Protect my family and my friends, let us all return together and bring Josh back alive.*

*   *   *

Rocco's breath was a gentle rasp in the dark as he dozed beside Ben, who remained vigilant behind the wheel. The PI was like a big cat, conserving his strength and energy for when it would be needed.

Stealth and cunning, knowing your enemy, thinking like him, it was all coming back to Ben. He felt revitalised by the anticipation of danger and prickly with excitement, even while he was terrified for the safety of his son.

Once a fighter, always a fighter, he thought. No matter how much time had passed, however much life had changed, although he resided in a new country, building dreams and conquering challenges and finally believing that peace and quiet were just around the corner, here he was again ready for an onslaught.

He could feel Dahlia beside him now. Almost feared to turn his head in case she was sitting where he knew Rocco slept. He could hear her voice.

'Even with so much at stake,' she says, 'your primal instincts have taken over and you're relishing the thought of the final confrontation.'

'I could never hide anything from you. You can see right through me … and you don't approve. But what other choice do I have?'

'Men, you never have another choice, do you? You have to pump up your chests and bump heads, establish who has the biggest dick.'

Ben smiles. 'You always said that was me.'

'Yes, I loved you, with all your machismo, because I saw the beautiful heart. And I love you still, despite this desire for confrontation and violence. But don't make this about revenge, Ben. Save our boy, however you have to. You know that's what I care about more than anything else. But remember that this thing started with revenge … with the attack at the Keller.'

'It started with Steyn victimising me for no reason.'

'For no reason you knew of. But it could have ended there. There was that moment when you saw him standing on the bar and you could have walked away. You have to accept your own role in this.'

Dahlia would always hold him accountable, show him his own demons if need be. Nonetheless, he wouldn't agree with her out loud. Not yet. But she still has more to say on the subject.

'I know what you're thinking: this thing with De Jager or Steyn, whoever he is, for whatever reasons he has chosen to devote himself to this malevolent path, this thing is going to end. You plan to make him pay, once and for all, for all you suffered at his hands.'

Ben has no answers. She knows him too well. He turns to look at the figure in the passenger seat. It's Rocco of course. But that doesn't change anything or make his conversation with Dahlia any less real.

CHAPTER
40

The Ghost of a Conscience

Under the hypnotic influence of the stars, Ben continued behind the wheel whilst Rocco seemed to have plunged into the most profound sleep and never stirred. He had insisted on sharing the driving, but Ben was adamant there was no need and there was no danger of him falling asleep.

If you die in a stupid car crash, you'll never be able to rescue Josh.

Ben turns in his seat. He must be really tired. He's hallucinating. He can see her now, where Rocco should have been. So beautiful, she brings tears to his eyes. His Dahlia.

'Hey, hon, stay awake, you need to be able to see the road. We need you alive remember.'

'Alive? Why? There are times when I wonder what for. I still can't come to terms with living without you.'

'You have the boys, Ben.'

'Yes, but there is such a void. Even they can't fill it. I've lost interest in just about everything.'

'It's hard, my darling, but you're not alone. I'm always watching, and I'm right here.'

'Nothing makes sense any longer without you around. I've tried to continue as usual, for the sake of the boys.'

'You're doing a wonderful job, Ben. You're a great dad, and they still need you.'

Now he has to cope with the paralysing fear that he could lose Josh and the reality of the danger posed by De Jager. It is out of his hands, all he can do is roll with the punches. The only positive so far is that at least he knows who the adversary is and what motivates his actions. They are racing towards a totally uncertain outcome and he is trying to concoct a plan that can stack the odds somewhat more in their favour. Somehow he has to get inside De Jager's mind.

'Ben, you need to be careful. Be sure that when you immerse yourself in the mind of a monster, you don't become one yourself.'

'But that's the only way I'll be able to understand who he is and how he'll act or react. Knowing your enemy and acting on informed decisions was never more significant than during my army days. It's ironic, but I learnt all that from Steyn back then, before going up north to the Caprivi during the war. Whether you're the hunter or the quarry, the more you understood your adversary the greater the chance of survival. That knowledge saved my life so many times. Whatever else I think of Steyn and his evil, he was an exemplary soldier and I was his star pupil.'

'So you're his protégé?'

As Dahlia's words hit home, a vision forms in his mind's eye of himself before a mirror. Looking into its depths he sees a face other than his own. It's Steyn's, but scarred, one eye covered in a patch, just as it has been described to him. He reaches into the glass and tears at the patch, and the scarred face comes away, revealing another face. His own.

Ben started awake. His heart hammered and he was totally dis-oriented, afraid that he had fallen asleep at the wheel. But he was not in the driver's seat. Rocco sat there, looking at him with mild surprise. 'Bad dream?'

'Yes.' Ben sat upright and rubbed his eyes. 'I thought I was still driving.'

'It's hard to be out of the driver's seat sometimes,' Rocco said pointedly.

'For some more than others.' Ben smiled.

'What was the dream about?'

'Oh, nothing. Forget about that. We need to focus on Steyn and on stopping him, permanently.'

'If we kill him in an attack, it's murder. Technically, we aren't defending ourselves, we're taking the law into our own hands. If we don't get away clean, there will be consequences.'

'There's no real justice in the world then, is there?' Ben said. 'If there were, I'd get a medal for exterminating a cockroach like Steyn who has lost all humanity.'

'Maybe.' Rocco shrugged. 'But there aren't too many men who, even when it seems their humanity has died, don't still have some ghost of a conscience left. And in the breast of every saint, I'll bet, there's still a seed of evil.'

'That's very philosophical,' Ben said without interest. His whole being was stirred by the excitement of danger. The compulsion to take decisive action and his unwavering focus on the task at hand was marshalling all his emotions into one direction. Doubt could no longer be allowed to sabotage his desire to get the job done properly. The one thing that Dahlia had said that stuck in his mind was, 'Save our boy, however you have to.' That was what he was going to do.

CHAPTER
41

A Sharp Bayonet

1961

They were rejoicing together yet again and Petrie had never felt closer to his brother. Even through the mist of the few beers that Joost had allowed him, he was able to appreciate the importance of the role that Joost played in his life. He made sure he did his school-work, ate proper meals and attended all of his matches. Petrie was thinking that his team's win that day was really due to his brother. Joost had supported his focus on rugby and now he had become the star of the team.

At fifteen years old and weighing almost 80 kilos, all of it solid muscle, he had run rampant through the opposing side. The only thing he didn't like was that some of the parents said that he was like his father Gerrit who also 'cut a swathe through the competition'. He recognised the sacrifices his brother had made for him. Joost too could have been a star player, but he never had time to train for the older team. He had to be around when Petrie trained, constantly reminding him, 'you have to cool it' and 'don't get overexcited' to help him keep his anger under control. His sacrifice had worked, and Petrie hadn't been sent off the field once that season. He hadn't killed any animals either. Petrus was doing well. With Joost by his side there was a light at the end of the tunnel.

The mood between them could not have been better. They felt like winners walking home in celebration, Joost's arm slung around Petrie's shoulders.

*   *   *

Gerrit had not had such a good day. The slut in the office had deducted a day's pay from his wage packet because he had not produced a doctor's certificate. She said she knew he didn't have the flu, and he was absent because of a hangover from the previous night's excesses. But he knew it was because he refused to fuck her any longer. He could not stand the sight of the fat bitch with her floppy tits. He wanted girls whose youthful allure still stirred him. Gerrit pulled out of the car park, spinning his wheels and leaving burnt rubber across the tarmac to let them all know what he thought of that particular piece of pussy.

He hadn't calmed down much when he careered into the home stretch looking forward to his fridge full of cold beer.

'Oh, my God!' he swore, when he saw his sons walking along the sidewalk towards home. 'Fucking arm in arm. Fucking faggots! What the fuck did I do to deserve these two pussies!' he screamed against the roar of his V8. 'I'll teach them a lesson.'

Gerrit put his foot down, steered the car towards them and leant across the left seat to wind down the window in order to scream his abuse as he drove past. In his stupor he grabbed the door latch instead. He was going faster than he realised and at the last minute had to swerve to ensure that he missed the fuckers. That's when the unlocked car door escaped his fingers, swung wide open and crashed into Joost.

*   *   *

Petrie heard the gunning of a car and turned to see what idiot was racing up their street just as the car door smashed into his brother.

He had a momentary image of Joost, eyes wide with surprise, as the back of his head smashed through the glass and disappeared off his shoulders, the rim of the window decapitating him.

Petrie stood witness as his vile father, who had robbed him of his mother and the ordinary love that a child could expect from his family, now tore away the only real friend he had known in his entire life. What decency was left in him died in the same moment as his beloved brother. The air was rent by an anguished howl that emanated from his soul to echo forever in his memory.

*   *   *

Later, Gerrit, in a drunken stupor, swaggered into Petrie's room to find him packing his meagre belongings.

'It's a pity,' he leered. 'He was the better of you two. It should have been you, instead of him,' he said.

That was the cue for Petrie to snatch up the bayonet he'd honed specially for the occasion. With a roar of rage, he swung the razor-sharp blade into his father's jugular, nearly slicing off his head as surely as his brother had lost his own. He left the house with his father's blood on the soles of his boots, intent on joining the army and finding a war in which he could unleash his boundless anger.

Baptised in the spilt blood of his family, he would be reborn as Petrus Steyn, a man with no history.

CHAPTER
42

Sins of the Fathers

2009

Besides his ma there was no one De Jager cared about other than his dog. Walking forlornly towards the house, his head in his hands and the brandy glass now empty, the loss of Hitler felt redolent of that long-gone regret over his brother's demise. A bottomless pit sucked at his chest and stomach. How could she have let Novak out of the cellar? How could she let the spawn of his enemy kill his dog?

'Ma!' De Jager called, thinking that she must have gone upstairs to her room. He was baffled by her interference, unable to decide what he should do about it. In the years since he had brought her home from the asylum she had been a quiet shadow, moving gently around the house. On occasion she would talk to him as though he was still a boy and, provided no one else was around, he found himself able to recapture fragments of those times when he knew happiness and joy; when he was surrounded by the love and care of his beautiful mother and his best friend, his brother, Joost.

Yet in those days when the shadow of his father loomed over the family, any moment of peace was likely to be fragile and fleeting. Sooner or later, Gerrit would arrive and the safety and security would vanish. Petrus felt his mother's pain; saw it etched in anguish on her face as Gerrit struck him. His powerlessness against his father was hers too, and she bore the burden of being unable to protect her children. It drove her insane. She held him close, rocking him, crooning in her sweet melodious voice, trying to undo the hurt. In the years of her absence he had not forgotten and yearned for the feelings he thought lost to him forever. A faint echo of them was restored to him with her return. He had been her saviour, the veil of madness lifted, and she became his 'Ma' again.

Climbing the stairs, he considered confining her to her room for a week. Let her know the disfavour she had fallen into by interfering in his business, even though punishing her would make him feel equally bad. He was so accustomed to her silent creeping from one room to the next, her quiet eavesdropping, her gentle presence. No, he would have to be firm so that she knew that this was not acceptable.

The old lady was seated in her rocking chair, eyes closed. She loved the chair he had bought for her, was always soothed by its motion. 'Ma,' he said softly, to wake her from her sleep. He looked around and saw the overturned bottle lying empty and the note. As though he had been ripped apart, disembowelled, his grief erupted from him. The little boy inside him, Petrie, wailed, as Petrus the man slumped to his knees and laid his head in her lap. For an eternal moment he rested before his trembling hand reached for her farewell message.

I am sorry.
I could not take it any longer.
I was not able to protect you from your father, nor from yourself.
Please forgive me.

'Oh, nooo!' he cried. 'My Maaaaaaa!'

Unable to rise from his knees, he enfolded her in his arms and moaned. Head buried in her lap, he rocked her, crooning as she used to croon to him, mourning both their tragic lives.

Novak and his family are responsible. They had always been. The generations of Novaks had been the cause of all his misery and loss. Just the thought of their name spurred him to revenge. He wished to have Ben Novak bowed before him, to make him pay for the sins of his father. *And his son, Josh. He shall pay for the sins of his father and grandfather. They will all suffer as I have.*

Everything would come to an end at Green Thorn. There would be no escape from there.

CHAPTER
43

White Son

In his room at Green Thorn, old Joshua was awake again. Growing old was no fun. The life of black South Africans was not easy, least of all for the aged. All the friends from his own generation had passed away, along with his wife. One daughter had made good and married a Swiss aid worker. Who would have thought? The other had died young, mixed up in some dubious affair to do with drugs and, perhaps, other things he would rather not know about. Now there was just Benjamin and himself. And his prostate, which was what had awoken him for the fourth time that night. Another of the gifts of old age. Awoken him to loneliness and aching sadness.

There was no mistaking the fact that, in many ways, he had it easy compared to so many of his compatriots. Fortune seemed to favour him at times. Benjamin's boss, De Jager, making him the offer of sanctuary at that time had seemed another good stroke. Perhaps Joshua would have been more suspicious of the boon if such serendipity had not already embraced him so often in the past. He did not like De Jager, nonetheless, and could see that he was no good. Not that the Afrikaner ever pretended to have any affection or much respect for the old man, but he seemed contemptuous of people in general, so Joshua sensed no prejudice there. What De Jager did intimate was that he valued his son's intelligence and abilities and that the resultant goodwill had been extended to his father.

Old Joshua was well aware that not all of De Jager's activities were on the up-and-up, but then there was so much corruption in South Africa and the rest of the world, for that matter, that it was easy to dismiss it as inconsequential. His own eyes had witnessed enough and Benjamin delighted in filling him in on all the cruelty and injustice in the world that he learnt of in his studies. It was true, Joshua thought, that he was an ignorant man, a simple man, and he could not resist the unwelcome education his son foisted upon him. Still, for all of the little understood lectures on Machiavelli and Hobbes and all those others whose names he could not remember, and all the rants about white men and capitalism, Joshua could not help but think that people were still basically good, at least underneath, if given a chance. Many were foolish or weak-willed, but few were wilfully and unremittingly evil.

As much as he disliked De Jager, old Joshua did not think of him as such. For the white baas kept Green Thorn sacrosanct. Plenty of debauchery that was sordid enough was conducted there at parties, but the sort of business that took place in the cellar in the city house was not part of the life at Green Thorn, and he remained in blissful ignorance of it.

The old man leant against the wall and waited tiredly to see what his penis would do. It got him out of bed and then hung inactive over the porcelain, refusing to perform the single duty left to it. Then, when it started and stopped, and started and stopped, it was as if it played a joke with him. Waiting for him to think he was finished only to send a dribble down the inside of his pyjamas as he returned to bed. Tonight he was lucky, he thought, as he made his way back to the bedroom. The highlight of his day, a successful toilet run! He heard the car pull into the compound and saw the lights paint moving shapes of brilliance upon his walls as they shone through his windows and the car swung around to stop near the central building.

Curious, he walked to the window and looked out into the dark compound. It took the occupants some time to emerge. He strained to see the shape of the man leaning over to the back seat. The big man though, Johan, and his Benjamin were clearly visible as they got out of the vehicle. Johan carried a gun and trained it carelessly on the third person. An urge to go out to take a closer look went through him. He walked to the door of his room, opened it and called out from the doorway, 'Hey, hey! Benjamin, what's going on?'

The men wheeled about at the sound of his voice. Johan hissed something and Benjamin called back, 'It's nothing, Dad. We caught a poacher. Go back to bed.'

Nonetheless, an irresistible impulse to find out more had taken hold of the old man, so he clutched his stomach and shuffled further towards them despite their instructions.

'I'm not well, that's why I was up, and now here you are! It's like the answer to a prayer. Maybe I need to go to the hospital.'

The white boy opened his mouth to speak, but Johan shoved the gun into his side and hissed something to Benjamin again before dragging his prisoner to the door and inside the building. Old Joshua had come far enough to see the boy's face clearly in the light of the porch in the seconds before the brutish Afrikaner dragged him away.

Benjamin ran forward and grabbed his father by the shoulders. 'Dad, what's wrong, what's wrong?'

To old Joshua everything was wrong. The brief flash of fear on the prisoner's face and the atmosphere of threat surrounding the situation tore at him. How could his son be party to such a business? On top of that, the vague familiarity of the 'poacher' made the occasion as bizarre as it was distasteful. This storm of emotions locked the old man in silence for a minute and Benjamin's concern grew deeper.

'What's wrong?' he demanded again.

'How do I know?' The old man grimaced as he answered at last. 'Am I a doctor now? You're the one with the education. Just help me back to my room. I may need medical attention.'

Full of care, Benjamin helped his father back to his room. Anger and love played havoc with his heart. So often, he erupted with impatience and frustration, but the notion that something might befall old Joshua petrified his son. It was as if his father represented that bit of him that was still good and believed in people, and if he perished, that last vestige of decency might die with him. Joshua had become fragile in his old age and Benjamin half carried him to his room. Once they were safely inside, however, the old man dropped his pose.

'Who's that boy?' he demanded. 'He looks familiar.'

'He's a poacher!' Benjamin said. 'What makes you think he looks familiar? Are you getting demented now?'

'Benjamin, Benjamin.' The old man shook his head. He didn't have an education and he was unsophisticated, but he was no one's fool. 'I've known for a long time that you lead a life full of lies, but I never knew how much you had lost your way. Maybe I really didn't want to know. Tell me who that boy is.

'Tell me!' he roared.

'All right!' Benjamin said. 'It's Josh Novak, Ben Novak's son.'

'Josh Novak?' Joshua's heart sank.

Benjamin grimaced. 'Ah yes, he says he was named after you. What an honour, eh?' His tone was heavy with sarcasm.

As if in a sudden inspiration, the unpleasant patronage of De Jager took on a sinister new meaning for the old man. For some reason the Afrikaner wanted Ben, his old boss, and now he had his son, Josh.

Benjamin's phone rang. The pair froze. He looked at the screen. Johan. 'Shit!'

He answered.

'What's happening?' Johan was straight to the point.

'My father's sick.' Benjamin gestured to old Joshua who began to groan.

'What's wrong with him?' Johan demanded suspiciously.

'What, am I a doctor now?' Benjamin said, echoing his father's words. 'He's old. People dragging prisoners around with shotguns pointed at them in the middle of the night is liable to be upsetting. But I explained about "the poacher". I'm looking for some painkillers and then I'm going to call the hospital for some advice.'

'Don't be long,' Johan said. 'I need you here.'

'Give me a few minutes.'

Benjamin hit 'end' then rounded on the old man in frustration and hissed, 'Why did you have to come out? You've put yourself and me in danger! If they suspect you know who Novak is, we're as good as dead.'

The old man shook his head. 'What kind of men are you caught up with?'

Benjamin hung his head. 'The worst kind. Look, I want to help him if I can, but I can't get away from Johan. They don't trust me, and we have to be careful. Please, just sit tight and I'll try to get back to you soon.'

'You make sure you do,' Joshua said fiercely. 'Ben Novak and his family are fine, good people. They don't deserve this, and not from you of all people.'

'Don't start that,' Benjamin hissed, 'or I might just change my mind!'

Johan was waiting, there was no time for further explanation. Full of conflicting emotions, Benjamin stormed over to the house. Throwing Johan off the trail by spewing out all that hateful talk on the drive had been easy for him. For long enough he had believed it fully, but he had come to realise that life was not so black and white. Associating with despicable characters like De Jager had helped to justify his contempt for the whites, but he had also seen too much corruption, greed and stupidity amongst his own people to believe that any race had a monopoly on evil.

In the abstract it was all very well to hate a race and to persist in hating them when surrounded by examples like De Jager. But there was something palpably good about the boy he had shared the ride to Green Thorn with. Josh was an innocent man just like he himself had been until harsher realities turned his mind to disillusionment and bitterness. Yet maybe he was not so irredeemably lost. There must be some way to pull away from all of this. The haunting disappointment reflected in his father's eyes had increased over the years as he had sunk further into De Jager's alien world. Even though his father had moved to Green Thorn, they saw each other less and less and seemed to have little to say to one another when they did. Maybe his father had tired of hoping that he would find a way to free himself from De Jager's shackles.

Benjamin's heart was heavy. Sadness engulfed him when he remembered how proud his father had once been of him; how he too had believed that, with his education, his son would one day do something for their people. Still, while South Africa suffered with its decaying infrastructure and the anarchic floodtide of crime that rendered its people so hopeless, he had squandered his opportunities and let his father down. The burden of guilt had become wearisome. Maybe any attempt to turn the tide would have been just as futile as he had come to believe, but he would have at least been able to say he had tried. Perhaps the time had come for him to make his old father proud once more.

*　　*　　*

Old Joshua thought of the tall, handsome young man who bore his name. In that moment when his face had been illuminated under the porch light, the likeness to Ben was inescapable. Ah, his beloved Ben. So many years had gone by. It was so sad that in all this time he did not even know that Ben had honoured him with the naming of his son.

Whatever providence had steered him to the Novaks, he would forever feel grateful for having been a part of their lives. There were those who believed that the soul came into a new life from time to time, maybe he and Ben had been family in a former life. Such was the bond between them during that period it was easy to imagine that was so. As it was, he had always thought of him as his white son.

Over the years, he had heard that Ben had come to look for him. When his card reached him, the temptation to see the boykie had been almost overwhelming. Instead, he'd merely secreted it away, though he had retrieved it and looked at the words 'Chief Executive' so many times that it was almost worn away. Yet what could be achieved by phoning him? To see him again would have been too painful; an occasion best avoided. He, too, had to move on. Life was hard for black people in the new South Africa, with no possibilities of sojourning to faraway lands. Places like Australia and America were as unimaginably distant and unreachable as Shangri La.

No, it had been better for him to pack away the memories of his white son, to say his prayers for him in silence and in peace, and hear no more of his deeds. Benjamin, his real son, should be the focus of his pride now, though he would always be grateful that Ben had made it possible for him to be educated, ensuring him a better chance in the harsh country in which they remained.

This poignant sense of nostalgia, so wonderful and terrible at the same time, was surely something only older people felt; the sadness and the joy he experienced at seeing a glimpse of Ben's son, his *Josh*. The knowledge that, just as he had kept Ben in his heart, Ben too had held him in his, moved Joshua to tears.

It was equally heartening to know that his Benjamin was at the point of helping the young man on his own initiative, although it would not be easy for him to get out of Johan's sight if the Afrikaner was suspicious. Were he a young man, he might have seen about getting his hands on a gun and storming the house, but even in his prime he was no warrior. Joshua was a gentle soul who had always been alarmed by the idea of violent action, another thing that had once drawn the derision of his son. But maybe there was something he could do. As much as he wished he could rely on Benjamin to help the boy escape, he was too used to his son's hostile attitudes to hope that his new-found desire to do right would persevere. What if it should require him to risk not only his own life but also his father's? For Joshua knew that, whatever else had passed between them over the years, the bond of blood remained strong and his son would do anything he could to keep his father alive. Including the wrong thing.

And what of himself? He was ready to help Ben Novak's boy regardless of his own safety, but what if he endangered his own son in the process? What really *was* the noblest course?

CHAPTER
44

Battle Plans

It was 2 a.m. when Ben and Rocco arrived at the entry gate to the magnificent Timbavati. The sky was clear and full of a billion stars which assisted the moon in lighting the night. The peaceful glow belied the savagery of the land. In the magic of that restful hour it seemed unreal that an ocean of blood had been spilt here over the millennia as predators and prey played out the eternal game of survival.

South Africa's game reserves are the legacy of Paul Kruger, the president of South Africa who had the vision to persuade parliament to secure the preservation of the Kruger National Park for future generations in 1898. That initiative had allowed ordinary people to escape from the demands of their daily lives and step back half a million years to a time when Stone Age hunters roamed the plains with the beasts. To Ben, it was inevitable that the evolution of man would be at the ultimate expense of Africa's phenomenal natural wildlife. The people of South Africa had a duty to ensure that this ancestral gift should be cherished and guarded for all time. The Kruger Park was a national asset, but the Timbavati was private property, and the sense of responsibility for preserving the balance of nature was not shared equally by its various owners.

For many it was their inheritance, land passed down through their families. For some it represented an indulgence of their wealth, and for a smaller number it was merely a means of satisfying their primal urge to hunt and kill. This discord between ideologies had fuelled much anger between neighbours and some were motivated to indulge in much manoeuvring to rid themselves of those they were at odds with. Conservation had its price and many could not afford it. These were the owners who found the weight of increasing levies driving them from their homes. Often the lucrative financial return on an animal trophy was seen as the only way to offset the cost of their preservation and too great a temptation to resist. In reality, since the border fences of the Kruger Park had been torn down, the hunting of game on private reserves was tantamount to plundering protected national assets and contrary to the interests of the nation and the charter of the Timbavati.

Harry had heard the car arrive and came out to meet them. As he and Ben embraced in a great hug, years of friendship and love coursed between them.

'I'm so sorry, Ben, that you're in this predicament,' said Harry. 'As soon as Rick told me what had happened, I knew I had to get here.'

'Thank you for coming, my friend. You cannot understand how much this means to me,' Ben said.

'Mate,' said Harry, 'after all we've been through, how could I not? And more importantly, I want to play a hand in seeing Steyn get his just deserts. It's hard to believe he's still around with all his evil. God, it will be a huge bonus to put an end to him once and for all.'

Ben had always been able to rely on Harry to watch his back. He'd proven himself an exceptional soldier in the Caprivi. Having him there felt as much a part of being ready for war as having a good assault rifle in his hands. Rocco had been silent all this time, hanging back, unwilling to intrude on their reunion. Hastily

Ben made the appropriate introductions and the new acquaintances shook hands warmly.

'Come inside,' Harry said, 'there's coffee waiting.'

They seated themselves around the huge mahogany dining table upon which were opened maps of the area and the plan Robert had drawn. The assistant game ranger was pouring the coffee.

'Hello, Mr Ben,' he said in greeting.

'Hi, Jeremiah,' Ben replied. 'Where's Robert?'

'He is sleeping. He told me he wished to rest before the rescue.'

'He's smart,' Ben said, 'but he better get up now while we finalise our plans. His input will be essential. I'm a bit surprised he's not already out here. He was always such a light sleeper.'

'Yep,' Harry said. 'It's strange he didn't come out to join me earlier when Jeremiah let me in. The guy must have ice in his veins to sleep in a situation like this.'

'Another cool head would be welcome,' Rocco said.

'Jeremiah, could you please get Robert?' Harry asked with a smile.

'Maybe the poor guy is exhausted,' Ben said. 'We're all getting older. You can't help but slow down a bit.'

'Speak for yourself,' Harry chortled. 'Remember, you're only as old as the woman you feel.' Harry had married a Brazilian woman fifteen years younger than himself. 'As far as that goes, I'm fucking fit,' he smirked, and indeed, he looked in great shape. Ben smiled, despite the twinge of pain Harry's jest evoked as he was reminded of the loss of his own lover, his best friend and so much more …

Realising what he had just said, Harry felt a moment of awkwardness, but the return of Jeremiah with an envelope in his hand saved him from pondering what to do about it.

'He's not there,' said the mystified ranger, 'only this envelope was on the bed.'

'Shit!' said Ben, guessing that, whatever the contents might be, this was not a good development.

Rocco took the envelope and opened it. He removed the paper inside and read the contents aloud.

Dear Ben

Don't worry, please. This is for the best. I have thought about what you are trying to achieve and I am concerned with your plan as there are too many unknowns.

I am assuming that you will stick with the plan to strike pre dawn at 4am, and it is clear to me that the chances of success will be much better if there is a man on the inside. I've volunteered myself for that role. I didn't want to wait and argue about it. I have no patience for that. Tonight you are not the boss but if we all get through this okay, I expect a big raise.

Ben, you have a good team with you but my bush craft and hunting skills exceed yours and those of anyone else, so it makes sense for me to infiltrate their camp alone. Whatever happens I will be in place to give you an edge no one will be expecting.

Don't worry about me, focus on getting Josh and yourself out. I won't do anything stupid.

Robert

'Shit,' Ben repeated. 'Nothing stupid!'

'It's damn stupid going off like that without any debate about how this fits in with our overall strategy,' said Harry, clearly annoyed.

'I don't know what to say,' Ben admitted. 'It is kind of crazy, but it also kind of makes sense. It pisses me off that he didn't let us talk it through and get our agreement but—'

'He should definitely have discussed this with us in detail,' Rocco interjected angrily. 'We're putting our lives at stake, and we have no idea what role a crucial member of our team will be fulfilling. It's madness. What was he thinking?'

'I guess we must all be a little mad to get involved in this,' Harry said, shaking his head. 'But I think Robert is spot-on. Him being inside their camp when we arrive will definitely give us a significant advantage.'

The development was a shock, but Ben felt encouraged by Robert's show of bravery and initiative. There was no doubt that having an inside man in their opponents' camp when the shooting started would disrupt whatever defences they had. Having an experienced operator like Rocco and an old soldier like Harry along as well further boosted Ben's confidence. There wasn't any time left to dwell further on Robert's actions.

'I think it's okay,' Ben said. 'It really doesn't change our plan. If anyone can sneak in undetected and give us that sort of support, it's Robert. He's right. He would have been slowed down by us, and I would have been loath to let him go alone. So he's probably saved us a lot of time and arguments this way.'

'Okay, well, let's make proper use of that time by getting on with our plans,' Rocco said gruffly.

They got back to work examining the information on the table. Robert had done an excellent job briefing them over the phone and the map, although crudely drawn, was crystal clear. But now that it came to finalising the rescue effort, Ben was suddenly immobilised with dread at the thought of Josh being hurt or killed. The prospect plagued him and clouded his judgement. In one flicker, he had gone from being focused and confident to being riddled with uncertainty and doubt.

For the mission to succeed, the plan had to be simple with everyone's role precisely defined. Rocco was a strong leader, clear-sighted and dispassionate, and it made sense that he should assume a position of command. Experience had also taught Ben that there were times when being a good leader required performing as a good follower. This was one of them.

Harry and Robert had no hesitation in putting themselves in danger. It was a testament to the depth of the friendship that had endured between them for so many years.

'I can't say how grateful I am for the support of all of you …' Ben halted, fighting with his emotions. 'It's impossible to convey how much it means to me.'

'You'd do exactly the same if it were one of my kids in this situation,' said Harry. 'We both know that. I've never forgotten the soldier you were, all those years ago. How you watched out for all of us.'

'Ach.' Ben waved a hand dismissively. 'You saved my arse more than once.'

Rocco cleared his throat. 'Gentlemen, let's get down to business.'

They had barely begun to discuss their strategy when Ben's phone rang. He pulled it from his pocket. The number was unknown. 'Hello?' he said worriedly. 'Ben Novak.'

CHAPTER
45

Ensnared

Moments after talking to Ben about their strategy, Robert Morgan was rinsing the foul taste of vomit from his mouth. The time to put his plan into action was imminent. Marie, his wife, thought that she knew her husband pretty well, and could not imagine what could disturb his composure to that degree. He had always seemed the embodiment of courage in the past. If he was sick with fear, it must be far more dangerous than he had admitted to her.

'Robert,' she urged, rubbing his back, 'I know you owe these guys a lot but do you have to risk your life for them? Do you really think you have to go that far?'

She glanced at the fine furniture, the beautiful artwork that hung on the walls. Their lives were filled with abundance and warmth. Despite her words, Marie could not help thinking about how much had changed over the past seven years since Robert had received that fateful phone call from Harry.

'Morgan,' Harry had said. 'You old son of a gun! Do you know how hard it's been for me to find you? I'm coming with Ben and

Rick. We're going to buy that game farm we always dreamt about, remember? And you're going to help us set it up and run it!'

The call was a blast from the past, and Robert had been delighted by it for the most part. But he was also somewhat resentful about the fact that, after twenty-five years, they could just show up, these 'mates' of his, and assume he would drop everything and go along with them. That was the thing about them, though; they knew they were going to be successful, even back then.

They had so much energy. Smart and tough, Robert's rich friends were simply used to getting what they wanted. When they first met, the unsophisticated youth from the Timbavati had been in awe of them. The cars, the pretty girls and the contacts with all the wealthy families in Johannesburg entranced him. Robert had never met a Jew or a Greek before and then, suddenly, he knew them all. They were fascinated with his knowledge of the bush and its animals. He felt unique and valued and became one of them, sharing the good times of the seventies, the parties in the bush. There was also the chance to screw a few Jewish chicks who thought there was something exciting about a 'game ranger'. Who was he to argue?

When they entered his life it changed completely. All those weekends he had spent teaching them everything he knew, maybe showing off a little. He had been a part of all their adventures. And his exploits on the Olifants River expedition had made him a hero in their eyes. Then, next thing, they decided that South Africa wasn't the place to bring up their children and they were gone – to Canada, Australia, America, wherever. Their families had stashed the money away over the years, always anticipating that one day the blacks would take over the country and the Jews would be the first to get it, like they did in Germany. They had their nest eggs to ensure that this generation of Jews living in South Africa would not fall foul of the fate of so many of their ancestors elsewhere.

The truth was, when Harry phoned, whatever his reservations, it couldn't have come at a better time for Robert. In fact, he was both relieved and grateful. His heart had skipped a beat. Finally, he was able to see a light at the end of that long dark tunnel he had been lost in for so many years. His work was abysmal, money was always in short supply and little Davey never had any luxuries, though Marie worked unceasingly. Robert had been crazy about Marie from the day they first met, but things had reached the point where he worried that she no longer found him attractive. All the beer had swelled his gut and his neck had disappeared into a large jowl that seemed to connect his head to his chest. The drinking was no longer only for relaxation, it was the only way he could get through the day. His life was one long struggle, and then Harry phoned and everything changed.

Now his family lived in five-star luxury at the lodge and he worked back in the bush. His body grew strong and lean once more, his brown hair bleached a little blond by the sun. Davey was at a private school and Marie could shop at the best boutiques in Nelspruit. She believed that they owed all their abundance to Harry, Ben and Rick.

'How could I not be part of the rescue?' he said. 'Think about where we were before they came back and look at what we have now.'

Yet Marie didn't know everything, nor would she ever, if he could help it. He could never tell her that he had become greedy. His new role at the farm had set them up nicely. But then he had met that devil, De Jager. The Afrikaner was a keen hunter, that was all he knew. Keen enough to offer an obscene amount for a little bit of 'discretion' on Robert's part. It might have ended there if he hadn't mentioned Ben Novak in conversation. The surprised look in De Jager's one good eye did not escape him, but the man recovered well and he soon forgot it. Only later did Robert remember and realise what it had meant.

Not long after, De Jager bought Green Thorn and began to court him under the guise of a courteous neighbour with a similar interest. Robert knew of his illegal hunting activities, but there was so much of that going on and he had never been a crusader himself. If he'd known how evil De Jager was he would have pulled back, but his new neighbour was cunning. He continued to play his part and kept the incentives coming. Soon there were also invitations to his powerful new acquaintance's secret parties. While Marie thought he was away at conferences he was drinking the best liquor money could buy, for De Jager was always quick to find a man's weakness. And when he was full of booze that snake had made sure he was set up with a woman who no man could resist, especially one as juiced as Robert at that hour. In the ensuing orgy he became so bewildered he thought he was having the best time of his life. He even posed for those disgusting pictures.

Robert didn't remember any of it the next morning. But De Jager had the photographs to remind him. There were no threats. De Jager acted as if the pictures were a mere amusement, but it was clear he intended to keep them and would maintain a hold on Robert so long as he lived. The trap was sprung and there was no way out.

Even then, the Afrikaner continued to play him. The money kept coming, there was no open hostility, and it was easy to believe they were co-conspirators rather than lord and lackey, mastermind and dupe. Many of the extras Marie was grateful for were from the 'bonuses' that had come from De Jager. All Robert had to do was turn a blind eye and act a bit stupid, as though he did not know the full extent of the 'trophy hunting', and then pick up the envelope buried at the bottom of the border post between their lands. Thousands of extra rands became available for the holidays in Europe, the beautiful clothes and anything else that could buy happiness.

All De Jager demanded was his cooperation in the hunting racket and any information about Ben Novak that came along. Through Robert he had learned about the link to old Joshua who Ben had spoken of so often. Robert had been there to see the arrival of Benjamin, even been at some of the same parties where Benjamin was seduced, just as he had been. Where it was all heading, he did not know, nor could he afford to want to know. But now the truth had come up and hit him square in the gut.

It was not his nerves at the looming confrontation that made him throw up, as Marie thought. Fuck, what would she have felt if she had known of his dealings with De Jager; not just the money he received for his myopia but the women. *Those pictures.* He knew Marie. She would never forgive him.

Now that devil had abducted his mate's son. Ben had been there when they most needed him, and now this disaster had arisen due to his indiscretion in mentioning Ben's name in the first place. Boasting about who his friends were and acting as if they were his partners rather than his employers had become a habit with him. Now, years later, he had become so used to reporting to De Jager about Ben and being rewarded for it, that he had given him all the details about Josh's imminent arrival without a second thought.

Robert was so ensnared by this villain that he had just put down the phone to him after letting him know there was going to be a surprise rescue assault on Green Thorn at 4 a.m.

The deed made him sick to his stomach. Still, he would make things right. He would help rescue Josh Novak and see himself free from De Jager in the process. The Afrikaner had played him for so long, but now he would outplay him. He had a trap of his own to spring. Yet Ben must not know about his motivation. No one could have any idea about it.

Informing the man with the eye patch that Ben was coming to rescue Josh from Green Thorn had been imperative. He wanted to ensure that De Jager would come personally to claim his prize. While it was true that Robert would be best placed to help Ben by going behind the enemy lines, it was also his best opportunity to kill De Jager and bury his dark secret with him.

The ranger struggled to hold onto his conviction that his current actions were all for the greater good. Although warning De Jager had increased the peril of the mission, his image would stay intact. That was vital for his family, and they were his first priority. He would do his best to help Ben rescue Josh, but if things went wrong, his attempt to redeem himself would turn into one final act of betrayal.

46

Old Friends

'Hello? Ben Novak speaking.'

The voice was so familiar and yet so changed, no longer the voice of a young man, and he had lost a little of the old accent. Old Joshua found it hard to speak, his chest was so full of emotions. Nostalgia, love for Ben, love for the son named after him, fear of what he was doing, fear that one of them might not survive this, fear that his son could not be relied upon, fear that he was not doing the right thing. What if Johan came in suddenly? Should he hang up …?

'Hello?' The voice was firmer now, impatient. Perhaps Ben suspected it was his enemy toying with him.

'Hello, boykie, it's Joshua … Joshua Mokwana …' The old man's voice faltered.

'Joshua! My old friend!' Ben's voice was full of incredulity and joy for a moment before fear and anxiety resumed their grip on him. 'Joshua, I can't believe it. How can this be you? At this time! What's going on?'

'That's what I'm calling about.'

'What do you mean? What do you know?' Ben fell silent as his mind struggled with a thousand questions that all begged to be answered at once.

'Ben, these last few years I have been employed by a man named De Jager.'

'What?' The question was a strangled cry. 'How?'

'Through my son, Benjamin. But none of this can be coincidence. Somehow, De Jager knew about our connection and saw a chance to exploit it. What does he have against you, Ben?'

'Ahh, Joshua! It's a long and complicated story,' Ben said. 'But what about my son, Josh?'

'He's here at Green Thorn.'

'You're at Green Thorn?'

'Yes, this is where I work now.'

'Oh my God. So you've seen my boy?'

'I was awake when they brought him in and I caught a glimpse of him. They said he was a poacher and took him into the house. Benjamin told me he is your *boykie*. He wants to help but they are watching him. It won't be easy.' He sounded old and tired.

'How did you get my number?' Ben asked

A momentary doubt erupted in Ben's mind. If Joshua's son worked for De Jager and was in danger, what would he do to save his own son?

'For so many years I have had the card with your number, Ben. For so many years I have wanted to call but always I think to myself, it is too long ago. The young baas has a new life now and his own children and family and he will not want to hear from an old man. And it is easier for me to believe that you would always think about me like I have thought about you. It would be too sore for me if I phoned you and you did not want to know me. And now I realise I was a foolish old man and that your own son is named Joshua and I am ashamed for everything.'

The pain in Joshua's voice crackled in Ben's ear. The tinge of doubt left him to be quickly replaced with fear and concern for how they might all get away from their insane enemy alive.

'Joshua, I could never forget you or Benjamin, but you are both in great danger now. So listen carefully. I'm trusting you with our plan. We're arriving there at 4 a.m. We're going to crash through the fences in a couple of vehicles. You must find out where Josh is being kept and let us know before we get there. Then you and Benjamin must be ready to escape with us.'

'Josh is in the main house, but I don't know if they'll keep him there or how well guarded he is. I'm hoping Benjamin will come back and I'll get some more information. As long as no one is watching me I'll try to keep you updated on everything I find out. If we can find some other way to help you, we will.

'I don't trust De Jager. If he suspects Benjamin or me, we are dead. Who knows, now he has no more use for this old Kaffir, he may be planning to eliminate me anyway.'

'That's true,' Ben said. 'You're wise to suspect that snake. You are best off well clear of him. We'll ensure you get away with us ... And, Joshua, you know if I could ever have helped you I would have, but help me get my son out of this and I'll do anything for you and Benjamin.'

'I know,' said Joshua. 'But you owe us nothing. We are just old friends helping each other, as it should be.'

There was a lump in Ben's throat. 'Stay safe, I look forward to seeing you.'

'Let God make it so.'

CHAPTER
47

Arming Up

'What was that?' Rocco demanded.

'An old friend,' Ben said. 'Well, an old servant actually, I guess, though it's hard to think of him as such.'

'Can you trust him?' Rocco was annoyed. 'You've told him everything. How do you know it isn't a trap?'

'If I can't trust him, I don't know who I can,' Ben said.

'As far as I could follow the discussion, he works at Green Thorn,' Rocco said. 'Are you sure he hasn't gone over to De Jager?'

'No, that's impossible,' Ben said. 'He's all right. He knows we're coming at four. He'll do what he can to help us from the inside. His son, too.'

'Presuming we can count on *him*!' Rocco said. 'At least they don't know about Robert.'

'Yes,' Ben said. 'I didn't mention that. It's best to keep everything on a need-to-know basis.'

'Ja,' Rocco agreed.

Ben sent Robert a text explaining about Joshua and Benjamin to ensure he did not mistake them for De Jager's men. He prayed that he would receive it.

Together they poured over the maps and diagrams and discussed the different approaches to the compound, eventually agreeing upon a strategy spelt out by Rocco involving six people in three vehicles. Three of these men would be resident game rangers who were proficient in all manner of arms, deterring poachers being part of their role.

Harry called a brief conference of his most trusted rangers and outlined the abduction of Josh and the planned rescue mission.

'Guys, this is dangerous, but we have no other alternative if we're going to help Ben rescue his son. We need you to drive the vehicles, which will allow us to do the shooting. You'll be armed and most likely find yourselves caught up in gunfire. Because of the danger, Ben has offered each of you 10,000 rand if you're willing to participate. I'll transfer the funds to those involved tonight, before we leave.'

Without hesitation each of the rangers immediately volunteered. The money was a substantial sum for one night's work but it was not their only motivation. Working for Harry, Rick and Ben at Makanyi had provided them a secure livelihood in excellent conditions. They appreciated their bosses, especially Harry, who went to extraordinary lengths to ensure the satisfaction of his employees.

Harry and Samuel would drive towards the south-facing main gate at Green Thorn, their headlights on. They would make no attempt to conceal their approach and serve as a diversion, keeping the guards at the gate focused on the lights of their vehicle as they approached. They would be in a noisy, unbaffled Ford truck. The clamour of its engine would mask the sound of the other two four-wheel drives coming from separate directions; one from the northeast and the other from the northwest. These vehicles would simultaneously break through the perimeter fences at the predesignated location, at precisely 4 a.m.

'We should assume that Robert is not a part of our plan. If he's able to provide assistance then so be it,' said Rocco. 'But if everything else works, the guards will be talking to Harry and Sam and will be disorientated by the commotion caused by the other vehicles bursting in. In the midst of the discussion and confusion, it's unlikely they'll fire on us unless we shoot first. But you need to be prepared and have your weapons loaded and ready. The guards will not know what's happening. They won't know who's in which vehicle or even how many of us there are, so I'm expecting they'll be hesitant to take any action no matter what else is going on.

'If Joshua and his son don't have Josh free, Ben and I will enter and search the main building where we believe his son is being kept.'

He pointed at the rangers. 'You guys, Jeremiah and Moses, will stay with the vehicles and provide cover for us in the event that any shooting begins.

'Ben will be with Jeremiah in the Land Rover and will enter through the northeast breach.'

The Land Rover was one of Harry's unique projects. With unbridled enthusiasm he had stripped, hot-dip galvanised and reinforced it to withstand a rhinoceros charge. Painted in marine Kevlar epoxy, the vehicle was bright yellow with polished silver manifolds protruding from its supercharged original V8 motor. It was a perfect attack vehicle, able to easily penetrate the perimeter fence and act as a shield for the other vehicles, and it had the necessary speed and power for the escape.

'Moses and I will come in from the northwest.'

Rocco paused and scanned the crew with an intense gaze before proceeding with the summing up. 'There are lots of ways in which things can go wrong and, as always, out in the field we may have to improvise, but at that time of night and given the element of surprise I see no reason why this should not work. Let's just hope old Joshua is able to get them out of the house.'

*   *   *

It was time to sort out their equipment and weapons. Between them they possessed varying degrees of experience with handguns and rifles. South Africans are well acquainted with most small arms and the rangers were accustomed to the .375 calibre rifles that were standard fare for most game hunting, the .458 calibre being reserved for larger beasts.

Harry had constructed a small armoury room. The handguns — .357 Magnums and 9mm Parabellums — were laid out on racks while the rifles were kept vertical, each in its own compartment.

Harry grinned at Ben. 'Here, I have something special for you.' He patted a large square object under a sheet.

'It isn't big enough or I'd be hoping it's Steyn's body in a box,' Ben said grimly.

'Not quite that good.' Harry smiled, pulling the sheet aside. 'But this baby might help put him in one.'

'Oh my God!' Ben exclaimed in amazement.

Harry had revealed a well-sealed ancient crate containing the rocket launcher and grenade that he and Ben had purloined from Steyn back in Walvis Bay in the 1970s.

'I can't believe you still have this!' Ben gawped, astonished at the irony. In a flood, the memory of how they had retrieved it returned to him, fresh as yesterday.

It was in 1976, and Harry had found Ben brooding once again.

'What is it?' Harry asked. 'I may as well hang out with a horse the amount of time I spend looking at a long face.'

'I'm sorry.' Ben grimaced. 'I don't mean to be such a wet blanket, but I can't get Gary out of my mind. It could so easily have been my carcass rotting out there among the shipwrecks that litter that coastline. I can't help but feel that I should have done more for him.'

'Well, you couldn't have, whatever you feel. Five years is enough time to grieve. I think we need to go back and face the scene of the crime.'

'Harry, we've been through this before. I don't want to go back; all I knew there was loss and anger. Gary's soul is the one that must find peace in that place, not mine.'

'You're wrong, Ben. Obviously, you need to come to peace with it, too. And we really should do something about those bombs we left buried out there. If we go out there we can unearth the RPG launcher and the ammo, and you can bury your guilt in the hole. We'll make it a little ceremony.'

'What's that going to do?' Ben shrugged. 'It's a meaningless ritual, it won't bring Gary back.'

'No it won't,' Harry admitted, 'but rituals aren't meaningless or
we wouldn't have them to mark all the big occasions like births and
marriages and deaths. They may not make logical sense but we're
more than just a brain. If logic worked, you'd stop brooding about
Gary because your guilt won't bring him back.'

Harry was like a dog with a bone. Ben wasn't convinced the trip
would do any good, but it was easier to go along than to keep on
arguing with his friend.

As it turned out, Harry had been proved right. Being in the desert, gazing in solitude at the barracks from the outside, was the salve
for Ben's soul that Harry had promised it would be. When they had
unearthed the RPG, they performed their own in absentia burial
for Gary. As Ben gazed down into the hole, he could visualise his
friend's frail form lying in a shroud in the dirt. He let the tears flow
freely as he said farewell for the final time. At last the chains of guilt
that had seemed destined to bind him to Gary's corpse for all time
were severed. Finally, those feelings of impotence and shame were
buried out in the desert. And now, here was their trophy, laden with
all those memories, still crated up.

'I had to hang onto it,' Harry said. 'It's fucking contraband. It's
not like I could give it in. People would want to know where it came
from, and if I had dumped it, chances are someone would have got
killed, so I've stored the fucking thing for the last thirty years or
more. And I have to confess that I've developed a sneaking affection
for it. Who knows, it could be useful tonight. You would be one of
the few people I know who is trained in how to use it.'

'If I can remember how,' Ben mused.

'Maybe it'll be worthwhile taking it along?' said Rocco. 'You just
never know.'

'That would be the ultimate in poetic justice,' said Ben, 'using
Steyn's own weapon against him.'

He opened the crate and saw the deadly implement, nestled in
its bed of straw, immaculately preserved and oiled as though it were
brand new.

'Come, Jeremiah, help me load this on our vehicle, please,' Ben said with some glee, visualising a direct hit on Steyn.

All the guns were checked to be in working order and loaded onto the vehicles with plenty of spare ammunition. In the rangers' staff quarters they dressed in traditional bush clothing: cargo trousers, multi-pocketed waistcoats and boots, before settling down for an agonising wait. They were impatient for the time of departure to come. Ben distracted himself by perusing Harry's collection of unique Bowie knives.

In the hands of an expert, a knife is a formidable weapon. During the months in the Caprivi while his platoon camped and waited for their orders, Ben had relieved his boredom with countless hours of practice throwing a 12-inch bowie knife. Eventually he was able to hit a target within four metres with the accuracy of other guys playing darts. He balanced and weighed the knives in the collection, eventually mounting one on his belt. Satisfied he was fully prepared, Ben lay down to rest, his phone close at hand in case Joshua rang with any additional information.

CHAPTER
48

The Man on the Inside

Robert lay motionless in the grass. In usual circumstances, stalking aroused his senses, causing him to quiver with excitement, alert to the sounds of the wild, enlivened by the hunt, emboldened by the deadly efficiency of his weapon. But not tonight. He lay brooding on whether he was about to meet his fate on the very road he had taken to avoid it.

He thought of the small convoy on its way to Green Thorn. *They will be leaving Makanyi about now.*

The windows were lit up in the big house.

'Johan?' he whispered to himself.

He'd seen the shadow against the curtains. It was the giant. Few men could cast so large a silhouette, and there were fewer still who De Jager would trust with guarding his prize.

Ja! That's where Josh will be.

A light had burned for a short while in a smaller building across from the main house but had now been turned off.

Are there more in there? he thought. Would they be involved in any fighting?

Yet there was no sign of activity and it did not seem possible that a body of troops lay sleeping quietly so soon before a battle. It felt safe to bet that any other forces De Jager might utilise would be en route with him from Johannesburg.

The sight of another shadow moving past Johan led him to wonder at the person's identity. The waiting game was killing him and he was eager to take advantage of the element of surprise. The house was guarded against a frontal attack, no one could suspect that he had infiltrated the main compound undetected.

There was risk in not knowing how many opponents there were. Nonetheless, he considered the feasibility of sneaking in and freeing Josh unaided, and taking out Johan and the others if necessary. But he could not forsake his true objective. So long as Josh was in the house and Ben was coming, there was a good chance De Jager would come too. He was now the target. Only burying that one-eyed monster could rid him of the cancer of guilt and remorse that was eating away at his guts. As much as he yearned to go to Josh's aid, he could not move himself to rearrange his priorities. He would do whatever it took to destroy Ben Novak's enemy for him, but if the only way to do that was to use Josh as bait, then so be it.

CHAPTER
49

Duped

'How's your old man?' Johan asked. 'Does he need to go to hospital?'

'No,' Benjamin said hesitantly, sensing a trap. Johan would never let them leave that easily, even if they had been willing to go without Josh. He pulled a face. 'You know how old people are,' he said disdainfully. 'The older they get the more neurotic they are. His prostate is playing up and it makes him constipated, so he gets a pain in his gut and thinks he has appendicitis.'

'I thought you were calling the hospital?'

Benjamin laughed. 'I had to say that in front of him to pacify him. I pretend.' He held an imaginary phone to his ear. '"What's that, doctor, you're sure it's just constipation like last time? Yes, okay, I'll tell him. Yes, I have laxatives ..." He won't give us any more trouble.'

Johan grunted, not amused by this pantomime. But then again, the giant never showed any sense of humour, unless he was the one making the joke.

'I'm tired.' Benjamin yawned. 'There's no need for both of us to watch this kid. I need some sleep.' He settled himself in a comfortable chair and closed his eyes. Johan just grunted.

Benjamin felt a growing sense of despair. He was well acquainted with the evil in these men and the realisation had dawned on him that the usefulness of his father and himself had come to an end. De Jager wanted to destroy Ben Novak by killing his son, before his eyes. He wanted Novak to suffer as much as possible and, knowing that Novak loved old man Joshua, why wouldn't he also kill him, too, if it would add to his satisfaction? And should Benjamin's own execution allow De Jager to squeeze one extra iota of sadistic pleasure out of the denouement, then he, too, would join the list of the slain. The Afrikaner was a madman, a Caesar who would sacrifice any number of others in the Colosseum for his own enjoyment.

This was not merely paranoia. It was clear as day to him. Benjamin's growing desire to help Josh had initially been motivated by a combination of guilt and compassion, but he would not have endangered himself and his father in order to achieve that. Now self-preservation had become part of the equation and the need to act was urgent. Helping Josh, or at least getting away from De Jager and his henchmen, was essential to their survival.

But what could he do against that brute, Johan? There was no overestimating his cunning and strength. Benjamin was no more a fighter than his father. He had always prided himself on his ability to use his brains to get out of a bind. Attacking Johan would be stupid, but what else could he do?

'Hey, wake up!' Johan said, holding a pistol out to Benjamin. 'I need to go to the toilet. You watch him.' He nodded to the door behind which the boy lay trussed up on a bed.

Benjamin looked at the gun doubtfully.

'You know how you use that, don't you?' Johan said. 'This is the safety.' He flipped the switch. 'That's off. You aim and shoot.' Johan aimed the gun at him and said, '*Pshew!*'

Benjamin had a hard time not flinching.

Johan handed over the pistol. 'Gotta go, I'm busting.'

Turning his back on Benjamin, he went off in the direction of the toilet. Benjamin looked at the gun. It was too good to be true. Had he actually done such a good job in fooling Johan? *No, it is too good to be true,* he thought again. It was a test. And if it were a test then, *there are no bullets in the gun.*

He knew more about firearms than the giant imagined. Enough to be able to eject the magazine and see that it was indeed empty. He double-checked, hoping there might be a round in the chamber that Johan had forgotten. No, he was grasping at straws. He couldn't be that lucky. Hearing the toilet flush, Benjamin quickly slouched low in an easychair as if he were perfectly relaxed, the gun cradled casually in his lap. He offered it back to Johan.

'Keep it,' Johan said, with a sly grin. 'I have another one.' He took a snub-nosed revolver out of his pocket. *What's the bet that one has bullets in it,* Benjamin thought.

'Sorry to disturb your nap,' Johan said. 'You can get back to it now.'

'Forget it,' Benjamin said. 'I'm going to get some coffee.'

Tucking the pistol into his belt at the back, he strolled nonchalantly to the kitchen and turned on the kettle. A block of knives sat on the bench. It seemed to beckon him and his heart raced with adrenalin, even while he trembled with fear in anticipation of the course he contemplated.

'Oh, God, I have no choice,' he whispered.

Benjamin hefted a large knife out of the block and slid it into his belt at the back, next to the pistol under his jacket. With shaking hands, he poured a mug full of steaming hot black coffee. Returning to the room, he stepped up to Johan who was seated on the edge of a chair.

'I wanted to ask you something about this gun,' he said, reaching back to where Johan had seen him tuck the weapon away.

'Oh?' said Johan, holding out his hand, the gesture of a man who believed he was about to explain some technical detail to his ignorant black comrade. But instead of a gun in the hand he received a stream of scalding hot coffee in his face followed almost instantaneously by a knife thrust at his jugular.

Benjamin had not reckoned with the reflexes of a man accustomed to a life of violence. No sooner had he hurled the coffee than Johan erupted from the chair and collided with him like a charging bull. Screaming from the burning liquid, he spun away from Benjamin to avoid the blade. The knife thrust at his throat missed its mark and penetrated deep into his right shoulder. With a roar, the giant lashed out blindly, fumbling for the snub-nosed pistol with his almost useless right arm at the same time. Benjamin barrelled into him again, stabbing at his arm but striking the pistol instead and knocking it from his hand. It skittered across the room and under the couch. Johan went after the gun.

Desperate now, Benjamin rushed to the door and wrenched it open. Josh was already there, drawn by the sounds of combat. With one swift slash Benjamin cut the bonds between the boy's feet. 'Let's go!' he screamed.

As they raced towards the door, he saw Johan use his good arm to overturn the couch, as easily as if it were made of papier-mâché, revealing the pistol. Benjamin wished he knew how to throw a knife. Instead, he tugged the front door open and lunged outside with Josh, the two of them sprinting side by side. Behind them, Benjamin heard Johan cursing and knew only seconds remained before Johan would be using his left hand to train his gun on them.

As anticipated the driveway was instantly flooded with lights and Benjamin was sure that the giant's determination to bring his quarry to ground would override De Jager's preference for their being alive, and he would shoot to kill.

*   *   *

Each minute Robert had waited for the action to start seemed to have added another kilo of guilt to the burden he carried. Yet, like one of those nightmares where every movement is frozen, his inertia was the equal of it. That all changed in the instant he heard a scream from the big house followed by a shout and a tumult of crashing.

While the meaning of all this remained obscure, one thing was clear: Josh Novak was in trouble, and he could not stand idly by while the power to help was his. He sprinted across the compound as the door to the big house burst open and two men ran out.

The white boy had to be Josh. The men saw him and hesitated, but he waved them towards him and they, recognising that he was not the enemy, turned in his direction. The floodlights snapped on and as Johan appeared in the doorway aiming awkwardly at the fleeing pair, Robert snapped up his rifle and fired. The doorframe burst into splinters and the giant ducked back out of sight.

Glancing at his watch, Robert saw that it was 3:56 a.m. Old Joshua had emerged from the servants' quarters. Keeping his gun trained on the main house, Robert backed up to join the fugitives who had reached the old man. 'Can we get to a car?' he demanded.

'There, the white Land Cruiser,' shouted Benjamin, dangling the keys.

CHAPTER
50

Green Thorn

Jeremiah had slowed the Land Rover almost to a standstill as they bumped and wound their way towards a dark outcrop adjacent to a heavily wooded donga. The ridge stood out sharply against the starlit sky. In the benighted bush there were no animals in evidence. The noise of the vehicle drove them away before the intruders got close enough to see their forms in the gloom. Cresting the ridge they looked downhill towards Green Thorn, nestled amongst the clumps of trees from which the estate had derived its name.

The lights were on in the guardhouse and a single sentry emerged, brandishing his weapon and peering towards the glare of the noisy vehicle approaching through the dark with Harry and Samuel on board. Even as Ben and Jeremiah ground their way towards the fence they saw another guard come out and join the first, taking up a position on the other side of the gate.

'They look prepared,' said Ben worriedly. 'What do you think, Jeremiah? Why would they both be carrying guns? I thought they'd just be curious about the approaching vehicle.'

'Mr Ben, they must have been warned and have been told to be alert.'

'Ja, that's what I thought. Shit, this is not good. I hope Harry is careful. I don't want these guys to start blasting away.'

Jeremiah nodded as he stopped the vehicle, leaving the motor idling softly. They were no more than 150 metres from the fence and, from the memorised layout, directly in line with the gap in the buildings where they had planned to bust through.

'Five minutes,' said Ben.

Harry and Samuel had arrived at the gate and the guards were moving towards the growling Ford truck.

Everything changed in an instant as gunshots from the house suddenly rang out. The guards spun away from the vehicle in the direction of the disturbance and Harry and Samuel bolted out of the doors on each side.

'Go! Go!' Ben screamed, his mind in turmoil. *Who could have started shooting? Could it be Robert jumping the gun? Might Josh be in the line of fire?*

Jeremiah hit the accelerator and the Land Rover roared ahead. Stones and gravel sprayed from beneath its wheels as they lurched forward, gathering speed over the short distance and smashing through the flimsy fence.

On the other side of the barrier they careered into a cluster of boulders that marked the pathways on the inside of the camp. *Just one of the details Robert neglected to mention*, Ben thought, as Jeremiah swerved to the left in an attempt to avoid them. Their right front wheel ploughed into a boulder and the vehicle reared high into the air, tipping to the left. Jeremiah wrenched the steering wheel to the left in an effort to return the wheels to the ground but couldn't prevent the Land Rover from smashing through the walls of the nearest bungalow, where it jerked to a halt. Crunching the gears into reverse, he floored the accelerator again, taking out the remaining part of the wall as they exited. With the building's support structure smashed, the roof collapsed and they emerged in a shower of bricks and dust in time to see Rocco and Moses' vehicle rupture the perimeter walls on the opposite side and vault into the forecourt of the compound, destroying the carefully manicured gardens and ploughing through the outdoor eating area.

With grim satisfaction, Ben observed that all was going according to plan, apart from the unscheduled gunfire. Harry and Samuel had taken advantage of the diversion and had the guards bailed up at the gatehouse, forcing them down on the ground and disarming them. From the rear of the camp, he saw Josh, Benjamin and old Joshua running towards a white Land Cruiser. Robert fired back towards the building, covering them while they bundled themselves into the vehicle. His heart flooded with relief at the sight of his son, yet they were still far from making it out of the compound alive.

*　*　*

His heart in his mouth, Ben watched the car carrying his son head towards liberty – white-haired old Joshua crouched down in the front beside the tall black driver, who would have to be Benjamin, and Robert still firing from the rear. *He really came through for me.* Ben sighed with relief.

'I think we've done it, Jeremiah!' he exclaimed in triumph at the very same moment that the ground in front of the escaping Land Cruiser exploded in a ball of fire, flipping the vehicle onto its roof.

'Oh, my God!' Ben screamed in panic, bolting from the Land Rover just as an attack helicopter loomed above the opening in the wall.

Troops with night-vision goggles dropped on cables from the machine, spraying bullets. Ben fell back. Any attempt to get near the Land Cruiser under that amount of fire was hopeless, but at least Ben could see the occupants moving around and he thanked God they were alive.

Shots clattered against the gunship. One of the descending commandos screamed and plummeted the rest of the way to the ground. Harry and Samuel were firing towards the hovering machine. The chopper turned towards the valiant pair, even as Ben screamed a futile warning. Their vehicle took a direct hit and erupted into a raging inferno. Harry and Samuel were gone.

Ben was stunned. Seconds ago he had been celebrating the safe retrieval of his son, and now his greatest friend and ally was lost. But any attempt to digest that disaster would have to wait. He was cut off from Josh and unable to determine what injuries, if any, the passengers of the Land Cruiser might have suffered or how to get them to safety. What could he do? How could he salvage the situation?

*   *   *

Robert crawled out of the upturned vehicle, dragging Josh behind him, and cried out in anguish as he witnessed Harry and poor Samuel consumed in flames. Josh, his friend's young son, had almost died because of his deception. As his own life crashed down around him, he saw De Jager dropping towards the ground on a line from the helicopter, like some dark demigod striking down his enemies. Robert's bid for salvation had become a debacle and now he bore the responsibility for two deaths, including that of a dear friend. The thought of Ben and Josh dying on top of that was too much to bear. There was no way out. De Jager held the upper hand and Marie would inevitably find out the truth. He could never live with that.

'Josh, tell your father I'm sorry,' he murmured.

Before the boy could ask why, Robert was out and running towards the helicopter, his .458 Holland & Holland chambered, firing at De Jager as he descended. The man with the patch swung the Uzi tucked under his right arm towards this new attacker and a spray of bullets cut him down like ripe wheat. Robert pitched forward under his own momentum and lay unmoving in a tide of spreading crimson. De Jager reached the ground and strode forward, continuing to fire into the corpse of his fallen foe.

The Afrikaner's men had run past him, screaming for Ben to surrender, their weapons raised, though they held their fire. *De Jager wants me alive!* Ben realised. With so many men between him and Josh there was no chance of a rescue. But if he allowed himself to be caught it was all over.

'Get us out of here!' he screamed to Jeremiah. At once, the ranger spun the steering wheel, grinding the gears into forward. The Land Rover careered out of the spin and charged forward, sideswiping Rocco and Moses' vehicle as they too made their desperate rush out of the compound. Suddenly their comrades' car slewed sideways, grinding to a halt with Moses slumped across the steering wheel, shot through the back of his head. Rocco leapt out of the left-side door and raced towards Ben.

CHAPTER
51

Aardvark Hole

'Go, go, go!' Rocco roared, as he grabbed the car door and pulled himself into the moving Land Rover. The helicopter still hovered, lowering the last of the men to the ground, and they had mere seconds before it would be free to pursue them.

'Cut the lights!' Ben shouted. Although he kept his weapon trained on De Jager's men, he refrained from firing, hoping to avoid more gunfire. Whilst it seemed certain that De Jager wanted him alive, he could not rely upon the mercenaries showing complete restraint if they found themselves under assault.

With the lights switched off, Jeremiah veered to the left and headed away from the road and towards the brush and tree-covered culvert – the donga – that he had seen earlier on their approach.

'Get us into the thick bush,' Rocco panted. 'We can conceal the Land Rover there. We're sitting targets in this thing while they have that helicopter. We'll be better off on foot, so we can hide and take stock.'

'Ja! So long as we don't go trampling on black mambas or disturbing a leopard.' Jeremiah nodded.

'I'll take my chances against them anytime, over an attack helicopter.'

The Land Rover bounced through the bush, leaving a trail that would be clearly visible from the air. They had very little time. Already the night sky was paling and the trees were limned in the first light of dawn. It was imperative that they get under cover as quickly as possible.

The clatter of the helicopter grew louder as it powered up. The pursuit remained temporarily delayed while De Jager ordered the bulk of his men back on board before sending them on their way.

Those precious extra moments had given them an unhoped for head start. Jeremiah slipped the vehicle into low gear as it crested the ridge, and let the V8 motor do the braking as the front end fell steeply towards the soft bed of the culvert.

The donga was a ravine, carved through eons of erosion and stabilised by the heavily populated brush. The canopy of trees covering this deep gully soon swallowed the Land Rover from sight. Satisfied they were safely hidden, Ben called a halt and they climbed out.

'Fucking yellow!' He shook his head and thumped the vehicle's bonnet. 'What was Harry thinking? It's so visible from above.'

He winced in pain at the loss of his mate and the cruel fate that had befallen Samuel and Moses. It had happened so fast. One moment they were full of life, the next a smouldering heap of ash.

In less than a minute they were on foot and moving through the dense bush, each of them equipped with a rifle and handgun. Jeremiah had armed himself with a machete for good measure and Ben shouldered the RPG 7. Loaded with a single heat-seeking warhead, it weighed around ten kilos.

'Do you think it's worth it?' asked Rocco. 'That bloody thing is heavy and not easy to get through thick bush with. It's going to slow you down.'

'But it also gives us the only chance to stop that chopper and even the odds between us.'

'Ja, okay, maybe.'

'Guys,' Ben said. 'My boy is at Green Thorn and I'm going back for him. I don't care what it takes or how many of De Jager's men are there, I have to save Josh. But I understand if you want to get out now.'

'Ben,' Rocco said. 'I signed on for this and I'm determined to finish it with you. If we get out, you're going to pay me plenty. But aside from that, I like fighting for the good guys. That De Jager is an evil prick and it's about time someone took him down.'

'Thanks, Rocco,' Ben said, relieved. 'Having you with us makes a huge difference.'

He turned to Jeremiah. Could he expect anything of him?

'It's okay, Mr Ben,' he said. 'If I walk away from here and your boy is lost, I will live with that all my life. In Africa too many lives have been lost in less worthy causes. I will see this through to the end.'

Ben couldn't find adequate words. Faced with the unspeakable evil of men like De Jager and his cronies, it was easy to forget just how much goodness others were capable of. That this man, who he hardly knew, should risk so much for him was indeed noble. Ben squeezed his shoulder and smiled, and Jeremiah patted his hand in a gesture far more eloquent than words.

In the distance, the helicopter circled, searching, while Jeremiah navigated them steadily through the pre-dawn bush that was coming to life with animals grazing and drinking. Whilst well habituated to men in vehicles, to these animals, a man on the ground was an enemy, either to flee from or to fight. Being on foot in this terrain, particularly in the dark, without being able to see any of their most lethal foes, was nerve-racking.

'It's going to be light soon,' Jeremiah observed. 'Be especially watchful for black mambas. There are a lot of them around here and they're one of the most aggressive snakes in the world. This is just the place you can expect to find them.'

'Thanks for that, Jeremiah.' Rocco smiled. 'I presume you're trying to distract us from worrying too much about that helicopter full of highly trained mercenaries. What do you think about finding a hideout and waiting until dark?'

'Uh-uh.' Jeremiah shook his head. 'That means waiting all day in the heat, giving De Jager's soldiers plenty of time to find us.'

'Rocco, don't you think we're better off doing the unexpected and taking the fight to them?' Ben suggested.

'Depends on what you have in mind? Right now we're best off putting distance between ourselves and the Land Rover. We're hopelessly outnumbered and outgunned, so taking the fight to them without changing the odds is suicidal and won't protect Josh either. We need some breathing space to plan another way of extricating him, and we won't get that with the chopper searching this area.'

'I think I have a plan but I need to find the right location,' said Ben. 'Let's just keep moving and I'll explain when I see it.'

As they moved on, seeking Ben's unexplained 'location', a parade of wonders unfolded around them in the dawn light. Silver cluster leaf sparkled amidst the green canopy of marula trees and herds of impala and kudu grazed undisturbed off the foliage, the man scent of the intruders carried in the opposite direction by the breeze. Startled, a family of foraging warthogs darted off through the grass squealing, their tails held aloft like aerials. Alarmed by the commotion, the skittish deer swiftly followed suit. Not far off, away from the dense foliage, a pair of giraffe grazed on a green thorn tree. It was not lost on Ben that at another time, in different circumstances, these delights of nature would have filled him with joy.

Yet this was no time for such contemplation and, as if to underline the fact, the helicopter swooped overhead and they dropped to the ground. In the dim light of the early dawn, concealed by the overhead canopy, they prayed that the aerial surveillance would not reveal their presence, until the chopper clattered by and they were free to move again.

'Aha!' Ben exclaimed suddenly. 'I guess I've found what I was searching for.'

Intrigued, Rocco and Jeremiah waited impatiently to discover what Ben had in mind.

Ben left the cover of the trees and strode across a short open plain to a termite mound. The structure, built to a height of three metres through the incredible industry of a thousand tiny insects, stood in the shadow of a large pink ivory tree. Ben searched the opening of the mound for the telltale signs of warthogs or other small animals that might inhabit the deserted burrows of the aardvark or anteater. Trampled grass at the opening and a broken spider web confirmed his fears that the shell was inhabited. He cursed; he needed that space. From a nearby bush, he broke off a long leafy branch and cautiously approached the entry to poke his bushman's broom into the chamber.

The mound could be home to any number of animals – all dangerous when cornered – and Ben held his breath in anticipation as he swept the floor inside, keeping well clear of the exit in the event of a sudden evacuation. With a rustle and a squeak, a mongoose broke from the exit and raced off. Given the identity of the evacuee, there was no fear of a snake sharing the tenancy. Satisfied that the large empty chamber he needed had been secured, Ben signalled for Rocco and Jeremiah to approach.

CHAPTER
52

Big Bang Theory

'Okay, guys, the idea is for me to slip backwards into this hole with the RPG aiming out. The chamber is large and deep enough to accommodate me and I'll be invisible from the outside. One of you has to attract the chopper so it levels off close enough for me to get a shot at it with the RPG. If you position yourself near that tree,' Ben pointed to the pink ivory, 'its shadow will stop De Jager's men from seeing into the hole and I'll be completely undetectable. When they come down in line with you, the chopper will be in front of the mound and I can't miss shooting the fucker down.'

'It could work,' Rocco mused, 'but volunteering to be the bait for a helicopter gunship seems a bit suicidal.'

'I don't think so, Rocco. We understand that De Jager wants to keep me alive, so the chances of his men shooting to kill is minimised until they are sure who the victim is. That moment of hesitation is all I need.'

Rocco grinned. 'Well, you mad sonofabitch, I'm persuaded, which probably begs the question, which one of us is madder?

Because it has to be me who acts as the decoy. They're not going to mistake Jeremiah for you.'

Turning to the ranger, Rocco clapped him on the shoulder. 'See, it isn't always so great being the white guy.'

Jeremiah smiled and said to Ben, 'Maybe, but I would have been glad to take the chance anyway.'

'I'm sure you would have,' Ben said sincerely. 'But for the moment the best you can do is stay out of sight until the helicopter is out of commission.'

Ben glanced at his watch. It was 5:16 a.m. and the world was bathed in early morning light. De Jager's soldiers would not take long to find the tracks into the donga. Within one or two low-flying sweeps, they would quickly pick up the sight of a lone white man moving out of cover.

Checking that the RPG's firing mechanism and safety switch were working correctly, Ben was amazed that this nearly forty-year-old weapon still activated as though it was new.

'The only thing I'm worried about is the after-blast of the rocket. The exhaust gases will flare out in a cloud of searing-hot smoke.'

Ben tucked in his shirt, turned up his collar and pulled his hat down to cover as much of his body as possible.

'I can only hope that it won't become an instant oven, but if we create an exhaust vent at the back, it might be enough to prevent a disaster. Jeremiah, you may have to pull me out of there if I catch fire.'

'Jesus,' Rocco said. 'How likely is that?'

'I don't know,' Ben admitted. 'I've never fired one of these from inside an ant hill. We're all taking a risk here, but I hope it'll be okay.'

'Me too,' said Jeremiah, as he used his machete to hack a hole in the back of the mound and looked to Ben for approval. Ben nodded in satisfaction and lowered himself backwards into the den. Rocco walked away a short distance to verify that he was out of sight. The PI was delighted to find that the shape of the lethal warhead facing directly at him was indistinguishable from only a few metres off.

Jeremiah found cover behind a nearby tree trunk from where Ben could be quickly reached if the explosion set him alight.

'You'd better look convincing about trying to hide,' Ben shouted to Rocco from the mound. 'We don't want them suspecting a trap.'

'Don't worry about me looking petrified,' Rocco snorted, 'I won't be play-acting, although I doubt they'll imagine *us* trying to trap *them*. How could they possibly suspect what we have in store for them?'

'Ouch!' In his hurry to secure his strategic hole in the ground, Ben had neglected to notice one tiny detail. In fact, many tiny details, in the form of the common black ant. In any other circumstance they would not have been of consequence, but lying still on the ground, Ben knew that the little sting was just the herald of an agonising program of torture. The black ant, albeit small, has a pair of disproportionately huge sharp jaws that snap open and closed like a pair of scissors. The sting came not from the incision of the jaws but from the accompanying squirt of formic acid and was absurdly painful for such a small bite. It caused him to wriggle despite himself, and slap at the source of the pain. The slap got rid of the ant but not the sting caused by the acid, and it was immediately followed by another bite and then another. Just as it was becoming intolerable enough for him to reconsider this entire insane strategy, the helicopter came thundering into view and Rocco made his quick run for the trees.

The gunship reared upwards as it halted in its forward momentum before turning in his direction. Rattling machine-gun fire sprayed in a warning arc above Rocco's head, confirming their assumption that Ben was wanted alive. With a screaming cacophony of whirling blades it completed the turn and settled its direction on Rocco's sprinting form. Watching with baited breath, Ben waited as the deadly gunship's menacing nose drew level with the open aardvark hole and fell in line with the sights of the lethal rocket launcher cradled against his cheek. With iron resolve he held the weapon steady despite the constellation of red welts that was beginning to pepper his body.

The essential principle behind the efficient use of the Russian-made RPG was to get as near to the target as possible to ensure an accurate shot. Ben prayed fervently that his location was close enough, for he could not break cover. Concealed by the shadows of the tree and buried deep inside the termite mound, he willed the whirlybird closer, waiting until he was able to look directly into the pilot's face. The gunship hovered less than 50 metres from him. Leaning out from both sides were six of De Jager's troops and no doubt more were hidden inside, completely unaware of Ben's existence and the seconds ticking away on their lives.

Recalling his training on the weapon, Ben reckoned the RPG's effectiveness over a distance of 50 metres, provided a hit probability at 100 per cent on a target crossing at 15 kilometres per hour. Ben's target was not moving. Given that he could withstand the blistering pain of the multitude of ant bites to keep the weapon steady for just a few moments more, there could be no doubt of the outcome. He squeezed the trigger. It struck the percussion cap, igniting the primer and the gases built inside the chamber to launch the rocket out of the tube at 117 metres per second. It took less than half a second to impact. Just long enough for the pilot's eyes to open wide in surprise, but not enough for his brain to register that he and his comrades were dead before the helicopter exploded in a flaming ball.

Burying his head in the sand, Ben felt the shockwave from the obliterated helicopter penetrate the aardvark opening, while the heat from the rocket's exhaust turned his shelter into a hell hole, searing his skin and singeing every uncovered hair from his body. The only blessing was that the colony of little black ants was wiped out along with his follicles.

CHAPTER
53

Redemption

Josh's mind was a whir. Lying in the upturned vehicle, dazed by the concussion of the explosion and deafened by its roar, he had believed that it was the end. Then Robert had hauled him out. What was the meaning of his words, 'Tell your father I'm sorry'? And why had he rushed off so recklessly to die at the hands of that monster with the eye patch? *Thank God my dad is alive,* he thought, after witnessing his desperate escape in the Land Rover, even though Ben and his comrades were now cut off from them once again.

Part of Josh had wanted his dad to flee and save himself, but knowing Ben, Josh was sure he would return, even if it meant sacrificing himself.

After witnessing their maniacal captor firing repeatedly into Robert's corpse, Josh felt sure there would be no happy ending to this. In many ways he was resigned to his fate. Benjamin was mumbling apologies to his father in English and Shangaan, devastated by a gaping wound in the old man's left side.

De Jager arrived after briefing his men and ordering them back onto the chopper to hunt down the quarry. Johan joined him, clutching his shoulder where he had been stabbed. His eyes burned with hatred.

'What happened to you?' De Jager snapped.

'That fuck betrayed us!' Johan cursed. 'I'm going to kill that black bastard,' he snarled, moving towards Benjamin.

'Get away from him,' Josh spat, leaping up and eyeing the giant warningly.

'Piss off!' Johan swore in response, swinging his left fist at the side of Josh's head, but the boy easily avoided the wounded brute.

'Hold on, Johan!' De Jager shouted. 'You'll get your revenge. But not until we have Novak here to witness it. Benjamin's execution will just add to his suffering.' He grinned at Johan. 'You'll see, it will work out nicely for both of us!'

He beckoned to Benjamin with his Uzi.

'Get your old man inside and bandage him up. I don't want him slipping away before Novak gets here. But I'm warning you, any more tricks and you'll find my patience has run out. If I have to settle for mounting one of your heads on a bayonet ... well, that's up to you.'

Benjamin glared at his former employer but knew that antagonising the madman any further was not smart, so he bit his lips instead. With a murmur of thanks to Josh, he bent to the old man and together they lifted him with tender care.

'Take him into the staff quarters!' De Jager snapped. 'You can try to fix him up in there.'

De Jager summoned another of his cohorts, an Afrikaner named Smeets, who was something of a field surgeon.

'Come,' De Jager ordered imperiously, and the mercenary, toting his medical kit, followed them to the servants' quarters, where Joshua had been settled on his bed. Benjamin and Josh were busy tearing a sheet to make bandages.

'See what you can do to get Johan back into shape,' De Jager ordered Smeets, ignoring the mortally wounded old man.

In the lounge room, Smeets gave Johan a hefty dose of painkillers, dressed his wounds and placed his arm in a sling. While he was thus employed, Josh and Benjamin bound Joshua's wound as best they could. The old man groaned, unable to disguise the level of his suffering despite his stoicism, and Benjamin was overwhelmed with hopelessness. His desperate efforts to save his father's life, should they succeed, would serve no purpose other than to allow De Jager to sacrifice him at his leisure in some sick spectacle. How degrading that his father was reduced from a human being to a pawn whose only value was to inflict more torment on Ben with his meaningless death.

The idea of trying to overpower De Jager tempted Benjamin sorely, but so long as his enemy was armed with an Uzi, and Smeets and Johan were on hand as backup, any such attempt would be suicidal.

'I need to get him to a hospital,' Benjamin begged, beside himself.

'I'm already too good to you,' De Jager snapped. 'I let your old man bleed on one of my beds. He should be on the floor like the dog he is, and you dare to talk to me of hospitals.

'I don't know why I even show you that much kindness. You were a nobody when I employed you. You've had every comfort; the drugs you so enjoy, the women. I gave your old man a home. But then, when you had the opportunity to show loyalty to me, you betray me and attack our friend Johan.'

It beggared belief, Benjamin thought. While the irony in De Jager's voice clearly acknowledged that every gift was a curse and all the favours had been part of a plot to enslave him, the madman seemed, nonetheless, to genuinely believe he was owed some allegiance. There could not be a clearer illustration of how this man was able to twist things in his mind so that the Novaks were the villains and he was the victim.

'I made the right decision,' said Benjamin. 'At last,' he added, looking towards his father. The old man lying on the bed could only manage a weak smile but his eyes were filled with pride.

Consumed by hatred, De Jager considered killing Benjamin right then and there, but mastering himself, he merely told Johan, 'If they try anything smart, do whatever it takes to control them, but keep them alive.'

Taking Smeets with him, the Afrikaner stormed from the room without a backward glance, determined to find out the status of his search-and-capture operation.

*   *   *

Locked up and helpless, Josh listened to the whirling clatter of the helicopter in search of his father and prayed that somehow Ben would survive. Then, the sound of the explosion seemed the realisation of his worst fears and he buried his head in his hands, imagining that the helicopter had blown his father off the road, just as it had earlier incinerated the men in the car outside the gate.

But it didn't make sense. De Jager had wanted his father alive.

There was a puzzling silence. The racket of the chopper had evaporated and Josh dared to hope. He exchanged glances with Benjamin who lifted his index finger to his lips and mouthed, 'It's gone.'

The explosion took on a new meaning of hope.

De Jager would realise that his enemy had found a way to fight back.

What will he do now? Josh wondered. *What can we do to stop him?*

Benjamin had shown his metal already. Maybe, together, the two of them could gain the upper hand.

Watching Them Squeal

'What the fuck?' De Jager had heard the explosion. 'How the fuck does anyone bring down a fucking helicopter?'

After arranging everything so that the odds were in his favour, a single thunderous sound had changed the entire picture. Before that blast De Jager had been confident that, whatever Novak tried, the result would be the same. With the boy as his trump card, his enemy was bound to come to him. No matter whether it was day or night, with such an overwhelming force against him, Novak was doomed. Still, with a single stroke, eight of his troops had been eliminated. How could the chopper be downed? Only a grenade or missile could achieve that, and where could he get such a thing?

For the first time in a long time, De Jager's confidence was shaken. A desperate man with extraordinary resolve was coming for him. *We'd better be fucking well prepared.*

'Smeets,' he barked. 'Set up in the main house and keep guard over the servants' quarters. Make sure no one gets near the hostages, except Novak. Don't kill him when he turns up, but take out anyone with him. And if he becomes too much of a danger, shoot his legs out from under him.'

With a curt nod, Smeets took off while De Jager went to rejoin Johan. The final confrontation would unfold with his hostages as witness. After that, they too would be disposed of.

Entering the lounge room, De Jager found Johan pointing his pistol straight at him.

'Johan?'

The giant dropped the weapon by his side. 'Fucking Novak has me rattled. I needed to be sure the footsteps belonged to you. That god almighty bang sounded like the chopper going up in smoke.'

'Ja, it must have been.' De Jager sighed.

'How could he do that?'

'I don't know. He's resourceful. So what are we going to do about it?'

The question was rhetorical but Johan didn't take it that way.

'Kill the kid and the Kaffir,' he snapped without hesitation, pointing to the bedroom with the pistol. 'I'll go in there and do it for you and then we can get out of here.'

'What! Without getting Novak?'

'Yes. We go right now. He just took down the bulk of your army, and you can bet your bottom dollar he's on his way here. He's got nothing to lose and he'll be more dangerous than ever. It doesn't make sense for us to stay. I'm not exactly in peak condition at the moment, you know.'

Johan had had enough. He was tired, his arm was in agony and practically useless despite all the tablets he had taken, and his nose throbbed abominably. The last twenty-four hours had taken their toll. He didn't care if Ben lived so long as he could kill the boy and the Kaffir, Benjamin.

'You can't be serious!' De Jager fumed. 'I've waited thirty years for this. Look at my goddamn face. Look at what he did to me. He turned me into a fucking monster, like my goddamned old man. Novak and his father have been the scourge of my life, of my family. No, I've waited too long. I want to be here when he arrives and I want him to understand why this is happening. And when I kill his son, I want to watch him suffer before he fucking dies.'

'Petrus …' Johan hesitated. 'I've done everything you ever asked without question or complaint. But this time you're making a big mistake. Someone like Novak, on a mission, won't be easy to stop. We should kill them and leave.'

'And then what, Johan? He'll still come after me. He'll contact the police, and they'll be all over here, and I'll be looking over my shoulder every minute of every day watching out for him. No, we're not going anywhere. We're standing our ground and ending it all, right here, right now.'

'At least let me kill the kid and the Kaffir and have them out of the way.'

'No, I want them alive. What is it with you anyway? You've always held the killing back until the last minute. That's the best part, watching them squeal before you end it. It's just because they got the better of you. That's why you want them dead.'

'No, that's merely another reason I'll enjoy it thoroughly,' Johan insisted. 'I just don't want to take any unnecessary chances with this guy.'

'While his son is alive, he'll be cautious. But when he sees the boy die, Novak will be a wreck and easy to handle.'

CHAPTER
55

Incursion

Jeremiah and Rocco dragged a dazed Ben from the smoking ant hill. Reeling drunkenly amidst the smoking debris of the destroyed helicopter, Ben's ears rang from the concussion of the explosion reverberating in the confined space of the aardvark hole.

'I'm all right,' he coughed, brushing off the few remaining ants.

'Well done, Ben!' Rocco exclaimed. 'It worked like a charm. I can't believe the devastation.'

The earth and trees around them smouldered. Searing fragments of metal and glass were all that remained of the gunship. While Jeremiah stamped out small fires that flared from tussocks of dry grass ignited by the explosion, Ben rubbed his bloodshot eyes and slapped the back of his head in an effort to restore his hearing. Despite his afflictions, he was delighted with the outcome of his handiwork and smiled in satisfaction. Rocco helped Jeremiah to put out the last of the flames, the two men blocking their noses from the stench of seared flesh, cordite and molten plastic.

'Let's get going,' Ben said. 'De Jager would have heard the explosion and we can't afford to waste any time. The quicker we get over there, the less time he has to prepare.'

'Slow down,' said Rocco. 'Let's consider a few other options. Should we go now or wait until nightfall? We have no idea how many men he has. We know they're well armed and just three of us going there in broad daylight against who knows how many hardened soldiers sounds potentially suicidal.'

'I don't think so, Rocco,' Ben replied. 'Come on. Let's get the Land Rover at least and I'll explain my viewpoint as we go. If you still think it's unworkable, we can consider waiting until nightfall.'

'Fair enough,' Rocco said, as they headed back across the open plain towards the donga. 'What do you have in mind?'

'We may not know how many men are left but the majority of his hired guns, the soldiers, would have been on that helicopter. Perhaps one or two stayed behind. Whatever the case may be, the other guards are not paid killers. They didn't do any shooting earlier, and I doubt they will. I'll wager that if there's any more gunfire, they'll run for cover. Time is on De Jager's side. If we wait for nightfall, it'll give him the opportunity to recruit more men. I'm convinced we should retaliate as soon as possible.'

Rocco took a long moment to weigh the arguments for and against a daytime attack.

'I hear you,' he said. 'Though I imagine De Jager would favour thugs as employees and no one took off during the shooting earlier. Maybe they held fire because De Jager wants you alive. *You*, not me and not Jeremiah.'

'But De Jager is also serious about his game reserve and will have hired men who are rangers foremost, though maybe thugs second,' said Ben.

'Well, let's call the chances fifty-fifty,' Rocco said. 'We also don't know where they will be holding Josh and we don't know where De Jager is.'

'Fair enough,' Ben said. 'But I actually don't think finding that bastard and his prisoners will be a problem. He's taunting me by demonstrating his power. Otherwise, Josh would have been dead by the time we reached Green Thorn. I'm the bait. He wants me to know where he is and he'll lead me to him. De Jager wants this encounter. But he's going to try to fix things so I can't possibly survive it.'

'Okay, ja,' Rocco agreed. 'That much makes sense. I can't see him getting into a duel with you where you have a loaded pistol each.'

'Exactly,' said Ben. 'De Jager knows I'll come back. What he doesn't know is whether I'll still have support. Our logical approach is to divide his troops and divert his men from guarding Josh and the others. Our previous attack has given De Jager's men three entrances to cover, so they're already stretched.'

Recalling Robert's layout of the property, they planned to drive as close to Green Thorn as safety allowed and then Jeremiah and Ben would proceed on foot, concealed by the brush, and enter the compound through the break in the fence.

'The fact that De Jager wants me alive is our main benefit,' said Ben. 'It means I can act as bait and draw their attention without getting shot. Once we're inside, Jeremiah can circle around the back while you hit the front gate with the Land Rover. The vehicle is practically designed for combat and you can draw their fire with relative safety. Keep the windows up and they won't know who's at the wheel. They might think it's me, or at least they won't know it's not. If they open fire, the armour plate and glass will protect you.'

'I'm sure it will be a trip around the park,' Rocco joked.

'The main danger will come from what remains of his soldiers. We need to be careful.'

Ben pulled his bowie knife and held it up meaningfully. 'I'll try to dispose of as many as I can before you hit the main gate. Jeremiah, are you prepared to use that machete?'

'It would not be the first time, Mr Ben. There is no sin in putting a wicked thing to a good use.'

'It's ironic, isn't it?' said Ben. 'I'm the one De Jager most wants dead, but I'm also the safest until he's played his sick game out to the last.'

'I wouldn't rely upon that too much,' Rocco said. 'If he gets tired of the game at some stage he might decide on a quick finish.'

'I have to risk that,' Ben said.

With Rocco at the wheel, the yellow Land Rover headed in the direction of the lodge and their last attempt to free Josh and the others. Ben's ultimate encounter with De Jager was inevitable; all that remained in doubt was who, if anyone, would survive.

At 6:41 a.m., the Land Rover rolled to a halt.

A gentle mist lifted as the temperature warmed, revealing a bright sun shining in a clear blue sky, the backdrop to a beautiful spring day in the African bush. Ben and Jeremiah jumped from the Land Rover and jogged easily towards the lodge. Both were lean and strong, Ben from years of working out daily, while Jeremiah was simply gifted with a superb physique, and, like so many of his people, seemed born to run. They moved swiftly through the undergrowth, invisible to even the most vigilant observer.

The camp came into view as they reached the ridge, each of the three entrances guarded by a sentry in camouflage fatigues who was obviously part of De Jager's hit squad. Making these mercenaries their primary targets would greatly enhance the chances of success.

Ben and Jeremiah arrived at the fence just as Rocco revved the Land Rover and accelerated towards the gate. The tall, muscular black sentry turned in the direction of the vehicle charging towards the front barricade. Diverted by its sudden arrival, he unslung the AK-47 from his shoulder as Ben sprang forward, his bowie knife aimed at the guard's throat. But his intended victim glimpsed the movement and swung his weapon towards his attacker, blocking the wicked blade's trajectory. Locked together, the combatants rolled onto the ground, the mercenary's firearm discharging in a cacophony of gunfire. As he struggled to keep the gun away from him, Ben lost his grip on the knife. The African used his weight advantage to roll his adversary onto his back and straddled Ben. He snatched up the knife, ready to plunge it into his opponent, when Jeremiah stepped forward and buried his machete into his head. The mercenary pitched over and the ranger dragged Ben to his feet.

Ben retrieved his knife and slipped it into his sleeve. *So much for the element of surprise,* he thought. The gunfire was a setback, but it could have been worse. Without Jeremiah along he would probably be dead right now, and he thanked his angels that the ranger was doing their job in the physical world.

'Thanks,' he murmured, grasping the man's arm, but there was no time for sentiment for the guard at the other breach now had them in his sights. Ever alert, Jeremiah snapped his own gun up and fired upon the mercenary, forcing him back under cover.

'Great!' Ben cried, pulling out his 9mm. 'Keep him pinned down while I make a run for the house.'

Ben glanced around for Rocco. The guards at the gate were firing on the Land Rover, but the armoured plate did its work and the PI ploughed on, collecting one of the guards before crashing through the barrier. The vehicle swerved to a halt, the window went down, and Rocco returned fire on the remaining guard who decided he'd had enough and bolted down the road away from all the mayhem.

Rocco noted where Jeremiah stood and exchanged fire with the guard at the other breach. He would have to drive between them to reach Ben. It seemed to make as much sense to use his vehicle as a battering ram to get rid of the last guard and then, together, he and Jeremiah could join Ben who was fast approaching the main house, unaware that Smeets had him in his sights. Rocco put his foot to the floor and aimed his car at the man he thought was De Jager's last guard.

* * *

In the servants' quarters, De Jager and his captives sat listening to the commotion.

It's time to take control of the situation, the man with the eye patch determined.

Grabbing Josh, he pulled him to the door, the gun barrel shoved in his neck. Novak was charging up the driveway towards the building, unaware of Smeets eyeing him like an eagle watching its prey.

De Jager salivated at the prospect of revenge. Novak was a sitting duck in Smeets' sights and De Jager could have easily picked him off from behind his human shield, if he had been willing to make a quick end of everything. But this was too good. He was ready to revel in his triumph. The idiot in the four-wheel drive, however, would have to be taken care of by Smeets.

'Hey, Novak!' he roared. 'I guess I have something you want.'

Ben froze. Josh was alive! He hardly noticed the man standing behind his son as a strange calm settled upon him.

'Come over here,' De Jager called. 'Surely you remember me, your old army buddy "Sergeant Steyn"? But drop the gun, okay? We don't need that just to have a friendly chat.'

'Don't do it, Dad!' shouted Josh. 'He'll murder us all anyway!'

'Quiet!' Ben snapped. 'No one is going to kill anyone.' He threw down the gun. 'Mr De Jager isn't stupid. I'm sure we can work this out.'

'Of course,' De Jager said with a cynical smirk. 'Let's talk inside, like civilised men.'

He stood back, and waved his enemy in with mock civility.

'After you.'

Numbed by the tragedy and loss of his friends Harry and Robert, Ben walked reluctantly into the lion's den. Rocco and Jeremiah were his only remaining hope for salvation. Of Smeets, he remained completely unaware.

CHAPTER
56

So It Ends

This was not the reunion either Ben or old Joshua would ever have imagined. Yet on Ben's entering the room, neither could help but smile gently, acknowledging that they were together once more. Their sons had been forced to drag the wounded man out of the bedroom to lie on the floor in anticipation of the final confrontation. Benjamin was ordered back onto the couch, unable to comfort his father though every instinct cried out for him to do so. Johan sat on the far arm of the couch, his pistol trained on Ben's namesake.

Ben recognised the bastard straight away, even with his broken nose, blistered face and sling. He looked a mess.

'Speknek.' He nodded to him. 'You certainly haven't improved with age.'

'You look like shit yourself, Novak,' Johan retorted, taking in the filthy bruised figure with his singed hair and insect bites.

'Yes, I got in a fight with a helicopter,' Ben said. 'But I won.'

'I hope that's some comfort to you,' De Jager said. 'You got my helicopter. I have your son. If this were a poker game, who do you think would win?'

Ben kept quiet.

'Sit,' said De Jager, pointing to a chair. As Ben obeyed, the Afrikaner sat also, forcing Josh onto the floor at his feet, gripping the boy's hair between his fingers. Josh winced but refused to cry out. Ben felt a surge of pride.

De Jager tapped the side of his prisoner's face with the barrel of his gun.

'He's a good lad, this one,' he said mockingly. 'Feisty, like his father. But I don't know if he's that tough in the final analysis. I think maybe he's like your pansy mate.'

Gary. His fucking name was Gary, you prick.

'I buggered that little faggot on his first day in the army,' De Jager gloated. 'That's why he killed himself. He couldn't stomach living the rest of his life knowing I had complete power over him. I told him that was his reward for being friends with you and that there was more to come, so he ran away, went AWOL. When we caught him and slung him in DB, I told him I'd visit him every day. I knew that weakling would do himself in. I even gave him all the tools. I put a spare set of laces in his pocket and told him to use them wisely.

'Maybe that's what I'll do to your boy, eh Novak? What do you think? Shall I shoot him while you watch or shall I shoot you and then ram his arse until he begs me for a pair of laces? I'll give you the choice. How's that for a fair deal?'

'Why?' Ben asked. 'Why would you do something so ugly? That's all I want to know.'

He wanted to keep De Jager talking. Maybe he would become distracted. Maybe one of the others would arrive. Maybe some miracle would happen.

'What is this obsession of yours that made you want to kill me from the moment we first met?'

'You're such a fool, Novak,' De Jager sneered. 'Haven't you worked it out by now? Your father destroyed my life. He destroyed my family. He hacked at my father's arm with a piece of glass and he became an amputee, so he became twisted and cruel as the worst

kind of animal. He made my life a hell; he killed my brother ...
my *brother* ... my only real friend, and he drove my mom crazy. All
because of what your father did.'

There it was. The mystery of so many years, resolved in a minute. Abe had told him about being beaten up by Gerrit and his
Brownshirts and how he had fought back. It made no difference
to De Jager that Ben's father had been defending himself. All the
misfortune of his childhood, everything he spoke of with such terrible anguish, had always been blamed upon the Novak family.
Every day the evidence of Ben's culpability had confronted him
in the mirror, just as his entire childhood was marred by the scars
inflicted by Abe's retaliation.

Both he and his enemy were victims of their own pasts. A history of violent confrontations repeated from father to son. The same
madness marked the record of so many generations of men. Could
it never end?

'De Jager, this is crazy. You're talking about something that happened more than sixty years ago. Look at the cost to all of us. Let
it go, we still have lives to lead. Please, don't throw that all away.'
Ben pleaded without shame, for it was his son's life that he begged
for and there was nothing he would not be prepared to do for that.

'You should have died in DB,' said De Jager, as if Ben hadn't
spoken. 'I was sure that smashing your skull would be your end,
but you were true to form: stubborn and resilient, you survived. I
shouldn't be surprised that you brought down the helicopter. How
did you do it?'

The truth was too hard to resist. 'It was your own RPG. I stole it
from your warehouse in Walvis in 1970.'

De Jager smiled oddly, seeming almost benevolent now that victory was his.

'I always thought you might have had something to do with that.
But I could never figure out how and, of course, I could never bring
it up, just in case it wasn't you. It would have let the cat out of the
bag. That's quite a twist. The funny thing was ... after all that, back
then, I actually respected your will to live and I might just possibly

have let it all lie, but you had to come to the German Keller and do this to me.' He pointed at his face with the barrel of his gun. 'That's what started it all over again. I've had to look at this face for thirty years, and I've been waiting for you every day.'

Hatred and evil had consumed him. Novak had shown him no mercy at the Keller, and he would show no mercy now. De Jager stood triumphantly.

'And so it ends,' he said, dragging Josh up by the hair, ready to splatter his brains in front of his father. 'So it ends.'

CHAPTER
57

Ambush

Rocco saw De Jager move aside and wave Ben past him into the house. He wondered for a moment if he would ever see him again. For now, though, he had to focus on the target ahead.

The target's name was James Obikwa, and he was not a man to be trifled with. Ben had been fortunate to have downed De Jager's gunship, for most of the men on it were battle-hardened experienced warriors, but the Afrikaner had kept one of the best behind, close by him in case he might be needed. Obikwa was an excellent marksman with nerves of steel. A soldier since the age of thirteen, he had been kidnapped from his home in Angola to serve a rebel leader. By eighteen, he had completed an intensive apprenticeship in the art of war and shown himself a natural and enthusiastic student. When the rebels were finally decimated and disbanded, he moved on to another battlefield. He knew no other life than war and no other appealed to him.

In that regard he was lucky to be in Africa, for there would always be an army somewhere on the continent, ready to take in a man with his abilities. At thirty-nine years of age, these were honed as sharp as they would ever be.

Rocco's vehicle powering towards him did not distract him from his current objective. He noted the rhythm with which Jeremiah popped out from his cover to fire upon him in his attempts to keep him pinned down. The ranger had become predictable. Obikwa waited, counting, and sure enough his mark popped up into his sights, right on cue. The mercenary pulled the trigger and Jeremiah was flung back out of sight. Now for the man in the car.

Obikwa drew a grenade from his jacket, pulled the pin, and, calculating the time to the explosion, hurled it under the front of the racing vehicle. The mercenary was gratified to see his timing was spot on, as the exploding missile lifted the back of the vehicle and flipped it onto its roof.

* * *

Rocco saw the mercenary fire at Jeremiah, seemingly unconcerned by the Land Rover's approach. For a moment he thought the soldier was simply unaware but then understood he had underestimated the man, when, with an extreme deliberateness, he suddenly switched his focus and launched a grenade towards him. The missile landed right in front of his vehicle, and there was no chance of avoiding it. Rocco's only hope was that it would explode well back from the Land Rover. A thunderous roar followed the vain hope, and he found his world turned upside down.

Groggy from the concussion, he struggled to release his safety belt and fell with a thud onto the upturned ceiling. Lying on his back, he saw the soldier coming cautiously towards him with his rifle raised. Rocco knew he had been lucky to survive the grenade. By rights he should be dead. He fumbled for his gun; it was his only chance. His hand found the grip but as his fingers slipped around it the assassin smiled grimly and squeezed the trigger.

A shot rang out and to Rocco's amazement the mercenary fell over backwards. He crawled out of the vehicle and saw Jeremiah propped up against the fence tying a tourniquet around his bloodied left shoulder. The ranger waved weakly and made an unconvincing okay sign. Despite his injury, he had managed the life-saving shot. Rocco waved back, grateful that Jeremiah's pinpoint aim had granted him survival.

Rocco leaned carefully over the fallen mercenary, making sure the man was dead before he took one of the grenades clipped to his combat webbing. He rose to his feet and turned towards the doorway where Ben had surrendered to De Jager and took off at a trot.

*   *   *

From the lobby of the main house, Smeets watched intently over the surrounding area, unsettled by the dangerous game being played out. Whoever these guys were, they were tough, resilient fighters and not what he had bargained for at all. Peering through the window, he could see the ranger down near the breach in the fence but he seemed pretty much out of action.

The driver of the Land Rover had been out of his line of vision, but the explosion of the grenade was unmistakable. Now, a heavyset fellow ran into view, heading up the pathway towards De Jager. The boss might be mad, but his plan to position him there was obviously well conceived. Smeets drew a bead on the newcomer and fired. The guy went down behind the rocks lining the pathway.

Attempting to check his handiwork, Smeets peered through the broken pane but dropped to the floor as a shot from the other ranger smashed through the window frame.

Cursing, Smeets raised himself cautiously, slipped his gun barrel through the window and, marking the ranger, who lay flat on the ground, returned fire. The mercenary noticed that his assailant was wounded, which explained why his first shot had been off its mark. His composure somewhat restored, the Afrikaner took aim at the head of the black man.

Smeets was quite the sharpshooter and now had the ranger dead in his sights when a grenade thrown by the driver landed outside the window and exploded, blowing out the front of the main house.

CHAPTER
58

Peace

The gunplay outside had not diverted De Jager in any way. But as he pulled Josh to his feet for the final reckoning, the exploding grenade distracted him for an instant.

This was the moment Ben had prayed for. Whipping the knife from his sleeve, he hurled it with deadly accuracy. De Jager stared in disbelief as the bowie scythed through the air towards him, delivering his fate. Even as the blade buried itself in his bad eye, his life passed before him: the feelings of grief and sadness at losing his brother and his mother, the only gentleness he had ever known; the torment derived from his interminable hatred for Gerrit and Ben. That hatred had deprived him of all peace in this life, and he held out no hope for any in the one to come.

A firearm roared almost simultaneously, and Ben felt himself thrown back. Johan had swung his gun away from Benjamin in a futile attempt to prevent the inevitable.

The moment the gun moved away, Benjamin leapt at his enemy, hitting him with a ferocious tackle that sent them both to the ground. The enormous Afrikaner gripped him savagely, clawing at him until he got a hand around his throat. He rolled Benjamin onto his back with ease and raised a massive fist for a crushing blow before a final blast rang out and he toppled to one side.

Josh Novak stood with De Jager's pistol stretched out in front of him, smoke curling away from the barrel. The young man tossed the gun aside, ran to his father and eased him into a sitting position. Tears sprang into his eyes as he saw the bright tide of red spreading over his father's shirt from the hole in his chest.

Ben looked at his son. 'It's okay,' he said. Even with his life ebbing away, his son's pain concerned him more than the likelihood of his own death. 'It's okay,' he repeated, and he meant it, because his boy was safe. But he could not go yet. One more thing remained to be done before he could have his peace. 'Take me to Joshua,' he urged his son.

'Dad, you need a doctor!' Josh cried.

'There'll be time enough for that,' Ben said, gently patting his arm.

'I've called an ambulance,' Benjamin said. He'd used Johan's phone to make the call. 'All we can do now is wait anyway.'

'Help me then,' Josh said.

Together, with immense care, they carried Ben to Joshua and lay him by his side. The sons knelt beside their fathers as the two old friends clasped hands.

Ben thought that Joshua looked barely older than he had since he had last seen him twenty-eight years ago. In all that time he had not changed, though his tightly curled hair had turned from grey to white. His skin remained smooth and shining, and his eyes still glowed with love and pride as he gazed at Ben.

'Joshua,' Ben gasped. 'I'm so sorry.'

He pressed his hand against his chest to stop the flow, to save his life from bleeding away. A feeling of dreamlike unreality was settling in. He squeezed Joshua's hand.

'Haugh! Boykie,' the old man whispered. 'It's so good to see you again.'

'You too, my friend,' Ben replied softly. 'Look, our boys are safe.'

'Ja, and we shall see them again … but only at the next station.'

Josh squeezed his father's shoulder, the tears running down his face. Hopelessly he whispered his name.

Jeremiah came into the room, supporting Rocco. Both of them were wounded but they were alive.

Ben smiled at them and looked at his son. 'Seems that De Jager was right. "So it ends" indeed.'

Here in South Africa, a land of untold violence and tragedy. He was starting to drift.

Yes, another voice answered, *and one of untold beauty.* It was Dahlia. He guessed it made sense that she was here now. Their son was safe so all had gone well, despite the odds, and what could explain that but that an angel had watched over them.

And so it ends this madness that has pitted two generations of De Jagers against my family.

As you sow, so shall you reap. That was Abe's voice.

Sure, why not? thought Ben. *Why shouldn't you be here too?*

He felt as if he were on a departing train, with his loved ones waiting for him, arms open wide, at the final destination. Dahlia, her cheeks stained with tears – tears of sorrow for her children's loss and tears of joy for her gain.

The sons gathered their fathers to them. Josh cradled Ben's head in his arms. His tears splashed on his father's cheek just as Ben's tears had fallen on his boys' heads when they were born. As if from a great distance Ben heard his stricken cry, 'Oh Dad! Oh Ben! My dad!'

Benjamin remained silent, his arms spread around his father, his face contorted with grief, his body racked with pain. And from that gentle place of peace, Ben was already trying to tell Josh it was going to be okay.

It's okay, it's okay. Just like I always told you, said Abe. *Tell your son it will be okay. We will never leave you.*

ACKNOWLEDGEMENTS

To Cristina, Sue, Jo, Annabel, Glenda and the whole team at Harlequin Books, thank you for reading my story and more importantly for supporting the belief that there is a world of readers out there that will share the adventure and relate to the times and places of the old and new South Africa.

I will always be grateful to Jan Scherpenhuizen, my editor, for his 'no compromise' attitude in ensuring that only the best would do. Because of him, the rewriting became a labour of love and pride, rather than a chore.

Special thanks to Eli for all the creative input and diligence in designing and producing the first book cover.

Thanks also to my sister, Cynthia, my nephews, Oren and Erez, and my friends who read the early drafts and encouraged me with the feedback I needed rather than just what I wanted to hear: Sam, Robert, David, Rodney, Alan and Merle.

And thanks to all my training buddies who have listened to the stories and waited patiently for over five years so that I could finally stop talking about my novel and actually give them something to read: Mark, Marty, Joel, Neville, Hoffie, Barry, Roy, Mike, Steve, Zelton and Debbie.

talk about it

Let's talk about books.

Join the conversation:

 on facebook.com/harlequinaustralia

 on Twitter @harlequinaus

www.harlequinbooks.com.au

If you love reading and want to know about our authors and titles, then let's talk about it.